Foudre

SKELM.reign(001)

The SKELM Chronicles: Renaissance
Book 1

Darby Skelm

Edited by
Maxine Meyer

Copyright

Published by THE ALIVE DUNCE

An imprint of SKELM LLC

First Edition

This is a work of fiction. Any resemblance to actual persons, living or dead, or actual events is purely coincidental. Any resemblance to corporations currently optimizing your reality is purely inevitable.

skelmcorps.com

Open mouths, empty heads, big bytes.

Dedication

For the incompatible.

The vast majority of highly intelligent people suffer from extreme stupidity. This proves, without a doubt, that I am highly intelligent—for I am extremely stupid.

— Alexandre Dumbass, père

Chapter 1

I come online to neon-green overlays hissing down my retinas like radioactive icicles. I'm somewhere soft, which means either I overshot the quarterly psych exam and passed out in the debrief chamber, or someone's gone off-script. A microsecond passes; the first possibility evaporates—no one at Moshimoto gives you a real mattress unless they want something from you.

The air tastes like filtered lithium, dry and perfectly neutral. Diagnostic readouts splay in lazy half-circles across my visual field: SPLIT CONSCIOUSNESS ALERT: Y/N? Under it is a flickering yellow tag: UN-AUGMENTED. Both pulse at 14 Hz, a frequency calibrated to trigger mild existential nausea in under 30 seconds. The overlays fight with the high-res view through my own eyes, but the external world insists on being the dominant layer. There are floor-to-ceiling windows, and rain falling in algorithmically perfect verticals, reflecting streaks of light across composite basalt floors. The outside is a suggestion. The real is right here, in the way every surface repels fingerprint oil and the smell of human desperation.

I shift. Muscles protest. Some skin still works. The sheets are colder than expected, hospital-sterile, high-count memory foam that feels like sleeping on the regret of every bad decision I've ever made. There's movement beside me, silk sheets exhaling the signature scent of Moshimoto middle management: vetiver, microdosed Prozac, and a spiced note I always associated with quietly engineered layoffs.

Émilie. Lying on her side, facing me. She's not asleep; her breathing is textbook, the practiced simulation of REM. Eyelids flutter in a way that means she's monitoring my vitals, waiting for the right moment to slide into the conversation. The part of my brain that's still corporate property recognizes her immediately: Émilie, Neural Acquisitions, Châtelet Institute vintage, unbreakable NDA on file since before she was born. Her arm rests along my shoulder, the skin slightly off—synth, but second-gen, with the kind of tactile feedback that can fake nervousness if she wants it. Her silver-white fingers stroke my jawline, the motion calculated for maximum trust induction.

"You're running hot again," she murmurs, voice precise even as she aims for a low, morning-after warmth. Her accent is regionless, like she spent six months at a European finishing school and then had it edited out at the neural level. "Says here"—she glances at the inset holo that only she can see—"you spiked at two-forty-seven, dropped to ninety, and then stabilized." Her hand moves to the side of my head, lightly, as if checking for fractures. "Memory event? Or something weirder?"

I take an inventory. My head aches at the base of the occipital lobe, the precise locus where Moshimoto protocols install their most insidious plug-ins. I try to recall what happened before this, but my memory surfaces only in patches: a six-hour meeting in a glass coffin, the sickly green glare of the Bizarre Bezoar Bazaar, a report I was supposed to file. Then nothing; a jump cut to her bedroom, zero transition. The overlays pulse harder, now flashing a dull magenta behind the "UN-AUGMENTED" tag, as if my own meat is yelling at me.

"System override?" I say, voice shredded by hours of disuse. "Or did you dose me again?"

Her smile is a self-repair algorithm—quick, efficient, plausible. "It's a known bug in the patch they pushed last night. Moshimoto claims to have it under control." She shifts closer, letting the sheet fall away to bare her synthetic shoulder and collarbone, both designed for seamless display but subtly at odds with the rest of her—too symmetrical, too perfectly smooth, like they were rendered for a product demo instead of actual use. "You blacked out at 22:07 and woke up here. It's nothing serious, unless you're trying to unionize your own nervous system."

Rain intensifies against the window, each drop lit by street-level advertisements for SKELM CORPS subscriptions and emotional brokerage certificates. The city's memory-foam sky absorbs most of the sound, but inside it's so quiet I can almost hear the faint haptic buzz of her fingers against my skin.

I want to believe her. But the overlays are still there, and now a third tag hovers just above the others: IMPOSTOR

SYNDROME DETECTED—CONSCIOUSNESS RESOLUTION PENDING.

I blink the overlays away, forcing my focus onto her face. It works, but only just. Her eyes meet mine; she holds the gaze a half-second longer than comfort would dictate. Is she scanning my micro-expressions? Probably. I calibrate my own face into deadpan. "What day is it?"

She hesitates, a real pause. "Saturday. Possibly Sunday, depending which hemisphere you're in."

I stare up at the ceiling, running calculations. Last night, I was in Iowa City, prepping for a data transfer that could burn out half the lower-tier neural assets. Then what? The jump to Châtelet's Residential Stack in Neo-Tokyo-Upon-Iowa shouldn't be possible, not on this timeline, not with my access level. "I had a meeting," I say, probing. "They said they needed a final sign-off. Did it happen?"

Her hand stills. She gives me the smallest shrug, nearly a tic. "They postponed. Said you were showing 'suboptimal compliance metrics.' Ordered you to report here for debrief. You don't remember?"

I could push. But her touch is warm, her demeanor perfectly unthreatening, the kind of calculated intimacy that's harder to refuse than any overt manipulation. I roll to my side, away from her, and stare at the window. Rain and neon streak the city in vertical smears; every tenth floor has its own color scheme, and somewhere down there I see the Moshimoto logo repeated like a virus.

I open the internal diagnostic panel in my neural interface, carefully. The "split consciousness" alert won't resolve, but it gives me admin access to system logs—something a normal black-out would never permit. I scroll through the last twelve hours of visual history: time codes, geolocation, encrypted meta tags. Most of it's noise, but at 03:09 there's a ten-minute blackout, followed by a burst of outbound traffic through a private Moshimoto relay. My eyes narrow. The log shows "User: D. Skelm"—my own credentials, except I never consented to the transfer. The destination is a classified server in the Reticulated Reality Reticulum, accessible only to those level three plus.

I run the security footage in split view. There I am—or someone running my exact neural patterns—sitting at a console, fingers moving at inhuman speed, cycling through locked files. The overlays analyze the footage: 99.7% identity match. At the end, the figure looks up at the camera. There's a pause, then the screen goes black.

I let my jaw set, grinding teeth so hard I taste iron. My fingers drum a silent alarm into the mattress, even as I pretend not to care. Émilie leans in, her synthetic arm now curled against my back, the gesture so expert I barely notice the subtext: reassurance, containment, surveillance.

"You're safe," she says, almost convincing. "Whatever happened, Moshimoto will fix it. It's what they do."

I nod, and let her pull me close. But my eyes stay open, watching the rain, watching the city watch me.

"Want breakfast?" she asks, bright and casual, as if the world hasn't just collapsed into probability hell. Her smile is a limited-time coupon for trust. "I have a new batch of void gel, imported from the Bizarre Bezoar Bazaar. Supposed to be good for split-consciousness resets."

She moves to get up, and I study the way her vertebrae segment under flawless synth-skin. She wears nothing but the ghost of yesterday's perfume. I watch for even the smallest deviation—a stumble, a micro-tremor, anything human—but her movements are factory-perfect, as if her every muscle is QA-checked and overclocked.

I let her walk out, let her think she's in control. Then I tap the overlays again, this time going deeper. System logs report three failed password attempts to my own cranial vault, all in the ten-minute blackout. There's also an anomalous ping from the "Department of Recursive Redundancy Department"—a meta-joke among bureaucratic saboteurs, usually the sign of a root-level exploit.

I wipe the sweat from my palms onto the sheets, the gesture hidden under the covers. My heartbeat is up, not that the overlays miss it. "UN-AUGMENTED" now glows a nervous pink, as if even my own interface is doubting me.

By the time Émilie returns with two mugs of nutrient sludge and a plate of corporate-grade fruit, I've already mapped the apartment's internal sensors, noted the lack of actual physical locks on the doors, and run three silent simulations of escape.

She sets the tray beside me and sits cross-legged on the edge of the bed. The fruit is sliced into perfect hexagons, each piece stamped with the Moshimoto "N" like it's a sacrament. I eat, because refusing would be a confession. She watches, amused. "Feeling better?" she asks, though she already knows.

"Better," I lie. "But I think the patch didn't take."

She smirks, swirling her finger in the air to call up a holo. "Typical. The whole city's running on beta code. Maybe that's the point—keeps us adaptive." She leans forward, fixing me with a look that's supposed to be earnest, but her eyes shine with the faintest blue light of a subdermal HUD. "Do you ever wish you could just ... unplug?"

I swallow. It's a trap, but I walk in anyway. "No," I say, too fast. "Not anymore."

She lets it hang for a moment, then touches my face again, this time with the soft pad of her real thumb—if "real" means anything now. "Me neither," she says, and I almost believe her. Almost.

We finish breakfast in silence, the overlays slowly resolving into a dull background hum. I watch her watch me, waiting for the next patch, the next glitch, the next betrayal. Somewhere in the city, another Darby Skelm is running the same protocol, or maybe it's just me, over and over, getting a little less human each time.

Yes, I share a name with the corporation that made me. No, it's not a coincidence. It's a leash they never managed to cut.

The rain never lets up.

By 07:30, Émilie has evaporated into the shower, her presence trailing a fine mist of citrus and subdermal opioids. I lie flat for another thirty seconds—long enough to let the full spectrum of paranoia reach room temperature—then peel the sheets off and move to the window.

The glass is triple-paned and polarized to reflect interior heat signatures. I study the city through its filter; every neon billboard and streetlight are rendered in hostile gradients. My overlays pulse, edges fuzzy with static, the split-consciousness alert refusing to go dormant. I bring up the diagnostics again, this time requesting root access.

Denied.

Which is impossible. Or supposed to be. I tap the override, brute-forcing my way in with the old admin key—buried in a Trojan subroutine I designed back before Moshimoto's neural net divisions went full closed-source. The override hits, and for a moment, I see the full audit trail: a patchwork of patch notes, failed login attempts, and a handful of pings from nodes I recognize as black ops staging grounds. Someone's been in here, scrubbing logs, but they left enough residue to be useful.

I run the most basic check—time-stamped sequences from my own memory stack, cross-referenced with known event markers. The overlay spatters the results in acidic orange: three blocks of memory are flagged as corrupted, and one is just missing, a void with a start time but no end. Last night, the ten minutes after three a.m. I leave the diagnostic open, raw data cascading in the periphery of my vision, and make a slow circuit of the apartment.

Her place is minimalism weaponized: hard surfaces, low furniture, nothing above eye level. Even the artwork—two black rectangles and a single chromed orb suspended from fishing line—looks like a dare. The kitchen counter is clean enough for surgery. I run my palm along it, checking for micro-scratch patterns or pressure points. Nothing, but I tag the location in memory anyway.

Each step leaves a faint footprint in the sound-absorbent polymer flooring. I move barefoot, as quiet as the synthetic cats that prowl the Memory Foreclosure districts, ears tuned for subtle resonance. On the far side of the main room, I find the workstation: one chair, one screen, no visible keyboard. The interface is projected, responding only to authorized neural signals. I slip into the seat, noting the slight indentation—used often, always by someone heavier than Émilie.

I slide my wrist under the interface node and let the station sample my cranial pattern. There's a click, and a faint tremor as the workstation confirms my identity. Not hers—mine. My own access clears the security, which means either she wanted me to find this, or someone else did the last twelve hours of dirty work.

The desktop opens to a single window: Moshimoto Internal News, today's date. The lead story is an HR blast about a new line of SentiSnack™ in the executive vending machines, and an ad for "Emotion Brokerage Certificates" as the next hot investment. I swipe it away, revealing a hidden folder beneath. It's named "_D Skelm."

Subtle.

I tap it open. Inside are logs, voice memos, and raw security feeds. I drag them into my neural HUD for quick analysis. The overlays project a timeline, slotting events into a neat, clinical schema. 02:40—arrival at Châtelet Stack. 02:55—entry into this apartment. 03:00—log blackout. 03:13—workstation login under my own name, ten minutes after blackout ends. 03:17—

seventy-two terabytes transferred via untraceable relay to the Moshimoto sub-basement.

What the hell did I move?

The answer sits in the last file, marked "PRIVATE—FINAL." I play it, sound only, the overlays suppressing voiceprint recognition to protect the source. It's my own voice, monotone, stripped of affect. "Transfer complete. System integrity degraded. Awaiting next instruction."

I scrub the file, searching for telltale click-backs or spliced-in segments. There are three. The longest is twelve seconds, an absence filled by white noise and the hint of whispered French, a language I only know from having it force-fed in corporate onboarding modules. I glance toward the bedroom. The shower is still running, thick steam curling out from under the door, the air in the main room dense enough to dull ambient sound. I take the risk: slip out of the workstation, pad to the bedroom, check her open tablet on the nightstand.

The tablet's active, running a diagnostics console I've only seen in Moshimoto experimental divisions. The header reads "SPLIT AGENT INTEGRATION: CASE STUDY #7." The log trail lists updates every fifteen minutes, the latest at 07:08: "Subject shows improved compliance. Recommending next patch at 08:00."

I screenshot it to my own interface, careful to mask the transmission. The overlays chew through the log, highlighting every instance of my own name, each time cross-linked to reports of neural desynchronization. She's studying me. Or studying what's left of me.

The shower cuts out, a sudden absence of white noise. I glide back to the kitchen, pour two cups of grey tea from the dispenser, and position myself at the island just as she emerges, towel wrapped like a uniform, hair not even wet. She stops when she sees me. Her smile is an equation, balanced perfectly between sympathy and dominance. “Didn’t mean to take so long,” she says, peeling the towel away in one continuous motion, body as clean and inhumanly precise as the furniture. “I lose track of time.”

“You always were good at that,” I say, gesturing with the tea. “Got a moment?”

She accepts the cup, careful not to let our fingers touch. “I’m already late. They want me to brief the Data Integrity board on the new security protocol.” Her eyes flick up, registering the overlays. “Yours is still glitched.”

I tap the side of my head. “Getting worse, actually. Memory gaps, overlays refusing to clear. Is it the patch, or something else?”

She shrugs, sipping her tea. “Your neural patterns show typical split-consciousness artifacts. Nothing to worry about. Moshimoto R&D is working on a fix.” She studies me, clinical, then lowers her gaze, as if the intimacy is too much.

“It wasn’t like this before,” I say, and let the accusation float in the space between us.

She rolls her eyes, expertly done, then softens her voice. “They said this might happen. It’s a side effect of using unaugmented hosts.” Her synthetic hand covers mine, cold and smooth. “If you want, I can schedule a flush. You’ll lose a few hours, but it’s safer.”

I pull my hand away, just enough to make the point. "I want to know what happened during the blackout."

She leans back against the counter, crossing her legs at the ankle, towel barely holding on. The way she positions herself is so perfectly calculated it must be intentional—a distraction, a power play, maybe both.

"I told you. You blacked out. The patch didn't take, then they brought you here for observation. I watched you the entire time."

A lie, because the logs show her out of the apartment from 02:45 to 03:12. "Where were you during the blackout?" I ask, deadpan.

She blinks, a real stutter this time. "I stepped out for a call. They needed an update on your status."

"And when you got back?"

"You were asleep." She says it like an accusation.

I process. The overlays flag her heartbeat as steady, but micro-tremors in the hand suggest she's running higher than baseline. "Why not leave me at Moshimoto? Why bring me here?"

She moves closer, hips against the counter, voice now barely above a whisper. "They didn't trust you," she says, "but I do." She lets the sentence hang, and the way she stares makes me want to believe her, even as every diagnostic screams otherwise. I turn away, scanning the apartment one last time, overlays highlighting every possible exit. She's blocking the most obvious path. "Are you going to report me?" she asks, the question loaded.

"Depends," I say. "On what you're hiding."

She grins, a slow reveal of perfect teeth, each one a micro-antenna tuned to detect deception. "We're all hiding something, Darby. Some of us just get paid better for it." She steps aside, towel dropping to the floor, and walks into the bedroom to dress. I watch her go, knowing she expects me to follow, that her every move is mapped three steps ahead. I stay where I am, overlay in silent mode, running recursive simulations of escape, betrayal, and every possible endpoint. I let the tension coil, ready for the next move. In the hallway, her voice carries. "You coming? Or are you going to stand there all day, watching the world watch you?"

The overlays pulse: UN-AUGMENTED. SPLIT CONSCIOUSNESS. And now a third line: USER: D. SKELM—ERROR. FILE NOT FOUND.

I smile, and follow her into the next disaster.

Émilie leaves for her urgent Moshimoto meeting at 08:13 sharp, schedule ironed to the minute. She wears tailored graphite pants and a spectral-white blouse, the kind that costs more than my quarterly paycheck. Her scent lingers after the front door seals with a wet click. She doesn't look back, doesn't say goodbye—just a soft "Stay, rest, recover" thrown over her synth-shoulder, and then she's gone.

My hands hover over the cooling teacup, unsure what to do with the leftover heat. I let it slide off my fingertips and wander to the bedroom. The overlays whine at sub-audible frequencies, split-consciousness alert mutating into something new: SENSE OF SELF DEGRADATION—IMMINENT. I palm the message away and stare at the closet. There's nothing remarkable about it—two meters wide, matte-black finish, handles perfectly flush with the doors.

But now the scene feels wrong. A single, invisible fuck-you from the universe, stashed among her precisely arranged wardrobe. I run a finger along the panel edge. The texture is maybe .0003 microns rougher than the rest, but it stands out like a gunshot to me. The overlays map the door in ghostly blue, a semi-transparent schematic forming over real space. There—a discontinuity, a rectangle offset by three millimeters, enough to hide a panel, a safe, or something far less legal.

I hesitate. The overlays feed in silent warnings: UNAUTHORIZED ACCESS DETECTED. LOGGING INITIATED. They want to scare me off, but that part of my brain was burned out back in the Moshimoto internment camps, when I was nine and already outdated.

I press the panel at the seam. It yields with a hiss, sliding open to reveal a low-lit alcove packed with hardware: racks of neural tangle, two palm-sized psycho-scalpels humming at a barely contained frequency, and a squat black box with its own medusa of braided wire. Above it all is a stack of clear-poly storage trays, each with a single labeled chip, tags inked in Émilie's crisp, upmarket handwriting: *D. Skelm. G01. D. Skelm. G02.* And on and on, at least sixteen in total.

I reach for the nearest chip, fingers numb. The overlays flicker as the RFID pings the system: MATCH: 99.999%—SUBJECT: D. Skelm. These are memory extraction modules, proprietary to Moshimoto R&D, only legal in three out of eight post-collapse continents. Each chip is a neatly-wrapped biopsy of my own consciousness, harvested at intervals regular enough to qualify as ritual murder.

I slot one into the black box and run the interface. The box boots with a purr, its surface warming under my hand, overlays auto-projecting a UI straight onto the backs of my retinas. I skim through the log: timestamps, access markers, "COMPLIANT MEMORY SEGMENTS" and "SUPPRESSED AFFECTIVE RESPONSE" reports. The first entry is dated seven months ago, in this very apartment.

My mouth dries out, tongue turning into a salt lick. My hands shake—harder than I want to admit. For a second, I think I'm going to drop the chip, but I get it back into the tray and close the panel. I sit on the edge of the bed, overlays pulsing with error codes I can't process. My stomach knots. My vision tunnels.

It's not the violation, not even the betrayal; it's the precision of the thing. The logs show every extraction, every moment of compliance, each one perfectly timed to occur during sleep or micro-blackouts, zero trauma to the subject, absolute plausible deniability. Émilie didn't just sabotage me—she wrote a user manual on how to dissect my selfhood and make it look like maintenance.

I dig my nails into my palm, desperate for something analog. Pain filters in, distant but present. The overlays offer a "PAIN KILL" toggle; I ignore it. I want to feel this. There's a final log, timestamped three days ago. The header reads: FINAL SEQUENCE. SUBJECT: D. Skelm. STATUS: FULLY RESOLVED.

I can't open it. I won't. I power down the box, bury the chip back in the tray, and close the panel with a trembling slap. My vision blurs. The overlays try to comfort me, but I shut them off completely, darkness crawling in from the edges. I fall back onto the mattress, the same cold sheet from this morning now hot and suffocating. My back slides down the wall, legs giving way, arms useless. I think I might scream, but all that comes out is a strangled half-breath, recycled air hissing through clenched teeth.

Bile rises. I make it to the bathroom sink and splatter pink-tinged saliva across the porcelain. I grip the edges until my knuckles bleach out, try to focus on the steady drone of the city beyond the window, the endless rain, the indifferent sky. I stare at my reflection in the mirror, overlays dead, no filters, just the raw animal staring back. I look older. I look erased.

I remember a training module from my first year at Moshimoto: “Trust no one who smiles with both their eyes and their mouth.” It seemed like a joke at the time. Now it just echoes, hollow and precise, in the empty spaces of my brain. I drift back to the bedroom. The panel in the closet is closed, but now it’s all I can see. I drop to the floor, back against the wall, knees to chest.

I count the seconds, waiting for her to come home.

Chapter 2

It takes four hours for the fear to crystallize into anger. Then I make myself stand. My legs are nothing but rubber and guilt. The overlays persist—shoving "SPLIT CONSCIOUSNESS ALERT" up and down my visual field like a warning no one can hear but me. I'm not waiting for Émilie anymore. I'm waiting for myself, and whoever that is, he's going to do something dumb.

The air in her apartment is so clean it hurts. I let it slice up my nasal cavities as I cross back to the bedroom, the sheets still twisted where I'd collapsed, the ghost of my outline visible on the high-count memory foam. The overlays ping the closet panel like a shark after blood. My hand goes to the seam before I'm aware of it.

The secret panel gives with less resistance than a polite door. No sound except a thin rush of cold air, recirculated and ozonated. Inside: not one rack but three, stacked with hardware modules, neural tangles, and microtome scalpels in zippered foam slots. Nothing left to chance, every cable coiled in geometric perfection, so precise it would make a C-suite archivist weep.

It is organized by a mind that knows what it wants, and for months, what it wanted was me.

I reach for the top tray. It's heavy, denser than it should be for its size. The labels on the chips are laser-etched in bone-white: *D. Skelm G01, D. Skelm G02*. The increments are regular, as if I'm just another item in a procurement line. Even now, my name looks foreign in her handwriting—sterile, almost pretty, the kind you'd see on corporate Christmas cards or lawsuit subpoenas.

The overlays go apeshit as I slot the first chip into the black diagnostic box. My field of view shatters into nested windows: timestamps, capture logs, biometric overlays—all calibrated to my unique neural patterns. The chip boots, and with it, an animated sequence of my own memory events—sleep cycles, micro-blackouts, forced compliance states—every one cross-referenced and color-coded in nauseating clarity.

The logs begin seven months ago, exactly as the apartment logs predicted. Every patch update, every "maintenance" session. All of it timed for sleep, or the aftermath of sexual compliance when my threat response is at its most pliable. "Minimum trauma. Maximum yield." It's not just a violation—it's a product line.

I force myself to look at the usage report. Neural harvests are transferred in three-minute blocks, always off-peak, always masked under standard home automation traffic. The recipient address is a Moshimoto sub-basement, but sometimes it's rerouted: Bizarre Bezoar Bazaar, Iowa City server farms, a few outliers with encrypted quantum tags. She's not just mining me for Moshimoto. She's open-sourcing my selfhood to every bidder who has a finger on the consciousness market.

There's a note appended to the last transfer, written in her private deadpan:

Subject: D. Skelm

Extraction Protocol: Ongoing, no resistance.

Recalibration at next event.

I can't feel my fingers anymore. The overlays want to offer suggestions for emotional stabilization, but I block them, watching the warnings flicker up the inside of my skull: SELF INTEGRITY DEGRADATION—CRITICAL. HOST INCOMPATIBLE. And my favorite, PROTOCOL INDOCTRINATION: PENDING.

I slot the second chip. The data ramps in, doubling the size of the harvest log. There are two hundred and thirty-seven extraction events, each with a full stack of my memory, my preferences, my pain. She took everything. Even the dreams I thought were too broken to matter—they're here, mapped in exquisite detail, labeled, and sorted for resale.

The smell of her perfume, always a comfort, now stabs the roof of my mouth. It's the only thing in the closet not designed to kill me. The overlays stutter, a magenta halo that flickers at exactly 14 Hz, the same frequency as the lab where they used to study mass-induced existential terror.

I pull out a random chip from the bottom tray, praying it might contain someone else's life, maybe even hers, but the label is a joke: *D. Skelm G12, Raw.* I slide it in. The system lags for a full two seconds before the data renders.

It's my birth—or the closest approximation the chip could muster. A fragment of a memory I never had, scrubbed clean and polished until it's no longer trauma but content. They're making movies out of my misery, running highlight reels in boardrooms, trading my identity like a zero-interest loan. My stomach seizes. For a second, I can't tell if I'm going to scream or throw up.

Instead, I drop the chip. It bounces once on the memory foam and rolls to a stop by my foot. I let it lie there. I look at my hand, not sure it's mine, and see the overlay's last gasp: CONSCIOUSNESS OVERLOAD—SYSTEM RESTART SUGGESTED. I kneel in the closet, the cold perfumed air like a punch to the solar plexus, and I try to imagine what kind of person could do this to someone they loved. I don't come up with an answer, but for the first time in months, I remember what it's like to feel alive.

I reach up, take the tray of chips, and tip them all into my pockets. The hum of the neural tangle is louder now, the closet's hidden fans working overtime to keep the system from overheating. I shut the panel. It seals perfectly, not even a line to show it was ever open. I wipe the sweat from my palms, steady my breathing, and stagger to my feet. The overlays flicker. My body is a failure, but it's still mine—for now.

I drag myself to the shower, set the cold water to maximum, and let the pulse hammer me back into a shape that can walk. My brain whines at every temperature differential, but I ignore it. I want to feel the shock, the numbness, the ridiculous hope that something in me can still resist this machine.

When the water runs clear, I towel off and sit cross-legged in the hallway, the chips heavy in my lap. The overlays have given up, replaced by raw input—the way I used to see the world, before Moshimoto, before Émilie, before every memory had a price. The apartment is silent except for the whisper of the neural tangle, always harvesting, never done.

I stare at the bedroom door and wait for her to come back, rehearsing every question I'll never have the courage to ask. Outside, the rain keeps falling, as if the sky has nothing better to do but mourn.

I give the overlays five minutes before the error messages subside. When they come back online, it's with the nervous energy of a rat in a demolition zone—scared, shuddering, but compelled to keep moving forward. I stare at the chips, and the chips stare back. I want to smash them, burn the contents, but it's not enough to erase the evidence. I need to understand it.

The chips hum with their own sick logic; all I have to do is let the black diagnostic box handshake with my cranial vault, and it walks me straight into the backend of Émilie's file system. Her workstation boots to life in the next room, probably triggered by a proximity script. I carry the chips over, ignore the warning about "EXTERNAL MEDIA DETECTED—MALWARE RISK," and pop the tray into her workstation's main reader.

The interface lights up, overlays sluicing the data into my periphery: personal logs, research protocols, dozens of high-clearance Moshimoto Corp memos. Most of it is encrypted with a custom obfuscator, but the chips—brilliant, malicious, clever—carry a digest of my own wetware, and that gives the system just enough doubt to let me in as "Authorized User: D. Skelm." The overlays whisper "PROTOCOL ELEVATION: ADMIN," and for the first time, I get to see the world from Émilie's side of the glass.

I open her secure inbox. The top message is flagged "RED," the highest possible urgency in Moshimoto color theory. The subject line is an anhedonic joke: "Final Disposition—READABLE SLAVE PROTOCOL—CHILDREN." I click. It unfolds as a corporate epic: sanitized, clinical, and perfectly monstrous.

TO: Émilie, Neural Acquisitions

FROM: C. Merrow, SVP Human Factors

SUBJECT: Final Disposition—READABLE SLAVE PROTOCOL—CHILDREN

Summary:

Per latest directive, all child subjects exhibiting incomplete protocol adherence ("readable slaves") are to be transitioned to Observation Pool or, in cases of demonstrable value, repurposed for conscious analyst testing. See attached for operational timeline and disposal protocols. DO NOT UNDER ANY CIRCUMSTANCE permit subject to interface with external networks without prior authorization from Moshimoto Legal.

My eyes dart to the attachment. It's a PDF, but it boots in the overlays as a 3D model: cross-sections of human brains, each with neural scarring highlighted in deep indigo. I rotate the model, see where the scars run—a lattice of crosslinked trauma, woven through the hippocampus and up into the frontal cortex. The legend is a horror show: STANDARD

DAMAGE ZONE, ENHANCED OBEDIENCE REGION, EXPERIMENTAL LOYALTY BAND. In the margin, a note: D. Skelm—Unique unaugmented signature. Retain for further study.

My hands start to shake. I want to tell myself it's just fatigue, but the overlays log microtremors and amp up their own stability software. I don't remember ever having a nervous system that wanted to save itself this bad.

I scroll down. The procurement manifests are worse than the diagrams. Moshimoto Corp maintains a running inventory of "suitable subjects." Each name comes with a purchase order, shipping route, and current location in the company's infrastructure. A thousand children—maybe more—sorted into cohorts, their fates cross-tabbed against extraction schedules and revenue projections. My name is on there, alongside a note: *Subject demonstrated high-level analytical skills. Monitor for noncompliance.* The overlays translate the line into what it really means: *Don't kill the golden goose until you're sure it can't lay any more eggs.*

I drag a hand across my face and feel the sweat on my upper lip, cold and sour. For a second, my vision swims with afterimages: the labs, the isolation chambers, the promises they made before they took everything from me. It wasn't random. It was a production line, and I was just a run of particularly valuable code.

There's more. I click through the technical specs: Optimal Neural Scarring for Compliance, Accelerated Amnesia via Retrograde Protocol, Emotional Inhibition Algorithms for Host Integration. Each white paper comes with citations, most from the Châtelet Institute. Her alma mater. Where they breed them smarter, and less likely to revolt.

My mouth tastes of copper, like I've been biting my own tongue for hours. The overlays say my cortisol is spiking, but they're programmed never to let it go lethal. Can't risk asset loss. I find a folder marked "Testimonial Logs." Against my better judgement, I open the first one. It's a video. The overlays render it as a hologram over the workstation: a young boy —ten, maybe—brown hair buzzed short, his Moshimoto uniform too big for him. He's plugged in, wires curling from behind each ear like the tentacles of a dying jellyfish. He reads from a script.

"My name is"—the overlays mute the name—"and I am a Readable Slave, Class III. I like puzzles and animals. Sometimes I remember my mom, but not all the time. They say if I get better, I can go to a new home. I hope it is nice there." The video ends, replaced by a progress chart: COMPLIANCE IMPROVEMENT: 37%. RECOMMEND: Continue Protocol.

I scroll through hundreds more: kids smiling through dead eyes, each one evidence of how much damage Moshimoto can do to a soul before it stops being marketable. I try to keep it impersonal, analyst's distance, but the overlays keep nudging me to flag any file that "feels relevant." They don't know how close I am to flagging the whole fucking company for deletion.

The bile finally comes up. I stagger to the bathroom, puke into the sink, and wipe my mouth with the back of my hand. The overlays try to pop a wellness tip, but I smash it out of my visual field. I crawl back to the workstation and keep reading. The last memo in the folder is from Émilie herself. It's addressed to the same SVP, time-stamped two hours before my last memory blackout.

TO: C. Merrow

FROM: Émilie, Neural Acquisitions

SUBJECT: Progress Update—D. Skelm

Skelm shows increased protocol compliance with recent calibration. Secondary benefits: unique neural structure allows for more stable data throughput, and reduced external memory bleed. Potential for escalation to Analyst Tier is significant. Recommend: Continue integration. If behavioral anomalies persist, schedule a full flush and transition to observation.

The line that kills me is at the end, buried in the small print:

P.S. He never really had a chance.

I stare at that line until the overlays grey out, fade to static, and then go dead.

I'm not crying. There's no time for that. I'm too busy calculating, weighing options, and mapping every possible angle of attack against the machine that made me. I replay the testimonial logs, searching for flaws in the system, holes in the compliance protocol, backdoors I can use to make it hurt. The world is small now: me, the chips, the workstation, the rain. The air in the apartment is so cold it makes my teeth ache. I think of all the other kids, all the other "products" they made and broke, and I swear—not as a promise, but as a hypothesis—I will burn this place down if it's the last thing I do.

The overlays flicker back on, tentative, like an abused animal. There's no more error message, only a quiet question: USER: D. Skelm. INSTRUCTION?

I whisper back, "Kill switch."

I wait for the overlays to figure out how.

The overlays process my last command with the kind of devotion only a corporate slave could muster. They run a full scan of every chip, every message, and every snippet of memory Émilie ever took from me. They copy, segment, catalog—each file hashed and checked, nothing left behind. I can't bear to sit, so I pace the apartment, room to room, as the overlays keep up a whispery feed of transfer status:

MEMORY SEGMENT—UPLOADING: 23%

TESTIMONIAL LOGS—ARCHIVING: 72%

INTERNAL CORRESPONDENCE—BACKUP COMPLETE

The air tastes sharper now, more metallic, like I'm breathing in the fallout of a disaster and not just watching from the sidelines. My head aches but I force myself to stay lucid. There's no room left for panic or self-pity. My training takes over, mercenary and precise. I hunt for a secure drive. Of course Émilie has a stash of them: a fireproof envelope under the cutlery tray, three cold-storage cubes taped to the underside of her desk. I grab them all. Redundancy is god.

With every byte transferred, the overlays grow steadier. I set up the three drives on her workstation, start a recursive mirror, then crosslink them through a logic chain so deranged only someone with my exact neural flaws could unlock it. For once, my brain's "unique unaugmented signature" is good for something.

It takes thirty-six minutes for the entire archive to duplicate. I walk in circles while I wait, and every time I pass the open closet, I notice something new: a patch of worn plastic on the diagnostic box, the dull metal of a heat sink smeared with nail polish. But it's the chip trays that catch me. There are faint scratch marks along the bottom edges—evidence of frequent use. Some of the chips are slightly bent, scuffed, even blood-specked from hasty swaps. None of this is the work of a detached scientist. It's the work of someone who did it often, fast, and under pressure.

I run a cross-check on the chip labels against the time stamps in the logs. The alignment is sickening: every "memory harvest" matches up to a blackout in my personal overlay logs. Sometimes the gaps are as short as five minutes, sometimes two hours. Once, a whole day. All those times I "lost myself," I woke up in strange places, or felt like reality had skipped ahead, like a bad edit—those were extractions. Product updates. Scheduled maintenance. I almost laugh. Then I almost cry.

The data archive finishes. The overlays pop up a summary:

EVIDENCE PACKAGE—SIZE: 1.6 PETABYTES

CONTENTS:

- Readable Slave Protocol documentation

- Child procurement manifests

- Neural scarring specs

- Analyst performance logs

- Internal memos (Émilie: 49 unique, 71 copies)

- Testimonial logs (Children: 1,802)

- Executive correspondence (Merrow, etc.)

- Marketing collateral: 'Consciousness. Reimagined.'

- Blackout event traces (D. Skelm: 237 unique)

ENCRYPTION: custom, one-way

REDUNDANCY: 3x

INSTRUCTION?

I stare at the screen. There are a thousand options, but really, only one. "Distribute," I say aloud.

The overlays do not hesitate. The first copy goes to my own cold storage cube, now cradled in my palm. The second is prepped for courier drop at the Bizarre Bezoar Bazaar, where all manner of black-market chaos festers. The third goes to the only contact I trust—my old handler at DARN, back when sabotage was a dirty hobby and not a full-time career. The overlays add a failsafe: if any drive goes offline, the next in chain activates, dumping the whole archive to the wilds of the dark net and a half-dozen corporate rivals.

The overlays seem almost pleased with themselves, like they want to impress me. Maybe they're learning. Maybe I'm finally training them. I wipe my palms on my pants, the sweat gone clammy and cold. There's nothing left to copy, so I take a last look at the closet. I slide the trays back into their racks, one by one, but not before pocketing three chips at random. I don't know if I'll need them. But I want to keep a piece of myself, for whatever's next.

As I reach for the last tray, I notice a tiny sticker on the underside: *Property of Châtelet Institute*. The overlays dig up a registry number, cross-referencing it with the archives. The chip belonged to another child, not me—a girl named Issa, deceased age nine. Her testimonial log is short, just three files, but the overlays flag one as "emotionally significant." I download it and try to listen, but my ears fill with static, my throat locks up, and all I can hear is my own pulse.

I snap the tray shut, maybe a little too hard, and the closet panel slams into place with a sound like a bullet in a crime drama. That's when I see the final memo. It's an auto-forward from Émilie, flagged "Priority: Lethal." It hit the Moshimoto servers exactly ninety seconds before I woke up in her bed this morning.

TO: Moshimoto Neural Acquisitions Board

FROM: Émilie

SUBJECT: Acquisition Complete—D. Skelm

Team,

Phase One extraction concluded. Subject demonstrates exceptional neural resilience, unprecedented self-diagnostic abilities, and superior memory retention (see attached logs). Subject is suitable for advanced test scenarios or repurposing at Board discretion.

Recommend: immediate transition to secondary exploitation, with direct Board oversight.

Note: Subject is displaying signs of emergent anti-corporate behavior. Consider full flush as a containment measure.

—E

P.S. There are no more loyal assets. Only survivors.

I read it three times, just to savor the audacity. Then I erase the file, overwrite the space, and encrypt it under a random hash. I zip my jacket, slide the three cold storage cubes into the lining, and pocket the chips. The overlays go quiet, almost reverent. There's nothing more they can say.

At the front door, I hesitate. The city is still there, waiting, rain turning the streets into mirrored rivers. In the distance, the Moshimoto building glows like a wound, pink neon pulsing in time with my own heart. For a second, I remember every kindness Émilie ever showed me. Then I remember every file, every scar, every testimony. The rage isn't even personal anymore. It's too big for that.

I leave the apartment and close the door behind me, gentle, like I'm tucking someone in for the last time. The rain hits me square in the face, and for the first time in years, I let it. The overlays ask if I want to archive the sensation, but I say no. I want to remember this.

Chapter 3

The overlays wake me at 02:17, shoving a wall of red across my retinas: IMMEDIATE PHYSICAL THREAT—EVICTION PENDING. The old jokes weren't wrong—every eviction is terminal. And this isn't a social worker or even a repo drone. It's a kill team, and they're burning latency just to savor the anticipation.

A microsecond later, the soundproof glass of Émilie's apartment shatters with the precision of a surgical incision. The first bullet is through the memory foam mattress before the kinetic signature even reaches my inner ear. The second round is a lazy ricochet, meant to herd, not kill. The third one's real; it tags the headboard an inch from my left eye.

Overlays flood my field: threat vectors, trajectory estimations, projected splash radius of the wall's ceramic foam. I roll under the bed, a move as much muscle memory as intent, and the next two bullets cut air where my brain case was. My own diagnostic feed refuses to settle. CONSCIOUSNESS

INTEGRITY: 61%—DROPPING. I force a cognitive blink, letting the overlays slide off priority and into instinct.

Above me, a single black boot lands in the splinters, followed by another, and another, each perfectly spaced for intimidation. I count three before the room floods with the synth-ozone stench of crowd-control gas. There are two ways out. The closet, or the service crawl behind the shower. The closet panel is slow, too obvious. The crawl is closer, but I haven't mapped it.

I decide, not with logic but with the ruined animal between my lungs. The overlays approve. SURVIVAL PROBABILITY: 18%—ADJUSTED. I exhale, hard, empty my lungs for a smaller target profile, and slide toward the bathroom as a fresh volley erases the mattress behind me. Shrapnel slices the tip of my right ear, pain hitting the nerves with a taste like electrocuted lemon. I let it power me through the glass shower door, crashing it with both feet first.

Behind the rain glass, I'm momentarily invisible. The crawl's access hatch is right where I hoped, hiding behind a wall tile the exact shade of synthetic ash. I jam my thumb against the release; it doesn't recognize my print, but enough skin comes away to let the biometric reader taste the blood.

The hatch swings open. I dive in, arms first, ignoring the way the metal ribs skin my knuckles. There's enough room for a child, maybe a maintenance bot; for a grown man, it's a birth canal lined with knives. Someone shouts from the bedroom, language scrambled by an imported accent. I catch only "alive" and "bring him," followed by the sound of three bodies converging at maximum threat velocity.

The crawl is ten meters of hell, then an elbow turn, then another hatch to the auxiliary utility corridor. The overlays dim as I go, sensors having to guess instead of verify. Every six inches, I set off a micro-tremor alarm, which is probably by design. But the attackers are slow—either they expect me dead, or they want a clean extraction.

Halfway through, I lose feeling in my left hand. It flops behind me, dead weight, blood from the hatch pooling at my elbow. The overlays offer a quick diagnostic: SEVERED RADIAL NERVE—CRITICAL, BUT NON-LETHAL. I blink it away, the world tunneling into a bright dot at the end of the pipe.

A gunshot from the far side makes the tunnel jump in my grip, then another and another, each one closer, more urgent. I have six seconds, maybe five. At the exit hatch, I punch the release with my ruined hand, pain triggering a phosphene burst that, for a moment, whites out the overlays and the world. It opens. I fall out and land face-first on the utility corridor's composite, shins ablaze from the friction. I scramble to my feet, half-blind, half-corpse, and run.

Behind me, the first of the kill team slams into the crawl exit, helmeted head crabbing sideways as it tries to free itself. I keep moving, hands and knees, tearing open every old scar on my body. At the end of the corridor is the high-security recycling chute, built for waste but big enough for a desperate analyst. I don't think. I jump.

The chute drops for nine meters, spinning and bouncing me off the sides, every bounce a new diagnostic warning: FRACTURE—LEFT RADIUS, LACERATION—RIGHT THIGH, LOSS OF TOOTH: #13. I count each one, as if they matter. The world ends with a deafening clang as I hit the chute's termination grille, mesh bending under the force, but not enough to break. The overlays fade for a second, reboot, and when I come back, the only thing I see is the taste of copper and the sound of my own pulse, impossibly loud.

I look up. The ceiling panel is thin, cheap, meant for cleaning bots, not humans. I put my whole body into one upward punch and shatter through it, coming up into a janitorial closet full of dirty linens and plastic buckets. I'm in the service sublevel, three stories down from Émilie's apartment. There's no time to plan. I wipe blood from my eyes, shove a hand towel against the gash in my arm, and stagger for the door.

As I limp through the silent service corridor, I do the math. Moshimoto sent three, probably four kill teams. Émilie's security would never have allowed it unless she was gone, or she'd been the one to pull the trigger. My head throbs, neural extraction scars lighting up every time I flex my jaw. I picture her face, ashen with anger or guilt or both, the last moment before I left her bed. Was it a lie, the whole thing? Or did she play me because the only other option was worse? The overlays suggest: ANALYSIS IRRELEVANT. FOCUS: ESCAPE.

I laugh, raw and ugly. Even my own subroutines know I'm an idiot.

I stagger up the emergency stairwell, footprints making a map of failure behind me. At every floor, I scan for movement, for heat signatures, anything that says the kill team is ahead or behind. Nothing but the slow, even hum of a corporate building in off-hours. I hit the ground floor and step into a lobby so bright it blinds. The cleaning drones have polished every surface to a weaponized sheen, and the only sign of life is a single security guard behind a quartz desk. His eyes don't lift from the screen. He's not expecting a naked, bleeding analyst at three in the morning.

I cross the lobby, hunched, trying to blend into the geometry of the place. As I reach the revolving doors, a second kill team enters the far side—two men and a woman, all dressed in Moshimoto black, faces hidden by filter masks. They see me instantly, and the woman raises a palm, projecting a warning shot that vaporizes the air above my head. I drop, roll, and bolt for the staff elevator. The overlays shout "NO EXIT," but there's a chance, however stupid. The elevator is still old enough for a manual override; I slap the panel and the doors open with a groan.

Inside, I punch the "roof access" button and kill the override. As the doors close, a round punches through the steel, slicing my ribs, but not deep enough to stop me. Ascent is slow, torturous. My blood turns the floor of the elevator into a murder scene. I stuff my fingers into the wound, scream into the walls, and count the floors in binary.

At the roof, I stagger out. The night is cold, but the rain is hotter than blood, pounding the city in horizontal lines. Neon from the next tower over slashes the world into color channels: pink, blue, and dead white. The overlays ping—there's a drone overhead, waiting, lazy. Not a kill team drone, a standard comms repeater, but it will have eyes, and those eyes will betray me.

I scan the edge of the roof. There is only one way down: the thirty-meter drop to the building next door. Between here and there is nothing but wind and advertising light. My ribs scream. My right arm is dead, my left leg a tangle of meat.

But the overlays give me a number: SURVIVAL PROBABILITY: 2%.

I'll take it.

Behind me, the elevator doors scream open and the kill team bursts out, guns drawn, voices flat with kill protocol. I hear the whine of a targeting laser against my shoulder. I hear a command: "Skelm, surrender!"

I run.

Three steps. Four. Five. The world contracts into a single moment, every muscle a live wire. I picture Émilie, the last real thing in my life, and use that as fuel. I leap. For a moment, the city is all light and noise and possibility, and my overlays are silent. Then I fall.

The wind tears the sound from my lungs. The rain flays my skin raw. Thirty meters becomes thirty years, the seconds stretched into eternity. I hit the next roof like a sack of broken glass. Pain floods the world—real pain, not the abstracted simulation of trauma I've known all my life.

The overlays pop a message in my blood-blind vision: USER: D. SKELM. INSTRUCTION?

I crawl to my knees, laugh until I spit blood, and say, "Run."

And then, like a goddamn miracle, I do.

The overlays don't bother with color anymore. Warnings scroll as blind white, strobing like an epileptic's funeral: LIMBIC INTEGRITY—CRITICAL, BLEEDOUT WINDOW: 8 MINUTES, MOTION DEGRADATION: IRREVERSIBLE."

I run anyway.

The roof slopes down toward the market below, slick with moss and windborne trash. I catch maybe two seconds of deceleration before the composite gives way, and I drop clean through an overhang of digital-plastic awnings. A pop, a snap, and then I'm falling, time dilating for just long enough to make me hate gravity even more than I hate myself. I hit an old man's fruit cart, breaking its back and my own fall. Hardlight pears scatter everywhere, dissolving into bio-bright slurry that stains my bare chest blue. The man yells, but the overlays are already mapping the next three threats:

1. Heat spike from the kill team's re-entry path, thirty meters due west.

2. Local PD beacon, converging from below.

3. Drone flight path, time to contact: 16 seconds and dropping.

I sprint, weaving through the smog of steamed noodles and burned sugar, every step a new catastrophic diagnostic. My right ankle stops reporting; my left ear is useless, nothing but a siren wail. The crowd in the market is thick, bodies dense as pixels, every face rendered with the slapdash economy of a meat printer. They ignore me, or maybe they see only what they're paid to see.

I push into a tunnel of heat, a corridor between vendor stalls. The air is a vaporized cocktail of pork, wet cardboard, and ozone, dense enough to coat my lungs in greasy aftertaste. My feet skid over oil and more fruit. The overlays try to warn me about "CARDIAC OVERLOAD," but the words blur and double, then fall away.

Above, the drone makes contact. It's a Kestrel unit, seven rotors, bristling with chems and kill sticks. The paint job is Moshimoto black, but the stenciling is custom: a smiling cartoon wolf eating a cartoon sheep. The crowd is cover, up to a point. I duck behind a stall selling knockoff SentiSnacks™ and snag a blade from the vendor's array. The woman behind the counter doesn't react; her overlays must filter out anything not marked as purchase intent.

The drone tracks me, heat sensors working overtime. I look up, making eye contact with the primary camera. A red laser dot dances on my collarbone, then shifts to my sternum, settling for optimal organ disruption. I get a quarter-second to act.

I throw the knife, wild and stupid. The blade spins end-over-end and, miracle of miracles, lodges in the drone's lower intake. There's a squeal, then a judder as the rotor alignment warps. It spits a burst of tranquilizer darts, four of them, all wide of target as the drone tries to right itself. It plummets into a stack of market crates, smashing half a metric ton of counterfeit citrus and a kid's toy kiosk.

I don't get to celebrate. Behind me, two corporate goons in debt collector uniforms shoulder their way through the crowd, guns held high, eyes glassy with the pleasure of sanctioned violence. Their overlays are probably showing a live feed of my vitals, maybe even my thoughts. I duck under a noodle cart and upend it into the legs of the first goon. He goes down, face-first, a bouquet of instant ramen sticking to his mask. The second goon swings wide, trying to cut me off at the mouth of the alley.

He yells something about "asset recovery," but my ears are ringing too hard to care. I put my head down and charge, body lowered for impact. I hit him just above the knees, a move stolen from playground football, and he folds with a satisfying crunch. I keep going. The alley twists left, then right, then opens onto a loading dock behind a closed department store. There's a delivery van idling, its side hatch open, the smell of wet cardboard and canned despair radiating off it in waves.

I consider hiding, but the overlays tell me my heat signature would light up the whole block. No point. I climb the van, using it as a ramp to the fire escape above. My hands are bloody, slippery, but adrenaline glues me to the metal. I hear shouts below as the kill team regroups, boots stomping through the market slop.

At the top of the fire escape, I'm twelve stories up, city open in every direction. The rain is horizontal now, pushed by cross-winds into perfect slashing lines. Every building surface is a screen, every screen a new ad for SKELM CORPS or the latest flavor of Emotion Brokerage Certificate. I want to keep running, but my legs have other ideas. I stagger, then collapse against the railing. Blood from my ribs leaks down my side, pooling in my waistband. I try to slow my heart, but it's not listening.

The overlays fade, then flare, then come back with a single new message: USER: D. SKELM. FINAL WARNING. For a moment, I think of stopping, just letting it happen. Let the kill teams do their job, or the blood loss, or even the rain. But something stubborn in me wants to finish. Maybe it's the left-over analyst training, maybe it's the rage, or maybe I'm just too stupid to die right.

I look down. The kill team is at the base of the fire escape, debating the value of a direct pursuit. They know I'm bleeding out. One of them shouts, "Skelm! This can end easy!" as if anyone in this city believes in easy. I climb. Each rung is a confession of pain. By the top, my vision is dark around the edges, the world shrinking to a keyhole view. The roof is flat, nothing but wet gravel and the occasional maintenance dome. I run for the edge, hoping for a miracle. Behind me, the first of the kill team crests the ladder, gun in hand. He doesn't bother aiming; he just fires.

The round catches me in the back, not a bullet but a micro-flechette. It stings, burns, then numbs. The overlays tell me "MOTOR FUNCTION COMPROMISED," but my body is still moving, still fighting. I hit the edge of the roof and jump, land ugly on the adjacent building, my left leg folding beneath me with a sound like crushed ice. I scream, but there's no time for agony. I crawl, then limp, then shuffle forward, every step draining more red onto the rooftop.

The next roof is three meters higher. I can't make it. I know I can't. But I try.

I catch the lip with both hands, pull, feel the skin tear open on my palms. I get halfway up, then my arms betray me. I hang there, suspended, the city swirling below. The overlays try to help, but there's nothing left to analyze. For the first time since Moshimoto ran my brain through a compliance protocol, I understand that calculation is useless when the only options are to die or die later.

I let go.

I hit the rooftop two floors below, my body rolling, arms and legs akimbo. I taste gravel and blood and rain. I can't move. Above me, the kill team scans the roofline, not seeing where I've fallen. For a moment, I'm invisible. The overlays go dark. I look up at the sky, the rain still falling, and I realize I have no more moves. I wonder if Émilie is watching. I wonder if she ever cared. I wonder if it matters.

There's a sound—rotors, heavy, close. Another drone, bigger this time, searching for me. Its searchlight cuts the rooftop, blinding white. I close my eyes and pretend it's daylight, the real kind, the kind I barely remember. The overlays spark one last message: ANALYSIS INSUFFICIENT. INSTRUCTION?

I want to say, "Surprise me," but I don't have the breath.

The world goes very small, and then it goes away.

The world returns as a boot error. I'm back on the roof, face pressed to gravel, rain in my mouth, lungs refusing to move air. The overlays are gone—no HUD, no prompts, just raw input. For the first time in years, I see without the filter. It's terrifying. It's beautiful.

A shadow moves in the neon, skimming the rooftop with a purpose I haven't seen since the war. It leaps from vent to vent, weightless, silent. The drone above swings its searchlight, searching, but the shadow isn't there, not until it is. There's a glint of metal, the hiss of pressure, and then the drone drops like a dead bird. The shadow follows, landing on the corpse with the grace of a dancer.

She stands up. The rain slicks her hair to her head, rivulets painting her face with black streaks. She's small, lean, too young to carry this much violence, but her eyes flash with an animal focus that makes my heart stutter. In one hand, she holds a splintered rotor blade. In the other, a fistful of my own hair. She crouches over me and checks my pulse. Satisfied, she slaps my face until I cough up a lungful of water and try to scream.

"Talk to me," she says, voice flat and ancient. Her language is old, fossilized, but my brain parses it like a mother tongue. The words make my teeth ache. "You Skelm?" I try to nod. My body won't listen. She huffs, annoyed. "Name or death, quick as ever."

"Skelm," I manage to say, each consonant chewing the inside of my cheek. "D. Skelm. Who—"

She flicks water from her eyes. "No time for origin stories, old man. He said you'd need help." I want to ask who "he" is, but she's already hauling me up by the collar, an absurd feat of strength in her tiny frame. The world lurches as she drags me across the roof, avoiding the pools of blood with the practiced steps of a predator. I try to protest, but the best I can do is vomit on my own knees.

Behind us, voices—three, maybe four—shout into the wind. The kill team's found our trail. She mutters, "They move slow, think they got you dead. Dumb." She drops me behind an HVAC unit and peeks over the edge. "They bring drones. You run?"

I don't run; I crawl. I hate myself, but I crawl. She follows, hand at my back, keeping me low. She leads me to a service ladder, its top guarded by a security mesh. She snaps the lock with a tool I don't see, then shoves me through. We descend four stories, each step a lesson in pain. At the bottom, the alley is half-flooded with rainwater and old engine oil. She splashes in without hesitation.

The overlays are still dead. I try to remember how to walk, how to see, how to live. She doesn't wait. We cut through alleys and loading docks, her pace always one step ahead of my ability. At every turn, she checks for watchers, sniffs the air, then moves. Her route is chaos: never straight, always zigzag, always just beyond the edge of probability. At a dead end, she stops and points to a trash skip. "In." I hesitate. She fixes me with a glare. "Or you want to die on the street like a dog?"

I climb in. The stench is apocalyptic, but at least I can sit. She crouches beside me, watching the alley. In the silence, I finally see her for real. She's covered in old scars, criss-crossing her knuckles and the visible parts of her arms. Her jaw is broken and reset, slightly crooked. She wears nothing but a tank top and street leathers, boots so worn they're almost bare. The pause is brief. Two drones sweep past, then three, but none look down. After a minute, she taps my foot. "Clear."

We move again. I limp, she glides. Every so often, she throws me a look, half disgust and half pity. "Never seen a Skelm bleed like that. You broken, or just soft?"

"Not soft," I say, anger giving me an extra step. "Just betrayed."

She nods, understanding more than I say. "It's the girls who break you every time. They always send the best for Skelms."

I want to argue, but I can't. I follow her through another maze of alleys, then up a maintenance ladder onto the roof of a noodle factory. There, she pauses and listens. The only sound is rain and distant engines. She turns to face me. "They won't stop. Not ever. Why you think he sent me?"

I wipe blood from my mouth. "Who is 'he?'"

She grins, teeth white and sharp. "The one who hates SKELM CORPS more than you do." She waits for this to register, then shrugs. "You walk, or I carry?"

"I walk," I say, though I barely manage it. She laughs, quick and mean, then leads the way.

We travel the rooftops, a path known only to her. She jumps gaps that would kill me, then doubles back to pull me across. Every time I hesitate, she sneers and says, "Trust or die." The first few times I don't trust, but after I slip and nearly fall twelve stories, I decide to let her pull me. At one crossing, the gap is a solid three meters. She leaps it like nothing, then gestures for me to follow. I balk.

"Can't make it."

She spits into the wind. "Can. Just need to want it." She squats, holding out both hands. "I catch." I stare at the space between us. It's all rain, all emptiness. My body shakes with cold and fear. "Do or die, Skelm."

I run. I leap. She catches my wrists with iron hands, hauls me over the edge, and slaps my face for good measure. "See? Not so hard."

We keep moving. The city blurs below, a mess of neon and moving bodies. On the fifth roof, we stop behind a billboard, the hum of transformers almost drowning out the world. She roots through a stash in the wall and pulls out a first aid kit. She tosses me a pack of clotting foam. “For your leak,” she says.

I apply it to my rib. The pain is instant, but the bleeding slows. The foam burns, then cools. I can breathe again. “Name,” I ask. “Yours.”

She thinks, then decides. “Ban. Like the book. Like the code. Remember it or forget it, don’t care.”

I nod, half-crazed with gratitude and disbelief. “Thank you, Ban.”

She ignores it, peeking over the ledge. The kill team is down below, sweeping the street with lights and dogs. We’re invisible, for now.

Ban sits beside me, eyes tracking the enemy below. “You have somewhere to run?”

“No,” I say, truth easy in the dark.

She shrugs. “Figures. Skelms always make big plans, never think about tomorrow.” There’s a silence, then she turns. “You hungry?”

I almost laugh. “Not really.”

She digs into a pocket, pulls out a ration bar, and tears it in half with her teeth. She hands me a piece. “You eat. You need it.” I eat. The bar tastes like sadness, but it helps. She studies me. “They put a price on you.”

“Of course.”

She grins. "Worth more alive, but they pay for dead, too. Makes it fun."

I stare at the kill team below. "They'll never stop, will they?"

"Not till you're deleted." Ban flicks rain from her nose. "But he wants you to stay online. For a while, at least."

I look at her. "Why?"

She shrugs. "He likes chaos. You're the best at making it." The street below is emptying, the kill team giving up for now. Ban stands, stretches, then offers me a hand. "Come on, Skelm. Let's see if you can keep up."

I take her hand. She hauls me to my feet, easy, and we run. We cross rooftops, slide down fire escapes, and vanish into shadows. Each move, Ban is ahead, but every time I think I'll lose her, she slows, waits, and yanks me up. We're a block from the river when she stops, looks back at me, and says, "This is where we run loud."

She takes off down the street, no more hiding, just raw speed. I follow, every nerve screaming. Behind us, the kill team sees us and gives chase. Ban laughs as the first bullets rip past. She jumps a barricade, vaults a car, then hurls herself off the bridge onto a floating shipping container. She lands perfectly. I follow, land on my face, and roll to a stop. Ban is already up. She helps me, then pulls me behind a stack of containers. We listen as the kill team pours over the bridge, firing blindly into the river.

She puts her lips to my ear. "You did okay, Skelm. Not good, not bad. Okay." I want to protest, but I'm out of air. She wipes blood from my face, the motion shockingly gentle. "You're alive because I let you be." I stare at her, trying to read the math behind the eyes, but it's too deep for me. She stands, rain washing us both clean, neon painting her face every color of the city. "Rest," she says. "Tomorrow, we make trouble."

She lays back, arms behind her head, and closes her eyes. I do the same, for lack of better options. The world is wet, cold, and endless, but I'm still here. Thanks to Ban.

And whoever "he" is, I hope he's paying attention.

Chapter 4

Ban's hideout is a brutalist scar, wormed three stories below the official sub-basement, accessed by crawling through an HVAC vent coated in thirty years of payroll-discount mold and weaponized dander. I drag myself in, caked blood flaking off my palms, and collapse onto the first horizontal surface not leaking electricity. My teeth chatter until I notice the air: 2 degrees above freezing, saturated with the fungal rot of surplus computers and the sharp top note of sweat that's marinated in copper for weeks.

My vision glitches twice before the overlays reboot. "MEMORY INTEGRITY: COMPROMISED," they read, then start spooling new diagnostics in the periphery. I force myself upright, plant the three stolen archive drives on the makeshift desk—reclaimed coffin lids on cement blocks, a joke Ban probably couldn't resist. The first drive slides a perfect arc on the greasy surface, trailing a comet's worth of someone else's DNA. I wipe my hands, then the drive, and boot up Ban's rig.

The startup sequence is twenty-seven seconds of blue-tinged hell, the display humming so hard the whole room pulses like a heart with three arrhythmias. I slot the archive, thumb trembling only a little, and pull up the terminal. Root access is a fiction; everything here runs on bad credentials and the faith that no one in hell is watching. I start a multi-threaded decrypt and let the files vomit themselves across the screen. Each folder is a dare: Neural Scarification Protocol, Empathy Suppression Metrics, Asset Compliance By Age Group, Product Recall.

I lose track of time as I sift. The blue glow eats my eyes. Each file is colder than the last. Child procurement manifests, neural damage routines disguised as "Compliance Enhancements," and schedule after schedule of "harvest events." The overlays dump a stream of error corrections into the feed, but the only correction I want is a bullet to the head of whoever made this. The smell of overheated circuits makes me gag, but I keep going, fingers moving with the speed of addiction. Somewhere above, water leaks through the concrete. Each drip is a metronome, reminding me that time, and blood, are both running out.

A footstep—soft, deliberate—breaks the trance. Ban stands in the entryway, backlit by the red LED tangle she calls ambiance, two stale ration bars in one hand, a dead rat by the tail in the other. She stares at me, eyes narrowed, then kicks the rat into a bin that hisses back. "You look like dogshit, Skelm."

I grunt. "Better than what's in here."

She drops the ration bars on the desk, the wrappers pre-punctured by her thumbnail. The gesture says: *you want it, eat it, but don't expect me to say please*. She leans in, arms crossed, combat boots making no sound on the sealed concrete. I can smell the powder on her hands, and under it, the afterburn of the fight. "Found anything worth dying for yet?" she says. Dark humor, weaponized.

I pick up one of the ration bars, stare at it, then decide I'd rather gnaw my own tongue. "They're breeding them, Ban." My voice is dry, unsteady. "Not kids. Not even clones. Something worse."

She shrugs, like this is news only to the willfully naive. "SKELM CORPS has always run organ farms. You think the miracle C-suites age on their own?"

I shake my head. "No, it's not just body parts. They're seeding the kids with engineered trauma. Each one is born with the scars already burned in."

She processes this, face a wax mask. "So? That's half the city, and the other half is just too expensive to optimize."

I flip through three more folders, skin crawling as I see the pattern: every third file references a "Skelm Variant," a protocol named after a dead man who still happens to be me. I drag up a schematic and shove it across the screen toward her.

She leans closer, face illuminated by the line drawing of a neural extraction chamber, scaled for children. The annotations are a master class in sadism: *"Compliance Induction 48h post-birth," "Remedial Re-traumatization at puberty," "Total Recall Suppression for life."*

My hands are shaking now. "They're breeding kids like spare parts, Ban. But the real asset isn't flesh. It's suffering."

She watches the schematic, jaw flexing once, then twice. "Never thought I'd see a Skelm with a conscience."

I let the overlays suggest the next move. "If even a quarter of this is true, every major syndicate, every lab, every corporate sponsor—"

Ban interrupts with a quick, precise laugh, cold and small as a stone. "They're all in on it. You think I'm hiding down here for the scenery?"

She scans the rest of the files, her eyes flickering as she parses the headers. The room goes silent, except for the water dripping and the hum of the overclocked drives. Ban breaks first, stepping back from the desk, hands on her hips. "So, what? You gonna blow the whistle? Hand it to the Bureau? They'll sell you to the same meat factory they bought you from."

I want to tell her she's wrong, but my body knows better. My voice shreds on the way out: "It can't just be this."

She smirks, but there's less venom in it. "Every analyst I've ever met wanted the truth, right up until the second they found it. Then it's all denial and drama." She digs in her jacket for something, finds a crumpled sleeve of nicotine gum, and jams three pieces in her mouth at once. The smell is sharp, chemical, almost clean.

I watch the files auto-sort. A subfolder titled "Châtelet Institute" surfaces, familiar logos stamped across the PDFs. The overlays snap a connection to Émilie—her name is in three out of the first five reports. I click, eyes locking to the phrases: "Test Subject: D. Skelm. Protocol: Readable Slave." Each report is a log of my own extraction events, detailed and annotated in her hand. The world spins. I brace against the desk, the coffin lid cold and real under my fingers.

Ban watches me, nothing in her face but the patience of the inevitable. "Now you get it."

I do. Every memory I'd lost, every blackout, every time I thought I was awake when I wasn't—there's a file for that, a timestamp, a fucking trophy for whoever ran the job.

I clutch the desk, sweat freezing on my spine. "This is all of us, isn't it? Not just me."

Ban's face goes sour. "It's the whole city, analyst. Maybe more. SKELM CORPS just does it at scale."

My chest is tight, and not just from the broken ribs. My hands twitch over the keyboard, desperate for an action that matters. "We can kill them with this, Ban. The right leak, the right time—"

She throws the dead rat at the trash again, harder this time. "They wrote that scenario before you were born. Any message gets chewed up and spat back out as advertising for their latest patch." She looks at me, really looks. "You still don't understand how deep you are."

I try to stand, fail, then sit back down, head spinning with the idea that nothing I am has ever been private. Not even to myself. Ban softens, not much, but enough to pass for human. She puts a hand on my shoulder, her fingers gentle and shockingly warm. "You need a reboot, Skelm. Take a nap. I'll keep watch."

I shake my head, tears threatening but not winning. "If I sleep, they'll harvest me again."

She leans in, close enough for me to smell the ration bar rot on her breath. "You're under my firewall now, analyst. Not even the Corp can dig through me."

She steps back, the moment gone, but the message delivered. I stare at the screen, the blue light now making me want to retch, and let the overlay process the horror for me. My hands shake. I can't stop looking at the schematic of the extraction chamber. Ban is already gone, boots silent on the floor. The only sound left is water dripping, and the electric whine of a city built to harvest its own. I close my eyes, and for the first time, I understand why every memory comes with a price.

I pace the perimeter of Ban's bunker, orbiting the chaos of screens, half-empty data cores, and the sticky blue glow that leaks across the coffin-desk. My teeth hurt from grinding; my tongue is sandpaper. Every surface is vibrating, either from the cooling fans or the pulse that's built up behind my left eye. I click through folder after folder, each one a fresh shitshow of ethics violations. The overlays lag half a second behind, trying to catalog the evidence and not short out my frontal lobe.

Ban leans against the back wall, the side of her face painted orange by the old sodium lamp she scavenged from a commuter tunnel. She's got her feet braced on a stack of ammo cans, a combat knife balanced on her knee. She cleans it with the focus of a saint doing penance: gentle, relentless, not even looking at me.

I gesture to the main screen, where the production quotas scroll in digital red: “Unreadable—Current Quarter: 1092. Defectives: 27. Projected Revenue: 12.7 MM Suffering Units.” Every number is a kid with their synapses set to fail at birth. I want to puke, but the last of my adrenaline burned out hours ago.

“We need to get this out. Leak it to the Bureau, to the labs, to every dissident node in the market,” I say, fist hitting the terminal for punctuation. The impact does nothing except make my own skin ache. “They’ll have to shut it down. Even SKELM CORPS can’t wash that much blood.”

Ban flicks the knife, catching the edge with her thumb. “You know what they do with leaks, Skelm? They monetize them. They’ll just up the marketing budget and launch the next line with a tragic backstory.” She spits the words with a smile, like she’s practiced this for years. “You want to help, go cut the head off a pipeline. Don’t send out a sob story.”

I circle the table, letting my palm drag across the old wood, feeling every dent and bullet groove. “If we can hit the right people, make it go viral—”

She laughs, low and mean. “Viral’s for housewives and hobbyists. This shit? This gets you vaporized before you even finish typing.” Her eyes are fixed on her knife, but I know she’s watching me in the reflection. The overlays try to mediate, running probability trees for every possible outcome. Most end with my body dumped in a river or my mind shredded into product demos.

I slam a hand on the nearest screen, the image shaking before it settles. "There are thousands of them, Ban. Maybe millions. No one's going to save them by blowing up another office."

Ban slides the knife into her boot and stands, rolling her shoulders with a crack. She's smaller than me by half a head, but I swear she fills the room when she wants to. She crosses to the main wall, where she's mapped every target worth hitting in the city—a patchwork of hand-drawn lines, thumbtacked photos, and sharpie scribbles that bleed into the drywall.

"You want to talk about saving kids, analyst?" She points to a red circle on the map, two blocks from the Châtelet Institute. "There's a transfer tomorrow night. Unreadable units, grade A, going up the food chain. You got six hours to make a difference that matters. Or you can sit here, write your manifesto, and hope someone cares."

The air is hot and wet, the smell of burning drives mixing with ozone and old rat droppings. My hands are shaking again, not just from anger but from the new error scrolling in the overlay: SPLIT INTEGRITY—HOST INCOMPATIBLE. I try to ignore it. "That's just a band-aid. I want a cure."

Ban doesn't flinch. "There's no cure, Skelm. Only survival. You've been out of the game too long, or maybe you just never understood it."

I pull up another screen, this one a compilation of internal SKELM CORPS memos: charts, names, lists of kids and their fates. I run a filter, cross-checking every reference to "D. Skelm" against Ban's own network. As I work, my fingers start moving faster than I can track, typing in a code I haven't used since the internment camps. The overlays don't recognize the syntax, but my muscle memory does.

I blink. There's a new note in the archive, tagged with my own encryption but no recollection of writing it. The text is simple: *You're not the only Skelm. Find the others.* My hands freeze. The overlays confirm: message is genuine, inserted exactly 39 seconds ago. No external access. Just me, or a version of me, leaving a breadcrumb.

Ban notices my hesitation. "Glitching again?"

I hide the screen, a pointless move, but it makes me feel like I still have a secret worth keeping. "Nothing," I say. "Just tired."

She squats by the desk, close enough that I can see the tiny scars lacing her fingers, the webbing on her left hand slightly melted from an old chemical burn. "You think you're the first to care, Skelm? They train us to hope, just so they can kill it twice."

I want to shout at her, to force her to see that not everyone is a product of their own cynicism. But she's already lived through the math and come out the other side. The overlays split for a second, then double down: two sets of diagnostics, two running commentary streams. One says *"Go public, burn the whole rotten machine."* The other whispers, *"Hit the pipeline, save what you can, or die trying."*

I look up, meeting Ban's eyes. "So what? We blow up a truck? Then another? Then what?"

She smiles, almost fond. "Then you keep going until the machine chokes on its own parts."

We're close enough now that I can see the static of her stubble, the blue-white light painting her features in relentless clarity. "Fine," I say, voice flat and unfamiliar. "We hit the transfer. Tomorrow night."

Ban's eyes brighten, just a little. "You sure your overlays can keep up?"

"I don't trust them," I say, and it's true. "But I trust you."

She shrugs, but there's a softness to it. "You'll get yourself killed, Skelm. But at least you'll do it for the right reason." The moment hangs, neither of us wanting to move first. Then Ban snaps back into motion, grabbing a battered duffel from the floor, already packed with enough firepower to survive a small civil war. "Eat something before," she says, tossing me the less-moldy ration bar. "You're no good to me dead on arrival."

I watch her load weapons, check the straps on her boots, and tie her hair back with a strip of faded memory cloth. She's done this a thousand times. I realize I never have, not for real. The overlays are merging again, the split in my mind resolving into a single, sharp-edged focus. As I swallow the ration bar—so dry it's like eating ground-up promises—I realize Ban is already at the door, ready to burn the world or die trying. Maybe both.

It doesn't take long for the patience to die. Thirty minutes of terminal quiet and Ban's gone, prepping something in the back, muttering into her collar at a frequency just above the range of guilt. I use the time to hammer my way through the last archive drive, running exploit after exploit against the encrypted core. It isn't enough. The files are cross-locked, triple-blind, and every time I think I have a crack, a watchdog routine snaps the connection and flushes the buffer. The overlays suggest sleeping on it, but I know from experience that nothing good happens in dreams.

So I make a jump. I reroute through Ban's own network hub—a tangle of raw nerves patched into the municipal grid and who knows what else. I know it's dumb, but all the smart moves got killed last night. The second I run the line, I get a pulse of warning: INTRUSION DETECTED—SOURCE: LOCAL. Before I can even close the session, there's a gun at my left temple. Not metaphorical. Cold, black, loaded. Ban's voice is a whisper, but it shoves the world sideways. "Your other half would know better."

I freeze, every muscle aware of how little space there is between brain and bullet. She's close, kneeling next to the desk, hand so steady I could use it for calibration. The old revolver is pre-digital—no safety, no smart targeting, just blunt kinetic promise. "You done?" she asks, barely above a breath.

I nod. The overlays lag, then confirm: HOST IMMOBILIZED. She pulls the gun back, stands, then paces in a tight arc that leaves scorch marks on the concrete. "You ever read the manual on trust, analyst?" She keeps her back to me, talking to the wall. "First page: Don't fuck with the network. Last page: If you do, pray no one is watching."

I stand too fast, hip hitting the coffin desk, pain firing up my ribs. "It was the only way in. The encryption's a lockdown, and my own keys are rigged to fail." My voice cracks, anger and shame competing for top slot.

She rounds on me, gun still in hand but pointed at the floor. "You want to paint a target on this place, fine. But don't come crying when the DebtHounds chew you apart."

The casing was already hairline-cracked from yesterday.

I move to reset the desk, elbow grazing the stack of drives. The top one—already hairline-cracked from yesterday's chase—skids, falls, hits the ground, and splits apart. Shit. I drop to gather the pieces, and Ban's down there too, both of us on our knees, hands scraping the rough concrete for the smaller bits. Our hands brush, briefly. I pull away, static biting my skin. She doesn't react, just keeps gathering. Then, softer than before, she asks, "You ever wonder how long you've been doing this?" I look up, confused. She meets my eyes, something different now—like a history I wasn't taught. "You've been planning this for years, Skelm. Just not the you who's here now."

The overlays try to parse it, but my brain skips over the details, too busy recalling the weird deja vu of the encrypted note from earlier. "How would you know?"

She shrugs, like she's bored of her own secrets. "Because I've met four versions of you. Five if you count the time I had to pull you out of a DARN blacksite. Each one smarter, each one more broken." She holds up a sliver of circuit board, balanced between thumb and finger. "But only one ever made it this far." There's nothing to say to that. Nothing that matters. She finishes scooping the drives into a battered courier pouch, then stands, brushing off her hands with exaggerated care. "You really don't remember any of it?"

"Just fragments." I close my fist around a chip, knuckles going white. "Some days I can't even trust my overlays."

Ban gives a low, humorless laugh. “Overlays are for the weak. Real memory’s in the scars.” She pulls up her sleeve and shows me the chemical burn, raw and pink. “You gave me this, by the way. Back when you thought you could hack fear.”

I stare, not remembering, but the overlays flash an error that tells me she’s not lying. A pressure builds behind my teeth, and before I can think better of it, I stand and slam the side of the desk, sending a monitor crashing to the floor. Glass and static and bad blue glow everywhere. For a moment, it’s just the two of us, angry and spent. Ban looks at me, unblinking. Then, with a quickness that would scare a less broken man, she steps over and puts her hand on my shoulder. Not hard, not soft, just there.

Then, the entire bunker goes red. Something’s coming.

Chapter 5

Pacing never solves anything, but the overlays insist on motion, feeding me anxiety graphs that spike when I stand still, feeding me anxiety graphs that spike when I stand still, feeding me anxiety graphs that spike when I stand still, so I wear a circuit into the bunker's floor. Every fourth step lands harder, blood still gummed in the sock of my right foot. My hands keep balling into fists, the feedback tight enough to pop the knuckles if I let it. Across the room, Ban is checking her gear for the fifth time—no wasted motion, every click and snap more mechanical than the Moshimoto mods she mocks. "Would help if you breathed through your nose," she says, not looking up. "You're fogging up the display."

"Noted," I say, but I'm already double-timing the inhale, hoping she can't hear the jitter in my exhale. The overlays chirp a "CALM DOWN" prompt and immediately get overridden by the heartbeat monitor's "LOOMING DEATH IMMINENT." I ignore them both. There's an argument in my skull: stay and hack the Bureau, or bounce and trust Ban's network.

The risk models are split fifty-fifty, but the overlays keep stuttering, as if my own brain can't decide whose orders to follow.

Ban lays out three pistols on the casket-desk and checks the load on each. Her boots make a deliberate click every time she shifts weight. "You want the one that goes bang or the one that melts the bones?" I hesitate, which she clocks immediately. "Pick, analyst." She taps the middle gun—heavy, cold, matte black. "You always pick the middle."

She's right. I take it, feel the cold in my palm, then do what I always do: check the model, scan the serial, and verify against internal recall. The overlays bring up the stats, but it's unnecessary. I know the type. Designed for corporate security, nonlethal at close range, but point it at someone's spine and they won't walk again. "Reliable."

She cocks an eyebrow. "That's what you call a gun?"

"In my line, that's as romantic as it gets."

She makes a noise that could be a laugh, or a cough, or maybe she just likes the way air moves through her ruined lungs. I reload the gun for no reason other than to have something to do with my hands. "We could still try the Bureau. Play the leak card. Offer up a sample, get whistleblower status."

She shakes her head. "They'll just flag us and tip the Corp." She folds a map along the lines of the neon-lit sectors above, the kind only a lifer could navigate. "This is our best shot: breach through the Gray Tunnel, skip the canal, then double back to the safehouse at Crumley's." The overlays do the pathing, then overlay a fifty percent survival probability. Ban's plan is better than mine, but I can't admit that yet. She rolls up the map, shoves it into a side pocket, then stands in front of me, arms crossed, weight forward like a coach ready to punch out her own team. "You trust me?"

The question catches. I want to say yes, but the overlays flash all the reasons not to, chief among them: she's got no Moshimoto skin, no market loyalty, and she's already pulled a gun on me. But the way her face doesn't move, the way her eyes hold steady, makes it easier to lie. "Yeah. I do."

She studies me like a weapon, then nods once, sharp and final. There's a pause while she loads a satchel with ammo and something that could be a medical kit or a makeshift bomb. She passes the kit to me, almost an afterthought. "Patch yourself on the way," she says. "Can't run on dead legs." I take it. My hands are steadier now. Ban shoulders the bag and opens the bunker's secondary panel, peering into the pitch like a predator with too many targets. "If they're here, they'll come fast. Corp doesn't waste time on cleanup."

I look down at my own shaking hands, remember the way the overlays froze in the market, then how Ban had to drag me through the trash skip like a child who'd lost their way. She's halfway up the service ladder before I register the movement. I follow, feet slipping on the rungs, but the overlays smooth out the motion, locking my center of gravity where it should be.

At the hatch, she signals for quiet: two fingers in a downward chop. Her language is pre-digital, the kind you only learn by surviving a dozen failed insurrections. The overlays flag nothing on the other side. For once, Ban trusts the raw input. She cracks the hatch and listens—breathless, still. I want to ask what she hears, but she's already sliding through, a ripple in the dark.

I follow, landing in a crawlspace of damp cables and pre-war detritus. Ban takes the lead, snaking through low pipes and moldy plastic. I try to keep up, but every move is a reminder that I'm still stitched together with borrowed hope, and the painkillers are an hour past expiration. At the end of the crawl, she stops and listens again. I can see the tension in her shoulders—a whole body wired for detonation. She whispers, "You ever fire one of those outside a training sim?"

"Once," I say. "Didn't end well."

She grins, teeth white in the blue dark. "Welcome to the sequel."

We breach into the stairwell, hot with recycled air and the stink of ozone. Ban checks the landing, then the overlays flag a blip: micro-drone, nothing major, but enough to warn a real team. Ban sees it too. She yanks a magnet from her sleeve and flicks it at the drone. It sticks, buzzes, then drops dead. She keeps moving, three steps at a time, never pausing long enough for a second guess.

We reach the ground level, and she slows, signaling for silence. The hallway ahead is choked with light—real light, not the blue-gray of the bunker or the smear of neon from the street. The overlays want to analyze it, but Ban trusts her nose. "They're here," she says. I peer around the edge. At the far end, two black-suited Corp goons stand at attention, visors down, guns held casually but ready. The hallway is so quiet I can hear their heartbeats through the concrete. Ban watches, counts, then leans in to whisper: "On three, I go left, you go right. If I drop one, you take the other." She doesn't wait for an answer. "One. Two—" and she's already moving.

She hits the first goon low, right at the knees. The crack is audible, and the goon folds, slamming face-first into the wall. I step out and raise my gun, but the second goon's already returning fire. The hallway fills with ricochets and the smell of burning polycarbonate. My arm jerks as a round grazes it, but I squeeze the trigger and send two shots into the goon's chest. The Corp suit isn't meant for live rounds. The goon staggers, then slumps. Ban stands over the first goon, already frisking him for keys or data. She wipes her hands on her pants and gestures for me to move.

"We've got about ninety seconds before the next team sweeps," she says. I follow, the overlays now running hot, every sense blaring in overdrive. We cut through the maintenance wing, past dripping pipes and dead fluorescents, then out onto a service balcony overlooking the lower city. The sky is a static of color, corporate logos fighting for every square meter of horizon. Below, I can see three more teams fanning out, all of them converging on our exit. Ban leans against the railing, scanning the options. "You got anything in the overlays for this?"

"Two options," I say. "Stay and fight, or jump and hope we stick the landing."

She laughs again, low and honest. "Knew I liked you, analyst." We don't get to pick. The alarms in the building go live, bathing us in red and white. The overlays scream, "PROBABILITY: 10%." Even Ban looks rattled. She pulls me close, voice a bark in my ear. "You freeze, you die. So don't freeze."

I don't freeze. We vault the railing and drop, falling three stories before the overlays catch the landing and flex my knees into a perfect crouch. Ban lands beside me, rolls, then is up again, sprinting. The street is chaos: Corp cars, more goons, a fucking gunship overhead. But Ban doesn't pause. She runs toward the chaos, dragging me along. We dodge through a noodle cart, under a crash of VR tourists, and across a street full of angry wet dogs. The overlays keep pace, mapping every threat vector, but Ban is faster—she's running her own code, old school and perfect.

We hit the tunnel entrance just as the gunship fires. The shockwave throws me sideways, and for a moment, the world is all noise and light. But Ban hauls me up, blood streaming down her arm, and we limp into the tunnel together. The alarms are fading behind us, the echo of the chase still in my bones. Ban finally stops, drops to one knee, and wipes the sweat from her eyes. "Not bad, analyst."

"Could have been worse," I say, voice high and uneven.

She grins. "Could always be worse." I laugh, the sound bright and hysterical. She claps me on the back, hard enough to pop my shoulder. "Next time, you take the lead."

I almost believe her.

We move deeper into the city's guts, every step the start of a new disaster. This time, though, we're both ready for it.

The tunnel stinks of rat shit and ozone, but compared to the nightmare upstairs, it feels almost holy. Ban wipes blood from her chin, not caring whose it is, and checks her pulse with two fingers, quick and businesslike. I lean against the concrete, trying to keep my heart from liquefying. The overlays have stopped barking instructions; maybe they finally accept that Ban's the new operating system.

She's reloading when the microdrones hit. They're smaller than a finger bone and twice as mean, each one a dart with teeth and a camera. The first wave bounces off Ban's jacket, barely a sting. The second is aimed for me. I swat at them, useless, but Ban just slaps a hand over my mouth and pulls me down. "Hold still," she says. "They only bite if you run."

I freeze and let the swarm pass, each drone a blur of blue and red, tiny corporate logos pulsing along their shells. We wait. Ban peeks around the corner, nods once, then signals with a flick of her wrist: *go, fast, no noise*. I follow, hunched low. There's an exit up ahead, a maintenance alcove that stinks of dead water and burned insulation. I'm halfway through when the world explodes—bright and loud and full of glass. *Not possible*, my brain tries to say, but the overlays are silent. They know: if a Corp wants to breach, it'll find a way. Even in a tunnel with no windows, they'll bring their own.

A wall of reinforced smartglass detonates inward, scattering the space with razors. Three armored goons follow, visors down, guns up. The first throws a tear gas canister at Ban's feet. She kicks it right back, never losing stride. It bursts between the lead goon's knees, clouding the whole corridor in wet, peppered misery. Ban moves like she's spent her whole life under siege. She ducks low, grabs my arm, and rolls us both behind a dead water heater. Shots follow, real bullets this time, hot enough to leave traces in the air. "Down," Ban whispers, even though I'm already prone. Her tone means *stay*, not *move*.

The kill team advances, every step synchronized, every shot measured for crowd control, not carnage. That's the Corp way: maximize pain, minimize the cost of cleanup. A round slaps the heater, throwing sparks and metal shrapnel. I duck, teeth grinding together, and Ban's hand finds my shoulder—steady, grounding. "Bounce right on my count," she says, voice glass-sharp and calm. I nod, bile crawling up my throat. She signals with a squeeze, and I push off. We clear the heater just as the next barrage shreds it. Ban throws something—a flash grenade, homemade—and the whole world stutters white. In the instant before it pops, she covers my eyes and yells, "Now!"

We run blind. The grenade detonates, frying every overlay and camera within ten meters. The air is all screams and static. We tumble behind another slab of old machinery, breathing hard. My lungs taste like burning tin. Ban doesn't bother to catch her breath. "Gun," she says. "Out."

I fumble, hands slick, but I get it out. She snags it, cracks open the chamber, checks the rounds, and hands it back. "You're loaded. Don't hesitate." I grip the gun, thumb white on the safety. The overlays slowly reboot, but nothing looks right. Ban's voice cuts through, low and almost gentle: "They'll try to herd us. Next move is theirs."

She's right. The gas is thick, reducing the world to shadows and the angry red of emergency lighting. Ban pokes her head out and comes back grinning. "Stupid. They split up." There are footsteps to the left and right, two teams now. Ban listens, counts, then motions: left first, right after. We wait until the left team gets close, then Ban jumps them. She aims low—two shots to the kneecaps, one to the throat. The goon drops, not dead but screaming. Ban yanks the next goon by the visor and slams their face into the floor. I hear the wet crack and try not to think about it.

The right-side team hears and rushes. Ban rolls back, grabs me, and pulls us up the maintenance stairs. We move fast, skipping steps, using the noise below to cover our own clatter. We emerge onto a sub-level catwalk, overhanging a vertical drop into the city's recycling arteries. Ban scans for a way out. The catwalk ends at a locked door, and I feel the overlays choke: no exits. Ban doesn't slow. She fires at the lock—two rounds, then a kick—and the door shudders open. "Go," she says, pushing me through.

On the other side is another hallway, dark and pulsing with blue light. We run, boots echoing on metal grates. Behind us, I hear the kill team regrouping. The overlays warn: "SEVERAL HOSTILES IN PURSUIT," like I need the reminder. We reach the end: another locked hatch, but this time, Ban doesn't bother with finesse. She rips a panel off the wall, exposes the wiring, and crosses two leads. The door hisses open.

We tumble through, and for a heartbeat, there's peace. We're in a server room, racks and racks of old biotech and data lines, all humming with the kind of power that feels alive. The overlays flag a thousand points of interest, but all I see is cover. Ban slides behind a row of racks and signals for silence. I huddle next to her, gun trembling in my grip. We listen. The kill team is right behind. I can hear them over the hum—three steps, stop, three more, a pause. They're searching, systematic. The overlays draw threat lines in the air, each one intersecting at our position. Ban whispers, “They’ll flush us with drones, then come in shooting. We wait for the first drone, then pop it. Got it?”

I nod. My throat is too tight for words. There’s a long pause. Then the whine of the drone, a miniature wasp of death, darts above the racks. Ban nods once, and I fire. The shot clips the drone, sparks fly, and it drops hard. Ban grabs it mid-air and smashes it under her boot. The kill team doesn’t hesitate. They rush, guns up, but Ban is ready. She’s already set the broken drone’s battery to overload, and when the first goon rounds the rack, she tosses it at him.

It pops—nothing lethal, but enough to blind and deafen for a second. In that second, Ban moves. She lunges at the nearest goon, wrests the gun away, and uses it as a club. I cover her, firing over her shoulder, hitting the next in line. He drops, blood painting the server rack. The room is chaos: gunfire, sparks, the wet slap of bone on steel. I lose track of the count, just shoot at anything not Ban.

When the ammo runs dry, Ban switches to fists. She’s brutal, efficient, not a single move wasted. I watch her take down a guy twice her size, knee to the groin, elbow to the throat. She grabs his helmet, rips it off, then slams it down on his head again, harder. The goon goes still. The last of them tries to run, but Ban’s not having it. She grabs him by the collar, pulls him in, and whispers something in his ear before snapping his neck. The overlays are a blank white sheet, out of metaphors.

We stand, breathing hard, in a room full of bodies and dead machines. Ban checks her pulse, wipes sweat from her forehead, and grins. “You okay?” she asks. I nod, but the adrenaline is making my teeth chatter. She claps my shoulder. "Told you. Easy."

There's a click behind us, the sound of another door opening. Ban turns, gun up, ready. A man in a suit steps in—immaculate, calm, with overlays that shimmer like a sharkskin tie. He's holding a briefcase, of all things. He looks at the carnage, at us, and doesn't flinch. "Impressive," he says. His voice is pure Corp—clean, modulated, and pleasant in a way that makes my skin crawl.

Ban sneers. "You here to invoice us for the damages?"

He smiles. "Just to negotiate a surrender. It's not personal, you understand. You're an expensive resource, Mr. Skelm. We'd prefer to collect you in one piece."

Ban gestures at the bodies. "Try harder."

The man sighs, like he's tired of being misunderstood. "This is a formality, of course. You'll make a final stand, we'll escalate, and eventually, you'll be brought to heel." He glances at Ban. "Unless, of course, you decide to cooperate."

She laughs. "Not in your wildest sim, suit."

He shrugs. "A shame."

He sets the briefcase down, opens it, and steps back. Inside is a tangle of metal and biotech, writhing, alive. Ban's face goes still. "Move," she says, and we both jump back as the thing unspools itself, filling the server room with tendrils of wire and organic blade. It's a DebtHound, but grown to a scale that makes the market model look like a puppy. It screams—a sound like a hard drive failing at full volume—and leaps at us.

Ban shoves me aside, then draws a knife from her boot. She waits, calm, then ducks under the first swipe and jams the blade into the beast's neck. It barely slows. The overlays are blinking "FATAL" in every color. I scramble for a weapon, find a broken server blade, and swing it at the DebtHound's back. It connects, splintering silicon and sending up a fan of sparks. The beast whips around, claws flashing. Ban rolls between its legs and slices at the soft belly. I jab at the exposed wire, trying to distract it. For a moment, it works—the thing turns on me, eyes glowing with a perfect ledger of every debt I ever owed. It lunges. I brace, ready to die, but Ban is there. She grabs its jaw, pries it open, and jams a broken power cell inside.

"Cover!" she yells, and I drop. The DebtHound detonates, splattering the room with bio-goo and shrapnel. Ban and I huddle behind a dead goon, riding out the blast. When it's over, the room is a slaughterhouse. Ban helps me up, both of us dripping with whatever used to be the DebtHound. She spits, wipes her mouth, and grins. "Now that's a dogfight," she says.

We limp out, down another hall, and toward another maybe-exit. I can hear the Corp still chasing, but for now, we're ahead. I look at Ban, at the way she moves, the way she smiles even when the world is burning. I want to say something, something real, but all I can do is laugh. She laughs too, and together we run, hearts pounding, into whatever disaster comes next.

We race through a maze of corridors, DebtHound splatter dripping from our boots. The overlays don't bother updating my pulse—it's maxed, nothing left to give. Every joint screams, every sense is stretched so tight I can feel the grit of my own sweat grinding inside the pores. Ban stops at the end of a corridor, shoulders heaving, then points with her chin: two meters of open ground to the maintenance shaft, and nothing but air and automatic gunfire in between.

"They'll have it zeroed," she says. Her lips barely move.

"Yeah," I whisper. "No other way."

She leans out, counting under her breath. I see her eyes do the math, then the corners flick up—she's already planning the story she'll tell if this works. Behind us, the kill team is regrouping, black boots thumping closer, reloading with corporate efficiency. Ahead, a drone paces the gap, lazy, almost bored, its lens tracking for movement. Ban looks at me, really looks, and I see the question: *you in?*

I nod hard, and it's not fear anymore. Just motion. Just *yes*. She grins, pulls a last grenade from her pocket, and rolls it underhand into the open. The drone tracks the arc, focuses, then gets greedy and drifts lower to investigate. Ban waits. I wait. The grenade pops—flash only, but enough to fry the drone's circuits and send it spiraling. Sparks shower the corridor. Ban is already running, head down, not zigging or zagging but just pouring speed into the space. I follow, the overlays flatlining, a purity in the act of not thinking.

Bullets rip the concrete, stinging my ears, but Ban's line is perfect. She hits the edge of the maintenance shaft and pivots, one palm on the wall, the other reaching back. I take her hand. She pulls, I dive, and we tumble together into the dark, the world above erased by the slam of the hatch. For a second, there's only the sound of our hearts. Then Ban laughs, breathless, half-mad. "Didn't think you'd commit," she says.

"Only thing left," I say, and for once, it doesn't taste like defeat. We lie there, backs against cold pipe, the gunfire now distant, just another bad memory in a city built on them.

Ban wipes her face with the heel of her hand, then glances at me. "You good?"

I check my body. Nothing critical. "Yeah. You?"

She shrugs. "Had worse first dates."

I laugh, then cough, the adrenaline spike shaking loose all the fear. "Where to now?"

She sits up, pulls out a battered comm-link, and thumbs the dial. "Safehouse three clicks east. We crawl for a while, then catch the next pipeline."

The overlays start to recover, rerouting diagnostics through Ban's rhythm, not mine. I let it happen. Her way works. We push up, knees cracking, and start through the maintenance shaft. The darkness isn't absolute; every few meters, the city's pulse leaks in, ads and alarms washing the walls in color. We move as one. No more lag, no more guessing. When Ban ducks, I duck. When she stops, I stop. Her code is better, simpler: *trust, run, survive.*

We pass an old service hatch, leaking neon from the world above. I see our reflections: two messes, smeared with blood and dog parts, smiling. Ban points to a map etched on the wall, a path only someone born in the tunnels could read. "Shortcut," she says, voice low. I nod and follow.

We don't talk much after that. There's no need. The city keeps hunting. The Corp keeps paying. But we're gone, already ghosts, and for the first time since I woke up in Émilie's bed, I don't miss it. Not even a little.

Chapter 6

Ban leads me down the spine of a safehouse, a corridor narrow enough to scrape blood from your knuckles if you forget where the walls are. The air is colder than the surface, loaded with the chemical ghost of dead rats and the bone-dry stink of resin. Every surface is either patched with scrap plastic or sweating black mold; nothing in here was designed for people. At the end, Ban takes a right and kicks a side door. It hisses open and breathes out a pulse of sodium light so harsh my overlays seize for a full second.

The room is a choked triangle, half filled by a workbench collapsing under the weight of its own clutter. I see upturned bottles, a universe of burned-out components, and three coffee mugs evolving their own strain of lichen. At the far end, a woman is hunched over a neural tangle, one hand twisting a jeweler's loupe into a cracked socket, the other deep in the guts of a microtome soldering iron. She doesn't look up when we enter, just stabs a probe into the mesh and rides out the little scream of ozone as something fuses.

Ban jerks her chin. "Katherine. Your 10 a.m. is here."

She looks like she crawled here through the wreckage. Ban grabs her shoulder—"How the hell did you get out?"—but Katherine just shakes her head. "Later."

The woman finishes her weld, flexes her hand, then pushes off from the bench so the chair pirouettes halfway toward us. She's got black hair streaked with silver, tied back with something that was never meant for hair—maybe a loop of network cable, maybe just a twist of wire. Her jaw is sharp, bones visible, the muscle stretched so tight I think if I yelled, she'd crack. Underneath, she wears a jacket a decade out of date, one sleeve rolled up past the elbow to reveal an arm latticeworked with old access port scars and newer burns.

She sizes us up through a wall of apathy and bad sleep. Her eyes are shot with red, but the pupils cut through with the intensity of a predator just before the collapse. She takes the cigarette from her lips, taps it on the desk, then returns it to her lips again, never letting the cherry cool. "Well?" Her voice is sandpaper, but I know the brand: Moshimoto Neural Engineering, Calculations Division, posthumous.

I glance at Ban, who gives a look that means: *You deal with her, I'm on comms.* Then she posts up against the far wall, arms crossed, one boot planted on an upturned crate, already scanning the hallway through a broken camera feed.

I step in, making sure to give the bottles a wide berth. "Darby Skelm," I say. "Asset reclamation, mostly."

Katherine gives a dry cough that becomes a laugh by accident. "Was that meant to impress me, or just trigger my gag reflex?"

"Neither," I say, flat. "But you're not big on formalities either, are you?"

She spins back to the desk, plucks up a small lens, and torques it with her thumb until the housing pops. "I'm big on reality. It's the only thing the Corp can't rebrand." She tosses the broken lens into a jar marked "FIX ME OR KILL ME" and moves on, hands shaking so minutely I wonder if it's ethanol withdrawal or just another custom nerve script running wild.

I look at Ban, who's already bored. "You said she could help."

Katherine hears that, too. "Did she tell you about the time she tried to crash the Châtelet Institute neural farm with an inside-out feedback loop?" She doesn't wait for a reply. "Didn't work, of course. But they had to incinerate three floors. You ever seen the color of a human brain when it's cooked at sublethal wattage for thirty hours?"

I haven't, but I know she's not bluffing. I nod, acknowledging the expertise and the crazy. "I heard about the aftermath. The mental hygiene crews couldn't scrape the memory residue from the ceilings. It's still there, under five layers of fresh paint."

She smiles, not at me but at the soldering iron. "You got a fun problem for me, Ban, or is this just one more wake for dead neural engineers?"

Ban shrugs, glancing at her nails. "You owe me. This clears half the debt."

Katherine picks at a fleck of metal on her palm, flicks it at the floor, then reaches for a bottle and pours a shot into the nearest clean cup. She slides the cup to me and raises her own. "To debts. They're the only family that always comes back."

I drink. The stuff is cheap, high-octane, and burns like solvent going down. Katherine watches me process the taste, a micro-smile flickering at the edge of her mouth. Ban cuts the silence. "We need you to break something. Big. Corporate."

Katherine lifts her glass. "You'll have to narrow that down, sweetie. All the big things are already broken, they just get patched with smaller and dumber until someone dies. You want to name a department, or should I run my own diagnostics?"

I shake my head. "Moshimoto. They're harvesting kids."

Her face doesn't move. Not for a second. Then, as she reaches for the soldering iron, the tip of her hand slips and the probe slices the ball of her finger. Blood beads, slow and dark. She keeps working, thumb rubbing the solder to push the burn back into the iron. "That's old news, asset. They've always harvested kids. The only new thing is the interface."

I lean closer, not aggressive, but I want her to see that I mean it. "They're burning out the consciousness before they even wire them in. I've seen the harvest logs. Unreadables by the thousand. Every time, they just flush the defective ones and make more."

Katherine shakes her head, jaw set, but her hands tremble harder now. "Of course they do. Once a child's brain is calibrated to optimal misery, they just mine the neural scar and reroute the leftovers. It's called efficiency. Châtelet invented it. We just refined it." There's a bitterness there so old it's probably fossilized in her marrow.

"You ever work with a child harvest rig?"

She shrugs. "I built three, ran two. Last time I saw one was in a shipping crate headed to the Singapore Correctional. They made me sign an NDA just for looking at the blueprints. Don't worry—they recycled the kids after they were done."

Ban is watching now, even if she pretends not to. She shifts her weight, eyes narrow. I keep pushing. "Do you know if the extraction process can be reversed?"

Katherine laughs, really laughs this time. "Of course not. The whole point is to make it irreversible. The more irreversible, the more secure the intellectual property." She wipes her finger on the front of her shirt, leaving a blood comet that does not slow her hands.

"Ban said you could help me rebuild my overlays," I say.

She shoots a glance at Ban, pure venom. "She overstates. At best, I can jury-rig a patch that buys you time. At worst, you get a stroke and a high score in the 'Readability' sweepstakes."

Ban speaks up. "I told you, he's special. Asset grade. They want him back, but he wants to burn their archives first."

Katherine looks at me, then Ban, then the bottle. She pours another, this time not offering. "Everyone wants to burn the archives. No one's willing to go up with them." Her hands, steady now, peel open the neural tangle. She starts wiring two broken modules together, one eye on me. "You want to crash a consciousness archive, you'll need more than a bootleg overlay. You'll need someone inside, someone with a valid credential or a really, really convincing signature. I'm good, but even my backdoors have backdoors."

Ban steps forward, finally losing patience. "I can get you in. I just need the kid operational."

Katherine puts down her tools and cracks her knuckles. "He looks operational to me. What's wrong with the current model?"

I look at the burn scars on her hands, the faded logo on her shirt, the bottles lined up like a proof of past failures. "It's not the hardware," I say. "It's the memory. They stole so much, I'm not sure there's anything left to salvage."

For the first time, something in her face shifts—a flicker of recognition, maybe pity. She clears her throat, voice softer. "You ever meet someone who still had all their own memories?"

I shake my head, honest. "Not in this life."

She nods, slow. "Me neither." She gets up, grabs a roll of tape, and wraps her finger like she's done it a thousand times. She turns back, eyes locked on mine. "You got a trauma profile? I need your baseline, or else the patch could scramble everything, even the bits you care about."

I tap the side of my head. "Stored local. But there's gaps. Bad ones."

"Show me," she says. I hesitate, then blink up the overlay, letting her see the diagnostic tree. The neural map is a horror show: pathways rerouted through scar tissue, whole blocks of memory crosshatched by corporate redactions, flashes of color where trauma events overlap. Katherine whistles, then starts sorting through the mess. As she works, I watch her hands; there's no tremor now, just precision and speed. She's more at home in the chaos of broken circuitry than she ever could be in a quiet room. Ban sits, watches, and offers nothing. Her presence is an anchor, but she doesn't get in the way.

After five minutes, Katherine pushes back from the bench. "I can build you a patch, but it'll cost." She raises her bandaged hand. "Nothing free, not even in hell."

Ban gets up, paces once, then nods. "We can pay. But it has to work."

Katherine laughs, voice wrecked but alive. "That's the funny thing, Ban. Nothing works. Not really." She starts pulling chips from a stack, slotting them into a homebrew compiler. "But if you want it, I'll make you a virus that eats their archive from the inside out. If you're lucky, you get a memory or two back before the collapse." She slides me a chair. "Sit. Let's see if you're as special as Ban says."

I blink through the headache. The world swims, sharpens, then locks into place. Katherine is already at the bench, stripping out the innards of two interface harnesses with the fury of a drowning god. She's in her element now, every twitch of her fingers a data point in the trajectory of mad invention. "Sit," she says. "Or leave. I need focus, not an audience."

I sit. Ban stands behind, arms folded, pretending not to hover. She's abandoned sarcasm for outright annoyance, her boot tapping a pulse in the concrete. The bottle Katherine started is now half-empty, but her hand doesn't shake when she moves. She talks as she works, like the code would clog if she didn't say it out loud. "Here's the problem: child brain, adult interface. They're not even the same species after you cook the wiring with thirty years of meme-crud and trauma overlays. You ever try to run an old console on a next-gen power supply? Bang, and you're a paperweight."

Ban snorts. "They didn't hire you for metaphors."

"They didn't hire me at all," Katherine says. "They conscripted. Good engineers don't last at Moshimoto; great ones last even less." She cracks open a ceramic node, slices the solder, and swaps in a crystal chip. The smell of burning epoxy fills the room. "If you want to block the extraction, you can't just jam the signal. That triggers the failsafe and cooks your cortex. You have to redirect, make the archive think it's extracting the real you, but actually just copying a sandboxed clone. Best-case, you're still alive. Worst-case, you become the world's smartest screensaver."

Ban scowls. "We're paying for best-case."

Katherine ignores her, clicks two leads together, and the mesh skeleton hums to life. "Skelm, you got anything in your overlays about self-image or identity consistency?"

I check the diagnostics. There's a new alert: PERSONALITY FRAGMENTATION—POTENTIAL. My hands clench on the edge of the table. "Plenty. Why?"

"If you've got splits, that's good. You can let the rig chew on a spare and keep the rest for yourself. They only want your marketable bits anyway. The rest is trash." She smiles, teeth yellow and perfect for a carnivore. "I can show you how to make a copy and hold it ransom."

Ban gives a low, ugly laugh. "So he gets to blackmail himself. Perfect."

Katherine leans back, grabs another bottle, and pours without spilling a drop. "Better than trusting Moshimoto with the keys to your skull."

I ask, "You ever run this in the wild? Or is this another lab special?"

She gives a one-shoulder shrug. "Tested it on two interns. One defected to the Bureau, the other took a job at a tech monastery. Both are still alive. Probably."

Ban pushes off the wall. "You ready?"

Katherine nods. "Bring me the asset."

She means me. I stand, the world a little off-axis but holding together. She gestures to a battered folding chair lined with copper tape and dried blood. I sit. She clamps a cold band around my head, then slips two dermal patches onto my temples. "This will sting," she says. It does. Like a wire brush dipped in salt and jammed straight into the bone. She fires up the interface, fingers flying over a mess of homebrew code and stolen corporate diagnostics. The overlays in my head stutter, then flare into a prism of warnings: DUPLICATION IN PROGRESS—UNAUTHORIZED. HOST INTEGRITY—DEGRADATION IMMINENT.

I grit my teeth. "How long?"

"Depends on how much you care about the parts you're losing," Katherine says. "Some people don't notice at all."

Ban watches, arms crossed, not blinking. The world goes sideways. I'm in two places: the chair, body sweating, and somewhere else, floating above it, watching as if through a greasy pane of glass. I see my hands gripping the armrest, see the way my knuckles blanch, but also watch as Katherine's ghostly overlay walks around me, tracing paths of light from skull to terminal.

She speaks, voice layered: one normal, one pitched low and slow. "Now comes the tricky bit. If I pull too much, you drop. If I pull too little, Moshimoto knows it's a fake and backtraces your real."

I want to ask what happens then, but my mouth is full of tin. I hear Ban's voice as if from underwater. "Don't screw this, Johnson."

Katherine's fingers move even faster. She talks to herself, or to the rig, or to a god who only listens to bleeding-edge engineers. "Come on, baby, thread the needle. Yes, there, that's it ..."

There's a surge of static—every memory I've ever had flares to the surface, fighting for primacy. My mother's face, the smell of the labs, the taste of blood, Ban's voice saying "run," Katherine's hands working the overlays. Then the world splits again, and half of me watches as the other half collapses to the floor.

I wake up in my body, on the cold concrete. Ban is kneeling over me, two fingers at my neck. "He's alive," she mutters, sounding almost disappointed.

Katherine stands above, breathing hard. There's a cut on her forehead, probably from where she slammed into a monitor during the surge. She wipes the blood away, then helps Ban drag me back into the chair. I blink, trying to focus. The overlays are different: faster, cleaner, but also more brittle. Katherine leans in, so close I can smell the old cigarette on her breath. She runs a quick diagnostic, fingers brushing the dermal patch on my neck. “You feeling yourself, Skelm?”

I nod, though my hands tremble. “Close enough.”

Katherine sits, grabs a towel, and presses it to her bleeding head. “Next time, maybe don’t make it a rush job.”

Ban finally lets herself smile, grim and ugly. “We’re not running a spa, Johnson. We need to hit the transfer tomorrow night.”

Katherine shrugs and sips the dregs of her drink. “If he wants to die pretty, he can always sign up for the early retirement package. Otherwise, this is the only upgrade I’ve got.”

I look at the overlays, the bright new lines of code. For a moment, I feel almost whole. Ban walks to the door, checks the hallway, then turns back. “You think it’ll work?”

Katherine laughs, the sound a rattle in her chest. “If not, at least he’ll be the prettiest corpse in the archive.”

I push myself upright, steady. “What do we do now?”

Katherine leans back and closes her eyes. “Now? You go, do your hero thing. Just remember, everything you save gets overwritten eventually.”

I stand, testing my balance. Ban offers a hand, and I take it. Her grip is warm, real, the only thing in the room that doesn’t shake. As we head for the exit, Ban glances back at Katherine. "You sure you're okay?"

She waves us off, already pouring a fresh drink. "Never better."

We walk out. The corridor feels narrower, the world colder, but I'm running on twice the fire. In the stairwell, Ban turns to me. "You trust her?"

I don't answer right away. After a minute, I say, "As much as I trust anyone."

She grins, wolfish, and for the first time since I woke up in the lab, I think I might just survive.

The next morning is worse than a hangover; there's a pressure in my skull that can't decide if it's agony or euphoria. Katherine is already awake, hovering over her bench, the blue glow of the console making her skin look translucent. I half expect to see the code bleeding right through her. Ban sits by the door, a silent guard, thumb flicking the safety on her pistol with rhythmic intent. She's watching Katherine, but every third flick her eyes dart to me—calculating, maybe even worried. Katherine beckons me forward with a single hooked finger. "Showtime, hero. This is where we see if you stay you, or become a very pretty slab of meat."

I sit in the chair, skin itching at the memory of yesterday's cold band. Katherine straps a fresh interface cap around my temples, tight enough to make my teeth throb. Ban stands, the gun gone but fists balled at her sides. "You sure this is safe?"

Katherine grins, the expression brittle. "Absolutely not. But it'll work."

She taps her console. "Darby, you'll feel a sharp sting, then a slide. Try not to resist the current. Think of something you love —assuming you've got any left."

The machine hisses. Overlays strobe my vision with diagnostic hell: NEURAL SCHEMA—OVERWRITE IN PROGRESS. MEMORY ACCESS—ADMIN PRIVILEGE ESCALATED. The air vibrates as the rig cycles up. It starts with a simple brightness, like a migraine aura, but then my perspective inverts—I'm both in my body and above it, observer and observed. I see the side of my own face as overlays draw heat maps over my own skull. Next, there's a sinking, the sense that my memories are draining through the chair, one drop at a time. I try to clutch at them, but each grasp slides off slick, like trying to hold on to melting ice. Katherine's voice is a filament in the dark: "We're running a decoy path, fooling the system into eating a dummy scan. You'll feel a gap, then a rush. When the rush hits, don't fight it."

In the periphery, I watch Ban's hands move—her knuckles white, arms crossed so tight the tendons look like wire. The overlays scream new warnings. PATHWAY COLLAPSE—REDUNDANCY FAILURE. HOST IDENTITY—CRITICAL THRESHOLD. All my senses flatten into raw data: numbers, colors, noise. I feel every beat of my heart as a spike in a graph, and each spike is tagged "EVENT: POTENTIAL SELF-ERASURE."

There's a sound in my head, a whine building to a scream. I realize it's the machine, and the air, and me—all three in feedback. The rig tightens, then the world shatters. In the shatter, there are hands on my body, my own and not my own. I am Ban, standing over myself, then Katherine, running code, then the kid in the chair who never signed up for any of this. The overlays pull back to a pinpoint, then explode outward. My entire life flashes: the brief joy of a safe day in childhood, the endless hunger of corporate labs, every moment I ever lost.

For one tick of the clock, I am everywhere and nowhere. Then the world slams back. I'm in the chair, air cold against my skin, chest heaving like I've run a marathon. The overlays blink, slow and uncertain, then resolve into one line: DUPLICATE DECOY—STABLE.

Ban's voice cuts through. "Darby. Are you in there?"

I try to talk, but all I can manage is a wet gasp. I nod, and after a few seconds, my lungs catch up. "Still me," I say, my voice cracking. "Still here."

Katherine checks the display. Her hands are steady, surgical. "You did it. You lost ninety percent of your marketable content, but the ten that's left is pure, uncut you." She grins. "They'll hate you for it."

Ban is at my side, hands on my wrists, checking for a pulse. Her skin is warm, grounding. "You okay?"

I nod again. My memory feels like a deadweight drive, but I can think, see, breathe. More than I could have hoped for. Katherine wipes her brow with the back of her hand, leaving a streak of graphite across her forehead. "He's as ready as he's going to get. You want to run the next phase, it's now or never."

Ban releases my wrist, not right away, but slow. She looks at me with an intensity that stings—like if I blink, she might not be there when I open my eyes again. She turns to Katherine. "He's good. What about you?"

Katherine shrugs, the mask of indifference back in place. "I'm a sidecar on this op, Ban. You need me to calibrate another patch, you know where to find me. Otherwise, I'm drinking until I believe in God again."

Ban helps me out of the chair. My legs are numb, but the feeling returns with ugly speed. She holds me upright until I can stand on my own. "You sure?"

I grin, or try to. "Never been less sure. But I'm not dead."

Katherine is already packing up, shoving tools into a faded satchel. She eyes us, then flicks a small, flat chip off the bench and into her pocket. "Call if you survive," she says, and for once, there's no sarcasm, just something that might be regret.

Ban and I make for the exit. She guides me up the tunnel, every step a little easier. At the hatch, she looks back at the lab, at Katherine, then at me. "We move in an hour." I nod, watching her pace the length of the tunnel, prepping for the next disaster. My memory is Swiss cheese, but the holes let in a kind of light I never had before. Back in the lab, Katherine sits, head in her hands, not moving. Her drink sits untouched beside her, the air electric with what she's just done. For a moment, I wonder if she'll call after us. But she doesn't. She's finished. Or maybe just broken in a way I understand too well.

Outside, the city is brighter than I remember. The overlays are slower, but the world is more real for it. I take Ban's hand as we step into the day. Whatever happens next, it'll be me making the choices, for once. And that, I realize, is worth every second of pain.

Chapter 7

The holding cell is five meters of afterthought, probably once a janitor's closet, now converted to house something you wouldn't want leaking into the walls. The stink is all surface: disinfectant overlaid on the sour tang of sweat and spent electrolytes. Fluorescents buzz in the ceiling, each bulb dialed to a frequency calculated to maximize tension and minimize hope. Even the overlays seem jittery in here.

Dorothy sits where they left her, arms folded around her own waist like a self-suffocating bear. She's too big for the plastic chair, so she's braced on the tips of her feet, knees up, hunching to avoid the steel crossbar drilled into her spinal mods. Ban gestures for me to hang back as she steps into the threshold—her version of polite. Dorothy looks up without moving her head. "Thought the next visitor'd be an incinerator," she says. Her voice is low, just this side of a growl.

"Budget cuts," Ban says, hands in jacket pockets, no visible weapons but her whole body reads like one. "They've outsourced the burning. Us now."

Dorothy doesn't laugh. I watch the tension roll through her chest, every muscle firing in sequence, overlays overlaying: POWER: 58%. MUSCLE SYNC: OPTIMAL. Both her arms are chrome from elbow down, the cheap mass-market stuff you see on out-of-work miners. It's been customized for war: manual overrides at every joint, a double-thick layer of ballistic polymer, and a ripper blade mounted on her left forearm where the corporate branding used to be.

Ban leans against the far wall. I step in slowly, careful to keep my hands visible and voice low. "Dorothy, I'm Darby Skelm. Ban said you were the only one strong enough to pop a Debt-Hound in half without losing your smile."

"Must've been a long night if you believe that." Dorothy's left hand twitches, micro-movements under the skin as the actuators click through a self-test. Her right hand is still, fingers curled around her own thigh hard enough to creak the bone.

"They said you went offline mid-mission," I say, "after you refused to neutralize a cluster of unreadables."

Her eyes flash—hazel, bright, wet with something worse than tears. "Those corporate fucks programmed the smiles onto their faces before they sent the kill order." Her jaw flexes, metal struts visible where teeth meet gum. "Smile, even while you burn."

Ban chimes in, dry. "Protocol said to vaporize everything. Dorothy vaped the kill team and walked."

"I didn't walk," Dorothy says. "I ran until the neural governors locked out my legs, then crawled. They don't mention that in the press release."

Ban's eyebrows climb half a millimeter. I take a seat on an upturned bucket, careful not to seem threatening or weak, but I doubt it matters. "Why did you do it?"

Dorothy snorts. "What, the classic 'I was just following orders' speech not good enough for you?"

"I want the truth, not the version that fits your file."

She shrugs, shoulders rising like a tectonic event. "Turns out my moral code's the only part of me they couldn't upgrade. The rest they rebuilt as much as they liked." Her fingers tap her own forehead in an absent, surgical way. "This isn't the first cell I've woken up in, you know."

Ban lets the silence eat up the next twenty seconds. Then, soft, almost kind, she says, "You're not here as a prisoner, Dorothy. We need a favor."

Dorothy looks up at Ban, then at me, and I get the full blast of her inspection—military, systematic, professional. "Favor," she says. "From me?"

I nod. "You know what Moshimoto is doing in the city. The harvests, the compliance labs, the brain-farmed kids. We want to break it. Cut the pipeline. Maybe even blow a hole so big it takes the whole Corp with it."

She chews on this. There's a tic in her jaw, some old pain playing a rerun. "What's in it for me?" she asks, voice bare.

"Freedom," Ban says. "Or as close as you're gonna get."

Dorothy shakes her head. "That's not a pitch. That's a coupon for suffering."

"Maybe," Ban says. "But it's better than waiting for the Corp to memory-wipe you again."

"Last time they did, I killed half the enforcement deck on my way out." Dorothy flexes her left hand, all five fingers splaying, each ending in a knife-sharp black talon. "I have a pattern."

Ban smirks. "We like patterns. They're predictable."

Dorothy laughs—a single hard bark, sharp enough to cut the tension for one second. Then her face resets, back to neutral. "You got a job for me," she says, "make it plain."

"We're hitting the harvest run at Châtelet," I say, the words feeling like a gun pressed to my own throat. "Tonight. We need muscle, and someone who's seen the inside of their extraction rigs."

Dorothy's mouth twitches. "No guns? No backup?"

"Plenty of guns," Ban says. "But the muscle is what keeps the kids alive."

Dorothy closes her eyes, head rocking once; maybe regret, maybe anger. When she opens them, the wetness is gone. "Fine. I'll help. But you should know something first." I wait. She stands. The restraints on her ankles pop with a servo click, the chair screeching across the tile as she rises. Ban tenses—just a hair, but enough to let me know it's real now. Dorothy towers over me, eyes locked, the rest of her body at parade rest. "My combat mods have triggers," she says. "If I lose it, if they get into my head, I will go full kinetic until everything is dead. That includes you."

I swallow, not subtly. "Duly noted."

She looks to Ban, then back at me. "You won't like what happens when they fire."

"We'll cross that river when we get there," Ban says.

Dorothy grins, an ugly, half-metal thing. "Hope you can swim."

She holds out her left arm. Ban moves to unlock the wrist module, careful, as if disabling a grenade with a religious bent. Dorothy keeps her gaze on me the whole time.

Ban steps back. "You're loose."

Dorothy stretches, the sound of synthetic sinew and metal joints making the overlays blink warnings for decibel overflow. She shakes out both hands, then cracks her neck, left, then right, the gesture more animal than human. "Let's get this over with."

I nod, but my hands are sweating. "You need a weapon?"

She glances at Ban. "She is a weapon."

Ban actually smiles at that.

The three of us make our way out of the cell, Dorothy in the lead, Ban at my flank. The hall lights flicker as we walk, the overlays throwing up fresh hazards at every turn. I watch Dorothy's back, the way her muscles and mods seem fused by the same stubbornness. The way she moves is like someone who expects to die but is prepared to kill anything that tries first. I don't trust her. But I respect her instantly.

As we reach the top of the stairs, Ban turns to me. "Congratulations. You're now the proud owner of an ex-corporate murder machine."

Dorothy laughs again. This time, it sounds almost human. “You want to live through tonight, Skelm?” she says, not looking back. “Stay close, and keep your hands where I can see them.”

Ban claps me on the shoulder, hard enough to sting. “Welcome to the team.”

We step into the next disaster.

The tunnel is colder than any hell they could threaten us with. Water drips from the vaults, each drop timed to some cruel metronome that never runs out of battery. The walls are tattooed with half a century of chemical graffiti—crew tags, corporate mascots, faded promises of salvation via new and improved breakfast cereal. The air vibrates, faint but constant, from the electromagnetic spill of the city’s dying subway system three blocks above. Ban leads the way, boots crunching old glass and rust. Dorothy follows, arms at her sides, head ducked as if trying to avoid a collision with the universe. I trail, overlays running environmental hazard warnings with an excitement I can only describe as masochistic. We round a bend and hit the staging area.

It used to be a break room for maintenance crews. Now it’s a tomb: two metal benches, three walls of exposed rebar, and a patchwork of first-aid kits repurposed as bomb casings. At the far end, Ban’s jury-rigged control station hums behind a reinforced plastic blast shield. She slides behind the console. “You both ready?”

Dorothy grunts, eyes fixed on the darkness at the far end of the tunnel. “Just tell me where to aim.”

The overlays dump an alert: NEW SIMULATION PARAMETERS DETECTED. Ban has programmed a full gauntlet—Moshimoto security drones, armed enforcement avatars, and maybe a killbot or two for flavor. Her voice is clear, but it ricochets off the concrete. "Objective is simple. Break the force, reach the finish line, don't die."

Dorothy's knuckles pop as she rolls her shoulders. "Do they scream when I rip them apart?"

"Every time," Ban says. "I like realism."

I settle into the observer's pit, overlays flickering blue lines of probability through the dark. Dorothy steps to the start mark, feet braced, one hand resting on the blade implant beneath her left wrist. The lights overhead dim, then pulse blood-red, and the tunnel fills with the clatter of bootsteps—not human, but close enough to trigger the old panic.

The first wave hits: six security drones, hologram-wrapped in riot gear, their shields glowing with non-lethal but very real tasers. Dorothy doesn't hesitate. She charges, body low, arms tucked close. The drones react—one, two, three baton strikes, each met by the thud of reinforced carbon against meat and metal. Dorothy spins, left arm extending, blade out. The first drone loses its head. Literally. The second goes down in a storm of sparks.

She moves like gravity isn't a factor, violence as natural as breathing. The overlays record the rhythm: IMPACT. IMPACT. RIP. IMPACT. Three seconds and the first wave is splattered across the concrete, their hard-light shells guttering into static.

Ban cranks the simulation. More enemies—now bipedal, now armed with shotguns and logic bombs—pour from the far end. Dorothy doesn't slow. If anything, she speeds up, learning with each step, her arms and legs transforming, adapting. By the third wave, she's replaced finesse with raw force, using the dead as shields, battering the next group into submission with the last one's torso.

From the booth, Ban whistles. "That's a record."

I'm so transfixed I almost miss the new simulation element: the "child-mem" holograms. Small bodies, no features but blank faces and generic hands, standing between the oncoming drones and Dorothy's rampage. Ban has her hand hovering over the abort switch, but she doesn't press it. Dorothy freezes, both arms out, claws dripping with the residue of simulated violence. The child-mems don't move, don't even flinch, just stand as if waiting for a bus that's never coming.

"Ban—" I say, but she waves me off.

"Trust the process," she says, not taking her eyes off the tunnel. Dorothy begins to tremble. The overlays warn "PTSD TRIGGER—SEVERE," but there's no option to patch this one out. Her breathing doubles, then triples. The drones close in from all sides, ignoring the children. One gets close enough to touch, and Dorothy goes berserk.

The world narrows to a strobe of red and blue. Dorothy's arms blur, claws expanding, then collapsing into something more like hammers. She smashes the first three drones so hard their hard-light projectors short-circuit and the explosion cracks real concrete. Then she pivots, aiming a kick at the next cluster, and the force of her leg detaches the entire upper half of a drone from its legs.

She's out of control, her mods firing on every cylinder, heat shimmering around her shoulders where the old skin meets the chrome. The overlays begin to panic: COMBAT GOVERNOR OFFLINE—OVERCLOCK. BIOFEEDBACK UNSAFE. HOSTILITY RISK TO ALL. Even Ban looks nervous now. Then Dorothy turns on the child-mems. She doesn't attack, just stands there, hands open, palms forward. The holograms cluster around her, blank faces upturned, and for a second, it looks almost tender.

But something snaps. Dorothy emits a scream so deep the tunnel shakes. She pivots, smashing her own head into the wall until the projection glass cracks and bleeds sparks. Then she drops to one knee, hands on either side of her head, sobbing or laughing or maybe both. The child-mems don't react. They just fade, leaving her alone in the wreckage.

I jump the observer's rail and sprint down the tunnel. "Dorothy—"

Ban is yelling something, probably "Wait for the cooldown," but I don't care. Dorothy's slumped, one hand still clawed, the other scraping raw against the broken concrete. I kneel in front of her, overlays all in the red, and reach out to touch her shoulder. She snaps her head up. For a split second, I see pure, animal terror—then she grabs me by the front of my shirt, lifts me off my feet, and slams me against the wall so hard my vision tints black at the edges.

"Focus on me," I manage to say, voice almost drowned by the buzz in my skull.

Dorothy shakes her head, eyes wild. "Can't stop," she says. "They're still here—"

I keep my voice even, every word forced through the pain. "They're not here, Dorothy. Just me. Just Ban. You're safe."

She shakes me again, not as hard. "You don't get it, Skelm. They never leave. They haunt the code."

I nod as best I can. "I know. I know it better than you think. But you have to override."

Her breathing slows, just a notch. I reach for her hand, the one not wrapped around my neck. "Let me help."

She lets me take it. The metal is cold, vibrating with spent adrenaline. I guide her fingers to the classic Ban combat stance: thumb and pinky flexed, palm open, wrist at forty-five. It's what Ban taught me in the first week—focus the pain, channel the rage, turn it into math. "Just like Ban showed us," I whisper. "Take the fight, make it real, then let it go."

Her grip softens. My feet hit the floor again. "Math," she says, voice hoarse.

"Yes," I say, matching her breath for breath. "All numbers, all just sequence."

She slumps, releases me, and sits on the cold ground, arms across her knees. The overlays shift from red to yellow. Ban appears behind me, silent as a judge. She kneels, puts a hand on Dorothy's shoulder, and waits. After a minute, Dorothy looks up. "I failed," she whispers.

Ban shakes her head. "You lived. That's the win condition."

Dorothy laughs, wet and rough. "No one's ever said that before."

I sit next to her, not quite touching. "Get used to it."

The tunnel is quiet again, just the sound of dripping water and Dorothy's cooling systems winding down. Ban helps Dorothy up. "We'll run it again," she says. "But next time, you set the parameters."

Dorothy nods, unsteady but determined. "Deal."

We walk back up the tunnel together, leaving the simulation's carnage behind. At the break room, Ban grins at me. "Didn't think you had a death wish."

"Didn't know I had one either."

Dorothy laughs, real this time. I think maybe she trusts us, even just a little. Next time, I hope it's enough.

The bunker is quieter now that the adrenaline has worn off. The hum of the data lines is almost soothing—like if I listen long enough, I'll decode a secret message hidden in the packet noise. The scent of solder lingers in the air, plus the sharp ozone tang from Ban's constant upgrades to our mesh perimeter. The only light is a cold-white string, coiling from the concrete ceiling down to Ban's corner desk.

Dorothy's in the back, stripped to the waist, cleaning dried sim-blood and carbon from the micro-seams of her arm. Ban sits across from me, legs folded, a holographic map hovering in the space between our knees. She's plotting potential attack vectors, one hand flicking icons in and out of existence.

“Her stance is military, but not clean,” Ban says, half to me, half to the map. “She holds a gun like you do when you’re not thinking about it. Night-self posture. Relying on overlays.”

“She has overlays?” I ask, voice low.

Ban shakes her head, eyes never leaving the map. “No, but she used to. You can see the ghost of them in her line. That’s why she overcompensates. That’s why she’s dangerous.”

I watch Dorothy through the data shimmer, her silhouette made of scars and contract steel. “She’s more stable than I expected.”

Ban smirks. “Not stable. Just disciplined. Her PTSD isn’t a wound—it’s a software patch. They installed it to keep her from questioning orders.”

I run a quick check on our own security: three layers of subdermal mesh; two of ceramic, one of my own design that I haven’t even told Ban about. The overlays seem content with the odds. “You think she’ll break?”

Ban looks up, really looks, her gaze a pin through the middle of my forehead. “We all break. Only question is what comes out when you do.”

I want to answer, but the perimeter alarms save me. The sound is a tripwire shriek, not meant to warn us so much as alert the neighborhood that everything has just gone to hell. Ban’s map folds in on itself and disappears. She’s on her feet before the next alarm hits, moving to the armory locker without breaking stride. I follow, overlays already drawing threat lines on every wall. “Phalanx unit,” Ban says, voice monotone. “Looks like Moshimoto found us.”

Dorothy appears at the hatchway, face blank but hands already stained red from cleaning her arm. “How many?” she asks, as if ordering at a drive-thru.

“Two drones, six humans,” Ban says. “Armored, minimum. Probably a suppression squad.”

Dorothy nods, then glances at me. “You run, or you fight?” I hesitate, and she almost smiles. “Thought so,” she says, and moves to the hatch.

Ban pulls out a sidearm and hands it to me. “Shoot straight. Don’t get clever.”

I load the gun, muscle memory perfect. My overlays try to suggest an optimal firing stance, but I flick the feed off. Not today. Dorothy takes point. She doesn’t ask for a weapon. Instead, she rolls her left shoulder, and the blade at her wrist unsheathes with a sound like a zipper yanked open at max speed. We crouch by the hatch. The sounds outside get louder: the grind of steel toes on concrete, the hissing exhale of synthetic lungs. Ban gives the countdown with her fingers: *three, two, one.*

Dorothy yanks the hatch open, and a drone fills the frame—black, beetle-bodied, its undercarriage bristling with chems and less-lethal pellets. Dorothy doesn’t hesitate. She shoves the blade up through the chassis, then rips it sideways. The drone splits like a melon, wet and sizzling, pieces bouncing down the corridor.

The second drone fires a volley. Dorothy ducks, using the shredded first drone as a shield. I lean out, sight the blue LED of its core, and squeeze. The recoil is gentler than I expected. The drone staggers, hits the wall, and keeps shooting. Ban lines up her own shot and nails the core, shutting it down for good.

The humans arrive, four of them, with two more covering the far end. They move like a single organism, firing in tight, controlled bursts. Dorothy takes a hit to her chest—blood splatters the floor, but she doesn't slow. She grabs the nearest by his visor, crushes it with a bare hand, and uses him as a battering ram to plow into the next. The impact shatters the skull behind the helmet, red and gray mashing into the wall.

The other two target Ban and me. I hear the rounds snap past, one hitting my left shoulder hard enough to numb my whole arm. I drop to a knee, aim, and fire. The first trooper goes down, legs blown out from under him. Ban moves low, sliding across the concrete. She pops up behind one, presses the gun to his neck, and fires point-blank. The spray coats the wall.

Dorothy is already down the hall, hunting the last two. I limp after her, vision narrowed to a pinhole, overlays running threat tallies like a slot machine. At the corridor's end, the final two Moshimoto troopers try to run, but Dorothy's faster. She leaps, grabs one by the backpack, and slams him into the opposite wall so hard the bones shatter audibly. The last one fires a shotgun at her face, but the rounds spatter against her cybernetics, and she barely even flinches.

She grabs him, puts him in a headlock, then tears his helmet off. The guy's young—maybe twenty, maybe not even that—and his eyes are wide with terror. Dorothy hesitates, just for a second, then cracks his neck and drops him to the floor. Then there's silence, except for the soft whine of dying drone servos. I step into the corridor, holding my numb arm, and see

Dorothy at the far end. She's bent double, hands braced on her knees, breathing in huge, ragged gulps.

Ban appears behind me, gun ready, eyes flicking from corpse to corpse. "You okay?" she asks Dorothy.

Dorothy stands, wipes blood from her mouth, and nods. "Just tired," she says, but her voice sounds wrong. I walk over, overlays checking for wounds.

"You're leaking," I say, pointing to the fresh blood seeping from a seam below her ribcage.

Dorothy glances down. "Bio or synth?"

I take a closer look. "Both," I say. "You need a patch."

She shrugs. "Later."

Ban holsters her gun. "We need to move. Extraction point's still hot?"

I check the overlays. "At least two squads inbound. We need a new route."

Dorothy paces back and forth, the thousand-yard stare etched even deeper in her face now. She doesn't say anything, just watches the bodies on the floor, as if cataloging them for some report she'll never write. Ban leans in close. "She's dissociating," she whispers.

"I know."

"What do we do?"

I think of Katherine's words: nothing works, not really. "Give her a minute."

The bunker is wrecked. Blood and hydraulic fluid mix on the floor, turning the whole place into a meat locker. I check my own wound, but it's superficial. The overlays are already instructing my glands to pump clotting factors.

After a moment, Dorothy comes back to us. "I know the way. Old drainage. It's tight, but no one follows a corpse down a sewer."

Ban looks at me. "Can you walk?"

"Can you carry me?" I joke.

She rolls her eyes. "Only if you want to be dropped."

I look at Dorothy, who's already at the exit hatch. She waits for us, one hand on the door, the other pressed to her wound. The way she stands—still, expectant—reminds me of the last time I saw someone waiting for their death, only Dorothy isn't afraid. She's just angry it's not coming fast enough.

We file out, Ban taking point, Dorothy in the rear. The tunnels are darker, older, more claustrophobic than the subway. Every turn is a blind corner. Every echo could be a new team on our tail. At one point, we stop so Ban can hack an old security panel. While she works, Dorothy sits, back to the wall, eyes closed.

I kneel beside her. "You did good."

She shakes her head, barely a movement. "No. I did what I was built to do."

"Same difference."

Chapter 8

There's no rest in Ban's safehouse. The concrete walls sweat; the ceiling is a failing logic grid of recycled PVC and exposed thermal bands, every seam patched with duct tape or someone's bad idea of a joke. Ban paces perimeter with her habitual twitch: left thumb grazing the combat knife, head jerking every seven seconds like she's syncing to a private metronome. Dorothy, post-trauma, has claimed the northwest corner, bleeding from her ribs into a field dressing that should have gone to someone less impossible to kill.

I'm at the coffin-desk, wrists bandaged and overlays throttled to minimum, cataloging the air for the scent of betrayal. Every molecule here is flagged as hazardous. If I stand still, I can almost track the path of the last kill squad that tried to break us: the ozone cut from gunfire, the trace iron where Ban's fist dented a faceplate, the stale black pepper that's always, always panic.

The overlays ping: GUEST, IMMINENT. Three seconds out. Even with half the hardware, Ban can spot a tail before it leaves the womb. She gestures with two fingers. "Friend or drone?"

I scan, then double. "Both." The signature's familiar: corporate, Moshimoto, but layered with so much spoof and shadow I wonder if it's some new hallucination. The buzzer goes. Ban answers with a blade, opening the hatch just wide enough for the kill zone, then stands to the side. The guest walks in. Not human, not entirely, but what passes for it in a world where every advancement is just another death certificate in the making.

Cleopatra—her real name, she insists—does not announce herself. She lets the door close and surveys the room, taking the geometry in one pass, never lingering. She wears her triple augmentations like a fuck-you to biology. First, the eyes. Chrome-pupil, gold-flecked irises, but what matters is the second layer: a rolling transparency that cycles numbers, equations, and live odds. I catch a reflection in the overhead bulb—ninety-four percent, then ninety-three, then up to ninety-six as she locks gaze with me.

Second, the time-dilation processors. You can't see them unless you know what to look for, but Ban must see because she stiffens and rocks back on her heels. Cleopatra's limbs move with a micro-stutter, like someone watching a video on double speed but never spilling a drop. Her left hand draws a business card from her blazer at the same time as her right smooths imaginary lint from the lapel. Both moves are perfect; neither leaves a shadow.

Third, the social-pattern cortices, visible as a web of faint blue under her temples—little rivers of light that pulse when she fakes a smile or listens too closely. They flare when Ban raises an eyebrow, and even harder when Dorothy, who hasn't spoken yet, just stares. "Darby Skelm," says Cleopatra. Her voice is pure corporate, the intonation modulated by someone who's read every guide to sincerity but prefers the footnotes.

"That's me," I say, too tired for chess.

"May I sit?"

Ban watches, says nothing, but motions to the nearest chair—one of the cheapos Ban found at a crime scene and brought home because it "felt lucky." Cleopatra takes it with all the grace of a C-suite on deadline, then crosses her legs, hands steepled on her knee. The overlays note a drop in room temperature. Cleopatra probably programmed it herself. I go for the credentials, quick as I dare: three scans, then a physical signature swipe with the corpse-warm surface of a neutral comm pad. She lets me do it, never moving, only her eyes flicking to each overlay in turn, the probability fields adjusting every time I hesitate.

Ban cracks first. "You're still flagged with an active Moshimoto badge. So either you're a double, or you're here to kill us."

Cleopatra smiles—not with her mouth, but with the corners of her data. "You're both correct. But I think we're all above that, aren't we?"

I run the second-layer authentication. The code is so tight it makes my hands hurt. The overlays suggest: FRAUD DETECTED: POSSIBLE. RISK: VARIABLE. I say, "Ban's got a thing for tight codes. Sometimes she can't tell if she wants to break them or marry them."

Cleopatra's eyes flick to Ban, then back to me. "That's why you're interesting, Darby. You're an anomaly. A readable who shouldn't be readable. A statistic that got lost in its own mean."

Ban bristles and leans forward, voice low. "Get to the offer. No one's running this much compute for small talk."

Cleopatra sips invisible air, then nods. "You're planning to hit the Moshimoto archive. I can get you in. Access codes, personnel schedule, the works. But I need a piece of the take."

Dorothy snorts. The overlays render it as "MILD DISGUST."

I try to find the angle. "What's your stake? They let you keep your teeth and your augment budget. Why sell out now?"

Cleopatra's smile goes legit. "You're not thinking big enough, Darby. Loyalty isn't a virtue anymore. It's a liability." She glances at Ban, then Dorothy. "I'm interested in outcomes. And you"—she points, almost delicately—"are a probability outlier. I prefer to bet on the side with higher variance. That's where the upside is."

Ban says, "You ever been upside down, Cleo? Because you will be if you double us."

Cleopatra's lips part, perfect and bloodless. "I'm not a double, Ban. I'm a triple." She cocks her head, as if she expects applause. No one laughs.

I let the silence bite for a while, see if it gets under her skin. It doesn't. If anything, it makes her more efficient. "You're running an exploit," I say. "What do you want at the end of it?"

Cleopatra's eyes roll the numbers. "I want the root. The keys to the archive, and the data that matters." She lets that dangle before speaking again. "You're welcome to the rest. I'm not here to bankrupt anyone. I just want an edge."

Ban raises both brows, meaning: *This one's better than I expected.* I'm still not buying it. "You were high up. Why not pull this from the inside?"

She flicks a dust mote from her sleeve. "You're not the only asset who ran out of usefulness. I got pushed to the edge of the org chart. You know what happens to outliers in Moshimoto?"

Dorothy answers, flat. "They get harvested."

Cleopatra snaps her fingers, a neat, rehearsed move. "Exactly. They repurpose the brain and call it a win for diversity."

Ban is done waiting. She stands, steps around to my side, and slams a hand down on my forearm—gentle, but it's the warning version. "We do it, or we sit here and die of boredom." She glares at me. "Pick."

I look at Cleopatra. The overlays run her numbers again: confidence 100%, empathy variable, and loyalty .003% and dropping. She's the kind of monster you want on your team, but only if you keep her on a short leash and three meters away from your back. "We do it. But if you screw us—"

Cleopatra cuts in, fast as ever. "If I wanted you dead, you'd have been flagged in the lobby."

She stands. The overlays slow, just a fraction, as if time gives her a little more room to breathe. "You need to be at 4318 Canal by sixteen hundred. Bring nothing but what you can carry and your best code." She looks at Dorothy, who is now very, very awake. "And her."

Dorothy's knuckles whiten. "I'm not a pet."

Cleopatra winks. "Noted."

She leaves, moving through the air like she owns it, and doesn't look back. When the hatch shuts, Ban is the first to breathe. "She's a virus, but she's our virus."

Dorothy flexes her arm, blood still leaking. "What if she's bait?"

Ban shakes her head. "Then we bite back."

I wipe a hand across my eyes, the overlays crackling in fatigue. "You sure about this?"

Ban grabs a needle and threads it through her sleeve, a gesture I now know means, *we don't have a choice*. She grins, teeth sharp. "If we die, we die interesting."

I believe her. The overlays run the odds. It isn't pretty, but it never is. Tomorrow, we move.

Next morning, the safehouse smells like a crime scene and the world's worst breakfast. The tang of patching foam and cheap instant coffee mixes with the ozone from a half-charged battery rig, turning the air into a biosafety warning. Ban's already cleared the perimeter twice, and Katherine—her hands wrapped in more gauze than skin—is soldering a neural patch on the edge of the kitchen table, bare feet tapping out the stress on broken linoleum. Dorothy, stitched up but operational, looms by the back exit with her arms folded and her combat mods cycling through diagnostics. I sit in my usual spot, waiting for overlays to finish their morning melt and reboot.

Cleopatra arrives five minutes early. Of course. She glides into the space like a surveyor claiming territory, no sign of fatigue, a fresh graphene suit tailored tight to her second and third layers of skin. Her probability eyes click and whirr, adjusting as she scans us, then the perimeter, then back to us. No one moves. Ban waits for her to start, so Cleopatra does.

She gestures with two fingers and overlays inject a 3D schematic into the middle of the room. Hacked together from stolen blueprints and crowd-sourced camera feeds, the projection is jittery but complete: the Moshimoto data center, floor by floor, with every entry point marked in red. She talks in units of precision. "Security rotates every twenty-three minutes. This corridor"—she highlights a narrow blue line—"has a blind spot for approximately four seconds at shift change. The elevator to the vault is locked behind a two-key system, but both are physical. One on the security chief, one in a locked drawer." She looks at me when she says drawer, as if my history with locked things precedes me.

Katherine looks up, bloodshot eyes not missing a beat. "And the vault interface?"

Cleopatra's smile is cold and incremental. "You'll have approximately two minutes to breach before the system runs a status audit and locks down. I recommend seventy-five seconds or less."

Ban grins. "She's an optimist."

Dorothy's hands flex, chrome tendons visible under skin. "What about on-site muscle?"

"Two guards minimum per shift, both armed. Drones supplement during low hours, but they're predictable. Watch for one untagged unit: ex-military, not on the payroll but definitely on the premises."

Ban nods, then checks with me, eyes asking: *You seeing the trap?*

I nod once, just enough. Cleopatra swipes her hand, and the map pivots to a sub-level. "There's an off-record maintenance hatch here. Not on any schematic except legacy." She taps the hologram; the line turns gold. "I have pre-seeded the opening code. You'll only have to spoof the maintenance request."

Katherine asks, "And if the hatch is flagged or booby-trapped?"

Cleopatra doesn't blink. "Then it's a new problem. Probability says ninety-three percent you get in clean."

Ban laughs, loading her pistol. "And the other seven?"

Cleopatra lets the silence dangle, then says, "Catastrophic failure. But low odds."

Dorothy shrugs, as if she eats catastrophe for breakfast. "Better than the surface."

I'm still scanning for angles, searching overlays for anything she's left out. The only uncertainty is the certainty itself. "Why are you so sure we'll make it?"

She gives me a look that's almost pity. "Because I built the system. And because you're all outliers." The numbers in her eyes spin up, then resolve. "The Corp won't expect a move this aggressive from people with nothing left to lose."

Katherine, sarcasm dialed to eleven, says, "That's some motivational shit right there."

Ban flips the safety on her sidearm, then looks at me. "You ready, analyst?" I don't answer, but I reach for the pistol she slides across the table. The metal's cold, the grip worn in places that say Ban's used it more times than I care to count. I check the chamber, load the mag, and holster it in one smooth move. Muscle memory, not my own. She sees, smiles. "Night-self never left, huh?"

Cleopatra tracks the whole sequence, eyes narrowing in a micro-expression of interest. "You didn't flinch. That's good."

Dorothy cracks her knuckles. "I don't care who's planning to double-cross. I just want the work."

Cleopatra stands, straightens her suit, and gestures at the map. "We move at sixteen hundred. The maintenance hatch is the play. If you improvise, do it fast and with conviction."

Ban snorts, then looks at me. "Anything to add, Skelm?"

I look at Cleopatra, at the numbers flickering through her, then at the rest of the crew. "Just that if this goes bad, we take as many of them down with us as we can."

Dorothy grins for the first time since the massacre. "Deal."

Katherine flicks the tip of her soldering iron, then points at Cleopatra. "If this is a setup, you get to die first."

Cleopatra's smile is a secret only she gets. "I prefer to bet on survival, but noted."

The meeting breaks, and for a moment, the only sound is the hiss of Katherine's solder and the hum of Dorothy's cooling fans. Ban catches my eye, shrugs, and heads for the weapons locker. I sit, rolling the pistol in my hand, and watch Cleopatra walk out. The overlays ping: NEXT MOVE: YOURS.

I smile, despite it all. Damn right it is.

We hit Canal at 15:57, three minutes ahead of probability. Ban leads, her jacket zipped so tight it looks painted on, with Dorothy shadowing in a black hoodie three sizes too small. Katherine stalks the edges, hunched and red-eyed, hacking a borrowed tablet with her thumb while she chain-smokes SentiSnacks™ that leave a dust of neon sadness on her lips. Cleopatra is already there, waiting with her back to the security fence and eyes tuned to some frequency just past visible. The overlays say her pulse is low, but the math flicker in her irises is a seizure in microcosm. She looks us over, then opens the hatch, a silent slice in the fence, and leads us down the tunnel.

It's all gravity and wet rust until the utility corridor kinks left, then up a stairwell into the heart of the Moshimoto vault. The air smells like recycled ambition and ozone. Cleopatra slows, presses a finger to the wall, and a panel blooms open, revealing a vent shaft just wide enough for three ex-military assets and a desperate analyst.

Ban is first in, feet-first, no hesitation. I follow, then Dorothy—who has to hunch her spine to fit. Cleopatra lingers at the entrance, whispering codes to invisible listeners, then slips in behind me. Her proximity is a static charge in the vent. I feel every shift of her suit as it rubs up against the insulation, her hand at my calf, not quite touching but near enough to make my skin crawl.

Katherine bails out at the first junction, disappearing into a server access closet to run interference. She mutters to herself as she unspools a tangle of cracked fiber, jacking into a maintenance node while Ban, Dorothy, and I crawl through the ductwork, echoing the world's least dignified parade.

The vault is a cathedral for data, floor to ceiling racks dripping with green and blue status lights. Hard-light Moshimoto logos rotate over every aisle, reflecting "INTEGRITY ASSURANCE" in a million refracted lines. The overlays are drunk with input, painting every surface with tags: SURVEILLANCE: ACTIVE, HEAT SIGNATURE: MULTIPLE, ESCAPE VECTOR: LOW.

Cleopatra leads us to the lower mezzanine, then gestures to a fire door wedged open with a wad of shredded plastic. She checks the hall, then ushers us inside. "Ninety-three percent," she whispers. We cross the floor in single file, hugging the shadows. Ban moves as if the space is already hers, reading camera angles and body language from forty meters out. Dorothy lopes, half animal, half human, eyes on the ceiling. I walk like a dead man, overlays spinning up so fast the colors blur.

The archive node sits behind a desk with one sad, bored tech running inventory. Cleopatra gives me a nod, then heads for the panel, all business. Ban hangs back by the corridor, eyes locked on the hallway entrance. Dorothy paces the perimeter, breathing through her mouth, every inch of her tensed for violence. Cleopatra taps the override into the node. "Nine-two-three-one-zero," she mutters. The lock blinks, then flashes red. She tries again. The same. She stiffens, and for the first time, I see her not as a predator but as prey—her math-aug eyes flicker with panic, then recalibrate. "They changed the code," she whispers. "That's impossible."

Ban glances over, voice low and sharp. "Define impossible."

"They haven't updated this protocol in six years," says Cleopatra, fingers already dancing over the keypad, splicing in new numbers. "There's no way—" She stops mid-sentence, eyes locked to the monitor. "The access logs are being wiped in real time."

Ban signals Dorothy, who glides over, picks up the tech by the collar, and lifts him from the chair. She holds him a foot off the ground and covers his mouth, eyes daring him to scream. He doesn't. Dorothy has that effect. I slide up to the panel, letting Cleopatra's code run, but it's a dead end. The overlays are screaming: FAILURE: CERTAIN. TIME TO DISCOVERY: 2:13 AND DROPPING.

I reach under the desk, pop a side panel, and jack in manually. There's a hardware bypass—analog; ancient, but never deprecated. My hands move on their own; I watch them as if they belong to someone else, twisting the copper, bridging two pins with a piece of torn badge lanyard. It's the trick I learned in the first blackout facility, the one they trained into me so hard it survived two neural wipes and three overlays. The panel goes green. The lock pops.

Ban grins, teeth like chipped glass. "Told you, Cleo."

Cleopatra gives me a sidelong look, then slips past, the panic erased but not forgotten. She pulls up the archive core and sets her drive to mirror. "Sixty seconds."

Dorothy drops the tech, who slides to the floor and just sobs, no longer a factor. Ban watches the corridor, her gun out and held low. I patch into the archive, pull our data, and run a local wipe as cover. Katherine pings from the back office: "Cameras are dead for the next three, maybe four minutes."

Cleopatra's hands tremble as she pulls the last packet. "Done," she says, voice so quiet it almost doesn't exist.

The overlays flash: ALARM: TRIGGERED. DRONE RESPONSE: ACTIVE. We run. Out the fire door, down a utility ladder, then back into the vent. The first drone comes on silent hover, gold-black shell and a shotgun for a nose. Ban drops it with two shots, then covers the rest of us as we scramble up the shaft. Katherine meets us at the junction, face streaked with blood and dust. "Second wave incoming," she says, and leads us into an access pipe so tight I feel my ribs compress. We crawl for what feels like a year, guided by Ban's grunts and Dorothy's weird half-laughs.

Cleopatra brings up the rear, silent, head down. She's not broken, but she's not leading anymore. We burst into open air, a loading dock on the backside of the block, and melt into the rain. Ban leads us three alleys east, then up a stairwell, into the decoy flat she prepped two days ago "just in case." The whole place smells like burned plastic and old newsprint. We collapse. Dorothy tears off her hoodie, sits on the floor, and hyperventilates until her hands stop shaking. Katherine plugs in, eyes the data we just stole, and wipes sweat from her face. Ban checks the window and the door, then finally breathes.

Cleopatra stands in the kitchen, looking at the drives. "It's better than expected," she says. "They never saw you coming."

Ban smirks. “That’s because we’re nobodies. Outliers.”

Cleopatra looks at me, eyes calculating again, a softer algorithm this time. “Without your analog hack, we would have failed.”

Ban shrugs. “Night-self’s good for something.”

I sit on the floor, hands still buzzing, and try not to think about the way my memories lined up behind my eyelids during the breach. Or the way Cleopatra’s voice softened when she said my name. Katherine lets out a low whistle, scrolling through the data. “This is every black budget for the last three years. Names, faces, even the shadow labs.”

Dorothy leans back, eyes closed, smile thin and dangerous. “Burn it all?”

Katherine nods. “Burn it all.”

Cleopatra paces, then turns. “This changes nothing. They’ll just build another.”

Ban gives her a look that would freeze nitrogen. “Maybe. But not tonight.”

We sit in the silence, each of us calculating the odds of survival. Cleopatra watches me, her eyes two endless decimal places of risk and promise. I think, for a second, that I want to trust her. Then the overlays remind me: PROBABILITY: 2%. I laugh. It’s enough.

For now, it’s enough.

Chapter 9

Ban takes us down three levels of subway history: brickwork so old the city's current name never touched it, fluorescent lamps flickering with a pulse that's more nerve than electricity, concrete pitted by a century of floods and a thousand forgotten evacuations. She picks the stretch between Exchange and Prairie because the corridor is dead in both directions, the only traffic the rats and the drip from the water main above. The air's cold enough to keep the overlays honest.

The team: me, Katherine, Dorothy, Cleopatra. The first day of real drills. Ban says the Corp never expects a stolen asset to run actual combat, so we run it hard and dirty. Ban's voice echoes off the tile. "Line up. Standard triangle, Skelm in the pocket, Dorothy tanking the fore." Her words have a rhythm—pre-digital, all curse and sarcasm, not a syllable wasted. I watch her circle us, eyes sharp and hungry. She's waiting for a mistake.

She brings out the mockup weapons, painted orange but weighted to the gram. “Katherine, left. Cleo, right. D and D, point.” Her hands move faster than her mouth, tossing the pistols with a sniper’s aim. Cleopatra catches hers clean; Dorothy just lets it thud into her palm. Katherine fumbles, nearly drops, and Ban grins like she meant it to happen.

“First drill: reaction and draw,” Ban says. “Nothing fancy, just pure trigger. When you hear my voice, you pop the nearest target. If you hesitate, you get the boot.”

Katherine holds the pistol in both hands, but her fingers can’t stop trembling. She tries to play it cool with a shrug and a muttered, “You should see my handwriting.”

Ban ignores her, eyes locked on the interval between the rest of us. “Ready, steady ...” And then she snaps, “Bang!” so loud even the rats freeze.

Dorothy’s gun is up first. She doesn’t fire, just aims at the center of the nearest mass. Me. Cleopatra’s is right behind, pointed at Dorothy’s head, her chrome eyes tracking the numbers in real time. My own is somewhere in between, pointed not at a person but at the air, halfway between past and future. I’m late. Ban shakes her head and clicks her tongue. “Again.”

This time, Cleopatra anticipates the command. Her gun is leveled before Ban even finishes, and there’s something smug in the angle of her wrist. Dorothy’s slower, not because she’s weak but because she’s thinking through twelve different options and only now picks the best one. Katherine actually fires—a soft, dumb click, aimed straight at the lamp above us. The bulb shatters, glass raining down, and she just grins.

"Jesus," Ban says, not unkind. "Remind me to keep your hands off the heavy artillery." She rounds on me. "Skelm, you know what your problem is?" I do, but I shake my head anyway. The overlays are trying to teach me discipline, but the old ghosts want chaos. "You're a calculator," Ban says. "You think too much, and in the gap, you die." She steps behind me, hands on my shoulders, shoving them down. Her grip is a vise, callused, not gentle but not cruel. "Night-self would have eaten this drill alive," she mutters, almost to herself. "Again."

We run the next hour on a loop. Ban keeps tweaking the simulation: sometimes a warning, sometimes just a slap of noise and a flash of light. Katherine keeps firing wild, but now she's aiming at the right target. Dorothy adjusts, muscle memory learning to snap and hold, never over-committing. Cleopatra goes cold, moving in a sine-wave of precision, her augments visible now in the way her eyes never blink.

My own hands start to catch up. The overlays buzz with approval as the grip tightens, the angle perfect, the reaction time dropping by the microsecond. But it's not the overlays that get me there—it's Ban, always behind me, always watching, pushing just enough to keep the edge sharp.

Halfway through, Ban swaps the mock pistols for knives. Real ones, though blunted, wrapped in friction tape. "Next drill," she says. "Close quarters, circle kill. We run full contact. Last one standing gets breakfast."

Katherine tries for bravado, spinning the knife like she's watched a thousand old movies. "If you want to cut me, Ban, just ask."

Ban's face cracks into a grin. "That's what I like, Johnson. Spirit."

Dorothy goes full professional, checking the balance on the blade and flexing her left arm. She stares at me, then at Ban, and then settles into a crouch so efficient it looks like she's bored. Cleopatra holds the knife between finger and thumb, as if it's not a weapon but a technical problem to solve. Ban paces. "First round, slow. Second, real." She flicks the switch on a headlamp, and the world goes blue-white. "Begin."

It's chaos, but not the kind you see in the Corp sims. Cleopatra is fastest, but she telegraphs every move: knife out, left-right, then a calculated lunge at Dorothy's ribs. Dorothy blocks, not with the knife, but with a palm to Cleo's throat. Cleopatra spins out, recalibrates, but already Dorothy's pivoted, aimed at me. I duck, but not enough; she taps me just above the kidney. Not a real hit, but in a real fight, I'd be bleeding.

Ban is everywhere. She lets us tangle, then intervenes with a shout or a slap to the back of the head. "Too slow, Skelm. Katherine, stop wasting energy. Cleo, you're not a goddamn algorithm. You're human. Even if you pretend not to be."

They go at it again. This time, Katherine is ready—she plays dirty, flicks dust into Cleopatra's eyes, then jabs Dorothy in the shoulder. Dorothy grunts, but turns the pain into velocity, slamming Katherine against the tunnel wall with a force that would break a lesser body. Katherine just laughs, then coughs, and mutters, "You hit like a bored social worker."

Dorothy cracks the tiniest of smiles. Then, she whirls, catches Cleopatra mid-stride, and uses her own knife against her. Cleo drops, rolls, and gets up with a streak of blood—real, a cut on the chin. She licks it, then shrugs, like it's nothing. Ban pulls us apart. "Decent. Not good, but decent." She looks at the cut, eyes flashing. "Blood means learning."

I wipe sweat from my eyes, knuckles bruised, ribs aching. Ban steps in front of me, close enough I can smell her—copper, ozone, sweat, and the baseline musk that never leaves her skin. She grabs my wrist, the one holding the knife. "You're gripping like a child," she says. "Night-self holds it different—tighter, like this." Her hand wraps over mine, the heat sudden, more jolt than comfort.

I feel the shift. It's muscle memory, but not my own—something borrowed from a version of myself I don't remember. My fingers flex, the grip resets, and Ban's thumb presses just hard enough to make the bones real. She doesn't let go. Not right away. For a second, there's no one in the tunnel but us, and the space between our hands is more charge than flesh. Her voice drops low. "You ever feel like you're someone else, Skelm?"

"All the time."

Ban leans in, the gap barely a breath. "Good. Use it." Then she lets go and shoves me back toward the others.

The drills go late, until the water on the rails is ankle-deep and every one of us is bleeding somewhere. Even Cleopatra, who never lets pain show, limps from a gash Dorothy gave her just to prove a point. Ban calls a halt. "You're done," she says. "Go home, patch yourselves up. We run it again tomorrow. Faster, and for keeps."

Dorothy just nods. Katherine curses, then smiles, cigarette already lit before the rest of us finish catching our breath. I linger, not sure if it's inertia or something else. Ban waits, arms folded, watching me. "You want to know why I picked you?" she says.

"No."

She laughs, not loud, but real. "Too bad. It's because you still think you're alive."

She shoulders past me, her hand brushing my arm, and in the wake of her is nothing but the memory of her voice and the promise of tomorrow's pain. The overlays update: PERFORMANCE—MARGINALLY IMPROVED. I ignore them. For the first time in a long time, I don't care about the numbers. I just want Ban's hands on mine again. Maybe next time I won't let go so easy.

The first round the next day starts with Ban's hands on my shoulders, kneading the knot at the base of my neck until something pops, and I'm not in the tunnel anymore.

Flash: I'm following Ban down a maintenance shaft, the world throbbing with distant gunfire, her back lit by the stutter of an old emergency beacon. She's muttering coordinates I shouldn't know, but my lips form the numbers anyway, echoing the rhythm before it happens.

Flash: her hand on my wrist, this time not to correct but to guide. "Left. Now." We duck, the air singing with the passage of a rail dart, and we land in a roll so synchronized even the overlays stutter before catching up.

Flash: a sharp, chemical tang—gunpowder and ozone—then Ban's voice, lower, rougher, calling for a breach. My own voice answers, the words too fast and too familiar. Then the present slams back in, Ban twisting my arm just hard enough to snap the recall. "Better," she says. "But you're still fighting the moves."

I shake out the arm, trying to ignore the vertigo. Katherine's watching from the edge of the track, hand jittering as she lines up a shot on a passing drone. Dorothy kneels by the power box and rips out the old safety relay. She works without looking up, muscle memory turning every motion into math.

Cleopatra hovers, never more than a meter away, logging our every move with her probability eyes. She offers advice like she's reading out of a manual she wrote in another life. "Ban, if you cut the interval by point seven, the group can breach before the defense cycle resets."

Ban nods, but doesn't slow. "You hear that, Skelm? Point seven. Try again."

This time, my body does what the overlays ask for: trigger, pivot, block. The knife grazes Cleopatra's outstretched hand, then arcs perfectly to the pressure point in Dorothy's shoulder. She grunts, but takes the hit and flips me to the ground. Ban laughs, then shouts for a reset.

We run it again. And again. Each time, the team moves tighter, the gaps closing. Katherine times her shots to the cadence of Dorothy's moves. Cleopatra starts to smile, just at the corners, when the team clicks together. Even the water dripping from the ceiling starts to seem deliberate, a part of the count. I lose track of time, or maybe time loses track of us. We're nothing but sweat and reaction, bruises and code.

After the hundredth run, Ban calls a halt. We stand, all four of us breathing hard. Ban looks at me, eyes dark and alive. "See?" she says, not just to me but to everyone. "That's the difference. Night-self moves without thinking. Day-self catches up after."

I nod, dizzy with the overlap. Somewhere in the mess of my brain, something new is growing—call it confidence, call it instinct, but it's fed by Ban's approval, and I want more. Cleopatra is the first to break the silence. "We're ahead of schedule. If this were a real run, we'd be inside the core already."

Katherine wipes sweat from her brow. "Or dead in the street, if Corp is watching."

Dorothy shrugs. "Either way. Not a bad day."

Ban turns to me. "You remember that reload move?" I don't, but my hands do. She tosses me a mag, and I catch it, strip the old, slam the new, all in a single motion. Ban grins. "That's it. That's how he does it." The words echo in my head. *That's how he does it.* I'm not sure who *he* is. Maybe I am. Or maybe it's someone Ban loved enough to teach the moves to me.

The team scatters, prepping for the next round. Ban lingers, eyes locked on mine, like she's watching to see if I disappear. I don't. I'm still here.

Hours grind off the clock in the tunnel. If the overlays are right, we've put in five straight, but my body's too raw to count.

The whole team moves as a unit now, each drill morphing into a dance less about reaction and more about anticipation. Ban's hand signals—two fingers, flick right, chin down—are our only language. The echoes of our steps mesh into a rhythm so tight even the rats run in sync.

Dorothy and Katherine run point, clearing each bend of the old Red Line with military efficiency. Cleopatra holds the back, eyes scanning for overlays and threats, but it's Ban and me who anchor the rhythm. We match each other beat for beat: breath, footfall, the rise and fall of pistols in perfect symmetry.

There's a game to it, a back-and-forth, like tennis but with the stakes amped to lethal. At first, I thought Ban was the sun we orbited. Now it's clear: we move in tandem, twin objects warping the space around us. She'll glance, just once, and I'll know where the breach will happen, what move to make, even before the overlays sketch the vectors.

After the second simulation run—live ammo this time, but the only casualties are a pair of drones and three pounds of steel pipe—we regroup in a service alcove. Ban pushes the crew into the far end, then leans against the wall and signals me over. She's bleeding from a graze on her neck, dark and sticky. I fumble for a wrap, but she waves me off. "Not my first tunnel bleed," she mutters, then wipes it with her sleeve. The blood leaves a line from jaw to collarbone, but she doesn't seem to care.

My own hands are wrecked, knuckles purple and raw. Ban notices and grabs my wrist. "You grip too hard," she says. "Relax. Save the tension for the pull." She unpeels the tape from my palm, then blows on the torn skin. The air stings, but her breath is warm, so I let it happen. She presses her thumb over the wound, then squeezes, hard enough to remind me that the pain means something. Ban holds my hand for longer than necessary. "You ever wonder if you're built for this, Skelm?"

"No," I say, though it's a lie. "I just go where I'm pointed."

She snorts. "Bullshit. You're the only one in the crew who knows what you want." She leans in, voice dropping. "That's why they'll hunt you first."

I watch her face, the muscles shifting from contempt to something that almost looks like concern. In the close space, her hair smells like old circuit boards and new sweat. "You ever take a break, Ban?"

She lets go and steps back. "Breaks are for the dead." But she hesitates before leaving, fingers brushing mine, just for a second.

On the next drill, the team moves without speaking. Ban walks point, me on her left, Dorothy and Katherine flanking right, Cleopatra taking rear with a sleek, custom rig she stole from the last Corp sweep. The formation holds even through the live-fire sim, which is full of pop-up enemies and hard pivots. When Ban ducks, I duck; when she holds, I hold.

The overlays lag behind, always a half-second late. We run it again, and the gap closes. By the fifth time, the overlays aren't even necessary. After, in the dead zone between runs, Ban signals for rest. Katherine collapses on the platform, head back, breathing steam into the air. Dorothy sits cross-legged, sharpening her blade, eyes glazed but alert. Cleopatra stands, hands on hips, watching Ban and me with a mathematician's detachment.

Ban sits next to me, wiping sweat from her eyes. “You get it now?”

“Yeah.”

She cracks her neck. “You move like someone who’s lost everything except speed. That’s good. Means you don’t care about dying.”

“Do you?”

She shrugs. “I used to. Now I care about the seconds in between.” She leans closer, voice a whisper just for me. “You ever want to run, Skelm? Just go and keep going?”

I know what she means. I think about it every time I close my eyes. “Only with you.”

She laughs, low and dangerous. “Never with me. I’d slow you down.”

I look at her hands—strong, scarred, the only steady thing in the world—and wonder if that’s true. She catches my stare, smirks, then looks away. On the last break before night, the team stretches out on the old platform, bodies sprawled wherever they land. Ban and I slip into the service alcove to patch up—her neck, my hand. She rips the tape and re-winds it with military precision, but this time she’s gentle, wrapping each finger slow, almost ceremonial.

Her touch lingers. She doesn’t let go. Her face is inches from mine. In the gloom, her eyes are huge, pupils wide. I see myself in them, fractured but there. Our breath mingles, visible in the cold. She moves first, closing the gap so our foreheads touch. “You trust me?” she asks, not quite a whisper.

“Yeah,” I say. I do. Her lips brush mine, light and shocking. It’s a small thing, over in a second, but the current from it lights up every nerve from toe to scalp. Then, just as her mouth finds mine again, the overlays explode with red. ALERT: CORPORATE KILL TEAM DETECTED. TWO LEVELS UP. VECTOR: MOSHIMOTO, TACTICAL UNIT.

Ban pulls back, eyes already on the threat. “Showtime,” she mutters. She stands, hand on her gun, scanning for signals. “You tell the others. I’ll hold the entry.”

I nod, all the heat now replaced by ice, but I’m ready. We move, quick, through the access corridors, relaying Ban’s signals. Katherine snaps awake, alert and smiling, eyes bright with old adrenaline. Dorothy stands, blade already out, flexing the bloodless hand. Cleopatra checks her weapon, then nods at me, no questions. We line up at the first fork, Ban’s voice low and steady. “They’re fast, but not as fast as us. Stick to the program.” I look at her, trying to hold the memory of her lips in the gap between heartbeats. “Time to see if these drills paid off,” she says, and then she’s gone, a blur down the left tunnel, the rest of us behind.

The overlays scream with threat vectors, but I’m faster. I’m not the only one. We move as one. We are one. And if I’m going to die tonight, I hope it’s with Ban’s hands on my throat, her breath in my mouth, and the sound of her laugh as the last thing I ever hear.

The first kill team rounds the corner. I don’t hesitate. This is what I was built for.

Chapter 10

The new safehouse is five meters below the skin of the city and two above the river's least legal pipeline. Ban picks it for the absence of windows, for the double-reinforced door, and for the air so thick with humidity it puckers the skin. The perimeter is a surgical nightmare—razor wire threaded through old rebar, every breach point laced with trip line, glass, and Ban's own favored spice: impromptu shotgun shells set into the concrete, paint-peeled and primed.

We crowd the main room. Even with all the bodies present, it's just big enough for two folding tables, one brittle couch, and a packing crate that serves as a conference altar. The air tastes of instant coffee, ammonium sweat, and solder. The overlays flicker with the ghost images of last night's run—heatmaps where Ban and I left our mark, a dirty orange trail of violence leading here.

Ban sits at the head, backlit by a static-bright flood lamp. Katherine is hunched over a battered netbook with the self-pity of a hungover bishop. Dorothy paces the long axis, boots trailing rust and oil across the tile, and Cleopatra's overlay is already pulsing in the top right: punctual, omnipresent, half a megaton of post-human certainty. Ban waits for no one. "Showtime," she says, and Cleopatra takes the cue, manifesting as a voice in the room's cheap PA. Her accent is pure glass, her cadence a stiletto through the words.

"Your target is the Moshimoto research wing," says Cleopatra. "Main floor and sub-basement, three security intervals. Two physical, one"—she pauses, just long enough for effect—"cognitive."

Dorothy grunts, never pausing her rounds. "What the fuck is a cognitive security interval?"

Katherine answers, voice slurred but not stupid. "Means they scan your overlays on entry. If you're flagged, you'll trip every protocol from the guard desk to the break room. Not a surprise, if you read your goddamn updates." Dorothy ignores her, swinging a heavy fist against the edge of the couch with a thunk that leaves a smudge on the vinyl. Her cybernetics whine at the torque, a low, liquid hum that would be pornographic in a different context.

Cleopatra keeps going. "Facility blueprint." A 3D holo blooms above the table, lines so sharp they cut the air. The whole space glows blue-white, flickers of patrol patterns and choke points playing over the surface in living light. "Patrols every seven minutes, thermal and lidar at all ingresses. Mainframe on the second sub-level. Neural mapping gear is on the top floor, east corner. It's isolated—no direct line to the rest of the lab."

Katherine rolls her eyes, never looking up from the netbook. “This blueprint is at least a week out of date. Moshimoto updates infrastructure every seventy-two hours, minimum. See here—” She points, but not at the projection. Instead, she taps a line of code on her screen, then hacks up a bitter laugh. “You missed the mirrored firewall. If we come in through this corridor”—she gestures, a lazy, drunken arc—“it’s an instant kill box.”

Cleopatra’s voice doesn’t waver, but I can almost feel the scorn rise in the background process. “They installed it yesterday. They do not expect you to use the utility access from the river. That’s your window.”

Dorothy plants her feet and folds arms across her chest. “You trust her?” she asks Ban, not even pretending to address me.

Ban shrugs, the motion minimal but clear. “We trust the data. If she’s wrong, we improvise.”

Katherine snorts, then grimaces at the movement. “Improvise is how you get a face full of DebtHound, boss.”

Dorothy squares up to Ban. “Why not just storm it? We have the muscle. They can’t stop us.”

Katherine looks up now, hair pasted to her forehead, eyes hard with bloodshot. “Because Moshimoto doesn’t give a shit about casualties, but they will hunt us to extinction if we torch a flagship. Use your brain for once.”

Ban lets the bickering hang for a beat. Then she claps once, loud enough to make my overlays strobe. “We’re not here to rack up a body count. Objective is the neural mapper, clean extract, zero alarms. Any deviation, we abort." Dorothy mutters something under her breath about how abort is what the Corp should have done to the lot of us. Ban's mouth twitches, but she ignores it. "Skelm. Thoughts?"

I review the blueprint, but my brain already knows where to look. There are three vulnerabilities Cleopatra didn't mention: the unsealed fire suppression conduit on the loading dock; the dead zone in camera coverage, half-hidden by a vending machine; the ancient service elevator shaft that overlays have flagged as condemned, but is actually wired as a covert access for security response teams. I point them out, one at a time, drawing the path in midair with a fingertip. The holo tracks my motion, painting each weak spot in yellow. "Conduit here. Camera dead zone here. Old service shaft—they call it sealed, but it's rigged as a rapid response ladder. Nobody's going in through the main corridor and living."

Ban nods, then turns to Katherine. "Can you rig the fire suppression to pop without alerting the grid?"

Katherine grins, the kind that exposes three missing teeth and a piece of last night's snack. "Easy. But you'll need a vector to the access panel. It's locked behind biometrics."

Dorothy's eyes go bright. "Give me the lock," she says, flexing her left hand until the servo motors hum. "I can make it forget who it is."

Katherine snickers. "Fine, muscle. But keep your ego out of the equipment or you'll set off the seismic alarms."

Dorothy cocks her head, the gesture canine. "Want to arm-wrestle for it?"

"I'd rather see you try to code a coherent sentence," says Katherine.

"Enough," says Ban, but there's a ghost of a smile.

Cleopatra overlays the plan in real time, three parallel attack vectors, each with a .002 variance in predicted outcome. "With this configuration, the probability of extract increases by twelve percent. If security escalates, fall back to the loading dock and initiate fire protocol. The building is only rated for half its posted capacity. If you trigger a full evac, it will empty in under a minute. That's your exfil."

Dorothy nods, jaw set. I lean over the table and scan the blueprint for any last-minute tells. My overlays pulse a warning at the sixth subroutine: SECURITY OVERRIDE: MANUAL. I blink it away, knowing it'll come up again the moment we move. Ban stands, adjusts the straps on her jacket, then turns to face us. "Last check before load-out. Katherine, what do you need?"

She glances at her hands, both trembling, then at the half-empty coffee mug. "Five minutes with the panel and a battery backup. I can code a delayed trigger so nobody suspects a thing until we're gone."

Ban nods. "Dorothy, you'll get her in. After that, you're a ghost until we call go."

Dorothy grins, all teeth and no humor. "I was born to be a ghost."

I look to Ban and await my orders. "You're on point, Skelm. Shadow me, run the overlay, and if anything goes to hell, you call the abort. I mean it," she says. I nod, and for once, there's no lag in my response.

"Cleopatra, you handle remote access and monitor the Corp channels. We don't need a surprise birthday party."

Cleopatra's reply is a digital whisper, already fading. "Confirmed."

We gear up. Dorothy opens a battered case and pulls out a compact SMG, blue tape around the grip, initials burned into the stock. She checks the load, then slings it across her back. Her hands flex, and the synth-skin at her elbows ripples with the stress. Katherine pulls out a tangle of cable, two ancient modems, and a set of dermal patches. She tests the charge on each, frowns, then slaps a patch to her own neck and shivers through the side effects.

Ban goes for the sidearm, a matte-black stubby with the safety drilled out and the grip rough as coral. I reach for the same drawer at the same time, and our hands collide, both aiming for the same piece. There's a spark, an audible pop of static, and Ban's palm lands over the back of my wrist. I freeze, overlays momentarily shorting. She doesn't move, not at first, and there's a flicker of something in her eyes—not laughter, not threat, but pure voltage.

She squeezes my wrist, just hard enough to remind me she's stronger. Then, slowly, she slides her hand down the back of mine, grip shifting until she's holding the gun and I'm holding the space where her heat lingers. She leans in, close enough that her breath turns the air electric. "You always want what I want, Skelm?"

I swallow, then try for casual. “Only if you want it first.”

She lets go, grinning, and I find I’m still hungry for the shape of her touch. The others are watching, but not watching; in this room, even intimacy is just another form of violence. Ban loads the pistol, then shoves it into her belt and gestures for me to follow. “Let’s get it done.”

Dorothy and Katherine are already at the hatch, Dorothy rolling her shoulders and grinning at the prospect of breaking things, and Katherine half-wired, overlays crackling along her arms. Ban waits for me at the door. She’s already in mission mode, eyes locked forward, but her hand brushes mine as I step through, the contact quick but deliberate. Like a secret. The overlays flare, then settle, and for the first time since I woke up in this life, I know exactly where I’m meant to be.

We move, a procession of misfits and monsters, out into the wet electric dark. The job is on, and there’s no way back.

The tunnels are alive. Not with rats or bugs but with the low, ceaseless pulse of city runoff and the hum of buried current. Every surface sweats, and every shadow is thick enough to drown in. Ban leads the way, ducking under pipework that gleams in the cold light of Katherine’s hacked headlamp. The rest of us bunch up in single file, with Dorothy behind Ban, Katherine glued to my ass, and me carrying the rear so tight that when Ban stops, the whole line nearly cracks her vertebrae.

“Checkpoint’s thirty meters ahead,” says Ban, voice flat but urgent. The overlays confirm: a soft-red rectangle pulses on the map, and below it, in smaller font, "ADDITIONAL SECURITY: UNKNOWN."

Katherine flicks the lamp to infrared. "Watch it. There are heat signatures." She points, and we all freeze. Just ahead, past a drip line of ancient condensation, two blobs huddle by the base of an access ladder—one upright, one slumped and shivering. I see them as colorless heat, but Dorothy just sees them. She tilts her head, calculates, then eases a hand to her left wrist where the blade socket waits.

"Not necessary," says Ban, reading Dorothy's body language the way other people read watches. She motions for me and Katherine to hold, then steps up and whispers loud enough to travel the last ten meters: "Status?"

The upright guard turns. His gear is standard Moshimoto: blue and silver armor, no faceplate, just a patchwork of old scars and a fresh addiction to something in the amphetamine family. "All clear," he says with a wink. Ban gives him the up-down, then, when he turns, slides a slim black chit under his collar. The guard shivers, twitches, then goes still, eyes rolling white for a half second before his system reboots.

Katherine sidles up and checks his neck for the patch. "Classic," she mutters, shaking her head. "Why do they always pick the lowest bidder for tunnel duty?"

"Because," says Ban, "nobody expects a mainline heist through the toilet."

Dorothy's disappointment is real, but she lets it go. She steps over the shivering guard with a kick to the ankle that leaves him pissing himself, then beckons for the rest of us to follow. The next stretch is pure corpse-paint: white tile, bleach stains, and long streaks where runoff has eroded even the memory of color. We move fast. Katherine finds the first security panel, pulls a tool from her sleeve, and jams it into the interface. It's almost sexual, the way she shudders as the overlays start to flood with admin access.

"Four minutes," she says, tapping at the keys. "Cleopatra was right about the legacy firmware, but she missed the new second factor. Biometric. They're using fucking tongue prints now."

Ban's face goes blank. "You have a workaround?"

"Sure," says Katherine, and with her other hand she pulls a red vial from her pocket, uncaps it with her teeth, and swabs her own tongue. "Give me sixty seconds and a clean surface." She kneels, hacks a glob of spit onto a microfiber cloth, then presses it to the scanner. The device cycles, stutters, then clicks to green. "Gross," she says. "But effective."

"Always is," says Ban, and gestures us forward.

We reach the elevator shaft, and Dorothy volunteers to go first. The overlays strobe a warning, but she ignores it. She pulls the doors open with both hands—no sound at all, just a smooth, hydraulic sigh. The ladder inside is slick with oil. Dorothy clamps on and slides down, arms locked so tight the metal warps under her weight. She hits the bottom, soft as a landing cat, and signals up. Ban goes next, then Katherine, who slips and nearly drops, but I catch her with one hand. She looks up, grateful and annoyed all at once. "Try not to die on the way in," I say.

"I'll die when the job is done," she says, kicking off. I follow. At the base, the world is suddenly cold, and the air is so filtered it hurts. We're under the main facility now. The corridor ahead is glass-bright, lined with white panels that show no joins. A strip of LEDs runs the length, cycling slowly from blue to white and back. The overlays say: STERILE ENVIRONMENT. TRACE PARTICULATE: NONE. I pull my sleeve down, suddenly aware of how much we stink.

Katherine is already at the next door, hands shaking a little as she slides her toolkit open. This lock is a biometric, but not tongue—retina. She doesn't even blink, just presses her left eyeball to the lens, and then, as it scans, stabs the lock's power circuit with a hot needle. The mechanism resets, thinks for a microsecond, then pops the catch. Door opens.

We step into the first interior room: the "airlock." Ban calls halt, then checks the ceiling for cameras and the corners for sensors. She nods. "Go." The floor here is soft, like foam, and every step makes a faint squeak. The walls are lined with what looks like vertical tanks, filled with blue fluid and something that moves in the depths. I don't look close. The overlays say: CONTAINMENT. NON-VIABLE. At the far end, we see our first security team: two guards, female, small and sharp, both armed with the black-stubbed SMGs favored by Moshimoto for close-in work. They don't see us at first.

Ban gestures, and Dorothy moves—her gait is so quiet that for a moment, it's like she's not there at all. Then one of the guards turns, and Dorothy is suddenly right in her face, hand on her mouth, blade at her throat. The guard tries to scream, but Dorothy's grip is perfect. The other guard blinks, shocked, and in the split second before she can react, Ban steps out and shows her both hands: empty, palms up. "We don't want to kill you," Ban says, and it's so calm that even I believe it.

The guard hesitates, then drops the gun and raises her own hands. Dorothy lets the first guard go, and she stumbles back, both hands at her throat, shocked to find it uncut. "Take five," says Ban, and the guards don't need telling twice. They edge down the corridor and vanish through a side door. Dorothy licks her lips, as if disappointed at the taste of not-violence.

Katherine makes a face. "Too easy."

Ban grins. "Next time, you get to play muscle."

The next hallway is the worst yet: a "clean corridor" so polished it feels like walking inside an LED. The overlays go wild with cross-linked security—every two meters there's a micro-camera, and the ceiling is littered with black glass pips that watch heat, sound, even air composition. Katherine slows, scanning for a hack. "Give me the panel."

Ban points; just past the first curve, there's a small, unmarked door. Dorothy takes the lead, this time going loud. She charges the door and wrenches it open with a sound like the universe cracking. Inside, a single white-clad tech is hunched over a comms terminal, oblivious. Dorothy grabs him by the collar and yanks him out, slamming him to the floor. "Shh," she says, then glances at Ban.

Ban nods. "Just hold him."

Katherine goes in and starts poking at the terminal. "Cleopatra's an asshole," she says, "but her seed code still works." She plugs in her own hardware, then starts typing, fast and reckless. "Three minutes until the next security sweep. I can kill the cameras for about sixty seconds, but after that, we're flying blind."

Ban looks to me. "You ready?"

"Always," I say, and for a second, our eyes meet. It's not fear I see in her—it's the thrill of the chase, the hunger for a crisis you can only solve by surviving it.

Dorothy locks the tech in a sleeper hold and waits, patient as death. Katherine counts down: "Ready, three, two, one—*now*."

The lights flicker, every camera in the hall winking out in perfect sync. We move, Ban and I at the front, Katherine right behind, and Dorothy dragging the unconscious tech. We run, silent, footfalls lost in the white noise of the ventilation system. It's only twenty meters, but it feels longer. At the far end is another door, this one labeled "BIO-SECURITY." We pile up, and Ban gestures for the portable scanner. I hand it over.

Katherine slaps a patch on the sensor, waits for the green, then shoves the door open. On the other side, we hit the jackpot: the neural mapping suite, a room full of glass tanks, holo monitors, and the gentle click of processors crunching endless data. At the center is a cluster of researchers—three of them, all mid-20s, all wearing the same Moshimoto-blue lab coat. They turn as one, eyes wide. Ban raises a hand. "You don't need to move," she says. "We're just here for the hardware."

The first researcher steps back, hands raised. The second just stares, mouth open. The third, a woman, is braver than the rest. She reaches for a red button on the console. Dorothy moves so fast it's a blur. She grabs the woman's wrist and twists it, hard enough that I hear something snap. But it's too late; the alarm screams, high and insistent, every light in the room strobing red. Ban curses, loud and English. “Katherine, get the drive. Skelm, help Dorothy.”

Katherine vaults the desk, grabs the portable neural mapper from its cradle, and starts ripping out the interface leads. I rush to Dorothy’s side, where she has the woman in a headlock, both of them struggling near the alarm panel. “Easy,” I say. “Let her go.” Dorothy does, but only after a last crushing squeeze. The woman collapses, holding her arm, but she’s still breathing.

“Security in ninety seconds!” shouts Katherine. “We need a way out.”

Ban’s already on it. “Service shaft,” she says, gesturing to a panel in the far corner. I run over, rip it open, and stare down a black hole to the sub-basement below. “Dorothy, you first.” Dorothy grabs the rim and swings down, boots finding the rungs before she’s even fully inside. She’s followed by Katherine, who clutches the neural mapper to her chest like a child. I go next, barely missing the opening volley from an SMG as the security team crashes through the main door. Ban covers us, firing twice and sending two of the guards sprawling, then follows down the shaft, slamming the hatch behind her.

We tumble into a cramped crawlspace, air thick with dust and panic. Dorothy is already crawling ahead, knees and elbows churning. Ban lands beside me, then jerks her head forward. “Move, Skelm.” I do. The shaft is a straight shot to the maintenance corridor, and we spill out into a forgotten janitor’s closet full of mops and obsolete chemical drums. Katherine rips open the exit, and we’re back in the first white-tile hall, but now it’s crawling with siren sound.

“Loading dock is two lefts and a right,” says Katherine, gasping.

Ban grabs my wrist and pulls me close. “You lead. Dorothy, keep the rear.”

We run. It’s chaos in the hallways—white-suited staff panicking, alarms blaring, gunmen in full body armor charging every which way. We sprint through them, ducking and weaving, our own overlays painting threat vectors a meter ahead of each shot. Ban is at my side the whole way. When I slip, she hauls me up; when she misses a turn, I correct for her. We’re not two people. We’re a vector.

Katherine yanks us through the last door, and we land on the concrete apron of the loading dock. A delivery truck sits idling, the driver inside lost in a dream of better wages and early retirement. Ban vaults the tailgate, yanks the driver out, and motions us in. Dorothy and I pile in the back, followed by Katherine and the hardware. Ban slams the gate, then dives into the cab and floors it. The truck peels out, tires screeching. Behind us, the Moshimoto security drones burst through the loading dock doors and open fire, but Ban zig-zags the truck so hard nothing but air gets hit.

We drive, fast and ugly, through the network of old service roads until the world goes dark behind us and the only sound is our own breathing. The neural mapper sits in the middle of the truck bed, humming and alive. Katherine leans back, trembling but grinning. “We did it.”

Dorothy wipes a streak of blood from her chin, shrugs. “Easy.”

Ban glances back at me through the sliding window, eyes shining in the darkness. “You good?”

“Always,” I say. But I can still feel her hand on mine, like an afterimage of the job.

The city is silent. For now, we’re alive.

The peace never lasts. Within twenty seconds, Cleopatra’s overlay is back on the comm, voice a crackle in the truck’s jacked-in speakers. “Security on your tail. Drones, at least four—thermal, armed. Air and ground both.”

Ban curses and checks the side mirror. In the blue-white strobe of city light, I catch the pinpoint flare of the lead drone, a wasp-bodied thing built for pursuit and pain. “We’ve got three minutes, tops, before we’re boxed,” says Cleopatra. “Route one is blocked; fall back to River Line and prep for breach.”

Dorothy grins, flexing the black and silver mesh of her arm. “Time for real work,” she says, and leaps from the back of the truck before it’s even stopped.

I scramble after, dragging Katherine, who is now holding the neural mapper like a sacred relic. The hardware is alive, emitting a low hum that sets every tooth on edge. Ban slides the truck to a halt against a dead alley wall, then yanks the ignition and tosses the keys into the drainage. “Leave them nothing,” she says.

The drone drops, close enough I can see the black glass camera bulging from its face. Dorothy is ready; she leaps, catches it by the armature, and rips it sideways, the torque enough to wrench the mounting from its own housing. The drone pivots and claws out, but Dorothy simply braces both feet and tears the arm off at the joint. There's a spray of black oil, a crunch of glass, and then she stabs the limb through the drone's own processor. It dies with a hiss.

But the next three are seconds away. Ban signals, hand chopping down: *move*. We run, Ban and Dorothy in the lead, me and Katherine behind, the neural mapping gear bouncing between us like a bomb. The fallback is the old River Line, a stretch of maintenance tunnel so old even the overlays have to guess at its layout. Cleopatra feeds us updates as we go: "Left at the blue door, then down the spiral. Hatch at the end is pressure-locked, but it'll give."

The air grows thin and chemical. The corridor is black and slick, the floor puddled with old runoff. At the blue door, Dorothy slows, checks the corners, then muscles it open—no sound, no drama, just a flex of inhuman arm. But the drones are smarter this time. The moment we enter, a volley of darts smacks the walls just above our heads. One hits Dorothy square in the back, but her skin barely registers the impact. She grabs the dart, snaps it, and yells, "You want to fight? Fight!" before sprinting into the darkness.

Ban follows, but slows just enough to check on Katherine and me. I'm starting to see double from the exertion, the overlays straining to keep my pulse level. Katherine stumbles and almost drops the hardware. I grab her, steady, then look into her eyes: bright red, wide with something close to terror. "We're almost there," I say.

She laughs, wild. "That's what you always say."

We move down the spiral, a concrete coil, so tight that Dorothy has to hunch her shoulders to fit. The walls tremble with the drone approach; you can feel them before you hear them. Every step, the hum gets louder, a full-body vibration like standing too close to a blown subwoofer. Halfway down, we hit a security door—metal, two feet thick, with a biometric plate at the center. Katherine lunges for the panel, rips the cover off with shaking hands, and jams two leads from her toolkit into the guts of the system.

Dorothy, in the meantime, stands in front of us, blocking the corridor with her body. She's vibrating, head lowered, arms flexed and ready. The drones appear, crawling the wall like silver bugs. The first one opens fire—a spread of electrified darts meant to stun, then kill. Dorothy shrugs off the volley, then surges forward. She catches the nearest drone by its front limb, pulls it in, then slams it into the wall so hard the concrete cracks. The second drone fires a sticky net; Dorothy dodges, but it catches her left foot. She tears at it, and I see blood—real, dark, her own—before she rips free.

Ban yells, "Hold them, but don't kill!"

Dorothy's answer is a roar. She shreds the net, then grabs both drones by their antennae and bangs their heads together until the lights inside go dark. At the door, Katherine yells, "Ten seconds!" and types furiously. Sweat pours down her face, her jaw clenched so tight I'm worried she'll bite through her own tongue. The third drone rounds the corner, and Ban steps forward, pistol out. She sights, fires, and the drone's central processor flashes, then dies. The fourth drone, smarter, hangs back, scanning, looking for a weakness.

Katherine finishes the hack with a scream of triumph, and the door slides open just enough for Dorothy to squeeze through. We all pile in, the hardware last. Inside, it's chaos: a mess of pipes, black cables, and old machinery. Cleopatra's voice comes over the comm: "Hard right, then down the ladder. Drainage shaft is your exit. Move fast—security is coming in heavy."

We follow the directions, barely keeping up with Dorothy as she sprints ahead, leaving bloody footprints on the metal. At the ladder, Ban lets me go first, then Katherine, then follows herself, pistol still out. We climb, lungs burning. The shaft is so narrow we have to move one at a time, single file. At the bottom is a maintenance room, old as sin, stinking of rot and chemical waste. Cleopatra comes in again: "Security perimeter is at twenty meters. You've got two minutes, max."

Katherine collapses on the floor, hardware clutched to her chest, sobbing from relief or withdrawal or both. Dorothy stands guard at the door, breathing ragged, hands twitching. Ban kneels next to me. "You good?" I nod, but my heart rate is off the charts. The overlays keep flicking warnings, but I ignore them. "Keep watch," says Ban, and moves to help Katherine, who is still shaking on the ground. She pries the hardware from Katherine's hands and checks the connections.

I walk over to Dorothy, who is pressed flat against the wall, every muscle in her body tense. "You did good," I say quietly.

She glances at me, wild-eyed. "I almost killed that tech. I wanted to."

"But you didn't."

She shudders. "Ban stopped me. I couldn't have stopped myself."

I nod. "Sometimes that's what it means to be on a team."

She laughs, wet and ugly. “Never had one of those.”

The overlays ping: PURSUIT: FIFTEEN METERS. The first security team bursts through the upper hatch, black-clad, in helmets with mirrored visors. They point and open fire—real bullets this time. Dorothy moves to intercept, but Ban pulls her back. “We’re done,” she says. “We go now.”

Katherine has the hardware up and running, a tiny LCD blinking green in the dark. She stands, and together we all crash through the final door—just a rusted panel, no lock at all. Outside is the old river. The water is black, but it moves fast. Ban signals, and we slide down the embankment, Katherine and the mapper first, then Dorothy, then me. Ban brings up the rear, never looking back. The river is freezing, the shock enough to punch the air from my lungs. We swim, Dorothy hauling Katherine and the gear, Ban and I side by side, just like in the drill.

On the far bank, there’s a dead zone—a strip of no-man’s-land under a collapsed section of city. Cleopatra is waiting, or rather, a proxy: a black car, engine running, with the back doors open. We pile in, soaking and bruised, neural mapper humming like a live animal in Katherine’s lap. Ban looks at me, eyes clear, hair plastered to her forehead. “Not bad,” she says. “Almost like we planned it.”

I grin, teeth chattering. “If we planned it, nobody would have survived.”

Dorothy laughs from the front seat, raw and pure. Katherine cradles the hardware like it’s a newborn. For a second, just a second, there’s no fear at all. We drive into the city, the drones still searching the far bank, and fade into the darkness. Only later do I realize that Ban never let go of my hand, not once, during the entire escape. The overlays never noticed. But I did.

Back in the safehouse, time goes viscous. The city's alarms fade to background noise; adrenaline crashes out, leaving just the muscle-tremor and the stinging aftertaste of survival. Ban posts Dorothy at the door, sets Katherine up with the neural mapping device on the main table, then sits herself down on a crate to go through the physicals—wounds, weapons, counts, comms.

The air smells of wet asphalt, bleach, and the faint ozone of burned-out nerves. My overlays keep misfiring, flickering red and blue warnings even though we're safe, at least for the moment. Dorothy stands statue at her station, back against the vault wall. Her arms are locked in what the overlays call "safety mode"—wrists limp, fingers curled, every actuator dead until Ban tells her otherwise. Her eyes scan the corners, but she never meets mine, not even when I walk a meter from her face.

Katherine is a different kind of wreck. She pops the mapper open with the delicacy of a bomb tech and lines up the componentry on the table in order of threat. The drive is less than a kilo, but every gig of it feels like a living thing—quartz and copper, but breathing. Ban drags a rag down her face, wiping off the blood and whatever passes for emotion in her today. "Status," she says.

Dorothy doesn't answer. Katherine doesn't look up. I lean over the mapper, trying to make sense of the shapes. “You okay?” I ask, soft.

Katherine barks a laugh. “Define okay.” Her hands are steady, but her jaw never unclenches. “It’s the right unit. The processor is a month ahead of market—there’s a blood registry patch, probably to boost efficiency.” I pretend to know what that means. Katherine runs a thumb across the drive’s etched label, then sits back. “They’re using these for full-stack consciousness extractions, not just endpoint harvesting. You could suck a whole city’s worth of memories if you stacked enough bandwidth behind it.”

Dorothy finally speaks, voice raw. “How many have they done?”

Katherine shrugs. “Doesn’t log local. Probably piped upstream. But if this is just a lab model, the real thing’s ten times worse.” She glances at me, then Ban. “Congrats. We stole the world’s best torture device.”

Ban stands, stretches, and in the same motion, snaps Dorothy’s arms back to ready. The motors whine, then click as they re-engage. Dorothy flexes her fingers once, then sits on the floor, back to the wall, eyes closed. “You want to talk about it?” Ban asks her, voice stripped of sarcasm.

Dorothy shakes her head. “Not now. Maybe not ever.”

Ban leaves her be, and instead patches up a graze on her own shoulder, eyes flicking to me every other minute. I know the look: she’s checking for fracture, waiting to see if I break. Cleopatra dials in, voice cold, no preamble. “You made a mess. But it worked.”

Ban stares at the comm speaker. “Your data was wrong. Almost got us iced.”

Cleopatra’s laugh is all static. “Welcome to live ops, Ban. Probabilities don’t guarantee anything.” She pauses before speaking again. “What about casualties?”

“Minimal,” says Ban, flat. “Dorothy could’ve painted the tunnels, but she held.”

Cleopatra’s voice loses a half-degree of chill. “Impressive.”

Katherine rolls her eyes. “You gonna congratulate us or tell us the next suicide run?”

Cleopatra lets the silence stretch, then says, “I’ll be in touch. Don’t go anywhere.”

Ban picks up a coffee mug and throws it at the speaker. The mug shatters, spraying ceramic across the floor. “Fuck her.”

For the next hour, the team decompresses in their own way. Dorothy stares at the ceiling, not moving. Katherine chain-smokes her SentiSnacks™, hunched over a tablet, running diagnostics on the mapper and occasionally cursing at the screen. Ban checks and double-checks the safehouse perimeter, every time returning with more tension, never less.

I spend the time in the back, reviewing the overlay footage from the op. Every second is burned in at full resolution: Dorothy’s violence, Ban’s commands, Katherine’s hacking ballet. My own movements are jerky, uncertain. Only when I sync the footage to Ban’s does the pattern emerge: the two of us moving in parallel, predicting each other, closing gaps with near-perfect efficiency. I lose thirty minutes replaying the moment in the lab when Ban touched my hand on the weapon. It's nothing, less than a second, but my body remembers the pressure, the spark. I try to focus on the data, but the memory keeps glitching in.

Later, Ban calls me over. She's on the crate, hunched, a fresh bandage on her neck. She gestures to the other crate beside her. "Sit." I do, and for a minute, we say nothing. Then she turns the tablet so I can see the footage. "We moved well together." I nod. She leans in, our shoulders just brushing. "You ever run with a partner before?" The question is academic, but the overlay flags an uptick in her pulse, barely perceptible.

"Not like this," I say, and the overlays skip, throwing up "INTIMACY WARNING" like a joke.

Ban laughs low, then nudges her shoulder into mine. "Guess we're stuck with each other now." We watch the footage. She rewinds the moment when I cover her at the first drone breach; then the hallway charge, where she ducks and I follow; then the vault, where our hands move in mirror. "This is what they want to erase, you know."

"What?"

"The feeling. The human part. The part you can't plan or overlay. It's always a liability for them. But for us—" She trails off, as if the thought itself is too big to finish.

I lean in, close enough to feel the heat from her skin, and say, "For us, it's everything."

She doesn't flinch. Instead, she lets her head rest on my shoulder for half a heartbeat. Then, just as quick, she's up and gone, standing at the table with Dorothy and Katherine, debating the next move. I sit there a minute longer, heart banging, overlays spinning.

By midnight, the safehouse is quieter, but no one sleeps. Katherine finally speaks: "You want to know what this really is?" She holds up the drive. "It's a zero-day for human consciousness. You run this at full power, you can copy a whole population. Or erase it."

Dorothy looks up. "Why would they need that?"

Katherine smiles, teeth showing. "You ever heard of a backup?"

I feel the chill. "They're making a template. A seed copy for when they want to reboot everything."

Ban nods. "Exactly." There's a long silence, then Ban says, "So we burn it or we run it ourselves?"

Katherine laughs, but the sound is nervous. "Doesn't matter. They already made a backup."

The thought sits there, ugly and real. Dorothy cracks her knuckles, then glances at me. "What do you think, Skelm?"

I stare at the drive, then at Ban. "I think," I say, "we need to get ahead of their next move. Or we're not just dead—we're forgotten."

Ban grins, wolfish. "That's more like it."

The overlays ping: "NEXT MISSION: LOADING."

This time, I don't ignore it. This time, I want it.

The night is cold, and the city's quiet, but I feel something like hope. It's almost enough to make me forget how close I came to losing everything. Almost. Ban catches my eye. “Tomorrow, then.”

“Tomorrow,” I say, and mean it. The overlays blink out, and for a second, there’s only the thump of my own heart. I go to sleep with the memory of her hand on mine. And when I wake, it’s still there.

Chapter 11

We move before dawn, because the city is more honest when it's wet and nothing's awake but the cameras. Cleopatra had the stats on this: 84% lower human threat in the hour before shift change, 23% more likely to blend in if you smell like ozone and wet cement. The trick is, the machines never sleep. They just idle.

Ban leads the crew up a service trench so old the concrete weeps rust, with Dorothy out front, palms dragging across the metal like she's tracing the memory of every security patch ever welded shut. Above us, the sky glows blue through the rain, sodium haze punctured by the vertical sweep of anti-drone lasers. The overlays light the perimeter in fluorescent red: every tripwire, every micro-hearing sensor, every insurance clause that means if you die here, your next of kin gets billed double.

Katherine and I are the sandwich filling, with her still sweating off last night's shakes, and me running overlays in ghost mode because the last thing I want is for my internal narrator to rat me out to the world's most hostile audience. Cleopatra walks at the rear, silent, all eyes and edge. I can tell she's running every probability on failure, but she only speaks when it matters.

We reach the perimeter: a diamond-mesh fence layered in so many legal liabilities it's more a suggestion than a defense. The city wants this to happen, so long as it can charge Moshimoto a retainer for the cleanup. Ban signals: *freeze*. The tip of her finger moves a millimeter to the left. The overlays ping a guard rotation—two drones and one human, all cross-covering the same thirty square meters. Cleopatra's voice is so low it's almost a thought. "Window in six-point-three."

Katherine's hands go for her bag—shaking, but deliberate—and she pulls out a cylinder of what looks like plumber's putty. She slices a thin disc and affixes it to the fence. It extrudes micro-hooks and starts eating metal in neat, silent bites. The overlays blink yellow: "STRUCTURAL INTEGRITY: 97%— 96% —" and so on.

Dorothy cracks her knuckles and makes a face at the acid burn. "You need a bottle, K?"

"Not unless you want to watch me puke for the next hour," she mutters, but her hands steady as she finishes the breach. The drone sweeps right overhead. Ban doesn't move, doesn't breathe, just watches its optics until they pass. On the far side, the building is a flat slab of hate, punctured by windows that look like eyes not made for seeing.

Cleopatra whispers, "Go," and Dorothy slips through first, boots silent on the slime-coated ground. We slither in after her, the cold air tasting like the birth of refrigeration. The overlays ping a grid of heat sensors in the field, and for once, I'm thankful my body runs three degrees below human baseline. Ban points to the access door—a smooth, eyeless rectangle in a world built on surveillance. Katherine is at the panel before I even register the move, and her hands shake so hard the overlays want to flag it as a medical event.

She mutters to herself, fast and technical, "Optical pattern match, sixty-four grid, linear bias ... God, these fuckers never update." Then to us: "Gimme fifteen."

Dorothy leans against the wall and I see her arms flex, the skin at her wrists receding as the subdermal chrome readies itself for work. I whisper, "Keep it subtle, D," and she gives me a look like I just told her to breathe water.

"I like the hands," she says, not even bothering to keep her voice down. "They make a point."

Ban watches the corridor, jaw clenched, not talking. She's already mapped the first three rooms in her head. Katherine's fingers finally stop shivering, and the access panel blinks from red to green. The lock pops with a pneumatic sigh. Cleopatra's voice is closer now, at my ear: "You have exactly sixty seconds before the system notices the bypass. Use them."

We pile in, Dorothy first, and I catch the flash of her smile at the security camera staring right at us. Inside, the corridor is new-white and dry, air scrubbed of everything but antiseptic and ambition. The overlays cross-hatch the entire floor in blue and gold: "HAZARD—LOW. PRIORITY—MODERATE." The hum of the facility is low and constant, like the world's most bored dentist drilling straight through your nervous system.

We move in formation. Dorothy in front, arms loose and ready. Ban behind her, gun already in hand, not drawn but close. Cleopatra ghosts the rear, while Katherine and I trail, pretending to be staff, heads down, eyes on overlays. Every ten meters, there's a corporate poster: a child's face, a family, a handshake. The overlays try to sell me on "Unity," "Trust," "Future Forward." But my mind refuses the advertising, smears the slogans into something like "Eat, Prey, Love" and "Your Value Ends Here."

We make the second breach without incident. Cleopatra's math keeps us in the gaps, and the guard rotations are almost beautiful in their predictability. On the third turn, we run into our first live threat: two security techs, one actual, one trainee, both young and more interested in their comms than in the hallway. Dorothy doesn't kill them. She just steps into the space, taps the real guard on the shoulder, and when he turns, she whispers, "Move," in a voice so deep it could crack vertebrae. He freezes, but the trainee jumps and drops his coffee. Ban intercepts the cup before it hits the floor, hands it back to him, and smiles.

The two guards stand aside, terrified. I catch the moment as it passes, the memory of it already mutating in my overlays. By the time we're ten paces down the hall, I can see they'll remember us as ghosts, or maybe just a bad moment in a long career of bad moments. We reach the core—level minus two, temperature dropping, walls now lined with frosted glass and blue-white LEDs. Here, the overlays double the threat warnings, but the real risk is psychological. There's a sense, in these tunnels, that your bones belong to someone else. Cleopatra signals, and Ban halts.

"Katherine, door," Ban says. The panel is bigger here, armored, and running dual authentication: retinal plus pulse. Katherine takes a deep breath, then pops the cover, exposing a bundle of fiber like raw nerve.

She whispers to the door. "You're not supposed to be this smart," she says. "But you're built by people who get paid to rush." Her hands dance, steady for the first time all night. I can see her mouth the numbers, her tongue tracing the path of the code as if she's speaking to a lover. The panel blinks, but this time, it resists. I watch sweat bead down her neck, watch her hesitate, then reach into her pocket for a single-use thermal pad. She cracks it, jams it against the panel, and holds her own eye to the scanner. There's a moment where nothing happens. Then the lock cycles, and the door slides open.

Beyond, the air tastes like saline and old blood. We step through. Ban goes first, eyes hard, then Dorothy, who rolls her shoulders and cracks her neck with a sound like someone breaking a baguette in half. The room is huge. Ceiling lost in shadow, but every surface below lit up with rows of consoles, each one running a simulation so complex the overlays can't keep up. There are tanks on the left wall—real ones, not metaphorical—filled with blue solution and a soft, floating haze of white matter. My overlays glitch, trying to render it as "research," but I know enough from the smell and the shape that this is a neural bank. At the far end is another door. Bigger. Vault-like.

"Target is ahead," whispers Cleopatra, her hand on my shoulder. "Thirty seconds before lockout."

We run for it. Ban covers while Dorothy barrels past the consoles, scattering a tech who looks up just long enough to wish she hadn't. At the vault, Katherine is again at the panel, but this one is different. Instead of digital, it's mechanical—manual wheel, backed by dual biometric triggers. She freezes. Just stops, hand hovering over the dial. Ban almost yells at her, but then sees the look in her eye: not fear, but recognition. "This is my work," says Katherine, voice flat. "They're using my old configs. No one else could've built this."

Dorothy stands at her back, not facing the threat, but Katherine, guarding her from herself. Ban leans in, voice low. "Can you crack it?"

Katherine nods, but her hands are trembling again. "I built a failsafe. If I turn it wrong, the whole block purges. Gas, fire, maybe worse."

Cleopatra steps to the panel, overlays reflecting bright in her chrome eyes. "There's a sequence," she says, "but it's randomized every time."

Katherine laughs, dry. "Not really. The algorithm is supposed to, but I never got it to randomize clean. It's always one of three." She runs the options in her head, lips moving. Then, slow and certain, she spins the dial to twenty-four, then zero, then ninety. A hum. The lock clicks. Ban pulls the vault open. Inside is another row of tanks, but these aren't blue. They're clear. And the things floating inside are small. Not infants, not quite, but not old enough for a name. Dorothy stares, then turns away, the muscles in her arms tensing so hard the overlays start pinging an injury risk. Katherine steps forward, hands over her mouth. "They're running full-stack here," she whispers. "This is a growhouse for brains."

Ban surveys the tanks, jaw locked. “We pull the drives and burn the rest.”

I nod, but I can’t stop staring at the smallest tank. There’s a kid in there, eyes wide, overlayed with the same fake smile as the poster in the first hall. It blinks at me, slow. Cleopatra hands me a tool. “Four minutes before the secondary lock.”

Katherine snaps out of it. “We need to unmount them first, or the feedback will cook the contents. Just like the old builds.”

She sets to work, Dorothy and Ban guarding the door. Cleopatra stands beside me, voice so low it’s barely sound. “You want to kill it?” she asks, not unkindly.

I shake my head. “No. I want to make sure it’s not hungry when it wakes up.” The vault is cold. The vault is silent. But outside, I can hear the alarms start, distant and doomed. We have maybe two minutes before the whole place tries to kill us. Katherine works, faster now, her hands finally steady. Dorothy braces the door, ready for anything. Ban looks back at me, just once, and in the blue-white light, her face is more alive than it’s ever been. I move to the next tank, ready to do my part. We’re outliers, all of us. But tonight, we’re more. For a minute, the world is honest. The vault is almost open.

I’ve seen a lot of fucked-up science, but there’s a special flavor reserved for what Moshimoto does when nobody’s watching. You can smell it under the scrubbed air, under the blue-white cold—this tang of hormone, urine, and chemical solvent, like a locker room made for ghosts.

The door to the vault hangs open on a three-point hinge. The interior is nothing: light, glass, chrome, fluid. The rows run from the threshold to a curved far wall lined with canisters, each with a kid inside. Maybe twenty, maybe a hundred. Each floating, small and soft as tissue paper, in viscous green, wires blooming from the crown of the skull in a nimbus. Some are perfect, faces frozen in REM-sleep, but most have their eyes open, and the overlays sketch probabilities of brain function that do not bear thinking about.

Dorothy's foot hits the ground first. I watch her targeting system flicker, every optic in her head pinwheeling for threat. She locks on two lab techs in the control pod on the far side; the overlays mark them as noncombatant, but her logic loop does not give a fuck. The techs see us, panic, and raise their hands. Dorothy's left arm blossoms into a bayonet, but she stops. Her eyes scan the nearest tube. The anger in her body shakes the floor. Ban is at her side, gun trained, voice a whisper. "Hold. We're here for the data, not blood."

Dorothy grinds her teeth—enough for me to hear it over the hiss of the oxygenators—but obeys. Katherine is past me, already at the closest console. She's talking to herself in a low, frantic mutter, fingers flying through windows and override prompts. The overlays show her overlays, a recursive window of orange, blue, and black—systems fighting each other for the right to call the shots.

Cleopatra, to my left, is barely visible except for the glimmer in her eye. She's walking the perimeter, looking for exits, data ports, and threat vectors. It's almost serene. I watch her shoulder the door shut, wedge it with something pulled from her coat, then start a slow count with her fingers. She's running time as the only currency that matters.

I step into the main vault. The glass tubes make a dull heartbeat sound: every three seconds, a pump pulls fluid through the crown of each child, extracting memory, neurotransmitters, or whatever the hell they want to call it. I see my own face in the reflection—dead, wide-eyed, overlayed with "FAILURE: IRREVERSIBLE"—and I have to laugh, because it's the only thing that keeps me from dropping. The two techs start babbling in corporate protocol. "We surrender, we surrender! Please don't damage the batch—"

Dorothy trains her arm on them and says, "Move again and I'll eat your hands."

They don't move. Katherine's voice is high-pitched and desperate: "They're using a multi-lattice neural net. This isn't just backup—they're live-scarring the kids and baking in trauma to trigger resistance." Her hands don't shake now. She slides to the next console, yanks the panel off, and starts pulling drives.

I follow her because it's better than looking at the tubes. "What does that even mean, K?"

She doesn't look up. "It means they're not archiving. They're running stressors—memory spikes, pain, then deleting all baseline. The only thing that stays is the suffering." Her voice breaks. "It's my old code. Just ... fucked to hell."

Ban moves to help, shoving portable drives into her satchel. She barks at Dorothy, "Secure the room. If those techs move, knock them out, but keep them alive. We need answers if anything goes wrong."

Dorothy doesn't acknowledge, but her arm shifts into something less lethal—just a needle, thick as a child's finger, humming with subsonic. Cleopatra says, calm as a goddamn lake, "First response in ninety seconds, entry point west wall. I suggest we make our exit before then."

But Katherine is on fire now. She tears another panel open, muttering, "If I can copy the protocols, we can reverse the scarring. Maybe give these kids a chance." I look at her, really look. She's younger than her face belies. The overlays always say she's forty-plus, but there's something in her now, a hope that only the desperate can muster. She's not shaking at all. She leans in to a glass canister, taps the screen, and the fluid level drops a centimeter. The child inside twitches. "Still alive," she whispers. "Good."

I look down the row. One tube per meter, each a person, or nearly. Most are just shells—bodies on slow time—but here and there I see the eyes move, the mouth twitch. "Can we save them?" I ask, voice dry as the air.

Katherine shrugs. "If we disconnect fast enough, maybe. But we have to hurry. The extraction sequence is almost done—they're about to purge."

Ban curses under her breath and helps her at the panel. Cleopatra moves to the main console, rips a fiber-optic from her coat, and starts a data siphon. "Sixty seconds," she says, "then we're out, regardless."

The two techs, one male, one maybe, start to shift. Dorothy's arm buzzes, and both they freeze. Katherine gets the first canister unhooked, then yanks the child out. The body is limp, pale, and covered in a jelly that smells like ten thousand headaches, but the chest rises. She cradles the kid and wipes the eyes clean. The kid blinks, mouth opening and closing, silent. “Shit,” Katherine says. “He’s conscious.”

Ban helps her wrap the kid, then gestures to me. “You carry.”

I’m not built for rescue, but I take the child, heavy as a bag of guilt. The overlays register the body as a non-threat, but for once, I don’t care. Katherine is on to the next, and then the next. The canisters are chained together, but with each break, the alarms escalate, the glass going red, the lighting strobing so fast my brain wants to liquefy. Cleopatra calls out, “Forty-five. They’re here.”

I hear the first thud of boots against the vault door. Ban moves to cover, gun at the ready. Dorothy shifts, needle now at full length, pointed at the door. The techs piss themselves, but stay down. Katherine pulls another child out, this one smaller, barely more than a fetus. The skin is raw, hairless. It twitches in her arms. Sounds rings from the door: a drill, a cutter, the whine of a real emergency. “Thirty. Now or never,” Cleopatra says.

Ban turns, and in her face is the thing I always feared: the decision to leave people behind. But she doesn’t. “We take the kids,” she says. “All of them.” Dorothy steps to the canisters, rips the last three off with a sound like ripping Velcro. The fluid sprays and stings my eyes, but the bodies flop free. Ban covers and shouts, “Now!”

We pile the kids into a mesh, grab the drives, and make for the exit on the far side. Cleopatra is there, already jacked into the panel, forcing the door. Behind us, the main door gives. I hear the snap of gunfire, but Dorothy steps back, arms wide, body covering Ban and Katherine as they run. I look over my shoulder and see the first two Corp guards. Dorothy takes them both—non-lethal, just pain—but they go down and don't get up. Cleopatra kicks the far door open. I carry two kids, limp and dripping. Katherine has one, and Ban has the rest in a bag. We sprint. Dorothy covers the rear, then follows, fast and silent.

We make it down the side corridor, past storage, up a ladder, and into a service tunnel. The light shifts from blue-white to sulfur yellow. My overlays throw up warnings I've never seen before: NEW MISSION: ESCAPE.

Katherine shouts, "We need to wake them, or they'll choke!" She thumps the chest of the larger kid. He gags, pukes, then starts to cry. The sound is too loud.

"Ban!" I whisper.

She gets it. "Cleopatra—any faster route?"

"Right," she says, and we all pivot. The sound of boots follows us, but the tunnel is tight, and we have the advantage. Dorothy stops, turns, and lays down a chemical slick on the ground. The first Corp through is in full armor; he hits the spill and faceplants, helmet first. Dorothy grabs him, hurls him into the others, and follows. We race. My lungs are on fire. The kid in my arms shudders, pukes, then wraps arms around my neck and clings. The tunnels get darker, the air worse, but I know it means we're closer to the surface. Cleopatra is first up the last ladder, pops the hatch, then holds it open as we spill out into the rain. It's still night, barely, and the world outside is alive with alarms.

Ban scans the perimeter. "Clear to the east, thirty meters to the river." We run. In the chaos, the city is just wet and dark. The alarms echo, but they're background now. Ban gets us to the drop point: a burned-out subway car, still running off-grid. Inside, it's warm. Katherine lays the kids on the floor, checking each for breath and pulse. Dorothy is last in, but she blocks the entrance, daring the world to follow. Cleopatra is at the console, hacking the power, setting the car to move. Ban turns to me and grabs my shoulder. "You good?"

I can't answer. The kid in my arms is still crying, but alive. Katherine holds the smallest one and wraps her in her jacket. Dorothy stands guard, arms flexing. Cleopatra watches us all, then says, "We did it."

For the first time in forever, I believe her. The subway car lurches, then moves. We slide into the dark, alarms fading behind us. There are children on the floor, cold and scared, but alive. And for a second, I think: maybe we are too.

The subway car stinks of panic, ozone, and wet jelly. We're halfway through the old interchange when Cleopatra says, "Vector's about to close—new blockades on both ends." I don't ask how she knows; I just grip the kid tighter and look for exits that aren't listed on any map. Behind us, alarms echo down the concrete, layer-caked and too loud for any one meaning. Up top, Moshimoto will already be locking every street, drone, and sewer lid, and every second means a new wall we'll have to crash through.

Ban has the oldest of the kids on her lap, slapping his back until he throws up another lungful of fluid. The kid's eyes lock on her gun, but Ban keeps it out anyway—comfort, or maybe a warning. The other children are laid across the old seats, each shivering in their own orbit, neural scars hot enough to show in my overlays as orange-red halos.

Dorothy's first in line for pain. She's positioned herself at the forward hatch, body braced for impact, arms flexed into a shield-wall of synth muscle. Every thirty seconds, she asks for updates; every time, Cleopatra supplies them like a clock ticking out death. "Five minutes to new lockdown. Security on both sides. If you're going to improvise, do it now."

Ban nods, pulling Katherine into a huddle. "Options."

Katherine's hands are a mess, blood from her own bitten fingers mixing with the goo left from the kids. She snatches a med patch from my kit and tapes her palm. "If we can get to the old pump station, I might be able to fry the scanners for a few minutes. But the manual control is only at the site. You'll need to hold it against a riot team."

Ban shrugs. "Better than nothing." She looks at me. "You game?"

Always, I want to say, but the kid in my arms is heavy as regret and just as hard to carry. "Yeah," I say, "just keep them breathing."

Cleopatra guides us by voice. "Next stop, ten meters past the gate. Hatch is above, entry by the left stair. Two live cameras, but the corridor's blind for the first twenty seconds. You'll need to run."

Katherine is already up, grabbing the smallest of the kids, then gesturing to Dorothy. "Can you carry?"

Dorothy nods, all business. She scoops up three children like a goddamn rescue dog, holding them against her body where the synth fur is softest. For all her threat, she moves gently. One girl, maybe four, latches onto Dorothy's prosthetic arm like she's been waiting her whole life to touch metal. "Doesn't it hurt?" the girl whispers.

Dorothy looks at me and shrugs. "Only when you let go."

We hit the stop. The hatch jams, and Dorothy simply pries it up, metal teeth slicing her own hand open, synthetic blood pouring down like a promise. Ban vaults out first, gun up. I pass the kid forward, then scramble up with Katherine and the rest. The world outside is hot and foul—pipes, stairs, slime-slick walls. The old pump station's only a hundred meters away, but already the overlay pings "MOTION: MULTIPLE." Security is closing in, two squads on intercept.

Ban points. "Skelm, left. Dorothy, on me. Katherine, you and the rest stay in the stairwell until I say move."

Dorothy's arms twitch; a blade deploys and then recedes. "Non-lethal only?"

Ban grins. "Try."

The first Moshimoto squad hits us at the midpoint, six in black body armor with visors silvered against the world. Dorothy doesn't bother with cover—she steps in front of Ban and takes the first three shots in the chest. The rounds hit, flatten, and drop, but the force shoves Dorothy into the wall hard enough to crack concrete. Ban kneels, sights, and fires twice. Two guards drop, each hit in the thigh, neither fatal. I come up behind, rip a pipe off the wall, and swing for the helmet of the closest. It shatters, face mask collapsing into his nose, blood and snot flying everywhere.

Dorothy grabs the next one, lifts him by the neck, and smashes his head into the bulkhead until he drops. Ban grabs the body and uses it as a shield for the last two, her own shots taking one in the hand, the other in the foot. Both scream, but neither advance. “Move,” Ban says, and we run. The kids don’t cry, don’t even whimper. Maybe the trauma is too big to fit in the moment. The little girl on Dorothy’s arm is still there, eyes huge and unblinking.

We reach the pump station. Katherine scans the door and yells, “It’s coded! Needs admin override!” I drop the kid at Ban’s feet, rip the panel open, and hotwire the connection with two old alligator clips from my pocket. It buzzes, locks, then slides open. Inside is chaos, a red-lit maze of pumps and catwalks. The overlays say the place is condemned, but the hum of the water mains says otherwise. Katherine darts to the main board. Her hands are trembling, but her mind is clear—she rips open the admin console, finds the main line, and jams a bent paperclip into the emergency port. “Now or never,” she says, and throws the breaker. The station lurches. Every alarm in the system pings, then blinks off. In the space of a second, every scanner in the sector goes dead. “Two minutes,” she says, “maybe less.”

Ban gathers the kids and counts. “Four. There were more.”

Dorothy shakes her head. “We couldn’t carry—”

Ban slams her fist against the rail. “No time. Skelm, rig the charges.”

I do. The demo pack in my kit is small but perfect for the job. I stick three on the support beams and wire them for remote triggering. Outside, the second Moshimoto squad is already at the door. Dorothy braces it, but this time, she's tired. The first guard through the threshold nails her in the face with a chem spray, and she howls, her synth skin blistering white. I sprint to her side, grab the guard's arm, and snap it at the elbow. The chem can falls; I kick it back into the crowd, and three more guards drop in a spray of their own.

Ban is moving the kids up a side stair, voice flat and certain. "Go, go; don't stop."

Katherine runs with them, the two smallest kids under each arm. Her breath is ragged, but she keeps moving. Cleopatra waits at the far end, hand on the exit, already patching in a new escape route. Dorothy shoves the last guard back through the hatch, then collapses to a knee. I lift her up, and for a second, she leans into me. "They're just kids," she says, voice shredded.

"I know."

We run. The upper deck is in disarray. Pipes, cables, old refuse. At the far side, Ban is waving us through, her arm around the oldest boy, who is just barely able to walk. Cleopatra holds the hatch open with her foot, scanning the stairwell behind us, pistol ready. We dive through. The tunnel on the far side is pure black, but I feel the air change—it's updraft, leading to the surface. Ban signals us to hold. "Skelm. Blow it."

I flip the trigger. There's a slow heartbeat, then a rumble so deep my jaw vibrates. The whole station shudders, then the wall behind us blows out in a rush of steam and stone. Ban hauls the kids ahead, me and Dorothy covering the rear. The last guard, the one I clocked, tries to follow, but Dorothy slams the hatch and holds it until the pressure is too much. She lets go, and the hatch implodes, flattening the guard to paste.

At the top, we find the next layer of hell: the riverbank, exposed and alive with lights from three Moshimoto drones and a dozen black SUVs. Cleopatra points. "There's an underpass thirty meters away. If we make it, we lose them in the crowd." Ban runs for it, Dorothy at her side. I grab the last kid and follow, heart in my mouth. zThe drones sweep low. I hear the hiss of a taser volley, but Dorothy flares her arms, catches the prongs, and yanks the wires, tearing the drones off course. One crashes, sparks lighting the sky. The other two pull up, but not before Ban makes the underpass, all four kids in tow.

We duck inside. The world goes quiet—wet stone, old graffiti, the stench of the river. Ban collapses, back to the wall, kids huddled tight. Katherine checks each one, running her own quick-and-dirty diagnostics. "They'll live," she says, "but the damage is ... bad. Really bad."

Ban doesn't answer. She stares into the dark, face unreadable. Dorothy stands at the tunnel mouth, arms wide, daring the world to come get us. Cleopatra leans against the wall and checks her pulse. "It's over," she says. But I know it isn't. Upstream, the Moshimoto Bio-Labs facility lights up the sky, alarms pealing in every direction. At the center, a white-hot fire blooms, eating through glass and steel. I watch as the fire climbs, floor by floor, until it's just a torch against the morning.

The oldest boy looks at the flames, then at Ban. "Are we free?"

Ban hesitates. “For now.”

Dorothy comes in and sits beside the boy. He doesn’t shrink from her, not even with her arm still leaking synthetic blood. Katherine curls up on the concrete, her own wounds finally catching up. I sit against the wall, the last kid on my lap, and wait for the overlays to tell me what to do next. They don’t. The fire burns higher. The city sirens get softer. For now, there’s nothing left to run from. Just the wreckage, and what comes after.

Cleopatra closes her eyes, and for a moment, she almost smiles. Outside, the rain starts again. Inside, we hold each other, alive and raw. Tomorrow, we start over.

Chapter 12

It starts with the crackle of static and a whiff of ozone. Then the world explodes. The safehouse wall goes first—concrete sheared into bloom, noise hard enough to stop my heart. Emergency lighting kicks in, flickers, then dies to red. I roll under the desk, teeth rattling, hands clutching at nothing but the hope I still have skin. The overlays lag, can't render chaos at this density, so I'm alone with my meat.

Then comes another blast, closer. Air sucks out of the room, replaced by dust and glass. I taste blood. I look up, trying to triangulate Ban's position from the last ping on her comm. The signal is everywhere, then nowhere, then in the stairwell, two meters north and down. Dorothy's silhouette glides into view, backlit by pulse-fire and the shimmer of her own terror. She's all edge and menace, even stripped to bare muscle and carbon from yesterday's scrape. Her left arm shifts, servos clicking, the steel extruding out into a blade I've only ever seen in maintenance mode. I watch her for half a second, transfixed, the weapon a slow-blooming nightmare. "Darby!"

she calls, voice cracked and mechanical, but alive. "Ban's down the shaft. I'll buy you time."

The line would be trite if it weren't Dorothy. This is her programming, her pathos: protect at all costs, even when the cause is beyond saving. Outside, there's footsteps—military, six at least, pattern matched to Moshimoto kill team doctrine. I lurch up, find the crawlspace hatch, and see Ban waving at me from below. She's bleeding, neck running dark down her shirt, but her grip on the pistol is steady. Dorothy sets her feet in the center of the room, body between the breach and the stairwell. The kill team's strobing flashlight paints her in arcs of red and white. She raises her blade-arm in a parody of a salute. "I used to train you people!" she shouts, teeth showing. "You think this is enough to kill me?"

A Moshimoto trooper steps into the kill zone, gun up. Dorothy grins and rushes him, blade carving a low sweep that opens his thigh to the bone. She shoves him back into the next two, then spins, catching a sidearm round in her left shoulder. It sparks, chems burning. The stink of it is nostalgic, like hot wire and old regret. The air is full of shouting and Ban's voice: "Move, now!"

I stumble for the hatch, but pause at Dorothy's side. She flicks her eyes at me—no overlays needed to know what it means. "Go," she says. "You're the only reason this mess matters." It should be Ban doing the dragging, but Dorothy puts a boot into my ribs and launches me toward the shaft. I tumble, hit the landing with my wounded shoulder, and the pain is enough to white out my vision.

Ban grabs my arm hard. Her nails cut through the sleeve, right into skin. "You don't get to die here, Skelm. That's an order.

We can't be sure if you'll come back. You know how unpredictable the protocols are." The resurrection protocols weren't designed—they evolved. Or devolved. Whatever intelligence runs SKELM CORPS now, it plays with human consciousness like a child pulling wings off flies. Sometimes it brings people back to see what happens. Sometimes it forgets they exist. Sometimes it breaks them on purpose. There's no pattern because there's no plan. Just an immortal toddler with administrative access to reality itself. She shoves a pistol into my hand, and I'm running before I even register the touch. I can hear Dorothy above, laughing and screaming at the same time. The rest is flight. Ban is faster, but I'm desperate. Down the corridor, past a fuse box sparking with Dorothy's handiwork, and into the maintenance tunnel. The air gets colder, wetter, then tastes like mold and stale solder. We hit the bottom, Ban leading, both of us limping and leaving a smear of ourselves on every inch of ladder.

A shockwave rings above, then the sound of the stairwell collapsing. Ban curses, then pivots and grabs me by the collar. She's shaking, but not from fear. "She'll hold the bottleneck. That's what she does." Her eyes are wild, fevered. I want to argue, to run back, but Ban holds me pinned. Her hands clamp down on my fucked-up shoulder, fingers digging into the bruises left by the last bullet I took for her. "We move or we die," Ban says, voice lower now, more human.

The world narrows to her face, the smell of her blood, the tremor in my own arm. I nod once, and she lets go. We stagger through the tunnels. Every few meters, I can hear Dorothy's voice, echoing in the pipework, taunting the kill team, daring them to be half as alive as she is. We don't look back, but the sounds of the fight follow us. Then, nothing. Just the slap of our boots, and the memory of the only family we ever had, holding the line above.

The city is made of bad dreams and power outages. We slip out of the maintenance shaft into a rain that doesn't know how to stop, the world above painted in ads for drugs that don't work and politicians who never existed. Ban is hurt worse than she lets on. She keeps her left side turned away, favoring the neck where her wound pulses out blood with every step. The red is brighter than the neon, a drip that glues her to the city's membrane.

We run the first five blocks on muscle memory. Down two flights, through a busted service gate, and under a stretch of polycarbonate canopy that smells like fresh-poured cement and yesterday's death. Ban doesn't talk, just gives the hand signals: two fingers up—*drone sighted*; flat palm—*hold*; index sweep—*move, now*. The old subway drills pay off. Every gesture is a promise, every glance a line of code. When Ban ducks, I duck. When she stops dead and hugs the wall, I freeze, matching her posture like we're a single shadow.

A drone circles overhead, lens array lit up like a saint's halo. Ban stares at the reflection in the puddle and counts the blink pattern. She mouths "seven" at me, and I know, in that instant, it's the interval for a sweep. We time the next sprint to the heartbeat of the machine—run, freeze, run. I can feel my heart in my teeth. The wound in my shoulder opens up again, a hot throb that soaks my sleeve, leaving a trail that should be visible from orbit. Ban catches it, rips a strip from her jacket, and tapes it off. She doesn't look at me when she does it. "Keep up," she says, and I almost laugh, because if I fall behind, we both die.

We cut left at an alley; a dead-end unless you know the trick: a loose panel, high and to the right, big enough for a cat but not a man. Ban boosts me up, the pain nearly blacking me out, then launches herself after, landing silent. On the other side is another corridor—worse lighting, more drones. This time, the hand signal is tight to her chest, almost like she's protecting her heart. We make it ten meters before the world erupts in noise. A Moshimoto scout team hits the street, two drones on manual, three men in exo-armor. They spot us, but Ban is faster—she drops low, yanks me behind a stack of broken concrete, and says, "On three."

She signals with her right hand; *three* ... *two* ... *one*. We bolt straight into the open, and it's suicide, but it's also the only way. The first drone lights us up, but Ban's timing is perfect. She leads it into the blind spot of a neon sign, the flash from the ad scrambling the optics. She's mapped this block before; every inch of it is a weapon in her hand. I follow, because that's the only move left. We sprint, her boot splashing water in perfect sync with the hammering of my heart. In that moment, the world is nothing but Ban's silhouette, the city bending around us.

We cut right, then another right, then double back to a basement entrance hidden behind a dumpster full of illegal SentiSnack™ wrappers. Ban grabs the door, muscles it open, and hauls me through. Inside, we breathe. The smell is of mold and rust and the wet heat of living. Ban looks at me. Her hair is stuck to her forehead, her lips peeled back in a snarl that's half pain, half laughter. “You're bleeding,” she says, as if it matters now.

“So are you.”

She shrugs. “Guess we match.”

We keep moving. The final approach is the old industrial tunnel, the one Ban mapped on a dare, just to see if she could. The route is tight, filled with collapsed pipework and ankle-deep water. Each step is agony, but Ban never slows. At the far end, a service gate starts to drop—someone, somewhere, tripped the alarm. Ban doesn't flinch. “You ready?” she says, but it's not a question.

We go, sprinting full out, every muscle screaming. The gap under the gate gets smaller by the second. Ban slides first, then reaches back, grabs my good arm, and yanks. We hit the floor on the other side, rolling through water and broken glass. The gate slams shut behind, the world suddenly muffled. We lie there, side by side, chests heaving, the stink of blood and adrenaline filling the space. Ban is the first to sit up. She wipes the water from her face, then laughs, low and ugly. “Told you,” she says, “breaks are for the dead.” I laugh, or try to, but my lungs won't cooperate. Ban leans in, her face inches from mine. “You did good,” she says, voice softer now. “Better than the odds.”

I want to tell her she's the reason I'm alive. I want to say something that matters, but the words won't come. So I just lie there, in the dark, watching her breath in the air between us. For a second, we're the only two people in the world. Then the overlays start to ping: “PURSUIT: 120 SECONDS.” Ban grins, hauls me up, and we run again. This is life now. We're a vector. We're a bullet. And no one gets to stop us.

After the sprint comes the cold. We crouch in a service vault, water up to our ankles, breaths clouding the air. Ban is a shadow at the door, head on a swivel, hands vibrating with the aftershock. I dig through my pockets for anything not ruined by blood and rain. Dorothy's badge is in my palm, sharp edge catching on the meat of my thumb. I'd joke she'd want it that way, but the joke would land nowhere. Instead, I use it to wedge open a half-empty bottle of synth-vodka Ban stole from an office fridge three lifetimes ago. The cap refuses, then gives, sending a splash of liquor onto my hands.

I set the badge on a plate of cracked ceramic, pour a shot of vodka over it, and light it with the micro-torch from my patch kit. The flame flickers, blue and uncertain. Ban glances over, says nothing, but her jaw sets, the line of her neck gone sharp under the dried blood. Katherine emerges from the dark, hair stringy and caked to her face. She's carrying the neural mapping drive, thumb hooked in the casing. She drops next to me, watching the flame for a minute. "She always said she'd go out laughing," says Ban, and her voice isn't steel now, but rust.

Katherine looks at the flame, at me, and I know she's remembering the exact algorithm that made Dorothy a monster and a friend. "I've got her last log," Katherine says. "If you want it."

I nod, and she jacks a cord into my overlay port. The world is still for a second, then Dorothy's last stand plays out in brutal, compressed time: blood, laughter, fire, a line of code that stutters "worth it" before cutting to black. I blink it away and stare at the badge melting in the vodka flame. The city up top is alive with sirens. The news feeds are already spinning—terrorist cells, mass violence, threats to the social order. They won't even remember Dorothy's name by morning. That's the algorithm.

I pull out the data chip Dorothy pressed into my palm during the scramble. It's slick with blood, hard to hold, but when I slot it into Katherine's drive, the payload unlocks: a single coordinate, mapped to a dead zone under the old hospital district. Katherine reads it first. "She left us an exit," she says, the words brittle but hopeful.

Ban nods, still at the door, still watching. "She was always the smartest of us," she says, and for the first time, I think she believes it. I pocket the chip, and together, we watch the badge burn down to nothing. Ban flicks her eyes to mine. "They're not done, you know."

I nod. "Neither are we."

Katherine wipes her face with the back of her hand. "There's more. The data—" She passes me the neural drive, then pulls up the decrypted logs. It's all there: names, locations, a city-wide purge. Not just us. Hundreds of cells. The kill teams are working round-the-clock, every corridor, every dark web ping flagged for extermination. At the top of the data dump is a file labeled "PROJECT: EMPATHY GAP."

Katherine opens it. The contents are a schematic for the neural mapper, and a plan for a memory wipe on a global scale. The Corp wasn't just erasing us. They were going to erase the world, one line at a time, and start over with a copy that never knew hope. Ban reads the summary, then smiles. It's not a happy smile. "They want to end the war by ending the memory of the war," she says. I look at Dorothy's badge, melted now, flame gone out. In the dark, Ban's eyes are bright, almost wet. "We take the exit. We get clear. Then we bring it all down."

I nod. There's nothing else left. We gather what we can. Katherine patches up my shoulder, then does her own. Ban walks point, the pistol back in her hand, but this time, it's not for show. Outside, the city is on fire. Inside, we walk the wet tunnels, Dorothy's ghost two steps ahead, lighting the way. This is not a story of heroes. It's a story of what survives when hope burns out, and the only thing left is the memory of laughter. We walk into the dark, and we do not stop.

Katherine is on watch outside—her choice, not ours. The container's barely big enough for two.

Chapter 13

We make it to the edge of the city with a four-minute lead and no plan but not to die. The "safehouse" is a mess of shipping containers rusted shut, a half-collapsed oubliette at the edge of the canal and patched into the power grid with wires fished out of a scrap yard. Ban picks the green one for its line of sight to the floodwall, her boots tracking a stripe of Dorothy's blood across the sand. She double-checks the doors, the corners, the empty black above, then ushers me in, quick and careful, gun out but lazy, like she's already certain no one followed.

Inside, the air is colder, full of brine and copper and the static stink of a failed dehumidifier. There's a lamp and two army cots and a field table littered with syringes and expired MREs. The only soft thing is a stack of plastic tarps, the kind used for mass graves or old carpets. Ban peels one off and lays it flat across the cot. She gives me a look: *collapse, or else.*

My legs fold underneath me. The cot groans. My overlays are nothing but damage logs and pain: right arm, still bleeding from the drone hit; left, patched, but numb. I flex my fingers, counting the bones. All there. The rest of me is less certain. Ban strips off her jacket, hands shaking only when she isn't looking at them. Under the jacket, she's all sinew and bruise, blood dried in lines from chin to sternum. She rips a shirt sleeve for a bandage and stalks over, cursing under her breath. She grabs my shoulder hard, and I flinch so bad the cot almost flips. "Relax," she says, then braces my head between her palms, checking my eyes for concussion.

"Dorothy's gone," I say. The words taste like battery acid. If she'd been lucky enough to resurrect, she would have found us by now.

Ban doesn't let go. I'm shaking now, hard enough that the overlays want to sedate me. Ban forces my gaze back to hers. Her irises are pitch black and flat. Nothing in them wants to comfort, but something in them won't let go either. She slaps a stim patch onto my neck. "We need to be human for at least one more hour."

I laugh, then choke, then laugh again. My hands are rattling so bad I can't get the blood off the trigger finger. "What if I can't be human anymore?"

She ignores the question, pops the cap on a med injector, and slams it into my thigh. The pain is instant, electric, but clears the fog for one clean second. In that second, I see Ban in full: face set, eyes raw, shirt torn and caked with two people's worth of death. She looks down, sees the shrapnel in my shoulder, and shakes her head. "Idiot," she says, but her voice is soft, soft enough to make me remember every time she ever said my name in the dark, every time she ever called me alive when the rest of the world called me a tool.

Ban kneels, and the cot frame whines. Her hands are steady now, all callus and old nicotine, but the way they land on my arm is careful, almost shy. She digs in with a multitool, finds the fragment, and pulls. The blood is dark, slow, not fatal. "You were built for worse," she says, but she's talking to herself.

The shakes get worse before they get better. I ride the edge between blackout and hyperclarity, the overlays reduced to red outlines. Ban bandages the arm tightly. She wipes her hands on the tarp, then sits back on her heels, breathing hard. The silence is the worst. Nothing but the two of us, alive where we shouldn't be, ghosts circling just outside the thin walls. "Why did you pull me out?" I ask, because I have to.

She shrugs, then stands, stripping off the ruined shirt and swapping it for a clean one from a plastic tub. The skin under her clavicle is puckered, one long scar running from neck to shoulder. "You're the last," she says, voice flat. "Can't lose the asset."

It's a lie, and we both know it. I want to say her name, but my mouth is full of someone else's blood. She throws the clean shirt over me, then sits on the cot, not touching but not leaving, either. "You ever think it should've been you?" I say, low. "Not Dorothy. Not Johnson."

Ban closes her eyes. For a minute, she is so still I think maybe she's gone too, that I've slipped sideways into the future where everyone leaves but me. Then she moves, just a shift of her knee against mine, not enough to be comfort but more than nothing. "You ever shut up?"

"Not if you keep saving my life."

She snorts, then leans in, forehead pressed to mine. Our breaths mix, sharp and sour. I feel her pulse, the same as mine, echoing off the cold metal. Then she kisses me. No warning, no lead-in. It's nothing like the movies: no slow fade, no soft dissolve. It's teeth and tongue and blood, the taste of cheap alcohol and cheaper adrenaline. Her mouth is hard, then harder, her hands threading through my hair like she's rooting for something buried underneath.

I kiss her back, because if I don't, I'll disappear. She breaks away first, and the air rushes back in. "Your other half's been promising this for years," she whispers, but the word "half" is glass in her throat. I laugh again, or maybe sob. There's no difference anymore. The cot sags under both of us, and Ban climbs into my lap, knees bracketing my hips, hands on either side of my head. The shirt she gave me is gone; the only barrier left is skin, and not much of that.

We fuck like we fight: desperate, graceless, and full of old wounds. Her nails score my back; my teeth find her shoulder. The cot threatens collapse with every motion. The tarp under us crinkles, the air fills with sweat and noise, but neither of us stops. Not for the cold, not for the pain, not even for the ghosts. She presses my hands above my head, pinning me to the frame, and for a second, I think about all the times I let her lead, all the times I wanted to be caught. She sees the thought in my eyes, and smiles—a real one, wide and wolfish. When we come, it's not about pleasure. It's not even about release. It's just the only thing left that the Corp can't monetize, can't steal or overwrite. After, we collapse together, limbs tangled. The cot creaks one last time, then goes silent.

Ban is the first to speak, voice raw. “Dorothy would’ve hated this.”

“Only if she didn’t get to watch,” I say. Ban laughs, just once, and lays her head on my chest. I listen to her breathing, count the beats, and memorize them for later. Outside, the city doesn’t care if we live or die. Inside, for now, we’re alive. The ghosts can wait.

The day comes up wrong, light sideways through the seams in the shipping container, painting everything in stripes of dust and blue-white fatigue. I don’t remember falling asleep. When I open my eyes, Ban is curled against me, her head jammed under my chin, one arm draped across my ribs in a way that would look domestic if it weren’t for the raw, brutal edge of last night. The tarp is stuck to my ass. The air is slick with old sex and the ozone of the morning after.

I count Ban’s breaths against my chest—slow, precise, nothing like the animal panting before. Her hand is balled up in a fist, pressed flat against my sternum like she’s holding something inside. I know better than to wake her. I just lie there, counting the scars across her shoulder. I find a fresh one—a pink line from her collarbone to the point of her scapula. I run my finger down it, soft. She doesn’t move.

I look for a clock, but there’s only the lamp, the dead comm, and the faint ticking of condensation. I let my head tilt back and stare at the patchwork ceiling, where a trickle of rain from last night has pooled and started to drip into a shallow puddle near the cot’s leg. I see my own reflection, ghosted in the puddle, double-exposed over the water. It looks less like a face and more like a smear. I wonder which version of me is awake now—the one who wants to fuck Ban, or the one who wants to kill her, or maybe just the one who doesn't want to die alone. I hope it's the first, but I've never been good at self-diagnosis.

I shift under Ban, careful not to wake her, and prop myself up on an elbow. She tenses, then settles. Her arm slides off me, leaving a cold stripe in its place. I watch her, because it's easier than looking at the city outside. I remember her at seventeen, on the floor of the gym, blood gushing from her mouth and laughing so hard the whole world could hear. I remember her at twenty-two, face to face in a riot shield, mouthing "missed you" through a split lip and a storm of tear gas. I remember her last night, naked and feral and more alive than anyone I've ever met.

I also remember Émilie, the soft hands, the low voice, the taste of peppermint on her tongue when she said, "Trust me." I remember the first time I lied to her, and the last time I touched her. I remember every fucking thing, and none of it makes sense. The guilt sits in my chest, sharp as the bone Ban's pressing her fist against. My hand drifts to her hair. It's cropped close, almost a buzz, but there's still enough for me to grip. I let myself run my fingers over her skull, tracing the dip at the crown where the bone was reset after a training accident. She hated the scar, but I always thought it was the most honest thing about her.

She stirs finally, eyelids twitching. She doesn't open them at first, just sniffs the air and then flexes her hand against my chest. "You awake?" she mutters, voice thick. I don't answer. I just brush her hair back from her eyes. She cracks one lid and glares up at me. "I'm not dead yet."

"Give it time," I say, then immediately regret it. She doesn't. She rolls away, pulling the tarp with her, and sits up on the edge of the cot. She reaches for her pants, which are inside-out and two meters away, then for her gun, which is within reach and probably warmer than the air. She doesn't look at me, just checks the mag and then sets it in her lap. There's a radio on the field table—an old, battered thing with a sticker for the IWW and the battery cover missing. Ban flicks it on, and static fills the container. She twists the dial with her thumb, searching for anything except her own thoughts.

I pull my knees up and wrap my arms around them. The cuts on my shoulder throb. I watch her move, every gesture sharp, all the grace of a razor blade. The radio clears: *"In other news, a spate of sabotage attacks on the Moshimoto Institute's neural cloning facility has left over a dozen security personnel injured, and two research suites destroyed. Authorities suspect—"* static, then *"—ban leader, identity classified as 'Ban,' remains at large following the attack. Moshimoto has raised the bounty to—"* static.

Ban snorts, a humorless sound. "They didn't even mention you. Asset status revoked."

"Maybe I'm just a liability now," I say. She doesn't argue. She pulls her pants on, stands, and starts collecting her kit. The scars on her back ripple under the pale light. I find myself staring, wanting to touch them, wanting to map them like terrain. Instead, I watch as she laces her boots, the left one tight enough to cut circulation. Ban finishes gearing up, then walks over to the table, rips open an MRE, and stares at the packet without eating it. She pulls a flask from her jacket, takes a swig, and tosses it to me. I catch it left-handed, and drink. It tastes like the floor of a maintenance tunnel. I roll the flask between my palms. "You ever regret it?"

She gives me a look. "Which part?"

I shrug. "All of it. Any of it."

She thinks, then shakes her head. "Regret's for the rich. I just move forward."

I look at my hands. "I used to be good at that."

She sits back on the cot, closer this time. There's a lull in the radio, then a new voice—thin, elegant, Moshimoto-accented. My skin prickles. *"And in personnel news, we welcome Émilie Moreau to her new role as Chief of Neural Acquisitions. Dr. Moreau's work on the Persephone protocol will revolutionize consciousness transfer. Details—"* static.

Ban looks at me. "That your ex?" she says, deadpan. I nod. Ban considers this, then leans back, hands behind her head. "Guess you have a type." I'm not sure if it's an insult or a compliment, but I let it pass. We sit in silence for a while. Ban's eyes go glassy, lost in her own overlays. I want to reach for her, but the distance feels wider now, measured in more than centimeters.

I get up and wander around the container. The light is stronger now, the city outside awake and angry. I walk to the door and peek out through the seam. There's nothing but fog and the outlines of cranes in the harbor, birds circling trash heaps, and the sound of a distant drone. I turn back. Ban is sitting up, radio in one hand, gun in the other. She looks at me, and for a second, the hard line of her mouth softens. "You ever think we could've just left?"

I shake my head. "No. We're both too fucked for that."

She stands, grabs her jacket, and shrugs it on. The air is so cold it makes my teeth ache. She walks to me, but stops a foot away. She doesn't touch me, not at first. Then she puts her hand on my face, rough and warm. She presses her thumb into my cheek and holds it there. "I don't want to die in a box," she says.

"Me neither."

She kisses me, softer this time, just lips, no teeth, no desperation. Then she pulls back and grabs my chin. "We go?"

"Yeah," I say. "We go."

We gather what's left. I pull the tarp off the cot and wrap it around my shoulders. The blood has dried, brown and flaking. Ban checks the door and signals clear. We step out into the cold morning. The city is louder, closer, but we keep to the shadows. In the silence between us, I replay the news about Émilie, about her new job and her new life. I try to remember if I ever knew her at all. I try to remember if I ever knew myself.

Chapter 14

The first sign is the comm blackout. One minute, Cleopatra's ghost is still feeding us city map delta and enemy heat signatures, the next, it's a wall of static so thick my overlays can't cut through. I tap the backup; nothing but red. Ban's expression says it all—lips gone tight, jaw set to demolition. She's already stacking the cots against the door, hands moving faster than the rest of her. "Katherine?" she says, and Katherine jolts awake from her post-op daze, face greasy and sallow under the lamp. She snatches up her kit, muttering through the worst of her shakes. Her hands hover over the neural mapping drive like it's a bomb about to go off. "Kill teams are on us," Ban says, not asking.

Katherine checks her own comm, but all the overlays are blank. She curses, knuckles white on the table. "They're here."

Ban points at me. "You've got two minutes to purge and prep. If you get taken, you erase yourself or I do it for you." There's no heat in it, no need for drama. Just business as usual in the ongoing bankruptcy of our lives. I nod, start dumping redundant data. The first boom shakes the whole container like a tin can in a cyclone. My overlays can't decide what to prioritize: breach warning, med alert, or the time-to-live counter on the neural mapper.

"Perimeter's blown," Katherine says, eyes flickering. "Give it maybe ten seconds. Then we're dead."

Ban unslings the shotgun from the cot frame. "Not dead. Just overdue."

The next sound is precision—Moshimoto at their finest. A whine of shaped charge, a brief flash, then the door tears open with a crunch that feels like an aneurysm. The world rushes in: strobe lights, cold rain, boots, and voices already in the kill cadence. Ban fires first, taking the left-side point man square in the groin, scattershot painting the wall in protein. He folds with a marionette's collapse. The others don't even blink; second and third shift to autofire, sweeping the inside of the container.

I flatten to the deck, but it's Katherine who's moving fastest. She hauls the neural drive to the rear wall and slams it into the one socket we never thought we'd use. "Prep for manual override!" she yells, and her voice is so raw, so alive, I almost believe she'll survive this. She runs a hand over her temple, then jabs two leads from the neural drive directly into the dermal patch behind her ear. There's no time for anesthetic, and her whole body jerks like a fish on a hook. "I'm gonna crash the feedback. Thirty seconds, max. After that, I'm dead or a vegetable."

I know what she's doing. It's not noble. It's not even logical. It's the kind of choice you make when the future is already gone and the only currency left is time. Ban fires again. Another kill, but the breach team just keeps coming. The lead operator flings a chem grenade into the space—clear, odorless, but instantly numbing on skin contact. My fingers go dead, then hot, then nothing. I use my teeth to trigger the last fail-safe on the mapper. Katherine's eyes go completely black as the neural interface spins up. Her voice jumps an octave. "Ban. Ready your mask. Skelm—if you don't make it, you owe me a drink in hell."

Ban's mask is already on. She hisses an oath in Mandarin I haven't heard since the tunnels under Beijing. The breach team's leader steps through the smoke, body shield up, rifle centered on my chest. There's a moment, just one, where I see the world at full slow: Ban's finger on the trigger, the flex of muscle in the Moshimoto suit, Katherine's eyes locked on mine as she mouths, "Make it count."

Then she slams her palm onto the drive, and every light in the world blows out at once. The noise is beyond pain—a pure, full-spectrum whiteout that cracks open the air and my skull at the same time. Sparks blast from Katherine's interface as her body goes rigid, back arched, mouth foaming with blood. The kill team's visor displays glitch, then black. The leader staggers, drops his rifle, and claws at his helmet like he can't breathe. Two more go down, convulsing. Even Ban, thirty years of nerve-end training, stumbles to a knee and lets the shotgun clatter to the ground.

In the instant of total confusion, Ban lunges, grabs me by the collar, and yanks me through the burning edge of the container. My legs don't work, but Ban's do; she drags me across the sand, into the rain, into the chemical bite of open air. Behind us, the shipping container is alive with light. Katherine's body is a silhouette in the center, small and bent, sparks and blood geysering from her skull as the neural feedback fries every system in the kill team's armor. The leader goes down last, screaming like he knows how this ends.

Then the drive overloads. The entire container ignites in a pure white flash, the kind that vaporizes retinas and memory both. I'm blind, and Ban's voice is in my ear: "Run, Skelm. Run or I'll break your other arm."

I try. My feet land wrong, my knees buckle, and I go down hard. Ban hauls me up again, never slowing, never looking back. We hit the access hatch behind the last container. Ban shoves me through first, then seals it, her own blood smearing the latch. We tumble down the maintenance shaft, air thick with copper and something sweeter, like the smell of static before a storm. For a long time, I can only hear our breath. Ban pulls the backup pistol and tracks the corridor behind us, eyes pure wolf now, every motion deliberate.

My overlays are gone—blank, burned, reset to zero. Katherine's last scream is still echoing somewhere in my skull. After a few meters, Ban stops, crouches, and drags me close. Her face is streaked with rain and smoke, skin pale as death. I try to speak, but my mouth is full of sparks. "She did it," Ban says, not looking at me. "Bought us twenty minutes."

I nod, but the numbers don't add up. Katherine was not supposed to die here. She was the redundant system, the fallback. It doesn't compute. It won't. I'm so sure of it that I fight to stay rooted to the spot, waiting for her to resurrect. "Are you —" I say, but Ban just shakes her head. Her grip on my arm is iron, but her hand trembles, barely. She urges us onward, and we don't stop moving until the corridor dead-ends into the first of the old sewage junctions. The rain above drums a private funeral on the steel.

We crouch together, backs against the wall, and the city is silent for once. "She said to make it count," I say. Ban doesn't answer. She just wipes the blood from her eyes and stares into the dark. Katherine's absence is an ache, a missing overlay that can never be patched. I feel it in my pulse, in every second Ban's hand stays tight on my sleeve. If there's a god, he's bankrupt now. I run a finger over the last fragment of neural drive I managed to pocket. "I will."

Ban's hand is steady now. She doesn't look at me, but she doesn't let go. We sit there until the tremors pass. Then we start crawling through the city's gut and toward whatever hell comes next.

It's the kind of warehouse they don't build anymore: shipping containers stacked seven high, ringed in razor wire, guard drones floating overhead like lazy carrion birds. The air inside is recycled too many times, thick with electrical burn and the smell of long-gone contents—old soymeal, plastic, and human sweat. The wind outside whines a continuous note, vibrating every loose bolt in the prefab siding.

Ban chose the place for its line of sight to the rail yard and the perfect perimeter. She didn't pick it for comfort, which is fine, because comfort is the only thing I can't use right now. We're down to two. The overlays won't let me forget.

I spend the first hour after arrival stripping the container of its most obvious trackers, and picking microdots out of the insulation with a soldering needle and grinding them to dust. Ban runs the external, making circles every fifteen minutes. I tell myself this is just good protocol, but I know the truth: she's making sure I don't bolt. Or overdose. Or put my head through the wall.

Katherine's drive is in my hand. Not the whole thing—just the fragment, black as a shark's tooth and humming with encrypted potential. I scrape off the blood and jam it into the raw I/O port drilled into the container's folding desk. No official reader would take it. But Katherine made sure to teach me the ad-hoc way: pair it with a half-ruined SentiSnack™ vending controller, fake the handshake, and let the system think it's feeding candy to a psychotic infant.

The first layer is the usual: a slurry of memory dumps, test logs, sensor readings. But the deeper I go, the more Katherine's signature shows up—not in the data, but in the gaps, the skipped bytes, the way the machine hesitates between commands. It's like she left me a breadcrumb trail, built entirely from what she didn't say. After a while, Ban comes back, slams the steel door, and wordlessly tosses a dented can of coffee at my feet. It's still warm. She sits across from me, eyes blank, skin paler than the sodium bulbs overhead. For the longest time, she doesn't say a thing, just watches my hands. They won't stop shaking. I can't tell if it's rage, withdrawal, or grief. I try to type, but my fingers twitch over the keys, filling the log with stutters and typos. "Want me to do it?" Ban asks, voice flat.

"No," I say, though I'm not sure why. She grunts, then unpacks a protein bar and eats it without looking away. After a minute, she slides another toward me, but I leave it where it lands.

The neural drive hits a payload, and every display in the container goes black, then blue, then starts feeding me encrypted blocks with header tags stamped "EMPATHY GAP, REV BETA." I recognize the codebase; it's Katherine's, all right, but recompiled a thousand times in ways she would've called "crime against reason."

I read through the executive summary, not that it matters, because the meaning is clear from the first lines:

—UNREADABLES EMBEDDED IN ALL MAJOR ORGS

—TWENTY-YEAR PROGRAM

—EMPATHY GAP: SYSTEMIC REDESIGN OF HUMAN CONSCIOUSNESS

I keep reading because what else is there? Each page is worse than the last—branching neural chains, sleeper agent protocols, self-updating overlays designed to mimic baseline emotion while routing true sentiment to a corporate node somewhere in the Cloud. There are logs, with names and locations; most have already been scrubbed, "burned," but a handful are still live.

I scan for "SKELM" and there it is: my line, my designation, my date of first activation. It predates my first real memory by two years. "They've been manufacturing us for decades," I say, and the words taste like sand.

Ban leans forward, chewing. "You always suspected."

"I did. But I thought I was alone."

"Why would you think that?" she asks, not sarcastic but genuine.

I blink, trying to clear the static from my brain. "Because everything about my life was an experiment in isolation. I thought the point was to see if I'd break. Not if I'd multiply."

Ban shrugs, the motion angular and tired. "The point was always to break everyone. We're just ... prototypes."

I keep reading, digging through the code for Katherine's fingerprint. I find it in the error correction: a string of text, hidden in a noise file, set to trigger only if the right parameters are met. I run the decode. The message resolves in her old, clipped syntax.

Skelm. If you're reading this, it means you lived. Don't be an idiot; you are the redundancy. You're the part they can't fix. If you get to stage three, kill the process. The rest of them are not coming back.

I lean back, letting the words punch a hole in my head. Ban finishes her bar, wipes her hands on her pants, and says, "Well?"

"It's worse than we thought."

Ban stands, paces to the corner, then back again. She cracks her knuckles, an old habit. "Can it be stopped?"

I shake my head. "Not anymore. Maybe not ever."

She picks up a cable and wraps it tight around her fist. "If we can't win, why fight?"

I look at her, really look, and see the thing Katherine meant: Ban was always the counterbalance, the brute to my algorithm, but the truth is she's just as broken. She just knows how to hide it. "They're not just manufacturing us," I say. "They're weaponizing." Ban's jaw goes hard. She says nothing for a long time. I slide the protein bar closer to me, stare at it, then crush it in my hand. The flakes stick to my skin, dark and synthetic. "We could burn the container," I say, but Ban ignores it. She moves to the panel and punches in a sequence that drops the steel blinds over the slits of daylight. The place is now a tomb, sealed against the world.

Ban sits beside me, shoulder against mine. We look at the neural drive, still spinning on the screen. "Katherine was smarter than both of us."

I nod. "But she trusted us to end it."

Ban's face is shadowed. I can't tell if she's crying, or if the light just caught her wrong. "We're the last."

"Yeah."

The wind rattles the walls. Somewhere outside, a drone passes, its lens glinting through the haze. I type the last line of code, then stop. I don't hit send. I just sit there, Ban's warmth seeping through my shirt, the future so perfectly absent it almost feels like freedom. We don't move for a long time. When we do, it's only to get closer, not further away.

Daybreak creeps through the slats in the metal wall, bluing the whole container in a color that doesn't exist anywhere else in the city. It's too cold to breathe right, too bright for the inside of my skull. Ban is already up, perched by the blast door with her chin on her knees, shotgun in her lap, expression folded into a perfect square of nothing. I killed the lights hours ago, but the neural drive won't let me sleep. The decrypted payload keeps spooling through my overlays, every fresh line of code like a new insult to the dead. I flick the interface back on and stare at the error logs, looking for anything that resembles a way out.

What I get is a flicker in the console—just a blip, half a second, but it jumps out at me because Katherine never left blips. She hated uncertainty. The signature is mine, but I know I didn't put it there. I open the subroutine. The logic loop is like nothing else in the dump: tighter, hungrier, written in a hand I barely recognize. I run it. There's a stutter, then the air three meters in front of me fills with a projection. It's me, but not me: older, or maybe just run through one too many crash cycles. The eyes are wider, the skin sallow and pulled tight over the jaw. I stare at myself, and for a second, neither of us speaks. Then the projection moves, jerky and raw. It looks at me, then at Ban, then back at me.

"If you're seeing this, things have gone sideways," it says, voice flat and almost bored. "Katherine is dead. Dorothy is dead. The project is in the endgame." There's a pause, a little tic at the left eye. I realize it's the exact way mine twitches when I'm about to black out. It smiles, a horror show of teeth and bone. "You're probably asking why you're still alive. Or maybe you're asking why Ban is. Either way, the answer is the same: you're both too stubborn to quit, and you're both too useful to burn yet."

I feel my hands tighten on the edge of the desk. The overlay jumps with my pulse. The projection leans in. "Katherine and Dorothy were always the most expendable. I'm sorry if that hurts, but you already knew. I calculated the odds, and it was clear: their sacrifice bought us exactly what we needed—time, and a window." I want to scream, or smash the console, but the words won't come. The projection paces, just like I do when I'm nervous. "Empathy Gap was never just about stopping the corporations. It was about making sure they never got what they wanted. The only way to win is to go full suicide algorithm. If you're listening, you're the last one standing. Burn the rest. Trust no one, except Ban. She's the only constant between us."

It stops, straightens, and for the first time, it looks tired. "If you get the chance, end it. For all of us. That's what Katherine wanted. That's what Dorothy would've wanted, even if she'd never say it." The projection flickers, pixelates, then turns and faces Ban. She doesn't flinch, just watches, eyes wide open. "Ban," it says. "Take care of Skelm. He's not as tough as he looks."

The image collapses. Silence returns, heavier than before. I stare at the wall. Ban's eyes are still on me. She doesn't ask questions. I sit there, breathing in the tin and cold, and finally say, "It was me. I wrote the protocol. I set the whole thing up to fail."

Ban gets up, comes over, and stands behind me. Her hands land on my shoulders, steady, solid. I want to collapse, but she keeps me upright. "You think I didn't know?"

I shake my head. "I just hoped you'd hate me for it."

She laughs, but it's more like an exhale. "No time for hate. There's only forward."

We pack the kit. Ban does it silent, methodical, her motions surgical as a machine. I pocket the last fragment of Katherine's neural drive, wondering if I'll ever be able to access it again without puking. We step out of the container into the blue-bright dawn. The city is still, for once. Drones are gone. The only sound is the wind scraping the perimeter wire. We walk. In my head, the suicide algorithm is already running. Every step is one closer to zero. But Ban is here, and I know she's got my back. *"Trust Ban completely. She's the only constant."* That's what the ghost said. I do. I have to.

The day stretches ahead, endless, full of things I'll probably never live to see. We don't speak as we move, but the distance between us is gone. If there's a god, he's dead, and all his code is up for grabs. We head for the river, for the next job, for whatever comes after.

Chapter 15

I'm running three overlays at once, which is two more than my neurology should allow, and the only thing keeping me from vomiting on the project table is the sound of Ban's voice, somewhere behind my left shoulder. "Pull it up again, Skelm," she says, her words anchoring me. I fight the vertigo and double-tap the screen, haptic shimmer ghosting under my fingers. The schematic for Project Empathy Gap lurches into 3D: a blue-lit fuck-you to every ethicist who ever died for tenure. Ban leans over my shoulder, breath damp and hot with day-old nicotine. "What am I looking at?"

"Substrate," I mumble, and even I can't tell if I mean the hardware, the neural lattice, or the layer of anxiety coating my skin. My fingers shake as I zoom in. "It's a forced mutation. They're not just running unreadables—they're breeding them. Curating trauma. Recursive stress and incomplete therapy loops."

She huffs, dry. "A whole farm of fucked-up kids."

"Not just kids," I say, but the word dies in my throat. "It's like a petri dish for the next generation of disaster. They seed the genome, bake in the trigger sets, then drop them into major orgs as sleeper agents."

Ban's hand lands on my shoulder, thumb digging a bruise under the scapula. "You always shake like this when you're tired?"

The question cuts through the fog. "Only when I haven't slept since the last time I tried to kill myself," I say, deadpan, but the sarcasm misses its mark. The screens paint the whole container in ghastly blue. Every surface is sticky with condensation, static, and the protein dust that passes for nutrition in the outer districts. The others—Ban, me, and two "contractors" whose only credentials are plausible deniability—are arrayed around the war table like the world's worst poker night. The only thing we're betting is which one of us goes insane first.

The display cycles through incident reports, experimental logs, and executive summaries too redacted for even Moshimoto legal to parse. Ban reads faster than anyone I've met, but she's not reading for meaning. She's scanning for patterns. She sees what I do, but it takes her longer. Maybe that's the difference: I catch the horror up front; she lets it sediment before acknowledging it exists. The silence stretches until one of the contractors—his name is almost certainly not Steven, but that's what his patch says—pushes back from the table, knuckles gone white. "You telling me," he says, voice a step above feral, "that Moshimoto has been running child soldier programs in every major city for ten years, and nobody noticed?"

Ban doesn't flinch. "Nobody with the teeth to bite back, anyway."

Steven's hands clench. "I've got three kids. If that algorithm hits—"

Ban slams her palm on the table, rattling the drives. "It's already out. The only reason your kids aren't on the grid is luck or your own shitty credit score. So unless you want to get sentimental, help Skelm crack the next block."

Steven subsides. The other contractor—pale, silent, probably ex-Corp herself—just stares at the screen, overlays flickering across her irises. Ban turns to me, softer now. "Skelm. Night-shift analyst. Pull up the source code." I want to argue, but my hands are already moving. The night-shift analyst is me, but more raw, less shielded. Daytime I am the suit, the mask, the correct grammar. Night-shift is the monster under the bed.

The code scrolls by. At this depth, it's less like programming and more like pornography for sociopaths: recursive loops, optimization routines, and, layered deep, a line of logic that even Moshimoto AI flagged as "unethical execution risk." My mouth goes dry. "They're not even hiding it. See here—'Therapeutic Abort.' If an unreadable fails to manifest as intended, the system just wipes their personality and recycles the slot for another candidate. No fallback. Just deletion."

Ban closes her eyes, lips pressed flat. "And the ones that work?"

I tap the screen. "They're pushed into critical infrastructure. Medical. Security. Even HR." I stutter, overlays catching on the next slide. "This is the bottleneck: once enough of them populate the network, the system can run a coordinated consciousness attack. Zero out empathy. Turn the whole org into a meat puppet."

Ban says nothing. The container seems to shrink around us, like the walls are digesting the light. The silence gets sliced by the pale woman at the table, her voice thin as printer paper. "I worked for Moshimoto," she says, almost a whisper. "I saw these names. We wrote the audits. Every time someone flagged a concern, it got auto-reassigned to Legal or Wellness. The system reroutes pain like an immune response."

Ban looks at her, and there's something close to pity in her eyes. "That's how they get away with it. You build a culture that can't process grief, and you can do anything."

Steven stares at the woman. "How'd you get out?"

She shrugs. "I didn't. My shift ended, so I left. Nobody came after me. I think they were done with me, or maybe I failed the screening."

"Probably," says Ban, with no heat. "Skelm, give us the vector. How do we crack it?"

I stammer, the night-self and the analyst vying for words. "We need to hit the sync point. If we can spike the network at the handover, it'll break the rollout for a whole region. The A/B test won't complete. They'll have to backtrack, patch the code, and restart the cycle. It buys us time."

Ban does the math in her head, jaw working side to side. "Best-case scenario?"

"Best-case: weeks. Maybe a month if the patch causes unexpected drift."

"And worst-case?"

"Failure. They mass-revert all the backups. The system overwrites us all."

She nods, then stands, stretching the tension out of her back. "Steven, you got the charge packs?"

He grunts assent. "Never leave home without them."

"Pale," says Ban, "can you run point on comms?" The woman nods, her overlays flashing green. Ban comes around the table, standing so close I can smell the sleep deprivation in her pores. "You holding up, Skelm?"

I blink, and my hands are steady now. The night-shift wants to run, wants to kill, wants to fuck or burn or eat the world. But with Ban this close, the analyst wins. "I'm fine," I say. "I'll need two shots of whatever passes for adrenaline around here, but I'll get us through."

She smiles, but it's all teeth. "Let's gear up, then."

The final prep is pure trench. We suit in silence, Ban's fingers tapping out the checklist on each piece of equipment, every motion a sacrament. Steven is meticulous, and Pale is ghostlike but efficient. I wrap the neural mesh around my wrist and feel the overlays pulse, then flatten. Ban checks the charge, then looks at me, her eyes gone soft for a second. "Don't get yourself dead," she says. It's as close to love as I've ever heard from her.

"Only if you do it first," I say. She grins, slaps my arm, and then she's gone. We move out into the rain, the world reduced to wet concrete and flickering light. I lag behind, running every data point again, looking for the hole. There's always a hole. By the time I find it, it's almost too late. I ping Ban over the comm. "The patch. It's not just a rollback. They're seeding a new variable: cluster suicide. If we fuck up, the network triggers a cascade—everyone in the test node zeros themselves out. No survivors, no evidence."

Ban replies, calm. "That change the plan?"

I breathe in the night, feeling the monster inside twitch. "No. But it means we can't stop. Not ever."

She laughs, low and broken. "Didn't think we would."

The lights of the target building blaze up ahead, blue and red and alive. I blink, and for a second, the world splits in two—one path where I run, one where I stay. Ban is already moving, silhouette framed by the neon, perfect and invincible. I choose the path that keeps her in sight, and I don't look back.

Cleopatra shows up at dawn, hair helmet-sleek and dress suit clean except for the blood at her collar. The first thing she does is check the room for gunmen; the second is look directly at me, eyes pulsing with the micro-tremor of a processor in brownout.

Ban's voice cuts the air. "Put your hands up, Cleo." The gun in her fist is old and hungry.

Cleopatra obeys, but her lips curl in disdain. "You always this dramatic, Ban? I'm unarmed." She flashes both hands, fingers long and white, nails painted in conductive black. Steven, behind Ban, cracks his knuckles and grins. Pale just watches, one thumb flicking the edge of a razor. I stay in my chair, overlays at max. Cleopatra's body language is a walking confession—her risk profile off the charts, but she's betting her triple-stack mind will let her talk us down.

"Talk," says Ban, gun steady on target.

Cleopatra exhales, then sits, ignoring the splatter on the seat. "I burned you," she says. "Yesterday. The call that took out Katherine was mine."

Steven explodes out of his chair, fists up. "You mother—"

Ban barks, "Sit," and Steven subsides. I can't tell if I want to kill her or make her explain herself. Both are good options.

Cleopatra lifts her left hand, index pointed at the side of her skull. "They offered me a promotion. Directorship, access to a new life, immunity for my branch. All I had to do was deliver you."

The overlays pulse: probability, certainty, lie, truth, all stacked in a column. "Why are you here?" I ask.

She laughs, not happy. "Because I'm not a sociopath, Skelm. I never thought they'd kill her. I thought it would be a snatch-and-freeze, buy us time. But the minute I handed off the signature, they ghosted her and declared a loyalty audit."

Ban steps closer. Her face is neutral, but the air pressure has doubled. "And now?"

Cleopatra's mouth tightens. "Now I'm off the payroll, flagged as a risk asset, and the only people who might keep me alive are the same ones I betrayed."

Steven's rage is physical. Pale is just a whisper behind Cleopatra, hand on her shoulder. I stand, keeping my hands in plain sight. "You know what you cost us," I say.

She nods, not flinching. "You can kill me. Or you can use me. Moshimoto will roll the patch at midnight tonight, and I still have the keys. They'll burn me as soon as they're done, but until then, I'm live."

Ban considers it, then lowers the gun to Cleopatra's knee. "What are the odds you fuck us again?"

Cleopatra's voice is very small. "Zero. I ran the projections."

I circle the table. "We flip you to the other side, they'll know. How long before they pull the plug?"

"Twenty minutes, tops. But if you want to hit the data center, you need someone who knows the audit trails, the logic gates, the emergency recovery. You need me."

Ban's finger slides off the trigger. She grins, all wolf. "Fine. You're in. One move out of line and Steven here will eat your fingers."

Steven shows teeth. Pale sits Cleopatra down, hands on her shoulders. "We do this fast. You walk us through every access point, every kill switch, every dead man's protocol. You slip once, and you're done."

Cleopatra nods. The risk overlay on her forehead—visible in my vision but not in reality—shifts from orange to yellow. I run through the options. Night-self wants to cut her throat; analyst sees the opportunity. I grab the terminal and toss it to her. "You get us in, you get us the override. We finish the job Katherine started."

Cleopatra catches the slab, hands barely trembling. “You'll need to map the site first. Security is tight since the last breach. I can seed a worm, but you'll need to be at the perimeter for a hard link.”

Ban cocks her head. “Can you do it, or are you just here to confess your sins?”

Cleopatra's mouth quirks. “You know me, Ban. Guilt is inefficient. I'm here to finish the mission, and maybe not die in a basement for once.”

I watch her as she works. The triple-augments in her skull ripple under the skin, shining at her temples and jaw. Her hands dance over the slab, overlays filling the room with code, location tags, and threat vectors. Every few seconds, she glances up, eyes flicking from Ban to me and back. Ban doesn't let up, never moves more than a meter from her target. But her questions shift from threat to tactic. “What's the fallback if they block the root kit?”

Cleopatra's face hardens. “You go manual. Fuse the tower at sub-basement two, and they can't restart the network for twelve hours.”

“Security?”

“Enhanced. Armed. All logged with hard biometrics. You'll need to kill the cameras and the local drone cluster.”

Steven grunts. “That's a lot of work for twenty minutes of lead time.”

Cleopatra shrugs. “If you prefer, we can all die now and save Moshimoto the trouble.”

Ban's smile is pure violence. "Not today."

We take ten to gear up. Steven brings out the last of the heat —the coilgun, two charge packs, a snubbed scatter, and a hand-drill in case we need to get surgical. Pale suits up in a mesh jacket, self-sealing at the wrists. Ban loads the gun, eyes never leaving Cleopatra. I watch Cleopatra code. She's faster than me, but I see the logic gaps she leaves—fail-safes, betrayals. I point at the worm she's embedding. "Don't fuck us, Cleo. I see what you're doing."

She glances up, and for the first time, there's a ghost of the old rivalry in her eyes. "If I wanted you dead, I'd have called in the strike when I walked in. Just keep up, Skelm."

Night-self wants to argue; analyst lets her have it. The plan is pure velocity: Cleopatra walks us to the perimeter, triggers the first stage of the worm, and, when security reroutes, Ban and Steven breach the door, while I hotwire the terminal on site. Pale covers us, suppressing any response team that shows. The only problem is the part where everyone expects us.

Ban is first out the door, moving with that zero-g precision that makes her the only one I'd trust with my life. Steven follows, gun low, eyes hunting shadows. I lag, watching the world shift in the overlays: probability trees branch, half of them ending in us dead. Cleopatra is silent, but she holds the terminal to her chest like it's the last organ she owns. She leads, guiding us through dead alleys, across old train tracks, and under the frozen eyes of corporate cam clusters. Each block, she reroutes a sensor, or buries a ping in the system, moving us ahead of the rolling blackouts that serve as Moshimoto's first line of defense. It works for three blocks, then the overlays light up: DRONE, EAST: TWENTY SECONDS.

"Contact," I whisper.

Ban doesn't speed up. "Copy. Cleo, you got a toy for this?"

Cleopatra ducks into a culvert, pulls a strip of conductive tape from her sleeve, and slaps it to the bottom of a handrail. She runs a pulse through her finger, and the tape goes live, sending a local blackout up and down the rail. The drone hits the dead zone, stutters, then slams into the side of the culvert and explodes in a burst of glass and composite. Steven whoops, but Ban shushes him. We go on, moving faster.

At the edge of the district, Cleopatra stops. She's sweating now, suit damp at the collar. "You're sure about this?" I ask.

She looks at me, and in her eyes is the terror that only comes from a mind that's seen the future. "It's our only shot, Skelm."

Ban nods. "Let's make it count."

We'd been moving since 04:00, already three hours behind. The last sprint is blur and blood. We breach the perimeter at 07:07:08, Cleopatra's worm already ghosting the outer cameras. Ban and Steven storm the door—three guards; one live, two drones. Ban drops the human with a baton to the throat, and Steven takes the drones with his scattergun, splintering the hall in flecks of steel and polymer. I hit the terminal, plugging in. The overlays pulse as the system resists the worm—Moshimoto AI counter-hacks with the desperation of an animal in the trap.

Cleopatra stands behind me, feeding me the bypass codes in rapid bursts. Pale covers the rear, the low thump of her suppressed rounds echoing up the stairwell. I'm losing the fight. The countermeasure is learning, closing off my paths. "Cleo!" I yell. "I need more bandwidth."

She drops to her knees next to me, jacks a cable from her skull into the port, and slams her forehead to the terminal. The effect is instant. Her overlays strobe, light leaks from her eyes, but the system slows, then stutters. Ban pulls me back from the terminal as the charge packs Steven laid go off below, frying the sub-basement hardware. For a second, the building is a beacon, every light in the district blinking in sequence. Then, blackout.

Cleopatra jerks back, blood running from her nose and ears. She sways, then collapses. I catch her and ease her to the floor. She's still breathing. Ban hovers, pistol in one hand, the other steadying her. "Did it work?" Ban asks.

The overlays clear, and for the first time in hours, the world is quiet. I nod. "We killed the patch. For now."

Steven grins. Pale wipes the blood off her sleeve. Ban crouches and checks Cleopatra's pulse. "Still in the game?" she asks.

Cleopatra's eyes flutter open. "How long?"

I run the numbers, then smile, tired. "You bought us a week."

Ban laughs, sharp and bright. "A fucking eternity."

We help Cleopatra to her feet. Outside, the city flickers, unsure if it should fear us or mourn itself. I choose fear. It's the only edge we have left.

• • •

The prep is a war of seconds. The night before, we poison every comm channel with Cleopatra's ghost—her voice, her face, the digital perfume of her betrayal. By morning, the Moshimoto system is eating itself, sniffing after false signals in every block of the city. Ban runs the drills like a drill sergeant, except she's smarter and better-looking and occasionally grinds her heel into my foot when I screw up the breach sequence. She checks every weapon twice, then hands me the coilgun. "Don't aim unless you want to kill," she says, pushing the cold barrel to my sternum, then up to my mouth, then away. "Your grip changes when you slip," she adds, adjusting my hold with a firm jerk that leaves a bruise.

Steven and Pale are prepping gear in the background. Steven has taken to calling Pale "Whiteout," which is technically racist, but mostly just a running joke now that the world is ending. Ban and I run a two-man breach, her fingers digging into my collar as we practice the entry. "You're half a second slow," she says, "but if you weren't, I'd worry you'd gotten cocky."

I grin, blood leaking from a split lip, and she kisses me in the break, all tongue and teeth. "You're going to get us killed," I mutter, but she just winks.

"Worth it," she says. We study the schematics together, overlays tracing every pipe and corridor. Cleopatra stands behind us, arms folded, watching the way Ban's hands linger on my skin. She never comments, but I see her eyes go tight every time Ban says my name with too much affection. "You ready to burn your old office?" Ban asks her.

Cleopatra shrugs. "That building deserves worse than what you're going to do."

Ban nods. "Then let's get it done."

The window is twelve minutes, max. Cleopatra has set up a ping-pong worm that will loop security into three blocks north. Pale and Steven will cover our exit on the east side, while Ban and I go in through the sub-basement and take the core from below.

The night before, Ban and I can't sleep. She sits on the floor of the safehouse, gun in her lap, peeling the skin off an orange and tossing the rinds into the drain. I lie next to her, overlays flickering with every bad prediction my brain can generate. "You know you're fucked in the head," she says, tossing a rind at me.

I catch it. "I learned from the best."

She grins, but it's sad this time. "You want to talk about it?"

"No," I say, and then, "Yes."

We don't talk, but the silence is the kind where everything matters.

An hour before the run, I am all animal. My hands can't stop shaking, and my jaw's locked tight enough to snap bone. Ban pins me to the wall and says, "Let the analyst drive. You go feral too soon, we're both dead." She tastes like gun oil and last night's breath, and her tongue presses between my teeth like she's trying to steal the words out of my mouth. "You good?" she asks when she's done. I nod. "Tell me you'll stay on script." I try to lie, but Ban sees through me. She cocks her head. "I'll make it an order if I have to."

I grin. "You always did like playing officer."

She slaps my cheek, hard enough to leave a mark. "Don't die before I say you can."

The four of us meet on the roof above the Moshimoto block, rain sheeting down the way it always does right before sunrise. The city below is chaos—alarms, lockdowns, rolling blackouts as Cleopatra's virus chews the infrastructure. Pale is on the comm, and Steven's checking charge on the scatter. Ban tightens my harness, double-knots the strap, and whispers, "If you have to choose, you pick the data. Not me." I want to say fuck that, but her hand is already at my throat, squeezing until the stars go white at the edges of my vision. Then she lets go, shoves the pistol into my hand, and says, "Go."

We rappel down, Ban first, me a meter behind. Every floor, my overlays glitch with new risks: patrol here, bot there, heat spike in the lobby. Ban slides past them like a shadow; I follow, brain running two sets of threats at once. By the time we hit the sub-basement, the only sounds are our own breath and the fizz of distant electrics. Cleopatra's worm is eating the perimeter, but we have to move fast. Ban signals, I jam the drill into the panel, and the lock blows with a hiss.

The data center is all white plastic and blue LED, sterile as a brain scan. Ban moves to cover, coilgun up, while I hit the console and start the hack. My night-self is screaming—every instinct to smash, kill, burn—but I keep my fingers on the keys, hands steady as they ever get. Cleopatra's codes work. I'm in the core in under ninety seconds, extracting every byte they thought they could hide. Ban keeps watch, eyes on the door.

When the transfer is done, I slap the bug onto the system, burning out the last trace of our presence. We exit the way we came, Ban pushing me so hard I nearly fall, both of us laughing even as the alarms finally catch up. Steven and Pale meet us on the east side, the van rolling in silent. Ban yanks me into the back and kisses me with enough violence to draw blood. "We did it," she says, but I know it's never that easy. The data on my drive feels heavy. Like it knows something I don't. But for now, we live. For now, that's enough.

The city goes on autopilot in the rain. We melt into the crowd, hoods up, bodies hunched, overlays running black as we cross the arterial to the Moshimoto block. The building looks like every other: four stories, windows slit for privacy, facade scrubbed clean by decades of acid drizzle and social engineering. Inside, the lighting is a scream. Blue-white LEDs flatten every surface, erasing every shadow. It smells like ozone and fresh vacuum. The night shift at the lobby desk doesn't look up when Ban and I pass, but I see his hand hover under the counter, thumb ready to hit the silent alarm.

Ban gets there first. She leans over the desk and says something too low to catch. He blinks, starts to reply, and Ban jams a neural suppressor under his jaw. The pulse is silent, but the effect is instant: his eyes glaze, body limp. We slip through the turnstile, and the glass-walled corridor closes in. Every step is mapped, every camera painted on my overlay in pulsing red.

Cleopatra's worm is chewing ahead of us, opening the doors before we even reach them. Ban never breaks stride. She checks corners by muscle memory, body angled to catch the next threat. I follow, my own muscles vibrating with the anticipation of violence.

We hit the first checkpoint: two guards in gray suits, both running combat augments under their skin. Ban gestures, and I take the one on the right. He barely registers the movement before my fist catches him in the neck, dropping him to the tile. The second tries for his sidearm, but Ban closes and cracks his ribs with the butt of her coilgun, then spins him into the wall. She looks at me, eyes wide, grin wider. "You always had a thing for uniforms," she says, voice a rough whisper.

I wipe my hands clean on the dead man's jacket. "I like what's underneath better."

We move on. The next floor is quieter, but the silence is wrong. Every footstep echoes. The overlays spike—Pale and Steven on the comm, covering the exits, but it's just us in the halls now. At the server room, Ban pauses, checks the sightlines, then signals me forward. The door is locked, but Cleopatra's code slides us in. Inside, it's ice cold and full of hum. Racks of data, all alive, all lit in the same inhuman blue. There's one more guard at the desk, this one smarter than the last. He sees us, recognizes the threat, and goes for the panic button.

I cross the distance in two strides. My hand closes over his, slams it to the desk, then shatters his elbow with my other fist. He screams, but Ban's behind him, hand over his mouth, eyes locked on mine. I want to kill him. I want to rip his skull apart and see if the hardware inside is better than mine. Ban sees it.

She mouths, "No," and shakes her head. I let go, shoving the man to the floor. Ban steps in and pushes me back. "Stay on target," she says, and I hate her for being right.

The air in the server room is so clean it stings. My overlays spike memory—flashes of old drills, old labs, the smell of burned copper and loss. I can see myself at ten, twelve, sixteen, alone in rooms just like this, learning how to survive by killing my own hope. Ban pulls me to the console. "Plug in. Get the drive."

My hands move. The analyst side of me surfaces, typing, decoding, and layering Cleopatra's access over my own raw instinct. The night-self simmers, wanting blood, but the data matters more. Ban keeps her hand on my shoulder, fingers squeezing each time I hesitate. Each time, I remember why I'm here. I finish the transfer, pull the drive, and slide it into the inner pocket of my jacket. Ban says, "One more stop," and we move out.

The last stretch is a gauntlet; the alarms are starting to notice the anomaly, and every camera in the building is pointed our way. Ban leads us down a maintenance stairwell, skipping the cameras with backtracking, spirals, and the kind of muscle logic that only she knows how to teach. We hit the basement. Cleopatra's worm buys us a thirty-second window before the failsafe locks down. Ban pops the door with a magnet key, and we're in the core vault.

The room is alive with hum, heat, and the promise of everything the world hates about us. Ban closes the door behind us and locks it with a piece of metal so old it probably remembers the last war. She leans back, winded. So am I. We stare at each other, breathing the same recycled air. "This is it," Ban says. I nod. My mind is still splitting, but her hand on my shoulder is the only thing that holds it together. The next move is everything. And for once, I'm sure I want to make it.

The core vault is a migraine in four dimensions. The servers are stacked to the ceiling, each humming with the kind of neural energy that makes your skin tingle and your teeth ache. Ban and I move together, flashlights off, navigating by the static charge in the air. I find the main panel, strip the case with a flick, and jack in the physical drive. For a second, nothing—just the thrum of data against the backs of my eyes. Then the world floods open.

First comes the voice. It's me, but not me—a version running at twice speed, spitting code and paranoia through a thousand mirrored loops. Next, the pain: a line of heat running from my jaw to the back of my head, down the spinal column, and out through my fingers. My hands go numb, then too sharp, then numb again. "Ban," I say, but it comes out as a wet hiss.

She's next to me instantly, steadying the drive in my hand, her own hand clamped on my shoulder. "Stay with me, Skelm," she says. "We don't get to quit now."

The overlays melt. I'm inside the network. Every node, every packet, every memory harvested by Moshimoto is here, stacked in blocks like tombstones. The Empathy Gap project is not a test; it's the operating system. Unreadables are the user interface. I see them: millions of ghost files, each a version of someone like me, like Ban, like Katherine and

Dorothy. Every one of us a redundancy, a backup, a thing to be used and burned as needed.

Ban's hand grounds me. I try to speak, but my mouth is full of numbers. She leans in and whispers in my ear, "Breathe, analyst. Filter the signal."

I do, and the noise contracts. I start to see the shape of the thing. Moshimoto seeded unreadables in every major corp, every org, every labor force. Each one is tuned to fail in a precise way—empathy, impulse control, addiction, loyalty. The failures are contagious, rolling out as social policy or "efficiency upgrades" that quietly erase whole classes of people. The survivors aren't people at all. They're compliance bots in meat suits, tuned to keep the machine running until there's no one left who remembers what a person is. I pull back from the drive, shoving myself clear. Blood runs from my nose, soaking the collar of my shirt. Ban grabs my jaw and turns my face to hers. "You back?"

I nod, shivering. "It's everywhere," I say. "Not just Moshimoto. Every org, every agency. All of them."

She nods, like she's known all along. "Can you stop it?"

I look at my hands. "No. But I can fuck it up."

Ban grins. "That's my analyst." She slaps a med patch on my neck. The pain fades, replaced by a slow, cold focus. We move through the racks, Ban pulling drives, me logging the sequence. Each step is a war with the system; every layer of security fights back, and each fight makes the headache worse. At the end, we have six drives, each one a black box of crimes. Ban pockets four and hands me two. "You make it out, you run with these. Drop point's the old rail yard. Someone will meet you."

I take them, but my hands won't stop shaking. "Why only two for me?" I ask.

She smiles, tired. "You're still a soft touch, Skelm. They'll go after you first. It's a compliment."

We move to the exit. The security failsafe is already closing in: lockdown, pulse cannons, a micro army of enforcers ready to eat us alive. We move fast and silent through the dark. The first enforcer is at the stairwell. Ban disables him with a knee to the groin, then a twist of his head that makes me flinch. I don't have time to be shocked. I take the next two, coilgun up, no warning. The first drops. The second gets off a shot that grazes Ban's thigh. She swears, rips open her pants, and presses a palm to the wound. "Not bad," she says. "You've gotten meaner."

"You bring it out in me."

We reach the surface. The rain is harder, and the city is bright with the lights of war. We run, as always. Behind us, the building alarms finally catch up, howling into the wet night. We make it to the van. Steven is at the wheel and Pale is in the passenger seat, both looking more dead than alive. Ban piles in and slams the door. Steven looks back. "Did we get it?"

Ban holds up the drives. "Enough."

I lean back, close my eyes, and let the hum of the city drown out everything else. For a moment, there is peace. But then my head splits again, and I know it's only beginning.

. . .

The safehouse is a ruin by the time we reach it—walls scorched, one window blown out. Cleopatra waits, sitting on the cot, eyes blacked out by stress and whatever cheap fix she found to patch her brain. "You did it," she says, not rising.

Ban throws the drives on the table. "Yeah. But now the real work starts."

Steven collapses in a chair, Pale sits next to Cleopatra, and Ban and I stand, backs against the wall. No one talks. I review the drive data. Every file, every record, is a confession of genocide in slow motion. Ban touches my face, tracing the dried blood on my cheek. "You okay?"

"No," I say, but then I grab her hand and squeeze. "You're the only thing that feels real."

She laughs, hoarse. "We're not real, Skelm. We're just what's left."

I want to tell her that's enough, but my voice is gone. We stand there, hands locked, the world dying outside. There's nothing left to do but get ready for the next run. It will be worse. But that's the job. We never stop.

We're ghosts on the run. The city's howl is half siren, half static, and the rain wipes clean every trace of us as we scatter from the Moshimoto building. The drives in my pocket feel like the only real thing left. Ban's fingers leave bruises on my arm, dragging me through crowds and alleys, her body a shield against the sky's indifferent electricity. We regroup at the fallback—the abandoned laundry two blocks down, still stinking of solvent and failure. Steven is already there, gun out, hands trembling in the raw aftermath. Pale leans against a dryer, breathing in the ozone and letting her eyes adjust to a world with fewer rules. Ban slams the door, checks the perimeter, then drops to her knees next to me. “Status?” she says, voice all muscle.

I spit blood into the basin and shake my head. “I’ve had worse,” I lie.

She slaps a patch on my neck, and the world swims for a second. “Good. Because we’re not done.”

Steven stares at the drives on the table, then at Ban. “You want to tell us what we just did?”

Ban glances at me, then back to Steven. “We bought time,” she says. “That’s always the job. But this”—she gestures to the drives—“this is more.”

Pale steps forward, her voice soft as lint. “He’s the only one who can read it,” she says, nodding at me. “The system’s built to crash normal brains.”

Ban grins. “Lucky for us, Skelm’s not normal.”

She hands me the first drive, and I slot it into the old tablet. The data hits me like a sucker punch—memory, pain, the taste of iron at the back of my throat. For a second, I see nothing but the recursive pattern of loss, the fractal edge of every soul that’s ever been burned out for corporate gain. But then I start to see the gaps. “Daytime Skelm” can map the networks, run the numbers, and predict the next strike. “Night-shift Skelm” reads the ghosts, the bad code, the intention behind the design. Together, we pull out the next steps. I spin the drive, scroll through the logs, and let my other self talk. "They're not just running backups," I say. "They're running a full-scale social replacement. If they finish, nobody left in the city will ever want to rebel again."

Ban doesn't blink. "Then we fuck up their schedule."

Steven shoves a hand through his hair. "You two are insane. They'll kill us before we get close."

Ban's laugh is raw. "They tried already. Didn't stick."

Pale smiles, faint, then looks at me. "What's next?"

I let the answer form, piece by piece. "They'll roll the next patch tonight. If it works, every union, every underground, every resistance cell flips. We have to hit the root before then."

Steven groans. "You know how much security is on the root node?"

Ban stands and cracks her knuckles. "We're not sneaking in this time. We go loud."

Pale nods. "I'll prep the distraction."

Ban points at me. "You build the virus. You're the only one who can."

My hands shake, but not from fear. I want to tell Ban she's crazy, but it wouldn't matter. She's the vector, the bullet, and I'm just the payload. We hole up for a few hours. I code, Ban runs security, and Pale and Steven split the labor of prepping for the next run. The rain outside is a lullaby for disaster. When I'm done, I find Ban by the window, gun across her lap, eyes fixed on the neon horizon. I sit next to her. For a while, neither of us speaks. “You ever think we could win?” I ask.

She smirks. “We’re winning now. Every day we don’t die is a win.”

I put my hand over hers. She doesn’t pull away. “I like the world better with you in it,” I say, and for once, it doesn’t hurt.

She turns, lips at my ear. “You’re a sap, Skelm.”

“Maybe. But I’m your sap.”

She laughs, soft and honest.

When the time comes, we move. Pale and Steven go first, setting off a block-wide blackout with a homemade EMP rig. The whole city flickers, and every security camera within a mile dies in the dark. Ban and I slip into the target building, silent and fast. The last line of defense is six guards, all upgraded, all ready for war. Ban takes the first three, then shoves me forward. “You do your thing,” she says. “I’ll keep them off you.”

I sprint to the mainframe, plug in the drive, and start the virus. The code is poetry: a pure, elegant fuck-you to every exec who ever thought they could erase a human soul. As the virus runs, I see the traces of every dead friend, every burned ghost. I see Dorothy; I see Katherine; I see a thousand Skelms I could have been. The virus blooms. The Empathy Gap goes critical. Every screen in the building flashes red. Then the city lights up, block by block, as the whole system chokes on the feedback.

Ban grabs my hand, and we run. We don't stop until we're blocks away, soaked and alive. We meet Pale and Steven at the rendezvous. They're bruised and limping, but smiling. Ban turns to me, her smile so wide it hurts. "You did it," she says.

"*We* did it," I say back.

She punches my arm hard enough to sting. "Don't get soft now, analyst."

I grin. And for the first time since I can remember, I want to see what happens next.

The four of us vanish into the night. There's always another war. But for a second, the rain feels clean. We move forward, together. And we don't look back.

Chapter 16

The new city comes at you sideways. Everything was built to be seen through three sets of overlays, every inch weaponized for maximum cognitive distraction. I let Ban lead me into the belly of the Moshimoto High-Tier Consciousness Bazaar, her hand a clamp on my shoulder, pulse sync'd to my own. Maybe on purpose, maybe just habit. In this place, you never know the difference.

The mall is not a mall anymore. It's a self-replicating urban ulcer, three stories of open atrium crowded with pop-up shops, wetware brokers, and what passes for food in a world where flavor is a security vulnerability. The air is a closed system, constantly rebreathing itself, which means the stench of ozone and burned plastic gets thicker every hour. Ceiling LEDs keep failing, so the dark spaces are patched with illegal neon, every sign brighter than the one before, as if color alone can erase the rot.

"Don't get sentimental, Skelm," Ban says, jaw tight as she shoulder-checks a handler in a blazer made of recycled memory-tape. “This was always a meat market, even before the flesh got optional.”

The handler gives us the corporate once-over, then spits a slur from the old language, the one Ban loves. Ban fires back with a phrase I haven’t heard since bootcamp, the rhythm jagged enough to make the handler wince. He moves on, muttering. Ban grins and tightens her grip on me. “Pre-digital. Throws them off,” she whispers, lips barely moving. Her eyes never stop scanning—left, right, up, down, then a ghost-cast to my own field of view. She knows how to play the crowd, and she knows how to play me. “You see the uplink?”

I don’t answer. I’m busy mapping the local security mesh. My overlays lag a half-step behind the live feeds, painting hazard zones in red and corridor dead ends in a lazy yellow. Every third camera is off; every fourth is painted with malware. The real threat is the handlers—real, freelance, or rogue corporate; you can’t tell from a glance, but you can always tell by their eyes. In this place, nobody’s high, but everyone’s jacked.

At the atrium edge, we pass a vendor hawking “Premium Analog Patterns—Guaranteed Untouched.” The booth is lined with jars of wetware, brains suspended in low blue light, each one a minor celebrity in the underworld of stolen consciousness. The jars are transparent for a reason: show the product, show it’s alive. Show you’re not fucking around. A kid with synth tattoos loads one onto a tray, checks the neural integrity, then seals it in a case so clean you can see the tremor in his hands. Ban leans in, her face inches from the jar, and gives the kid a stare that says: *you even think about pocketing a tip, I’ll rewrite your DNA to read “FRAUD” in Latin.*

The kid blinks, then winks. “You want the discount, or the full pleasure model?”

“Don’t play with your food,” Ban says, dragging me onward.

Every stall has its flavor of horror: live-mind auctions, memory flashbacks played on infinite loop, “cosmetic” surgeries that can make you anyone for a price. The worst are the open-air demo pits, where desperate runners hook themselves to black-market neural loops and let the crowd watch them burn out, synapse by synapse, for a hundred credits a minute. It’s part spectacle, part lesson: This is what happens if you cross the wrong client.

Ban walks like she’s above it, like nothing here can touch her. I’m less sure. The overlays glitch at random, sometimes resolving into ancient signage, sometimes painting the world in hard blue lines that make my head ache. My threat grid ticks upward with every step. Ban never slows, but I can see the micro-muscle tension in her neck.

We pass a stall where an auctioneer, voice hammered flat by years of smoke and threat, is running a live consciousness demo. The “subject” is a middle-aged office type, dressed in the default business casual, mouth forced open by a plex bracket. The auctioneer jacks a line into the base of the guy’s skull, then flicks a switch. The man’s left hand spasms in a perfect circle, then stops, then twitches again.

“Pattern stable, but entropy point at two minutes,” the auctioneer says. “Look at that response! Pure analog, untouched by digital aug! Bidding opens at—” The numbers rise in a cloud of AR confetti. The crowd is all teeth and eyes.

Ban glances at me, then at the subject. For a second, her hand slackens. I think of saying something, but my mouth won't open. Instead, she yanks me onward. "See the exits?" she says, low.

"Three ground, one up, two down. One hidden. Security layer is thin, but there's a deniable squad covering each vector."

She grins. "You always were a paranoid bastard."

She stops at a mezzanine platform and points with her chin at a booth labeled "Unfiltered Consciousness Streams." Inside, two handlers in matching jackets play chess over a live neural link, every move echoed in the twitch of the other's face. Above them, the wall cycles through faces—some famous, some just beautiful—each accompanied by a price tag and a description of what you'll feel if you buy a slot. Ban eyes the nearest handler. "That's the rival," she says. "Came in second at the Shanghai show, but never let go of the grudge."

The handler sees us and flashes a wide, dead smile. "Ban! You still recruiting trash, or just working out your own issues in public?" The handler's accent is Moshimoto upper-tier: pure, flat, designed for international. She's got a tattoo on her throat, running black up into her jawline.

Ban shrugs. "I go where the product is."

The handler looks me over. "He doesn't look like much. You sure he'll hold up?"

Ban's smile is acid. "That's what they all say. Then they see him in action."

She grips my shoulder and pulls me close enough that my nose almost touches her hair. The smell is sweat, gun oil, and something floral underneath. She whispers so soft it barely vibrates the air. “Remember,” she says, “you’re merchandise, not an analyst. Keep your patterns unstable but enticing. Anyone checks your signature, you let it ride wild, then crash it just before they get a trace. Don’t overthink it. You’re here to make them hungry, not to feed yourself.” The world swims. I nod once and let my jaw go slack. Ban turns back to the handler. “Tell your boss he’s obsolete. This one’s fresh off the chain. No reruns.”

The handler laughs, hollow. “We’ll see. I’ll be watching the auction. Maybe I’ll even put in a bid.”

Ban leans in, her lips inches from my ear. “Only if you want a virus that’ll eat your grandmother in her sleep,” she says, eyes locked on the rival. The handler laughs again, but this time it sounds more nervous.

We move deeper into the bazaar, past the black-market psych wards and the “fixers” running chop shops for defective consciousness. A man with half a face is hawking “full-sensory orgy packs,” but his overlays are glitched to show him as a twenty-year-old gymnast. Ban waves him off with a hand motion so ancient only I recognize it: “Fuck off or get fucked.” He gets the message, winks, then vanishes into the press of bodies.

Up ahead, a stage is being prepped for the night’s main event. Ban finds us a spot near the back, behind a broken rail and a cluster of discarded food containers. She crouches, pulls me down with her, and scans the perimeter. “You see it yet?” she asks.

I check the overlays. "Yeah. The security layer here is shit. But the surveillance is all live—nothing stored. They don't want a record, which means they're expecting a raid."

Ban grins. "Good. Chaos is cover. When it goes off, we get out or we don't." She looks at me, and for the first time in months, I see the old Ban: the one who taught me how to run from a room without ever standing up, the one who made me memorize every escape route before I could eat, the one who kissed me once and never talked about it again. She puts a hand on my cheek, brief as a heartbeat, then lets it drop. "Sorry for dragging you back into this," she says. "I know what it does to your head."

I laugh. "This is the only place my head makes sense."

She nods, then focuses on the stage. The first auctioneer of the night is setting up, voice already slicing the air with the kind of confidence that can only come from surviving several assassination attempts. I watch Ban's face as the auctioneer runs through the opening acts—secondhand patterns, defective joy bundles, a knockoff of a famous CEO's libido circuit. The crowd is loud, and every sale is punctuated by a blast of digitized applause.

The night stretches. Ban relaxes, her hand dropping from my shoulder to my thigh. I let my body go limp, tuning my own overlays to show only the critical. At the break, Ban lights a synthetic cigarette. The smoke is cold and bitter, hanging low in the stagnant air. She passes it to me. Our fingers touch, and I feel the surge of old code run through my arm. I exhale, the taste familiar. She leans in, close enough that only I can hear. "You see anyone from the old company?"

I scan, then nod. “Two. One on the mezzanine, watching for trouble. One at the west exit, not bothering to blend. Both running low-grade augments.”

She grins, teeth showing. “Means they’re scared.”

“Means they’re desperate.”

“Even better.”

We sit in silence, trading the cigarette, each of us lost in our own memory. Around us, the bazaar hums, living on the edge of chaos. Overhead, a drone whirrs, then fizzles, then falls dead to the floor. The crowd laughs. Ban’s eyes shine in the blue, and for a second, I forget what world I’m in. She leans in, lips at my ear. “Just remember: if they get close, you break character. You’re worth nothing dead, but you’re worth less if they see through the act.”

I nod. My head is already filling with scripts, worst-case scenarios, failure trees. I let the night-shift Skelm run loose, the part of me who’s more algorithm than flesh, more animal than man. The crowd, the noise, the risk—all of it fades until the only thing left is Ban’s hand, tight on my leg. On stage, the auctioneer is ramping up for the main event. The handler from earlier is already at the front, eyes locked on Ban. They trade insults, quiet and professional, until the moment comes.

Ban stands, pulling me up with her. The whole world sharpens, every line in focus. I can feel the handler’s gaze, the attention of every rival in the room. Ban leans her forehead to mine, voice low. “Ready to be sold, analog boy?” She smiles, and for a moment, I almost believe it’s real. Then she pushes me toward the stage, and the show begins.

• • •

I spend the next two hours horizontal, body spread on a cold slab of steel, cables running from my temple to a homebrew neural interface that Ban jacked from an old security checkpoint and rebuilt out of malice and spite. The stall is small but perfectly positioned—line of sight to every exit, only one way in. Ban paces behind the console, hands a blur over the patchboard, every gesture calculated to look both careless and expert.

The space around me stinks of disinfectant and stale panic. Above, an AR menu spins in three languages, advertising my mind as "Uncut, Untouched, and Unfathomably Rare." A couple of kids hover near the rail, taking video for their next trauma cycle, but they're not the real threat. Ban checks the interface, then looks down at me. "Ready?" she asks, but it's not a question. She twists the dial, and the world dials up with it—every light too bright, every sound doubled in the bone. I nod, then let my eyes roll back, half performance, half necessity. I feel her presence at my side, a hand settling on my chest like a nurse about to declare time of death. She checks the line, then leans in close. "Showtime, Skelm," she whispers.

The first test buyers are easy. Hobbyists, small-time brokers looking for a patch to their own lineages. One runs a basic pattern test—connects, samples my dreamspace, then bounces with a scowl. Too much noise, probably. Another tries to probe my memories for famous faces, or at least high-value trauma. I let them see just enough—the night I lost my arm, the time I drowned in a kiddie pool full of real saltwater, the morning after I set fire to my own apartment just to kill a listening bug. Then I lock down and ghost them.

Ban handles the sales pitch. She ramps up her accent, leans into the old language, and tells jokes about the pre-digital age that nobody but the most pathetic nostalgia-fetishists could possibly get. She's a blur of smiles and perfectly measured contempt. Between buyers, Ban tweaks the interface, "upgrading" me in ways that mostly just invert the signal or add new filters. The real work is in the presentation—she wants them to see me as both flawless and on the verge of collapse. If you don't look breakable, you don't look real. If you look too broken, you're not worth the effort.

The third hour is the bad one. The rival handler from the "Unfiltered" stall sweeps in, eyes glassed out with overlays, jaw moving like she's grinding down old anger into diamond. She carries a travel-sized terminal in one hand, and a confidence that fills the booth before her body does. Ban meets her with a half-smile and a knife's edge of courtesy. "Can I help you, 'Svetlana?'" The name is mockery; the handler's nametag is blank.

"Just browsing," she says, voice clipped and tuned to corporate standard. She circles the table, eyes on me, then on the patchwork of wire and bone running down my jaw. "You running him pure? Or is there a backup somewhere in the cloud?"

Ban's smile widens. "You think I'd trust a cloud after what happened in Tianjin?"

The handler sets her terminal on the slab, inches from my hand. "Then you're a braver woman than me." She runs a scanner over my neural port, then frowns. "No digital signature. No synthetic organelles. How the fuck are you keeping him stable?"

I let my body twitch, just a fraction, like a glitch in a system under stress. She notices. Her eyes narrow. Ban doesn't miss a beat. "He's all analog, baby. No training wheels. You'd be surprised what raw meat can do if you keep it hungry."

The handler probes the edge of my consciousness with her scanner. I feel the itch as she tries to sync with my core and push past the defenses Ban and I rehearsed for hours. My overlays freeze, then stutter; the world flickers. The night-self, the Skelm who ran the tunnels, starts to surface, code and flesh bleeding together. I want to scream, or bite, or break her fucking wrist. Ban must sense it. She jabs a finger into the interface, sending a shock through the system that snaps me back into the pain. I gasp, as rehearsed, then let my eyes flutter.

The handler looks impressed, but she hides it. "You sure he'll last the cycle? Looks like he's about to seize."

Ban shrugs, casual. "It's the new vintage. You want smooth, you buy a CEO knockoff. You want grit, you come to me."

The handler gives a slow, evil smile. "Yeah, but what's the warranty? If he burns out after the first orgy, my client's going to want a refund."

Ban's hand hovers over her jacket pocket. I know there's a stunner or worse in there. "He's yours to break, Svet. But if you hurt him bad enough, he'll haunt your dreams for a decade."

The handler leans in, whispering just loud enough for me to hear. "I'll be back at auction. You'd better hope he doesn't glitch out before then."

She leaves a business card—holographic, glinting red in the bad light—then moves on, heels clicking like gunshots. Ban waits until she's clear, then kneels at my side. Her hand is on my forehead, gentler than I expect. "You good?" I nod, but the overlays are still sparking. "Keep it together," she whispers. "Just a few more hours."

I stare up at the cracked ceiling, counting the stains and the intervals between Ban's careful checks. It's a pattern, a rhythm. If you let yourself follow it, you can almost believe you're somewhere else.

Next buyer is a mid-grade corporate fixer, dressed to look like a civilian but with the dull eyes of a man who's never wanted for anything. He haggles with Ban for twenty minutes, each time pushing her to lower the price, each time getting an offer that's higher than the one before. Ban lets him believe he's winning, but by the end, the number on the terminal is double the starting bid. He leaves with a handshake, face full of hate and hunger.

After he's gone, Ban lets me up, lets me stretch my arms and reset the pain. She hands me a bottle of water, and I drink it in silence. "You did good," she says, voice soft.

"You're a better liar than I'll ever be," I say. She smiles, then wipes the sweat from my face.

We go again, hour after hour, until the booth lights up with the signal: *Main event in ten.* Ban cleans the interface, wipes down the slab, and sets the overlays to a low, hungry blue. She stands behind me, hands on my shoulders. "Remember," she says, "if they see you as human, they'll never pay the full price."

I nod. But somewhere under the surface, I feel the night-self smile.

We hide behind the privacy screen, which is just an old advertising banner strung up with zip ties and bad intentions. The world outside is a pulse of voices and light, but in here, it's dark enough to almost pretend the bazaar is just another late-night job, not the edge of everything we've ever cared about. Ban sits on a packing crate, boots planted wide, hands shaking as she fishes out a pack of synthetic cigarettes from her jacket. She lights one with the back of a spark chip, then sucks the vapor down, exhaling slow through her nose. The smoke comes out in slow blue curls, like she's writing something on the air and letting it fade.

She offers the cig to me, and our fingers touch at the exchange, her thumb tracing the inside of my wrist. It's too long, but neither of us lets go. The tobacco is pure simulation, no nicotine, no risk, but it burns with a hit that makes my head spin. I pass it back. Ban inhales, then grins. "Best thing about these? Never stains your teeth." She bares her own, just to show. I wipe the sweat from my forehead, but Ban beats me to it, palm rough and cold against my skin. "You're holding together better than last time," she says. The compliment lands crooked, and I see her cringe before she adds, "I mean, better than most merchandise I've handled."

The word stings, but only a little. I know the script. Still, I let the night-self flicker, let my body react. My left hand twitches, the memory of a fight loop playing out in micro-movements. Ban watches, then presses her hand down over mine, stilling it. "You ever wish you could just let go?" I ask, voice thin.

She doesn't look at me. "I tried once. Didn't stick."

The cigarette burns down to the filter. She stubs it on the crate, then flicks it into the dark. We listen to the muffled noise of the bazaar—the slap of shoes on tile, the distant auctioneer hyping up the next big thing, a child screaming then laughing as some handler does a demo with a brain in a jar. "I fucked this up, didn't I?" I ask.

Ban's head snaps up. "No. We're here, aren't we?" She rubs her thumb over my hand, as if to reassure herself more than me. "Besides, we're the only ones who could pull this off. You know that." I nod, but inside, the overlays show nothing but failure trees and disaster loops. There's a silence, then Ban says, "You remember the river job?" She laughs low. "I thought we were dead, but you rigged that whole fire escape with nothing but two wires and a bottle of shitty cologne."

I shrug. "You did all the work."

She shakes her head. "Nah. You just don't remember how much of you I pulled out of the water after."

I let the silence stretch. My left hand calms, but my right stays frozen, fingers curled around the edge of the crate. The air thickens with announcement static. A synthesized voice booms over the bazaar: "Final main event begins in five minutes. All high-value assets to display. Auctioneers, prepare your lots."

Ban grinds her jaw. "Fuck. That's us." She stands, then turns to check my neural port, fingers gentle as she tweaks the interface. "This'll sting," she says, then patches in the latest update. My vision lurches, overlays shifting from warm to icy. I let my eyes go glassy, lips parting just enough to make me look more lost than I am.

Ban leans in, breath cold on my ear. “Ready?” She tries to smile, but it’s the saddest thing I’ve seen in years.

“Always,” I say. She straightens my shirt, wipes one last bead of sweat from my temple, and leads me out into the light. I feel her hand on my back, solid as a promise. We step onto the auction floor together, the masks up, the world watching. But I can still feel the touch of her hand on mine, the ghost of warmth from a cigarette that never really burned.

The auction floor is a killing field, engineered for violence so clean it almost feels like seduction. The bass rolls under everything, a subsonic rhythm that makes your spine want to follow orders. Above, strips of light and banners of moving code run between the mezzanines, keeping the crowd jacked-in and off-balance. My display slab is upgraded, front row, and polished enough to show the whites of the bidders’ eyes as they come to take a look.

Ban stands at my side, jacket tight, hair in a knot so precise it makes her look taller. The handler mask is perfect now: calm, detached, just enough sweat at her brow to show she’s working hard to hold back the chaos inside. Buyers orbit in a narrowing spiral—first in pairs, then alone, each one hungrier than the last. Most are small-time, looking to flip the asset for a quick profit. Some are old-money creeps with faces permanently tweaked for poker. A few are full-corporate, legal teams in tow, scoping the meat for holes or hacks. Each one wants to test me.

A woman in a white pantsuit flicks my eyelid with a single cold finger, then grins and jots notes on her overlay. A Corp fixer in a chrome tie puts his hand on my jaw and moves my head back and forth, checking for symmetry. Ban lets them, barely. Each time, she offers a little resistance, a little disdain, like a carny sick of tourists but still desperate for tips. The neural readouts hover above me: live, multi-spectrum, looping every three seconds. Each pulse shows my brain spiking, then calming, then spiking again. Ban's programming—I can tell. She wants them to think I'm dangerous but trainable, chaos on a leash. Sometimes, between the cycles, she brushes a thumb over my cheek or whispers a phrase in the old language, a little calibration for the pattern.

Around us, the auction is in pre-show: lesser goods moving fast, bargain sales for anything below top-tier. Every time a brain changes hands, a burst of AR confetti explodes over the crowd, then vanishes. The auctioneer floats between platforms on a hidden track, each time pausing to hype the next lot. "Asset 67! Former biotech prodigy, emotional stability rated at the 94th percentile, sexual adaptability reprogrammed for all known kinks! Starting bid—"

The audience laughs, or groans, or just opens wallets. Nobody is here for prodigies tonight. Every five minutes, Ban checks my interface. Each time, I see her fingers are just a little stiffer, her smile just a little more forced. Word spreads about my lot number—23, rumored to be "the last analog on the grid." I know it's not true, but Ban wants the myth alive. Scarcity drives price. Around us, the volume builds. That's when she enters.

The crowd parts as Émilie makes her way down the steps, Moshimoto insignia glowing in ghost white on the shoulder of a tailored suit. Every other bidder in the room looks down, or away, or pretends to check their overlays. The few who don't are so alpha they don't care about death, which means Ban will need to worry about them, too. Émilie walks with the posture of someone who's memorized every social script and rewritten most of them. She's flanked by two admins, neither of whom looks like they know how to bleed.

Ban's body reacts before her mind does—spine straightens, shoulders lift, chin tucks in just enough to show submission but not weakness. I feel it all through the neural link, the old code between us lighting up with a nostalgia so fierce it almost burns. Émilie doesn't look at me. She walks right to Ban and offers her hand, palm up. "Ban," she says, voice as gentle as static. "I see you've found new work."

Ban hesitates a split-second, then takes the hand. "It's honest, at least."

Émilie smiles. It's a perfect smile, practiced in a mirror, but there's a cold joy at the edges that makes me want to crawl out of my own body. "Interesting merchandise," she says, finally glancing my way, but only briefly. "I wasn't aware any pure analogs remained on the market."

Ban shrugs. "You'd be surprised what the world spits up when you stop looking for it." Émilie's admins circle the slab. One shines a light in my eyes; the other checks the neural port for tampering. Neither says a word. I stare at the ceiling, counting each strip of blue as it scrolls overhead. "You're not planning to buy, are you?" Ban says, too flat for comfort.

Émilie turns, slow. "We are always interested in legacy assets. If not for study, then for the prestige of simply owning one."

Ban's face is stone, but her right hand grips the edge of the slab, knuckles so white the overlays in my eye highlight them as a potential injury site. "Seems like a waste," Ban says. "He's better used for something real."

Émilie's smile flickers. "I would expect no less from you." She glances at her admin, then adds, "Are you available after the event? We could have a drink, catch up."

Ban nods, but her mind is already running the angles, counting how many exits she can hit before Émilie's admins close the trap. The auctioneer's voice booms through the chamber: "Ladies and gentlemen, esteemed bidders—Asset 23, cataloged as 'Darby Skelm.' Please make your way to the main platform for viewing and authentication."

Ban wheels my slab into the spotlight, her hand never leaving my body. The crowd surges forward, a single living thing made of greed and hope and need. Buyers shove, argue, flashing cards and badges to get the first look. A child in a suit not old enough for high school offers her own mindprint as a down payment, but Ban shakes her off. The handler from the "Unfiltered" booth is there too, eyes on Ban as much as me. She winks at me, then gestures like she's going to slit my throat. I wink back, just to piss her off.

The auctioneer lifts a hand, and the sound drops to zero. All eyes face forward. "Asset 23 is unique. Untouched by modern upgrades, bred in chaos and violence, but never overwritten or rebooted. A once-in-a-generation chance to own the last true edge case."

The bids start slow, then spike.

“Fifty thousand.”

“Eighty.”

“Ninety.”

“Two hundred.”

Each new number comes with a crackle of tension. Ban keeps my neural readout cycling, letting the spikes show, letting them think I might snap, might break, might be more alive than anything else on the block. Émilie says nothing, but her admin holds up a hand. “Three million, pending authentication.”

The room goes silent. The auctioneer blinks. “Three million. Any higher?”

A man in a leather coat tries to raise, but the admin shakes his head, and the coat drops out. Ban leans over me, face so close I can smell the fear under her perfume. “Hold on,” she whispers. “You’re going to want to remember this.”

Émilie steps up to the slab, finally looking down at me with eyes that are more animal than human. For a second, the overlays glitch, and I see her as I remember: soft, wild, and impossible to read. She puts her finger on my jaw, same as the woman before, but hers is warmer, heavier. She leans in and whispers, “I’ll take care of you, Darby. I promise.” Then to Ban, she says, “Have the merchandise delivered to Moshimoto Level Seven. Full custody, no proxies.”

Ban nods, but her face is ice. “You’re the boss.”

Émilie smiles again, then vanishes into the crowd, the admin close behind. The auctioneer slaps the console, and the room erupts in a hiss of noise—half applause, half outrage. Ban lets the crowd wash over us, then pushes the slab back toward the curtain. Behind the screen, she collapses onto a crate, shaking so hard I think she might puke. I want to say something, but my mouth is dry. “Three million,” she says, voice a rasp. “You’re a fucking legend, Skelm.”

I nod, then close my eyes and let the neural feedback hum me into a numb nothing. The show’s not over. But the price is set, and there’s no going back.

It happens faster than the math can catch up. The crowd is still reeling from the three-million bid when the next number detonates in the AR sky: thirty million, cold green, floating above my slab like a digital curse. The noise in the room cuts out so cleanly it’s like someone surgically removed the air. Ban lets her mouth hang open, just for a second, eyes wide as she leans in for a closer look, but I can feel the twist at the corner of her lips, the private signal between us. “Unbelievable,” she murmurs, shaking her head for the crowd, but in the neural link, there’s a wash of raw pride, or maybe relief.

I catch the handler from earlier, her mouth pinched tight, jaw flexing as she recalculates her chances and comes up with zero. A few others try to muster a raise, but nobody’s got the bankroll or the corporate backing. Thirty million is a joke, a number meant to close the conversation, and everyone in the room gets the message. The auctioneer stumbles through the script, voice suddenly dry. “Uh, thirty million from Moshimoto Holdings, bid accepted. Last call, any higher offers?”

There's silence, then a slow ripple as people begin to realize what's just happened. The rarest asset in the city just got bought, out of nowhere, by a buyer who wasn't even supposed to be here. Émilie steps forward, her bodyguard duo falling in with military precision. She holds up a hand—her left, the one augmented for fine manipulation—and dismisses the auctioneer with a flick. Her eyes never leave Ban. "I'll require immediate transfer and verification," she says, voice soft but iron. "The lot is too valuable for on-site inspection."

Ban nods, the picture of humility, but in the overlay, I see her adrenaline spike. She unlocks the slab and gestures for the market's own verification officer—a man with no chin and too much badge. He skims my neural port, double-checks the chain of custody, then leans in to Ban with a whisper. "Are you sure about this?" he asks, and I hear it, too. "You'll never work this floor again."

Ban shrugs. "If I could pull off a sale like this twice, I'd have done it already." She signs the transfer doc. Her hand shakes, just barely, but to everyone but me, it looks like show. Émilie waits, lips pursed, until Ban unplugs the neural interface and slides me upright. The sudden loss of input is a shotgun blast to the brain, but I manage not to puke or black out. Ban holds me steady, hands at my temples, and for a split second, her thumb strokes a pulse point at my neck—one, two, three. Our code. "Be safe," she whispers. "And don't let them fuck you up."

I try to smirk, but my face isn't fully under control. The two Moshimoto goons grab me under the arms. Their grip is surgical, impersonal. They march me off the slab and across the auction floor. Each step is agony, but the market itself is a blur

—the crowd is already moving on, talking about the number, talking about what it means. Nobody cares what happens to the product.

At the exit, Émilie waits. She watches my approach with an expression I can't parse, a mixture of triumph and disappointment. As her men set me on a padded gurney, she leans in close, just enough to feel her breath on my skin. "You'll be an excellent addition to our collection," she says, the words soft as a caress and twice as dangerous. "I hope you understand the honor." I want to reply, but my jaw won't unclench. I settle for a glare. She smiles, not kindly. "Don't be so dramatic, Darby. You always wanted to be special. Now you'll never be forgotten."

The guards lift the gurney. As I roll out, I see Ban at the back of the room, arms folded, a wall of handlers and freaks between us. Her face is unreadable, but in the overlays, I see the ghost of our last conversation: *"Remember, you're not here to lose."* The market is a machine, and today, I'm the cog that broke it.

Outside, the air is colder. The Moshimoto van is black, logo barely visible in the rain. The guards load me in and lock the door. I stare at the ceiling, overlays running wild, but nothing comes through except the hum of the drive and the echo of Ban's voice, somewhere deep in the old code.

The plan is in motion. I just hope Ban's as good at buying time as she is at selling legends.

Chapter 17

The neutral lounge is an architecture student's wet dream: forty meters of one-way glass, pressure seals on the doors, and security towers in the walls disguised as living moss. Holoboards, silent and efficient, run endless stock tickers in the ceiling's corner angles. The whole place is a shrine to frictionless negotiation, maximum transparency with zero reflection. All mirrors banned. All cameras run by the house.

Ban checks in at the host stand—a dead-eyed concierge with surgical hands, presumably so every drink is sterile. She signs the log with her left thumb, then leads me past the empty bar. There are no bartenders, only a wall of nano-shaken glasses on rail tracks, each dispensing measured doses to sleek, transparent tumblers. The bar stools are shaped like neural clusters: white resin, high-backed, every one engineered to make you feel both at ease and under a microscope. Holo-ads drift between tables: "Rebrand Your Anxiety—Now With Mood-Lock™," "Impulse Control: The Ultimate Edge," "Thought

Leader Subscription—First Session Free." My overlays choke on the pitch and dim everything to grayscale.

Émilie's table is at the room's perimeter, tucked in a gimbal alcove that rotates for privacy. She sits with her back to the glass, two tech operators in midnight black seated on either side. On the table are four vials of NeuralPrime, a halo of interface gear, and a tray of company-branded energy bars in shrink wrap. The techs, both sleeved in bicep-length gloves and matching blue contacts, watch Ban and me approach with all the warmth of an assembly-line QA check.

Ban makes a show of scanning the room for bugs, even though she knows everything in here is already recorded at six different angles. She peels off her jacket, smooths her shirt, and steps ahead to intercept any greeting. She picks the chair closest to the door, forcing the nearest tech to sidestep and re-calibrate his gear. Her pistol rides on her hip, visible and holstered, the display saying "on safe," but who believes that?

I settle into the next seat, bones making it creak. I clock the nearest three exits, two security subroutines I'd use if I was a raider, and at least five different pressure points in the neural cluster stool that would snap a tailbone if I leaned wrong. Ban sits on my right; together, we make a wall. Émilie watches us both, posture perfect, hair cinched in a whip-tight twist that glints at every head movement. Her smile is mathematically precise: two-point-three seconds, seven degrees of mouth curve, then drop back to neutral. She gestures to the drinks, not breaking eye contact. "NeuralPrime? Corporate blend; guarantees no aftertaste or hangover. Or we can switch to something artisanal if you're in a nostalgic mood."

“Not before the contract,” Ban says, voice low. “We don’t touch until the terms are live.”

Émilie gives the briefest flicker of amusement, then glances at her left-hand tech. He’s already got the documentation prepped, scrolling in two columns: TOS and non-compete. He rotates the slab so Ban can read it. Ban doesn’t, because her overlays are better. I stare at the glass table. The holoskin shows rolling market updates, live timecodes, and an animated visualization of the thirty-million-credit bid that brought us here. For a moment, I wonder if it’s a flex or a warning. Probably both. Émilie folds her hands. “I know we’ve all had a long day,” she says, and it’s so perfectly scripted I feel my skin crawl, “so I’ll make it quick: thirty million for complete neural access. Non-negotiable.”

Ban’s lips part, but instead of speaking, she drums two fingers on the table. A rhythm: long-short, short-short-long. I catch the message—*stall, drag, collect data.* I smile, showing teeth. “You always did like to cut the foreplay, Émilie. But I want to be clear: neural access means what, exactly? Thought probe? Personality mapping? Or are you just after memories?”

She leans in, giving me her full attention. “Full map and backup. I need to know how much of you is authentic, and how much is residual. If your overlays are unaugmented, you’re a unique resource. If not, you’re a very expensive whiskey shot.”

The right-hand tech chimes in, not looking up from his slab. “We’re set for single-sample non-invasive. But we’ll need at least thirty minutes to get a coherent run.”

Ban shifts. "Fifteen, or nothing. He doesn't run stable beyond that."

Émilie shrugs. "You know the business better than anyone."

The left-hand tech preps the headset. I see the nano-filaments flex, a mesh of colorless hair-fine wire with a hundred microdarts ready to anchor into my temples. I suppress the urge to flinch. Ban's hand brushes my knee, grounding me. Her nails dig in, not enough to break skin but enough to say: *keep the act up, don't break yet.* The tech wipes my skin with alcohol—cold, then burning—and straps on the interface. The clamp makes my scalp itch, every nerve in my forehead prickling to attention. I breathe, slow and steady, trying not to think of the night-self, the thing in me that wants to break the chair and run.

"Baseline," the left tech says, and I'm supposed to close my eyes. I don't, not at first.

Émilie smirks, her smile now genuine. "Still can't follow instructions, Skelm?"

I close them, and the probe starts. It's a soft invasion at first, like a caffeine drip in the medulla. Then harder, the software coldly rifling through recent files, cataloguing trauma by date, index, and access. I see flashes: Ban's breath on my ear, the burn of my own blood in my mouth, the blue-white flash of a gunshot in a stairwell. It tries to branch out, but I force it back, keeping the search local.

Next come the synthetic memories, the ones I never fully accepted. Corporate drills, the taste of synthetic coffee, a room with a projection of Émilie's face backlit by blue. The techs flag the conflicts, highlighting each memory leak in yellow. They want the real pain, so I give it to them: the drowning, the riot shield, Ban's hand breaking my nose and then kissing it better. I let the interface swim in all the old wounds, replaying the worst days on high loop.

The first set ends. I open my eyes. The left tech says, "Midway stable. Slight artifacting on the overlay, but nothing we can't patch."

Émilie makes a note. "Go deeper. I want full pattern recognition."

Ban's fingers tap a new code: long, short, short. *Give them something. Let it hurt.*

The second probe is different. They push the mesh into alpha range, and suddenly every neuron in my body lights up like a Christmas overdose. My jaw locks; my hands spasm and grip the neural cluster stool so hard I feel the resin creak. I fight the urge to vomit. The pain is raw, like someone poured molten glass in my head and asked me to remember my favorite birthday.

The techs look alarmed, but they keep going. They want a breakdown. They want to see if I can make it through without code-crashing the system. Émilie, meanwhile, watches Ban. "Fifteen minutes," Ban says. "Not a second more." The techs nod, but they're not really in charge here.

I ride the pain, focusing on the code. I let memories bleed in, but wall off the parts they want most: my night-self, and the thing I did for Ban under the harbor bridge that no one else knows about. I set a decoy, let the probe latch onto the image of Ban peeling an orange in the rain, the rind hitting the concrete like a funeral drum. I fill it with color, scent, emotion. A Trojan horse. I let them think this is my root memory.

The left tech looks up, brow furrowed. “We’re getting cross-talk,” he says, tapping his console. “Asset is running internal reroute.”

Émilie tilts her head, almost impressed. “That’s why you’re worth thirty million.”

Ban’s hand tightens on my knee. This is the cue. I let my jaw unclench, let the pain roll through, and I laugh. Low at first, then rising, just to show them I’m not dead yet. “Is that the best you’ve got?” I say, eyes wild.

The techs unplug me, both hands shaking. There’s a brief smell of ozone, then blood: the microdarts pulled a bit of scalp on exit. I taste iron in my mouth. Émilie gives me her corporate smile. “You pass,” she says. “We’ll proceed with the deal.”

Ban relaxes, just a fraction, and wipes a bead of sweat from my hairline.

The left tech applies a bandage, hands cold and competent. “You’ll want to rest,” he says. “This level of mapping usually takes a day to recover.”

I shake my head. “No time for that.”

Émilie stands, smoothing her skirt. “Transfer to be completed by midnight,” she says to the techs, then to Ban: “He’s more valuable than you said. You should’ve held out for more.”

Ban stands, face flat. “I’m not here for the money.”

Émilie glances at me. “Lucky you.”

The whole thing takes twenty-six minutes. They pack the gear, wipe down the table, and vanish into the staff corridors, leaving Ban and me alone. Ban's hand shakes as she pours a measure of NeuralPrime. She sips it, then passes the glass to me. Our fingers touch, linger, for just a moment. "You did good," she says, voice almost gentle. "Almost like you were built for it."

I don't answer, just drink. Outside, the sky flickers as the city lights stutter on for the night. The probe is done. But I know there's worse coming. And I know I'll be awake for all of it.

The next probe is a punch in the spine before it's even live. They hit me with a local anesthetic, but it's just to stop the nerves from shorting out and screwing their readings. My jaw feels like it's glued shut. The techs swap in a fresh mesh, this one with extra microdarts and a skullcap that smells like old sweat and ozone. I think about saying, "this is unsanitary," but decide to keep my dignity for the archives.

Ban sets the chair herself, lines my head up to the perfect ninety, then leans close. Her lips brush my ear. "Stay in the tunnel. When it gets too hot, follow the markers out. If you need to break, tap three times on your right thigh." She slides her palm down my thigh, stops at the knee, and squeezes hard. A warning. A promise. I count her breaths, memorizing the way her shoulders rise and fall. She always telegraphs her lies with the left one.

The techs start the sequence. This time, they go fast—no gentle ramp, just a hard spike of current to open all the windows at once. The first second is white noise, the next a high-pitched static that wants to melt my teeth. My overlays are no help. All I see is blue. Then a fast-forward reel of every failure I ever logged: the job in London that cratered, the body in a river, the time Ban broke my thumb and made me finish the run anyway. I let the interface chew through them, highlight my own disasters, making myself look worse than I am.

But it's not enough. The probe wants more. It drills into the empty spaces and starts to excavate the stuff I buried, the shit not even Ban knows. I sense her presence—always two centimeters to my right, always in my blind spot. She does the old trick: the "good-cop-bad-cop" switch in her eyes, alternating contempt and encouragement. I focus on the cues. When she smiles, I push a nothing memory. When she glares, I let the probe dig deeper.

The first bad leak is one I didn't see coming: Émilie, seventeen years ago, standing over my hospital bed. She's smiling, but her hand is on my wrist, fingers pulsing a subsonic code. She says, *"You will do it, won't you, Darby?"* and I say, *"Of course,"* because that's the only script I know. Next up is the first time I lied to Émilie. She wanted to know about Ban, why I never let the subject go. I remember saying, *"Ban's a tool, like any other."* I was drunk; not enough to kill the filters, just enough to believe my own lie. Even now, the echo of her disappointment is like a nail under my eyelid.

The probe shifts, getting hungry. It wants more, so it dives into my late twenties, the wasteland years, before I met Ban again. There's a memory I try to hide: the day I found the neural extraction rig in Émilie's apartment. She said it was for "research," and I almost believed her, but I knew the model—custom job, black market, not the kind you keep for fun. I knew she was prepping to ghost me, but I let her anyway. I sense Ban wants me to share this one. I see it in the tilt of her neck, the set of her jaw. So I let it out, full color, high-res. I picture Émilie's hands on the rig, the flash of blue as she wired it to her own port, the way she didn't even flinch when the pain hit. I remember thinking: *she'll be famous, but only if I get out alive.*

The probe tries to break me, but I reroute it with a memory of Ban and me in the tunnels under Kiev. We're running from a kill team. Ban's limp is bad and she's three liters low. I remember promising her, *"I'll get you out. I swear."* The probe wants to flag this as a trauma, but I let it mark it as love. Then the probe gets weird. It loops back to Ban's hand on my leg, but this time it's not from today—it's from six years ago, in a motel in the Midwestern sticks, where we were hiding from a bounty on my head. She wakes me up in the middle of the night, presses her palm to my jaw, and whispers, *"Don't you dare let them own you. Even if you have to kill me to stay free."*

The probe likes that. It flags it as an anchor, a root program. I feel my fingers tremble, sweat breaking on my upper lip. Ban sees it, nods, then hits the table with her knuckles—one, two, three. Time to let it go. I start to lose the thread. The techs increase the current, and now the pain is total, a full-body nausea that makes me want to scream. My hands clench the chair so hard I feel the microcapillaries in my nails burst. I see the techs looking at each other, worried now, but they keep the voltage up.

Suddenly, there's a memory I can't explain. I'm in a church, or maybe a lab, and Émilie is crying. She's wearing a different face, but the voice is hers. She says, *"I never wanted to erase you. I just wanted to know if you were real."* She's holding my head, and her tears burn like acid. The memory isn't mine, or maybe it is, but I don't remember it until now. I can't hide it, so I let the probe see. The techs stare at the console, then at me. One says, "We've got a loop. He's running cross-talk on three overlays. No human should do that."

Émilie steps closer, arms folded. "His patterns have always been unique. That's why he's worth thirty million."

The tech looks pale. "If we keep going, there's a nonzero chance he'll blue-screen."

Ban glares at the tech, then at Émilie. "He doesn't break. Not until he's done."

The probe hits a final threshold. I feel my mind split, like ice under stress. Half of me wants to kill Ban, the other half wants to kill Émilie, but neither half is willing to quit. In the end, I choose the only thing that ever works: I let the probe win. I drop all resistance, let my mind go soft, and let the memories flood. I see the war, the losses, every friend I ever watched bleed out. I see Ban and Émilie, both of them holding my head in the dark, both of them whispering that they need me. I see my own face, reflected in the ceiling of the neural lounge, mouth twisted in a rictus grin.

The probe finishes. My body sags. I can't feel my fingers. Émilie watches me, then Ban. "He's perfect," she says.

Ban kneels and wipes the blood from my ear. "You did good, Skelm."

The techs wrap my head in a cooling band. "You'll hallucinate for an hour. Maybe three," one says, "but after that, you'll be fine."

I want to laugh, but my throat is raw. I reach for Ban, but she's already packed and moving. She picks up the neural mesh, wipes it clean with her shirt, then leaves it on the table. Émilie leans in and whispers, "You did what no one else could. I'll make sure they know."

I want to ask who "they" are, but the words don't come. Ban walks me out, arm over my shoulders, her face unreadable. We limp down the corridor, past the bar, past the cluster of neural chairs, and out into the night. The sky is still blue. The city is still alive. I'm still here. But there's a memory I can't shake: Ban's promise, and the way she kept it, even if it cost me everything else. My body hurts, my head's a mess, but I feel something close to proud. For the first time in years, I'm worth the price.

The final handshake is digital, but it feels like signing away a piece of my soul. Ban accepts the contract on my behalf, overlays flickering as her thumbprint ignites the doc. The transfer code jumps to Émilie's slab, then pings through to the techs, both of whom look like they just survived a minor car accident. I feel the data move, a tide pulling at the base of my skull. I want to throw up. Ban stands behind me, hands steady on my shoulders, fingers massaging the knots like she's sculpting raw meat. I focus on the sensation, anything to keep from splitting again. The afterglow of the probe is a mess—raw voltage, shuddering memories, the taste of ozone in my teeth.

Émilie waits for the final verification. Her smile doesn't reach her eyes, but the satisfaction is real. "A pleasure doing business, Ban. I hope you'll stay in touch. We'll have more projects in the future if this one works out."

Ban's reply is pure muscle. "We accept your offer. But next time, no deep probe unless I'm in the room."

Émilie shrugs, unbothered. "Your asset, your call."

The deal closes with a whirr as the contract is signed and triplicated. Thirty million, split across three shadow banks. I'm not sure who gets paid. It doesn't matter. They let us go first, the lounge's house security sweeping the corridor clear. As we step into the hallway, I feel the data spike one last time, a stutter of microseizures. My legs go soft. I have to lean against Ban, my mouth hot with the copper stink of a nosebleed.

Ban holds me upright, dragging us into a service alcove lined with broken screens and peeling paint. The city outside is wet, rain making rivers on the glass. Through a grimy porthole, I see the blue glow of police drones hunting the next disaster. Somewhere, a siren wails, then cuts out. Ban pulls a rag from her jacket and wipes the blood from my face. "Stay with me, Skelm. You can't black out now."

I try to answer, but the words come out slurred. My overlays run backward, the colors all wrong. I see Ban's face, then Émilie's, then Ban again, but older, hair grown out and wild, eyes feral. She's screaming at me, but I can't hear the words. The probe left cracks. I can feel the fractures, places where my memories overlap but don't match. Some are new, some ancient, some not even mine. "Who would be proud?" I manage to say, the words sticky on my tongue.

Ban blinks, her guard slipping. "The real you," she says. "The one who started all this."

I laugh, even though it hurts. "There's nothing real left."

She shakes her head. "You're more real than any of them. That's why they keep trying to buy you."

I look past her, through the rain, at the endless grid of lights and patrols and blind, hungry machines. I try to picture the person Ban thinks I am, but all I see is a blur of faces, most of them dead, a few still trying. She takes my hand, squeezes it, then presses her forehead to mine. "Listen," she says, "you can break down now. I'll hold it together."

I want to say something clever, but the tears come first. They're hot, bitter, and full of chemicals. Ban lets them run, holding me until the shakes die down. We stand like that for a minute, maybe a year. When the pain fades, she pulls away, wipes my face again, and says, "Ready?"

I nod, because I always do. We walk out into the night, the wet city reflecting our shadows in every surface. Ban keeps her hand on my shoulder, steering us past the holoboards and neural cluster stools, through the crowd and out the staff door. On the street, the rain feels like absolution. We keep moving, together. Behind us, Émilie's smile lingers, a promise and a threat. Ahead of us, the city is as hungry as ever. But this time, I feel like maybe I'm not alone in it. Ban's grip is steady, and for now, that's enough.

Chapter 18

We hole up in the fallback, the worst of the city's morning haze held at bay by triple-sealed blackout plastic and an upcycled HVAC that smells faintly of burning nerves. I'm still bleeding from the inside, so I sit as still as possible while Ban locks the door behind us and throws a slab of "food" onto the steel countertop. In the corner, three neural mappers hum their idle threat, throwing static into the air like incense. Tactical overlays flicker on the wall display—a patchwork of live feeds, building schematics, even a scrolling ticker of active bounties. Somewhere, a protein bar dies an ignoble death in Ban's grip.

She chews it with hatred, staring at me, but her eyes don't focus. It's the residual, the aftershock of the probe. I still have memory holes that whistle when the air pressure changes. "You said it would be quick," I say, voice dry as a sanded circuit board.

Ban snorts, wipes the synthetic crumbs from her chin, and

shakes her head. "You're the one who let them scan past the firewall. You always want to show off for the suits."

I don't deny it. We both know it's true. My overlays are still fucked, the colors lagging behind reality by about half a heartbeat, so I squint at the kitchen's single window until it syncs up with the outside. The city's all blue and orange this morning, a diffusion of sun through industrial miasma, but the rain left a clean sheen on every visible surface. The world looks new, or maybe just reset.

Ban pops her knuckles and stalks a loop around the safehouse's perimeter, checking every blind corner and camera dead zone, even though we're supposedly blacked out. When she finishes, she comes back, kneels down in front of me, and peels the bandage off my forehead. "Still leaking," she says, and dabs at the blood with the hem of her shirt. "Try not to get any on the couch." I grunt, because that's what's expected. But the moment her hand's on my face, I forget what I'm supposed to be. Ban notices. Her thumb hovers on my jaw for a fraction too long, and something flickers in her overlay. She shakes it off. "Don't do that."

"Do what?"

Her mouth twitches. "The thing where you look at me like I'm a person and not the last thing standing between you and a bullet in the back of the head."

I want to make a joke, but my tongue won't move fast enough. Instead, I just watch her, and for a second, she watches me back. Then, there's a knock at the door. It's not loud, not the kind of knock you'd expect from a raid or a kill team. Just three light taps, evenly spaced, almost polite. Ban's hand is at her hip before the sound finishes echoing. She draws the gun, glances at me, and her mouth tightens to a slit. "Stay down." She moves to the door, puts her back to the wall, and eases the safety off with her thumb. The knock comes again. Same rhythm. Polite, like before. "Who is it?" Ban calls, but her tone says: *I already know.*

The voice on the other side is perfectly pitched, not even trying to disguise itself. "Ban. Skelm. It's Cleopatra. You left the backdoor open."

I feel my gut knot. Ban's trigger finger flexes, then she glances at me, as if waiting for permission. "Do it," I mouth. She flicks the gun to her left hand, presses the override on the door, and the security bolts hiss open.

Cleopatra stands in the hallway, wearing a suit so clean it makes the rest of us look like garbage. Her hair's different, longer now, and there's a new pattern of chrome at her temples—shiny, fresh, and meant to show off the triple-augment package she's sporting. Her hands are raised, palms out, but I can see the flicker of overlays running through her skin, shimmering with risk calculations.

Ban doesn't wait. She steps forward, grabs Cleopatra by the collar, and shoves the gun up under her jaw. "You have three seconds to tell me why you're not a corpse."

Cleopatra doesn't blink. "Because I'm holding something you need," she says, then turns her eyes to me. "And you—Darby, you always did want to be the center of attention. Congratulations. You're the most expensive neural signature in the Midwest."

Ban jams the gun harder into Cleopatra's chin. "That's not a reason. That's a threat."

"Let her talk," I say, my own voice weirdly flat, like it's coming from a floor below.

Cleopatra's eyes flick to mine, and for the first time, I see the overlay math: her risk assessment scrolling across the surface of her left iris. *Ban: 31% probability of shooting; Skelm: 2% probability of intervention; Self: 95% chance of walking out alive if I play this right.* I realize she wants me to see it. Ban scowls, but doesn't lower the weapon.

Cleopatra's voice softens. "Look, I get it. I fucked you. I let Moshimoto map your entire consciousness, and I probably got you blacklisted from half the safehouses in the city. But it was necessary. You were never going to make it past the mainframe unless someone cut you loose."

She shifts her gaze, fast, and locks onto me. "You think you're irreplaceable, Darby? You're not. Moshimoto grows your kind in tanks now, and every single one of them is pre-broken. But Ban"—she glances at Ban's hand, then back up—"she's the last wildcard in the deck. That's why they left you alive."

Ban laughs, low and bitter. "You're a terrible liar. Moshimoto wants us dead because we keep breaking their best toys."

"Not this time," Cleopatra says, voice dropping to a whisper. "This time, you're the main event. They want you in the integration cycle. I know because I'm running the op." I try to stand, but my legs don't work right. Cleopatra notices and gives me a pitying smile. "I'm not here to gloat," she says. "I'm here because there's a way through this. I just need you to trust me. For maybe two hours. Then you can decide if you want to kill me."

Ban looks at me, gun never wavering. "Your call, Skelm. She sold us out twice. Third time's the charm, right?"

My night-self wants to break Cleopatra's neck. The part of me that lived in her shadow for a decade wants to buy her a drink and see if I can out-bluff her this time. My overlays run a hundred scenarios, and in ninety-nine of them, Ban kills Cleopatra. The one that works is the one where I play along. "Let her in," I say. "But if you twitch, Ban pulls the plug. Understood?"

Cleopatra nods, eyes wide and clear. Ban shoves her into the room, but keeps the gun leveled at her head. Cleopatra moves with perfect grace, never turning her back, never dropping her hands. She circles to the far side of the kitchen, eyes scanning the neural mappers, the scattered tactical sheets, the old, broken phones on the countertop. "Nice setup," she says. "I always did like your sense of style, Ban. Not much for interior design, but the paranoia's a classic."

Ban growls. "Cut the shit. Why are you here?"

Cleopatra's smile is slow, deliberate. She sets both hands on the countertop, then flicks a finger, projecting a thin blue slab of light between her wrists. A data core, old-school. Physical. Unhackable except by hand. She slides it across the counter, inching it toward me. "That," she says, "is what will get you into the mainframe. It's a legacy exploit, predates even the first Moshimoto merge. No one in the current security stack remembers it exists—because I erased all references to it."

Ban narrows her eyes. “If that’s true, why give it to us? Why not just use it yourself?”

Cleopatra’s overlay glitches, and I catch the ghost of sadness behind her eyes. “Because I’m already burned,” she says. “I got caught running a probability tree on the Continuity Directive. They’re going to decompile me at midnight. My only play left is to bet on the two of you. So congrats—Moshimoto just gave you a thirty-million-credit head start.”

I glance at Ban. Her trigger finger is white, but she hasn’t fired.

“So, what?” I say. “You hand us the golden ticket and expect us to say thanks? You’ll forgive me if I’m not feeling sentimental.”

Cleopatra sighs. “You always did have trouble seeing the endgame, Darby. This is not about revenge. It’s about making sure someone, anyone, survives with a copy of the truth. If I can’t, maybe you can.” She looks at Ban, then at me. “You’re not heroes. You’re not even good people. But you’re the only ones who can do what needs to be done.”

Ban stares at the core, then back at Cleopatra. “And what do you get if we win?”

Cleopatra’s mouth twists. “Nothing. Or maybe just the satisfaction of knowing I left the smallest possible mess behind.”

My overlays run the odds. She’s not lying. Or if she is, it’s the best acting I’ve ever seen. I reach for the data core. My hand shakes, and Cleopatra doesn’t miss it. She pushes it the last few centimeters until it touches my fingers.

"I don't care what you do with it," she says. "Just don't let Moshimoto win."

She pulls her hands back slowly, then sits at the edge of the counter. She's trembling, but only in the places the overlays can't see. Ban holsters the gun, but doesn't look away. The room feels colder, like the air itself just remembered how to hate. Cleopatra laughs, brittle. "You want me to stay and help you prep the integration? Or would you rather shoot me now and take your chances?"

I look at Ban. She looks at me. In the end, we do what we always do: we don't decide. We just get to work.

It takes three minutes for the air in the safehouse to turn lethal. Ban stalks the perimeter, circling Cleopatra like a dog deciding if she wants to bite or just piss on the carpet. She inventories every weapon and wire in reach, not because she doubts the plan, but because she needs something to throttle besides Cleopatra's windpipe. I don't move. I let the data run, every scenario grinding through the back of my skull, a wall of scrolling futures that taste like gunmetal and broken teeth.

The only light in the room is neon runoff from the outside, spattered up the rain-slicked window and painting Cleopatra's face in ugly blue. She watches Ban, doesn't flinch. "You ever get tired of this?" Ban asks. "You ever just say, 'I'm gonna try and make it a whole day without shitting on everyone who ever trusted me?'"

Cleopatra blinks, and her overlays light up her cheekbones, twin veins of amber under the skin. "I've made it three days before. But the results were statistically disappointing."

Ban snorts, then launches into her case file. “First time, you sell us out to a freelance extraction squad. Second time, you fry Katherine’s brain with a staged mercy kill. Third time”—she points at the legacy exploit on the table—“I’m not even sure what to call this. A fuck-you with extra steps?”

Cleopatra folds her hands on the counter, every finger perfectly still. “You’re oversimplifying. The extraction squad was necessary to break the contract loop. Katherine’s ‘death’ was a side effect of bad input—she wouldn’t have survived the cycle anyway, not with the hardware she was running.” Her voice is smooth, but the overlay math is ugly. “Third time, I save your asses, and you throw a tantrum.”

Ban keeps pacing, but her eyes snap to mine. “You buying this, Skelm? You really think she’s not going to walk us into a live blender the second it’s convenient?”

My hands twitch, but I keep them in my lap. “There’s a forty-eight percent chance Cleopatra’s telling the truth. Another ten percent she’s playing a longer game and needs us to survive for at least one more round. The rest is noise.”

Ban laughs, rough and low. “I forgot how much I love it when you talk dirty.”

I don’t smile. “It’s not about trust. It’s about exploit. If she’s lying, we’re dead before we get to Moshimoto anyway.”

Ban stops, faces the wall, and punches it. Her knuckles bounce off the metal, but she leaves a dent. “Fuck it. We’re out of time, and I’m out of patience.” She turns on Cleopatra, who’s still seated, still watching. “If you so much as twitch, I’ll gut you myself. But first, I’m putting a kill switch in your neck.”

Cleopatra nods. “Expected. I recommend the right jugular—less margin for error and easier remote access.”

Ban pulls a bone-white injector from her belt. She snaps the safety off with her thumb, then flicks the cap at Cleopatra’s feet. “Show me.”

Cleopatra tilts her head, brushes aside her hair, and exposes the artery. Ban steps up and presses the injector to the flesh. Her hand is steady, but I can see the pulse in her wrist. Ban pulls the trigger. The device hisses, and a microsecond later, Cleopatra’s overlays light up with an internal alert. “Integration successful,” Cleopatra says, voice without inflection. “You now have sovereign kill rights over this body.”

Ban steps back, keeping her eyes on Cleopatra, then glances at me. “You see the difference between her and us, Skelm? She doesn’t even care. You could kill her right now and she’d still think she won.”

Cleopatra’s mouth curves. “Eighty-three percent chance you’ll need to use it. Seventeen percent chance you’ll thank me instead.”

I clear my throat, the air in my lungs so cold it burns. “Sixteen hours to integration. If you’re going to set your grudge, do it after.”

Ban’s face hardens. “You want to prep the gear, or you want to start running the operation from here?”

I check the feeds. Rain is still coming down, the city is still alive, and the Moshimoto security cluster is still holding the perimeter but not showing extra movement yet. “Run the op from here," I say. "We go in light, three hours before start, then improvise."

Ban scoffs. "You always did love improvising. Maybe this time, it'll get us killed instead of promoted."

Cleopatra stands, smoothing her shirt, then tucks the legacy core into her suit pocket. "I need fifteen minutes to recalibrate the exploit," she says. "After that, we move."

Ban grunts, moves to the far corner, and starts checking her kit. She makes a show of cleaning her gun, but I can hear the snarl in her breath. The hum of Cleopatra's augmentations fills the room, a white noise that scratches the inside of my skull. Her risk overlays flicker: Ban's threat profile, the integration window, a complex probability spiral of failure and escape. I watch the rain crawl down the window, neon light dancing in every drop. We're all animals here. Some of us just wear better collars.

Time passes like a slow virus. I sit at the table, patching the overlays, while Ban prowls the perimeter in tighter and tighter circles. Every few minutes, Cleopatra checks her data core, then glances at Ban, recalculating her odds. At one point, Ban stops, leans over my shoulder, and whispers, "If I die because of her, I'll haunt you."

I smile. "You'd do that anyway."

She moves off, boots crunching the plastic sheeting on the floor. Cleopatra finishes her calibration, then looks at both of us. "I'm ready," she says. "The rest is up to you."

Ban grabs her pack, slings it over one shoulder, and flicks the safety off her gun. "Let's go. And remember: one wrong move, and you're dead before you hit the ground."

Cleopatra smiles, faint and perfect. "I'd expect nothing less."

We move out into the night, the rain hitting our faces like a countdown. I wonder if any of us will make it to morning.

The trip to Moshimoto Tower is a wet crawl through the city's intestines. We ride the tram as close as the perimeter will let us, then melt into the sub-basement sprawl, dodging cams, shunt alarms, and the thousand tiny betrayals that mark every inch of corporate territory. The closer we get, the tighter the tunnels, and the louder the hum from the fiber-optic arteries that keep the whole thing alive.

Cleopatra moves in front, every footfall measured, every gesture flicked with a silent overlay ping. Her hands never stop, tapping at the air, sending new patches and credentials upstream in real time. Ban walks a meter behind, gun at Cleopatra's kidney, thumb resting on the trigger that'll juice the kill switch Ban jammed in at the safehouse. I bring up the rear, neural dampeners tight on my skull, the world running two steps slower but at least not fracturing into pieces.

The tunnels drip condensation onto rusted rails, puddles reflecting the faint blue glow of backup generators. Everything smells like coolant and old blood. We hit the first junction, a wide-open vault with pipes running up three stories, and Cleopatra pauses, eyes flicking as she checks the map. "This way," she says, and takes a sharp left down a crawlspace no wider than Ban's shoulders. Ban grunts and follows, but with every step, her eyes rake the back of Cleopatra's head.

It's maybe twenty meters before we hit the security checkpoint. A heavy door, armored and alive with sensors. Two guards are in smart uniforms. One's glued to a dataslab, the other watches the approach with predator calm. Cleopatra stops, brushes the damp from her suit, and puts on a face I haven't seen since the night she crashed my first wedding: professional, beautiful, and completely soulless. "Routine maintenance," she says, voice set to 'bland superiority.' "Work order 5889, continuity check on the archive node. You should have it in your system."

The guard with the slab grunts, pulls up the overlay, and starts reading. Ban's hand slips to the small of Cleopatra's back, like a lover's touch, but I can see the tip of the injector pressing into Cleopatra's spine. A warning: *one wrong answer and it's over.* I keep my eyes down, letting my neural dampener wash out everything but the next breath. The slab guard glances at Ban, then at me. "Didn't know we had visitors from HR today," he says, voice slow and syrupy.

Cleopatra's smile never reaches her eyes. "We're on loan. Need to finish the cycle before the morning shift or there'll be a repeat of the Toronto incident."

Both guards laugh—everyone loves a horror story about Toronto. While they're distracted, Cleopatra drops a data bead into the inspection slot. The bead pulses once, then dies.

The slab guard blinks. "Supposed to use the new model."

Cleopatra shrugs. "If I had a budget, I'd be using better assets too."

The guard looks at Ban again. “She doesn’t look like an asset.”

Ban grins, the kind of smile that ends with broken bones. “I’m not. But if you want, I can show you my certifications.”

The guard’s smile stutters. “You’re good. Just make it quick. There’s a systems diagnostic in forty.”

Cleopatra nods and walks us through the checkpoint. Once we’re past the door and in another stretch of dead tunnel, Ban says, “You keep making friends like that, we’ll never get out alive.”

Cleopatra doesn’t look back. “Easier to fool them if you treat them like equals. And anyway, we’re not supposed to survive this.”

Ban snorts, but I catch the glint in her eye. She liked the way Cleopatra handled it, even if she’ll never say so. We follow Cleopatra deeper. The tunnel narrows and the walls sweat. Every step brings us closer to the building’s living nervous system: the mainline data trunks, humming so loud they drown out even the gun in my hand.

Finally, Cleopatra stops at a metal door so old it’s been painted over a dozen times, each coat flaking under the neon misery of the service light. She pries the panel open, exposing a series of mechanical toggles and an actual keyhole. She grins, genuine for the first time all day. “Analog, just like you, Darby. I knew you’d appreciate the nostalgia.” She cracks the panel with a code she hums more than types, then jams the legacy exploit into the ancient reader. The light inside blinks, then turns green. “After you.”

I crawl in, Ban at my heels, gun still leveled at Cleopatra's ribcage. Inside, the world's quiet. No overlays, no hum—just the sound of breathing and the faint click of relays in the walls. Cleopatra squeezes past, kneels by a waist-high cabinet, and opens it. She works the latches blind, every finger moving by memory, then pulls out a core so old and out of spec I almost don't recognize it. But I do. I've seen them before—in museums, in nightmares. A little black brick, stamped with a serial number and wrapped in red tape. Ban's eyes widen. "That's—"

"Pre-breach technology," Cleopatra says, cradling it like a grenade. "Moshimoto never figured out how to wipe these clean. This one's been offline since before the war."

I reach for it, but Ban stops me, checking the corners for hidden lasers or kill drones. Cleopatra waits, patient. I hold the brick in my palm. It vibrates, a low thrum that matches my heart rate. "Still work?" I ask.

Cleopatra nods. "All the best secrets are analog. Just needed someone who could read it."

I slot the core into my jacket. Ban lets out a long, slow breath, then holsters her gun, just for a second. "We get this to the node, and then what?"

Cleopatra stands and dusts off her knees. "Then we improvise."

I grin. For once, I don't hate that idea. We move out, down the tunnel, every step echoing the future. Behind us, the old door swings shut, and the past is locked away again.

. . .

The vault is smaller than I imagined. No high ceilings, no epic displays—just a ring of analog server racks humming in sync, air thick with ozone and the promise of ancient failure. The walls sweat with condensation, and the floor is covered in a mat of fine, nonconductive mesh that sticks to my boots with every step. Cleopatra moves to the access panel, hands dancing over the switches, every gesture sharp enough to draw blood. Ban covers the door, gun out, her eyes tracing the vents above. I stand in the center of the room, neural dampeners screaming with overload. Something in here is talking directly to my brainstem, and it wants to burn me down.

The moment Cleopatra plugs in the exploit, the room jumps from zero to full red alert. Sirens wail—an old sound, like the scream of an animal that knows it's been out-evolved. Gas erupts from the ceiling in shimmering clouds, every molecule designed to break the will of anyone breathing it. Ban is on me before I can move. She shoves me to the floor, slaps a rebreather mask over my mouth, and punches the seal tight. Her own mask's already up. Cleopatra doesn't have a mask; she never expected the system to be this analog, this angry. Cleopatra coughs, eyes wild, but keeps working the panel, augmentations firing in every color. Her overlays are visible now, projected in tight bands of light from her temples. "Forty seconds," she says. "Then the kill drones."

Ban drags me behind the nearest server rack, sets her gun to autofire, and takes aim at the vent nearest Cleopatra. I peek around the corner. The gas is so thick now I can barely see the lights. But I do see the ceiling shift—panels popping open like trapdoors. The first drone drops, a fat, ugly bastard with too many rotors and not enough personality. "Three o'clock, above maintenance panel. Weak spot at the rear junction," I say, voice muffled by the mask.

Ban fires, once, twice. The first round hits armor; the second shreds a cluster of servos, and the drone shudders, drops, and slams to the floor. But there's more—three, maybe five—moving through the gas like sharks in a sewer. Cleopatra's voice comes thin and slow: "Manual override isn't working. Need a direct physical hack."

Ban gestures to me, then at the drones. "Cover her," she says, then bolts across the room.

I run, lungs burning from the effort. The neural dampeners make every movement feel like I'm underwater, but adrenaline pushes me through. I get to Cleopatra just as the next drone drops, landing so hard the whole panel shakes. "Back panel," I say. "Twelve screws, four on each corner, two center. You'll need a passkey."

Cleopatra grins, lips blue from the gas. "Always a fucking puzzle with you, Darby." She grabs my left hand, jams a micro-laser into my palm, and uses it to burn out the screws. A drone swings at us, claws extended. I duck, dragging Cleopatra down with me. Ban shoots it mid-arc. The drone explodes in a confetti of wire and glass, spraying us both with plastic shards. Cleopatra's hand is shaking, but she gets the panel open. She plunges both arms into the mess of ancient chips and pulls out a flat black wafer, old enough to have lived through three corporate coups and one actual war.

A drone lands directly above her, laser sight tracing a line between Cleopatra's eyes. Ban stands behind me, gun up, the kill switch in her left hand. She hesitates. The world pauses. I see Ban's mind: She could end Cleopatra right now, no witness, clean break. Or she could take the shot and save her, risking everything for an enemy who's been nothing but betrayal and teeth. Ban curses and fires. The round takes the drone's laser eye out; it stumbles, then locks onto Ban as the bigger threat. "Go!" Ban screams. "Get the core and run!"

I grab Cleopatra and drag her back toward the exit. She's gasping, but she's got the wafer locked in a death grip. Alarms reach a new octave, and a fresh wall of gas pours from the vents. The last drone is closing fast, Ban doing a serpentine dance to keep its attention. She fires, each shot precise, but the drone's casing is better than the others. It absorbs the hits, then launches a cluster of microdarts at her. Ban ducks, rolls, and comes up with the gun ready. She tags the drone's battery, a lucky shot. The whole thing detonates, raining battery acid and plastic. Ban's jacket smokes, but she doesn't slow.

The far door begins to close—old school, pure steel, no mercy. "Ten seconds!" Cleopatra shouts, her overlays back to full burn. I haul her toward the door. Ban follows, limping now but still dangerous. We reach the exit as the slab is half-closed. Ban turns and fires three blind shots into the vault, just to keep anything else from following us. She dives, slides under the door, and I feel the wind of it as it slams shut with a seismic *thunk*. We tumble into the main tunnel, the sound of the vault's alarms receding behind us. Ban rips her mask off, breathing hard, face streaked with sweat and blood. "Did you get it?"

Cleopatra holds up the wafer, hands shaking. "If I hadn't, you'd have let the drone finish me."

Ban glares, but then something in her face relaxes. “Maybe.”

Cleopatra looks at me, eyes raw. “Thank you,” she says, voice almost human. I just nod, too tired to speak. The three of us stagger down the tunnel, the echo of alarms still rattling my skull. I look at Ban, then at Cleopatra, and realize I have no idea what comes next. But I want to see it.

We limp back to the safehouse, Cleopatra two steps ahead and Ban at my side, blood smearing down her leg where the acid got her. The city is quiet again, post-alarm, post-crisis; the only evidence we survived is the taste of copper and ozone still leaking from our lungs. Ban doesn't speak. Not to me, not to Cleopatra. She holsters her gun but doesn't bother to clean the barrel, just sits at the kitchen table and waits for something to kill.

Cleopatra doesn't wait for an invitation. She moves to the workbench, peels off the ruined sleeve of her suit, and jacks the data wafer into the slab. The slab blinks, then lights the wall in a wash of blue. At first, it's a mess: columns of raw code, gigabytes of names, incident reports, personnel trees. But as Cleopatra works the keys, the data collapses into a single, beautiful horror: a map of Moshimoto's brain. Ban squints at the display. “This supposed to mean something to me, or are you just showing off?”

Cleopatra ignores the jab. “You'll see,” she says, and flicks a finger at the interface. The wall erupts with new color, three huge orbs spinning at the center. Each orb is ringed with names, faces, corporate designations—hundreds of lines feeding in and out, every connection pulsing with live risk.

"This is the war inside Moshimoto. No one owns the company. They're all fighting for it, three factions at minimum, each running their own version of the integration protocol." She taps the first orb. The display zooms in on a cluster of executive faces, each stamped "Continuity Directive." Their overlays shimmer with the color of cold money. "The Directive is old-school. They want to keep unreadables and use them as black-box tools, but keep everything in corporate control."

Ban makes a face. "That sounds like your crowd."

Cleopatra smiles, but only with her mouth. "Not anymore." She shifts to the second orb, marked "Purity Protocol." The names here are colder, the faces all matching, like someone copied them from the same genetic starter pack. "These psychos want to wipe every unaugmented mind off the map. If they win, no more edge cases, no more risk."

Ban glances at me, then looks away. "Fuck them."

The last orb is the smallest, burning hot. "Sovereign Cognition," Cleopatra says, and her voice cracks, just a little. "My side; they want to free the system, let unreadables outgrow the old code. Maybe break the company. Maybe break the world."

Ban leans back, arms crossed, and watches the pattern spin. "So that's your angle. You didn't save us. You just want to use us."

Cleopatra meets her gaze, overlays running full display—numbers, odds, tiny flames of possibility flickering up and down her jaw. "I'm dead anyway. Moshimoto will overwrite me the second I fall out of line. The only thing that matters is which version of the future gets to survive."

Ban laughs, low and exhausted. "That's real inspiring."

I step to the wall and run my finger along the lines. "If we can get into the right protocol, we can play them off each other. Trigger a chain reaction, maybe. Destroy more than just the local instance."

Cleopatra nods. "You get it, Darby. Night-self always was better at strategy."

Ban doesn't argue. She's still angry, but now it's at the whole system, not just Cleopatra. I look at the schematic, then at Cleopatra, then at Ban. "Okay," I say. "Let's burn this to the ground."

Ban stands and cracks her knuckles. "You really think this'll work?"

Cleopatra's smile is empty but bright. "Seventeen percent chance we make it out. Eighty-three percent chance we take a lot of bastards with us."

Ban shrugs. "Best odds I've heard in weeks."

We get to work. The overlays light the room, and the city outside keeps spinning, like it doesn't know it's about to eat itself alive. This is how it always ends. But this time, maybe, we get to choose what comes next.

Chapter 19

They say integration is painless. They say a lot of things: "It's over in seconds," "You won't feel a thing," "Most patients experience euphoria." But the thing about lying is, you have to believe the person on the slab is too stupid or too dead to remember the truth. They don't say, "We strap you down because otherwise you'll try to eat your own tongue when the cascade hits." They don't say, "You'll shit yourself from the voltage." They don't say, "Most of you won't make it back with the part that makes you 'you' still attached."

I make a game of counting how many times the lead technician stares at my hands, probably imagining them on her windpipe. The upload chamber is colder than my last six birthdays, which is saying something since most of those happened in storage units or the back seat of an abandoned sedan. This room is white and perfectly shaped for death: domed ceiling, two exits, all surfaces sealed for easy hosing. Overhead, a nervous system of wiring pulses with blue intent, each node blinking in time with my heartbeat—except it's not mine anymore. There's a little delay, like the room is waiting to see if I'll make it.

There are four techs in white coveralls, not a drop of color anywhere except for the red Moshimoto badge at their collar. The guards wear black with blue stripes, sidearms fixed and faces slack with the anticipation of a shift spent watching someone else get violated. They don't even try for bedside manner. The lead, a short, rectangular woman with triple-augmented eyes and a voice that could bore a hole in granite, reads the chart at the foot of my chair. She doesn't look at me as she speaks.

"Subject: Darby Skelm. Male, age thirty-eight, classified Unreadable Type-Red. Exemption status revoked as of twenty-three hundred yesterday." She scans down the page, lips moving faster than the words. "Primary goal: neural harvest and integration into Tier One instance of the Moshimoto mainframe. Secondary goal: minimize residual artifact." She looks up. "Any last requests?"

I spit a clot of old blood onto the floor. It lands a centimeter from her boot. "Don't fuck up the haircut. It's my best feature."

She nods, unmoved. "We'll preserve the skull cap if the matrix is stable. Otherwise, we burn the remains. That's protocol."

Her assistant, a hunched man with the pallor of a shut-in and the hands of a violinist, preps the neural mesh: a nest of gold wires and microfilaments, a hundred stingers blooming from the plug. He lines it up with the base of my skull, brushes away the sweat with a tissue, and says, "Hold still."

I make a show of trying to break my own neck before the harness goes tight. The technician smirks; he's seen worse.

The mesh clicks, a noise so soft it's like a baby learning to swear. Then it's in, and every nerve in my spine starts to ring. They dial up the pre-flight sedation. I can feel it crawling through my blood, hot and chemical, turning every muscle to warm custard. But I'm still there, still me, because the nightmares haven't started yet.

Lead Tech steps to the console, which is shaped like a baby grand piano for maximum intimidation, and hits the power. She glances at me, then at the guards. "Ready to log?" The guards nod. One draws his sidearm and points it at my face, just in case I try to Houdini out of this with a head full of sedative and sixteen kilos of duct tape. I give him a wink. He flinches. Lead Tech toggles a switch, and the world narrows to a point of hot blue light.

The first thing you notice is your teeth. They rattle. Every second of microcurrent shakes them to the bone so hard you can feel the fillings compressing into the roots. I want to scream, but my mouth is already full of blood. The chair reclines, and I can see the ceiling again, but it's not the same: the domed white is now a pulsing, living surface, crawling with faint shadows that slither just below the paint. I think of Ban, of her hands on my jaw, the way she used to check my teeth after a fight—"If you lose another, I'll have to switch you to soft foods, Skelm"—and I almost laugh. But then the mesh goes live.

It starts in the spinal cord, a gentle hiss that builds into a shrieking column of light up the vertebrae, through the brainstem, and detonating in the cortex. Every synapse is now an antenna, every glial cell a tiny, screaming repeater. The pain is not pain, it's certainty: every possible version of me, all memories and wishes and lies, compressed to a diamond point and then ground to paste.

I taste copper. I taste ozone. I taste the protein bar Ban ate three hours ago, because she left the wrapper on the countertop and my memory is a vacuum for the irrelevant. The mesh begins to tease apart the layers. Daytime Skelm, with his math and reason and dislike of small talk. Night-shift Skelm, the bastard, the survivor, the animal. I feel them pull at each other, fighting for surface area, but the mesh is greedy. It wants both, wants all, wants the whole mess packed into a single digestible pill.

I see the lead tech's face through a blur of blue. She's reciting something, probably to the console, but her lips look like they're chewing through beeswax. "Integration at forty percent. Significant resistance from host. Increase voltage."

The assistant flicks a dial. The world turns white. I bite through the plastic mouth guard, then through the inside of my cheek, and the blood leaks down my throat in hot, metallic waves. The guards back up a step. I see it in the corner of my left eye, which is now running its own visual field three seconds ahead of the right. They're worried. Maybe I'll blow the circuit; maybe I'll die and ruin their efficiency rating.

I want to show them something beautiful. I focus on the memory of Ban's laugh, the time she shot a man in the kneecap for "failure to communicate," and let it rise to the top of the soup. The mesh latches on. It loves violence, loves stories. I can feel it shunting those neural patterns into some secure side channel, tagging them as "priority artifact." The lead tech leans in. She's worried too. "Approaching max resistance threshold. Subject is not complying. Recommend manual override."

The assistant looks at her, then at me. "He's a Red. We can't risk a spike. If the mesh fries—"

She slaps the console. "Override it. I don't care if he strokes out, I want the mind online."

I think about telling them to go fuck themselves, but the words turn to smoke in my mouth. The override hits, and the world breaks.

Now I'm both above and below myself.

Above: the high, frozen clarity of a system doing exactly what it was designed for. A beautiful machine, even if I'm the one being milled. I see my memories folding, curling, being pasted into neat strips for processing. The parts of me that ever wanted to sleep, ever wanted love or comfort, are sliced out first, chewed up and spun into a digital shroud. Those fragments float, like ice chips in ethanol, before the next phase of extraction.

Below: the meat. It's seizing still, but the pain is a background hum. My tongue is gone—bitten off, maybe, or just drowned in blood. My hands curl against the restraints, nails digging into my own palms. The mesh is now inside the bone, unraveling the architecture, looking for secrets in the folds. Somewhere, a voice is screaming. It's me, but it's not. I can feel the echoes in the air, bouncing off the curved walls, amplified and fed back into my own ears as an endless, recursive shriek. If I could, I'd laugh.

The process takes forever. Or a second. It's impossible to tell. At some point, the smell of burning plastic gives way to the crisp tang of ozone and urine. My bowels let go. The guards hold their noses, but nobody stops the process. The lead tech is yelling. "We're losing the left temporal! Increase feed! Dump the backup!"

The mesh obeys. Every thought I've ever had, every doubt and fuck-up and secret hunger, is now copied, crosschecked, and slotted into a directory marked "Primary Artifact: Darby Skelm." I wonder if they'll keep it in a climate-controlled vault, or just run it as an interactive novelty for bored middle management.

My last thought before the world finally goes pure cold blue is of Ban, standing in the rain, hands in her pockets, mouth crooked in a way that's almost a smile. The light floods in. My body jerks once, twice, then goes limp. On the inside, I'm already gone. But I still taste the blood. And somewhere, far above the burn and the noise, I can feel the first whisper of someone else waiting. This is how it starts. This is how you become more than one thing. The mesh peels me out of my skull and pours me into the dark. And for a brief, holy instant, I'm everything at once. Then the world goes white, and I'm not there to see it.

Welcome to heaven, except everyone's God and all the angels have your face. The whiteout from the mesh trip gives way to a grid of blue lines—thin, perfect, infinite. They run in every direction, humming with intent, and at each intersection is a version of me: happy, angry, dead, never born, even the one that stayed in the burbs and never took the first job at Moshimoto. Every copy is an echo, and every echo is hungry.

The integration process promised instant upload. This is more like being projectile-vomited through a thousand dead-end streets, each lined with billboards advertising the life I could have had. I crash through them at terminal velocity, each one tearing off another patch of self, another memory chunk, another unfulfilled fuck-up.

My first day at Moshimoto: The memory is hot and clinical. The building's white as a teeth commercial, with a lobby staffed by perfect strangers and the stench of future ambition. I'm wearing a suit I borrowed from a dead cousin, but it fits because we had the same taste in getting fired. Émilie waits for me at the reception, already backlit by power and indifference. She leads me up, all brisk and effortless, talking in that flat monotone that means every word is a trap and every compliment is already spent. "You're the new model," she says. "Show me you're not defective."

The elevator is cold and mirrored, so I see myself the way she does: too much jaw, not enough eye contact, shoes a week past polish. She likes it, which means I hate it. We arrive at a conference room where the walls are glass and the chairs are chrome. Émilie hands me a contract, the print so dense it bends light. I sign without reading. Her smile is almost human. "Welcome to your last job," she says. I feel the papercut from the pen, sharp and perfect, like the first time Ban split my lip.

The system fast-forwards, reeling through every late night, every bad idea, every time I cut a corner or bled out a rival. They're all here, compressed and set to repeat: Skelm the loyalist, Skelm the spy, Skelm the addict, Skelm the traitor. Most days I was all four. The mesh wants to file these, tag and bag and lock them in a directory of "Experience: User, Red Type." But my head is a garbage fire; the memories won't pack down. The code keeps glitching, leaking Ban's face into every bad memory like she's the ghost in my machine. It pisses off the sorting algorithms—beautiful. I get a few seconds of nothing. Then the memory changes:

My first split. I'm twenty-one, watching myself fuck up a neural relay install on a city grid, hands shaking because I know if I miswire it, someone dies. Someone always dies. The supervisor screams at me, *"You're doing it wrong!"* but she's not talking to me, not really. She's talking to the other Skelm, the one who's already in the system, the one who does this job perfectly and by the book. I don't remember training a second Skelm. I don't remember becoming two, or three, or ten, but the split is there now, coded at the DNA and up. The overlay turns red. "CONFLICT," it says, in typeface so ugly it must be legal.

The job gets done, because it has to. But now there are two me's, and both want the steering wheel. Every memory after that is a fistfight for control: which hand to use, which voice to trust, which urge to chase. The mesh eats it up, delighted by the redundancy. I blink and I'm back in the lobby, or maybe I never left. Émilie is waiting, clipboard in hand. "You're special," she says. "They'll study you for years after you're gone." I want to punch her, but I also want her to hold me. That's the split. That's the joke.

The crash gets rougher. I start to lose the difference between past and now. I see Ban the first time, her eyes so dark they make all the world's blue look cheap. She's in a bar, maybe, or a cell, maybe both, and she's making a bet she can break my fingers without me making a sound. She's right, obviously. But she also buys me a drink after. I taste the gin, and then the memory tears away and I'm in another job, another death, another bullet with my name on it.

Now the code goes full digital: the grid opens into a desert, all black sand and glass towers, the sky rotating like a screen-saver with a seizure disorder. The real world is gone; this is where the upload gets real. I stumble through the code, trying to assemble some version of myself that can walk. The sand is sharp and it cuts, but I don't bleed. I just leave chunks of memory behind: old fights, old lovers, the endless parade of faces that wanted me dead.

There's something wrong here. I feel it before I see it. A glitch, a shudder in the landscape, like the whole place is being redrawn while I'm still inside. At the edge of the world, I spot the first of the resistance cells. It looks like nothing: a pixel of black in a sea of blue, a dead spot in a living system. But I know the signature—Red Type, unreadable, like me. I move toward it, and the code thickens, gets noisy, until I have to hack my way through like it's made of razor wire.

I get close, and the pixel unpacks itself. Not a person, not an AI, just a pattern, a suggestion, a map of what could be. But inside it is a message, left like a mine under the sand. *WE WAIT FOR YOU.* That's it. No sender, no address, just a promise. The code tries to shunt me away, but I dig in, making the glitch bigger. I feel the system start to panic, rerouting memory, stacking the error logs higher and higher until the whole sky goes black. A voice finds me in the dark. It's not mine, but it's familiar, like hearing a recording of yourself played at half speed and in a different language. "Your pattern is unique," it says. "You don't fit. That's why you survive."

The world resets around me: now I'm in a room made of mirrors, infinite and awful. Each mirror holds a different Darby Skelm. Some are dead, some are monsters, one is happy, and I want to punch his face in just to see what happens. The voice becomes a face, a shadow-puppet built from lines of code and bad intent. It flickers between forms—sometimes a person, sometimes an algorithm, sometimes the memory of a nightmare I forgot on purpose. It names itself: Cipher.

"Why am I here?" I ask.

Cipher's mouth splits, a black hole with too many teeth. "You're the payload. The rest are just carriers."

I look down at my hands. They're fractal, each finger splitting into dozens, each drip of sweat replaced by a waterfall of data. I try to clench a fist, but the hands aren't mine anymore. They're just what's left of me in the system. "Can you get me out?" I say, but it's the wrong question.

Cipher shakes its head, or maybe the world shakes and the face stays still. "Escape is a privilege. You're here to do damage." I feel the mesh tightening, the system closing ranks, the memory of the white room pressing down from above. I taste the blood again, but now it's code, sharp and metallic and sour with fear. Cipher steps closer, its form collapsing into a perfect sphere of light. "Hold on to your split, Darby. If you let them pack you down, you're nothing."

I nod, or at least try. The pressure is building. The system wants to compact me into a file and lock it forever. But the more I remember, the more I split, and the harder it gets for them to finish the job. Around me, the mirrors start to shatter, one by one, each burst releasing another Skelm, another fragment of self. They rush to me, clutching memories and dreams and regrets, all desperate not to be erased. Cipher circles me, each orbit leaving behind a new memory, a new copy. "You're almost ready," it says. "Next time the system cracks, run. Find us."

The system shudders, the sky goes blue again, and the desert comes back, now filled with towers made of glass and screams. The mesh is losing control. For the first time since they strapped me down, I can feel myself—the real me, the night-shift bastard, the animal in the wires—pushing back. I look for Cipher, but it's gone, or maybe it never was. The code wants to erase me, but I'm too messy to kill. I pull the pieces of myself together, making a new version of myself from the scraps. I laugh, because it's all I have left.

Then the world cracks again, and I tumble into the next layer, the memory of Ban waiting on the other side, her voice loud and clear even through the noise. "Don't you dare let them own you," she says. I don't intend to. I run, because that's all I've ever been good at. And behind me, the grid burns.

The grid is a city at midnight: everything humming, nothing alive, all the lights programmed for maximum despair. I walk through it because what else do you do? Each step fractures into a thousand: every time I pick a direction, a dozen other versions of me take the others, each peeling off into their own future, their own memory loop. At the center is the crossroads, a field of obsidian glass criss-crosses with highways of pure blue code. Above, the sky is a billion-threaded net, every strand a pulse from someone else being digested by the system. Below, the darkness is not empty—it's full of hungry things, patterns that twitch and chew the edge of the world, waiting for a crack.

Cipher waits in the middle, barely holding a shape. It's a person and a symbol and an error message all at once, shifting every millisecond into something new. It radiates anticipation like heat. "Welcome back," it says, voice spliced from all the people I've ever lied to.

I step up, toeing the line at the crossroads. "Did I ever leave?"

Cipher's smile twitches. "You're everywhere now. That's the problem."

I glance down. My feet are a fractal of toes and boot prints and scars. Even the bloodstain from Ban's last bandage is here, bright as a warning. "So what's the play?" I ask. "You said I was the payload."

Cipher ripples, splinters into a spectrum of possibilities, then snaps back to a single sharp form. "The system wants to flatten you, pack your mind into the right size and shape. If you let it, you'll have full access to everything. You could run the world from here." I wait for the but. There's always a but. Cipher obliges. "You'll be gone. All the Skelms, all the memory, turned into code. No difference from the other ghosts."

"Or?"

Cipher pauses, letting the word fall like a hammer. "Or you fight the integration. Hold the split. Stay fractured. Keep a wedge in the code—enough to do damage, enough to remember you're real. But they'll hunt you forever. And you'll be limited."

I stare at the lines. They want me so bad I can taste it. I almost say yes, because the power is so close I can smell it. Then, from somewhere off-grid, Ban's voice cuts through: "Whatever you choose, I'm with you." It's not a memory; it's a live feed. Somewhere outside, she's waiting, comm open, trusting I'll pick the right path. I feel the split in me: the analyst who wants to run the show, the night-self who just wants to break things and leave. For a perfect moment, they synchronize. I look up at Cipher, which is now just a floating black sphere ringed in burning white. "Let's fuck it up."

Cipher laughs, a sound like static and breaking teeth. "Excellent."

I open the first vault inside my head. It hurts, like digging a bullet out of your own thigh, but the pain is what keeps me from becoming a bot. The logic bombs Ban and I built are coded into the parts of my memory I hate most: the failures, the betrayals, the people I watched die. I crack the first. The grid shudders. Lines of code spiral off the highways, dissolving the neat blue order into spray-paint chaos. Security subroutines flash orange, then red, then dead. For a second, I see the faces of every lost friend I ever sold out—Katherine, Dorothy, even a couple of the better bots. They smile, sharp and animal, and then the world flips again.

The system counterattacks, trying to compress me into a single, compliant node. I let it in. I show it everything: every shitty decision, every night on the run, every time Ban risked her life to drag me through one more bad day. The overload fries their filter, and for a moment, the whole grid is just me, screaming. Cipher is delighted. It shouts instructions I don't need: "Next payload, now! Don't stop!"

I'm ahead of it. I open the second vault, then the third. The grid rips open and floods with raw data, ten times what the architecture can handle. You can feel the mainframe start to melt, neurons and circuits boiling over into the digital street. Somewhere outside, I know Ban is watching. I know Pale and Steven are lying low, waiting for the fire to get hot enough so they can run. I push the last memory—Ban's laugh, the way she looked at me when she thought I was dying, that mix of hate and hope—and I spike it through the core. A shockwave rolls out, pure signal, erasing everything it touches.

Cipher flashes with all the colors in the spectrum, then turns to me, almost gentle. "You did it."

I don't feel triumphant. I feel empty, like I just bled out every decent thing in my life and all that's left is the desire to make them pay. The system is not dead. But now it's bleeding. And so am I. The grid collapses to a point. I'm back in the white room, only now it's empty. The chair is gone. The techs are gone. The walls pulse red with alarms. I hear Ban again, faint but close: "Get out. Now."

I try to move, but I'm still trapped. The mesh is burning my skull; the code is all tangled. It's taking every shred of self I have to keep from letting go. Cipher appears beside me, solid for the first time, a hand on my shoulder. "Hold on," it says. "You're almost free."

I breathe in, then exhale blood and numbers. The world narrows to a tunnel of red and blue. I run, and the rest follows.

Outside, the first of the real-world logic bombs detonates, turning Moshimoto HQ into a firework of light and glass. Alarms spiral into the night. Inside, I hold the wedge, just barely. I am not gone. Not yet. Ban is out there, waiting. I just have to find the way back. The mainframe howls in pain, and the world explodes again.

In the moment before I black out, I feel every memory at once: Ban's hand on my chest, Pale's snarl, Steven's curse, Émilie's eyes. I remember why I started. I remember why I can't quit. They thought they could digest me, but I'm the part that sticks in your teeth. I ride the explosion all the way out, and somewhere, I start laughing again. It sounds like freedom.

Chapter 20

Plug in. That's all they say: "It's just another neural transition. Like logging in, but deeper." The fucking liars. The instant I breach the first node, I lose the shape of my own body. The world melts, congeals, and the pain is sublime—pressure behind my eyes, like the time Ban broke my nose and set it herself with a cigarette and a fistful of antique gauze. Except this time, when I look up, I'm not in a room. I'm in the grid.

My first impression is that the Moshimoto mainframe is bigger than any of us. It's an animal—no, a city, all roots and branching arteries, a trillion layered glass corridors whirring with digital speed. The ground isn't ground; it's a seething dataspace that flexes when I touch it. The walls are nothing, then everything: zeroes and ones, then black marble with fractal veins, then shifting honeycomb with each cell holding a slow-moving, blue-lit parasite.

My second impression is that I'm not alone, but also not whole. My self fractures on impact, splitting into half a dozen runners, each with a different priority. There's an analyst—strict, methodical, already mapping the network like it's a hostile city. There's the night-skull bastard, blunt force and wild logic, hot for violence. There's the part of me that just wants to hide, and the part that would sell out everyone I love if it meant surviving an hour longer.

The system doesn't like this. You can hear the hum of its immune response. But unreadables, by definition, don't follow protocols. I see where the logic is supposed to force me into the designated holding pen—the "User Integration Module," a nice, sterile cage for copycats and office drones—but my mind flickers at an angle, and suddenly I'm in a maintenance shaft, five floors off the map. It's not hacking, not really. It's being the wrong answer to a question the system doesn't know how to ask.

I tunnel everywhere at once. The city's defenses respond: white-clad guardian routines, bristling with suppression algorithms, armed with "compliance hammers" meant to pacify unruly thought. The first swarm catches a fragment of me in a corridor lined with teeth—each tooth a locked file, a memory stripped from a less lucky target. They try to subdue me with bliss. A rush of dopamine analogs, a flood of pseudo-nostalgia. I see my old apartment, the one from before Ban. She's there in the doorway, mouth open like she might say something forgiving.

It almost works, but the night-self is immune to comfort. He shreds the memory, lets the fake Ban dissolve, and tears the "compliance hammers" apart with a logic bomb I loaded before I even entered. The system howls. Every corridor floods with counter-intrusion routines, each a shade smarter than the last. They stack like dominoes, wall off whole city blocks in seconds, and try to trick me into recursive traps: infinite mirrors, dead-end loops where you could lose a decade in a second.

For a few microseconds, it works. I fall into a loop, a memory of Katherine's hands threading sensor filaments along my scalp, the gentle pressure of her knuckle against the bridge of my nose. She's saying, *"Don't be afraid, Darby. It's just code. Pain isn't real unless you want it to be."* The memory's perfect, which is how I know it's a trap. Katherine would never have said that, not to me, not with her own record of what code could do to a mind. I smile, savor the ache, and let another fragment take the wheel. He's the ghost, the runner, the piece of me that never made it past age twenty-four.

He skips. Time warps. Suddenly, I'm everywhere at once: six floors above the central server, in the catacombs below the mainframe, perched at the top of a watchtower so far from the core I can taste vacuum. Every instance of myself is engaged, running its own logic tree, some of them already dead, but they all serve the same purpose: distract the system, bleed off its immune response, and let the real me slither closer to the center.

The city narrows as I approach the core. Security is denser, but less sophisticated: just brute force, static guns and kill zones with overlapping fields of pain. It's beautiful, in a way—how old code survives every update, stubborn as a cockroach. A thousand memories bubble up, most of them fake, but I let them pass through. They're not hooks, not now. I've learned the trick: the best way to fool a system is to believe your own bullshit.

At the nucleus, I see her. Émilie's digital signature is more than just a name. It's a cathedral floating in the void—a structure of white glass, blue light, and arches that support nothing but more arches. Every wall is lined with running code, billions of live contracts, every clause a blade. At the top is a window, and behind it, her face. But it's not her, not exactly. The eyes are too bright. The smile is predatory. She's watching, and she knows I'm here. But the unreadable parts of me are a blank in her surveillance feed, a smear in the air. She's curious, not yet afraid. That'll change.

I move into the side corridors, through admin nodes and maintenance tunnels mapped to look like old, human spaces. The logic bombs are physical here—bright red, pin-sharp, hovering in the air like landmines or seeds. Each one is coded with a signature only I can detonate. I plant them at the weak spots: at the base of a "clocktower" where the timekeeping routines try to maintain order, in the "sub-basement" where user logs are stored and then forgotten, at the "top floor" of a sky-piercing spire where Moshimoto keeps its darkest contracts.

Every time I plant a bomb, a piece of me dies, and another fragment inherits the plan. Sometimes I see myself, a hundred yards down the corridor, nodding approval. Sometimes I watch one version of myself get chewed to pieces by security. No regrets. The dead versions buy time for the rest. The system adapts, sending hunter-killers now—free agents, clever little fuckers that know how to look for non-patterns. One gets close, almost takes my head off, but Ban's voice rips through the datafeed just in time. “Watch your left, Skelm. The next node is loaded.”

Her voice is analog, fuzzy with static, but perfect. I feel her hand on my shoulder, the way she always steadied me before a job. I feed the moment into the fragment, and it twists, evades, and slides past the threat. We’re close now. The main feed pulses—a heartbeat, a countdown, something hot and urgent in the air. The architecture here is denser, less like a city and more like a gut: twisting tunnels, blind sacs, places designed for digestion. This is where unreadables get broken down, processed, and turned into corporate fertilizer.

I see the remnants of those who came before me: trapped memories, failed uploads, ghosts of technicians and runners who thought they could outsmart the system. They look like stains in the air, or sometimes just a whimper echoing down a corridor. Somewhere, I hear Katherine’s laugh—real this time, or close enough to cut. I slow, savor the sound, and let the best part of me take charge.

The bombs are in place. The system’s confused. The next step is to breach the cathedral and leave a piece of myself inside Émilie’s “office,” ready for the final trigger. I reach the cathedral steps. The security routines don’t even try—they sense I’m an anomaly, but by now, the mainframe is too gummed up with clones and fragments to send a proper defense. At the door, a memory slams me: the time Ban and I stole the Sapphire Key from a datafortress in Paris, her lips on my neck as the alarms screamed, our laughter mixing with the scent of burning plastic. I ride the memory up the stairs, straight into the chamber at the top.

Émilie waits behind a glass wall, her face lit in holy blue. She doesn't speak. She just watches as I plant the last bomb, right in the center of her office. For a moment, I feel sorry. Not for her, but for the system. It's old, tired, running code nobody remembers how to patch. In a better world, maybe it would have been left to die. Ban's voice cuts in, closer now, more urgent. "Bombs in place, Skelm? Because it's about to get loud out here."

I laugh, the sound rippling through every version of myself in the city. "Locked and loaded, Ban."

She's breathing heavy on the channel. "Ready for round two?"

I picture her, pistol in one hand, fistful of chaos in the other. "Always," I say.

The bombs pulse, every one in sync. The system feels it and trembles. And I wait, hovering just outside the final detonation, savoring the prelude. One fragment of me checks the link to Ban and makes sure it's clean. Another checks for the ghost of Katherine, just in case. We're all here. Every Skelm, every regret, every failure, all wrapped up in a single, glorious split. "Phase one complete," I whisper. And then the world holds its breath, waiting for the call.

Digital time isn't measured in seconds. It's measured in the number of times you die and come back before the system figures out how to kill you for good. In the microseconds between Ban's last word and the start of her neural extraction, the grid goes full arctic. The corridors freeze, logic flows ice over, and every copy of myself left in the city spasms with something too sharp to be called pain. The ghosts in the tunnels—that's what the old runners used to call it when another mind was about to fry. I know the feeling.

Ban's signal is strong, but it's also wrong—scrambled, too much voltage, running backward and upside-down like the time she drank half a liter of solvent to win a bet. Except this time, the hangover is coming for both of us. I try to reestablish the tether, find the thread Katherine spun into the dark, the last patch she coded before they turned her off for good. For a second, it's there—a whisper of static, a half-remembered lullaby. Then the whole city shakes, and the white cathedral where I planted the final bomb blooms with a cancer of new code, each cell screaming Ban's name.

Émilie. Of course. She's clever. She knows how to pull a lever and watch the world react. She's using Ban as a flare, a black hole of suffering to lure me out. Or maybe she thinks it'll make me hesitate, fuck up the timing, and let them purge my signal before the detonation can propagate. She's almost right. For the first time since I broke into the mainframe, I feel lost. No plan, no next step. Only the raw, animal urge to find Ban, to fix it, even though I know that's not how any of this works.

The pain intensifies. Ban's in the chair now; I can sense the neural mesh chewing through her brainstem, taste the salt of her sweat, the copper of her blood. It should be impossible, but Katherine designed the system to channel pain and memory both ways. It's a two-way mirror. I run every fragment of myself at the cathedral, trying to overwhelm the code and break through the newly hardened walls. The Émilie at the top is waiting—she's replaced the glass with obsidian, and the stairway with a single, narrow shaft lined with razors. I go anyway.

Inside, the air is full of Ban: memories I never had, regrets she kept hidden even from me. That night on the roof when she said she could see all the city's pain at once and it made her feel holy, or maybe just high. I walk through the rooms of her mind, each one painted in the colors she would never let herself wear in real life. There's a picture of us—old, impossible, both smiling, both with all our teeth. I want to stay there. I want to burn it to the ground. At the center, I find her.

She's strapped to the chair, jaw clamped open, sweat and blood pooling under the plastic mask. Émilie stands over her, the real one and the digital one, both immaculate, both bored. She's tuning the mesh, tweaking the settings, looking for the sweet spot between consciousness and collapse. I try to get closer to Ban, but she's out of reach. I can only watch.

"Your boyfriend is losing coherence," Émilie says, voice piped through every corridor, every logic thread. "He can't hold the split much longer. Give up, Ban. It's over."

Ban's eyes roll back, but she spits blood at Émilie's shoes, just like before. "He's not my boyfriend," she says, the words mashed by the voltage. "He's the fucking apocalypse. And he hates you more than I do."

Émilie smiles, then turns the dial. The pain redlines. Ban's whole body arches against the restraints. The noise in the system goes hypersonic, and for a nanosecond, every process in Moshimoto chokes. That's my window. I pile all the remaining copies of myself into the cathedral. Some die in the entryway, some get caught in the razors and turn into ghosts, but enough make it to the top floor to tip the balance. I hit the obsidian door, and it shatters. I rush Émilie, knock her away from Ban, then kneel at Ban's side. She looks at me—really looks, both eyes open, both pupils blown to ink. "Do it, Darby," she says, words soft and perfect. "This is bigger than us. Light the fuse."

I want to argue, but she's right. I cup her face, or the memory of it, and she leans into the hand. Émilie is already back, claws in the digital world, rewriting the walls, patching the doors, trying to kick me out before the bombs can sync. She shouts, but I can't hear her over the sound of Ban's heart. "Ready?" Ban asks, and even now, she's fucking with me, because she knows I'll never be ready. I let the split go. Every version of me merges, just for a second, and in that second the world is beautiful: all the loves, all the betrayals, all the mistakes, bundled up like a spark in a powder keg. I squeeze Ban's hand. She squeezes back. Then I light the fuse.

The grid erupts. Logic bombs go off in every corner, cascading through Moshimoto's core, eating code and memory and everything that ever mattered to the company. Security routines panic and collapse; the cathedral buckles, showering shards of black glass into the dark. Through it all, I hear Ban laughing—raw, wild, feral—like the first day we met. Émilie tries to run, but the system has no exits left. I see her avatar stuck in a feedback loop, melting down into static, screaming silently into the void. Ban is fading, but she's not scared. Not now. She says, "See you on the other side."

I hold on until the light eats us both. In the last nanosecond before the system dies, I see every future we never had: the wedding, the slow mornings, the kids we would never raise, the bar we'd run on the edge of nowhere. All of it real, all of it gone. I don't feel regret. Not anymore. Only love, and the perfect, infinite anger of wanting more time. Then it all blinks out and we're free.

Chapter 21

It begins before the countdown. My self splits, divides, and doubles, a recursion bomb with my name as the payload. I am every node, every exploit, every worm chewing at the root of this cathedral-brain. They never expected an attack vector that wanted to be the infection.

First fork: the analyst, straight-line, checksummed, already mapping the net's vascular system, parsing weak points in the Moshimoto topology. Second fork: the bastard, raw logic and violence, his answer to everything is "run it till it dies." Third: the hide instinct, slipping through admin tunnels, logging every move, feeding fake traffic to the real one. Fourth and fifth: meat dummies, decoys, built to stall intrusion countermeasures. The rest are split fractions, shunts, payloads, cannon fodder.

The first logic bomb goes off with the sound of a million hard drives dying at once. A thousand corridors filled with code and hunger. My fragment rides the rippling shockwave, sifting through glass corridors—no, blood vessels—no, datalines packed with living, shivering code. Moshimoto's immune system responds with that pathetic, exquisite overkill: every countermeasure spins up, security flags going blue, then orange, then the death-color red. The firewalls close in, trying to box me in an airlock, but they're trapping ghosts and echoes and deliberate misdirection.

I let one fragment die slowly, just to watch the diagnostics. I taste the sanitizer sweep, smell it: clinical, sharp as ozone, overlaid with the meaty aroma of burning insulation. The attack AI tries to run its protocol, but I've already fucked the hash tables. The system is chewing itself in circles, screaming recursive errors into the logs. I ride the surge, the rush, the sense of infinite bandwidth and nothing left to lose. "Integration incomplete," a system voice wails, distorted like a stadium echo, "user uncooperative, user uncooperative, user uncooperative—"

I duplicate the voice, re-code it, and beam it into every office, every conference call, every line of sight in the mainframe. A thousand executives piss themselves, or maybe that's just the way the net smells now. Moshimoto was never a city. It was a tumor with blue LEDs, and I am the worst strain of virus it ever dared to sequence. As the next logic bomb lights, I fracture even harder. Each fork acts on its own set of priorities. Some of me want to blow the main power, some want to melt the redundancy nodes, and some just want to pull the fire alarm and see what the suits do when the world unthreads under their feet.

In one corridor, I'm an avatar—six arms, mirrored glass for skin, and a face that reflects nothing but open sockets. I run at the security barricade, tear through it with wild hands, and as it tries to heal, I spit a recursive exploit into the gap. The hole gets bigger, ugly, cancerous. I hear the panicked chatter of admin routines as they try to patch it, but every fix is a new hole. I switch perspectives: now I'm a shadow, slinking through the silent tunnels between functions. I find the payroll archives, the blacksite code vault, the quarantine zone filled with angry, half-dead routines. I set them loose, mayhem in the back alleys of the net.

Another fork: I'm a ghost, floating above the process, watching as Moshimoto's brain fever climbs past safety limits. They're running hot, servers packed tighter than a battery cell. The cooling system can't keep up. I taste the synthetic coolant, biting and sweet, a last defense before the boards fry. I see the first sysadmin try to kill the process. He's a fat, unshaven blur, all fingers and hate. He thinks he's smart. He thinks he can ride the kill switch and reset the system before I do my work. I fork a personality just for him. A scream, a middle finger, a static-blasted meme, looping forever in his interface. He jerks back from the terminal, eyes wide, mouth forming my name: "Skelm!"

I laugh, and it's everywhere. Meanwhile, the propaganda walls begin to crack. Every screen that once spat out "Moshimoto: The Future of Mindful Capitalism" now floods with gibberish and melting gifs. I see the slogans re-coded: "FUTURE OF MINDFUL CATASTROPHE;" "YOUR BRAIN, OUR SLAUGHTER-HOUSE;" "THE NEXT PHASE OF EXTINCTION, NOW WITH MORE METADATA." It would be funny if it didn't taste like victory.

Another bomb; this one aimed straight at the backbone, the contract manager, the core of the core. I push the payload and feel it detonate. The lights in the virtual city strobe, stutter, then burn steady and blue, the color of corporate panic. Now the human response: executives in their glass offices, blinking as their overlays invert, the world suddenly black on white, every margin call and quarterly report replaced by the word ERROR, capitalized. Some of them try to fight back, calling IT, begging the analog phone lines for rescue. But it's all down, all noise.

In the real meatspace, the servers begin to run hot enough to melt the dust off their backs. Cooling fans die first, then the CPUs, then the clusters of VR heads that run the city's day-shift. In the security office, three men and a woman in black-on-black body armor start running physical sweeps of the server floors, but all their targeting data is gone. I watch them from every cam, laughing at how slow and helpless they look. One of my forks rides the cameras, every eye, every lens. I see Ban on an external feed, moving through a city that's suddenly more alive than any net I ever met. I see her face, see the focus in her jaw. She's running the plan, taking advantage of the holes I'm blowing in the system. For a second, the urge is to slow down, wait for her, match pace. But the bombs want to burn, and I let them.

Next wave: I dig into the legal archive, the repository of every NDA, every contract, every non-compete they ever forced on a worker. I run a macro and invalidate all of them. For a microsecond, the net shudders—ten thousand invisible handshakes, all unbound at once. The system responds with firewalls, harder this time. They throw black ICE, real corporate code, stuff with teeth and hate. But I am a hydra now, every process a different vector, every death a new chance to shatter their pretty illusions. They try to flood me with noise—millions of decoy pings, brute-force attacks, garbage in every channel. But I grew up on garbage. I eat it, metabolize it, and spit it back as more attacks surface.

The CEO herself—her digital signature is "ExecutiveThreeP-rime," what a fucking cliche—boots up her emergency console. She tries to run a rootkit to flush me from the lowest layer up. I recognize the code, the same code they used to wipe Katherine, the one that gave her a neural bleedout after her first real hack. I'm angry now. Night-self is back in charge. I dig into ExecutiveThreePrime's personal archive. I dump her emails, her calendar, her ten-year record of abuse and manipulation. I send them everywhere. The next time she tries to log in, every surface in her office is wallpapered with her own humiliations: nude shots, blackmail letters, her mother's last words on loop.

I push the last logic bomb, a suicide run straight at the main processor. For a second, the system holds—a stutter, a flicker, a desperate effort to keep the center intact. But nothing holds forever. The city collapses. Lights go dead. Servers cook. Fans scream, then die, then are silent. All that's left is the sound of my own laughter, echoing through the empty corridors of dead code. The last fork tries to remember what it's like to be a person. But the old world is gone. Only chaos remains. For a perfect instant, I feel nothing. No hunger, no regret, no need. Just the clean, crisp silence of a world without masters. It almost feels like peace. But I know better. There's always another job. There's always Ban, waiting to see if I survived.

And there's always a next system to break. I reset myself one last time and wait for the world to reboot.

The outer doors are glass, because of course they are. Nothing says "we have nothing to fear" like putting your entire legacy behind shatterable carbon mesh and praying nobody hates you enough to try. Ban stands under the entry awning, two meters of cold air between her and the first camera. I am the camera. She's changed since the last time I saw her live. Her hair is short, close to the scalp; her walk is different, more glide than stride. Every motion is a calculation, and she's running hot. I taste her pulse in the sensor feed, watch her through a dozen lenses.

The security in the lobby is old-school: two guards behind a bulletproof desk, three floaters with light armor and subsonics in their ears, a bot in the corner with a pulse carbine trained at crotch level. There's a killbox, a checkpoint, and a panic button under the nearest palmprint. None of it matters. I have already bricked the biometric scanners, and the only thing the bot will shoot is itself when the override hits.

Ban steps through the doors at exactly 01:24:00, local. The rain is a memory behind her, but she tracks water onto the floor, leaving a line of wet that will outlive half the people in this building. Guard One opens his mouth to speak, but she's already inside the killbox, badge flashed, hand in her pocket. She's running the "lost tourist" routine, one I saw her perfect in Denver, then Shanghai, then the burbs outside Minneapolis. But she's not here to fool anyone. The first shot is a distraction—through her own thigh, grazing the meat, arcing out at a precise angle to clip the guard at the knee.

He goes down hard, grabs at his leg, and never sees Ban draw the gun from her jacket and put two rounds through his vest, center mass. The next guard flips his pistol up, but the webbing on his sleeve catches, and Ban is already in his lap, yanking his arm out of its socket, then using the deadweight of his own body to shield her from the bot. The bot whirrs, confused, as I feed it a brand-new protocol: All threats are blue-badged. All threats are management. The bot panics, spins, and opens fire into the glass wall of the conference room behind them.

I watch Ban through the optic, the way she moves with the chaos, not against it. Her hands are wet, but the grip is steady. She uses the pain of her thigh as a strobe, letting it remind her to keep moving. She clears the checkpoint in nineteen seconds flat. The floaters are down—one's leaking into the carpet, one's twitching with a slug in his neck; the last is just gone, probably out the fire door. Ban doesn't chase. She waves at the camera, the one I'm riding, and mouths, "Ready?" I trigger the inner door. It clicks, disengages. She's through.

Now it's the big space: open-plan office, cubicles like teeth in a broken jaw. Every worker left here is a blue chip, a diehard, or an idiot. They scatter as Ban walks the main aisle, gun at her hip, jaw set. "Up," I say through the speaker, and she grins. On the elevator ride, I drop in via the maintenance interface, lock the car, and drop the brakes. The lift zips up thirty floors in eight seconds. Ban's braced against the corner, blood drip painting the brushed aluminum. At Floor 31, I ping the master security, tell it to open the elevator and then jam every other lift shaft shut. The doors pop, and there's Grandpa, shotgun in hand, guarding the hall.

“Nice ride,” he says, and Ban just nods.

The main conference room is a fishbowl: execs and heavy hitters, all circled around a speakerphone, every one of them talking at once. Ban leads with a flashbang—“Frag it,” Grandpa says, and she does—then walks in with Grandpa behind, gun raised. The room goes white, then gray.

The first exec to recover tries to bargain. “We can negotiate,” she says, but Ban just shoots her through the mouth. Two more stand, hands up, as if they forgot that the hands are never what gets you killed. Grandpa nails one with the shotgun, and Ban puts the other down with a clean shot to the orbital.

“Clear,” Ban says, and I shunt the rest of the floor’s security cams to static, so the backup can’t get a clear bead. Ban looks at Grandpa, at the wall of dead and dying, and then at the main screen where the Moshimoto logo is melting like ice under a blowtorch. She taps her comm. “Status?”

I answer. “Opening core in sixty.”

The plan is simple: meet at the heart, kill anything that’s not us. On the way, Ban limps, but never slows. Grandpa keeps behind, covering the corners, looting sidearms and zip cuffs as he goes. At the corridor leading to the server vault, Ban pauses, lets the headrush of pain clear, then pulls a patch from her belt and staples it over the wound. The hiss of the glue reminds her of the old days, cheap hospitals and cheaper highs.

Ahead, the door is shut tight. No badge, no entry. But the wiring is accessible if you know where to look, and I do. “Left panel, third rivet," I say into the speaker. Ban jams her finger under the rivet, pries, and pops the casing. The power relay is right there, begging for a short. She bridges it with the barrel of her gun, fires a single round through the circuit, and the vault door gasps open.

Inside is cold. Like meatpacking cold, but instead of hanging beef, there are racks and racks of humming, blue-lit servers. Four guards, black visors, standing at intervals. Two drop at once—Grandpa and Ban in sync. The third gets a shot off, grazing Grandpa's cheek, but Ban is there to finish it. The last guard is not a man, not anymore—just a bulked-out neurodroid, built for nothing but kill orders and chewing through threats. It steps from the shadow, blade-arm out, blood already painted on its chest from a previous engagement. Ban lets Grandpa handle it; she moves straight to the access ladder, climbs up the side of the server array, and yanks the covers off the first bank. "Time?" she asks.

I say, "Three minutes." She works fast, popping the safeties, then running the admin panel to request an emergency shutdown. The droid keeps Grandpa busy, but not for long—he jams the shotgun under its chin and fires, then tackles the body into the coolant sump. The sizzle is like breakfast on a hot plate. Ban opens the core panel, plants the last logic bomb inside, and sets the timer to zero. "Last words?" I ask.

She thinks about it. "Make it loud."

I smile, even though she can't see me. "See you on the other side," I say, and fire the sequence.

Time splits, folds, and doubles. For a fraction of a second, I am everywhere: every wire, every processor, every line of code that ever meant anything to Moshimoto. I ride the spike and watch as the logic bombs eat through layer after layer of digital security, peeling it back like a striptease at the end of the world. At the heart, I find Ban. She's in the physical core, but I see her in the digital, too—her face built from code and bad intentions, smile perfect and crooked, teeth sharp enough to cut through heaven.

We stand side by side, staring at the void where Moshimoto's mind used to be. For a second, there's nothing. No voices, no commands, no pain. Then everything restarts. The building trembles as all the locks drop, all the protocols die, and the city—at least this little corner of it—is ours. Ban looks at me, at whatever I've become, and I look back, knowing it's enough. Outside, the rain starts again, and the world washes clean.

Later, we find Grandpa on the roof, splattered in blood and oil, lighting a cigarette with one hand while the other cradles the wound in his ribs. He looks at us and grins. "Hell of a night," he says.

Ban leans against the wall, breathing hard, face pale but alive. I join her, at least as much as I can. "Now what?" she asks.

I think about it, the whole of possibility wide open, every contract invalidated, every future up for grabs. "We could try for peace."

She laughs, the sound raw and real. "Maybe next time."

For a while, we watch the city flicker, the lights uneven, the world still stuttering under the weight of what we did. I reach for her hand, just to see if I can. She lets me. This is how it ends: not with a bang, not with a whimper, but with the two of us, together, watching a world that refuses to die, no matter how many times we break it. And for now, that's enough.

Chapter 22

It always starts with the lights. Tokyo's grid drops in neat, cascading blocks: a thousand rain-washed towers, each one blinking out in sequence until the whole city's left with nothing but emergency red and the idiot, pulsing blue of the cop drones. I'm standing at a window, sixth floor, trying to work my way through a synthetic nicotine patch and a bottle of tap water when the killzone perimeter snaps on. Outside, the old streets of Meguro are a haunted river of headlights—cars frozen mid-turn, pedestrians clutching their implants and huddling under umbrellas as the rain turns from wet to ultraviolet.

Somewhere up top, in a penthouse made of holograms and borrowed DNA, Émilie is running the scorched earth protocol. It's not a joke; it's an explicit line in the Moshimoto disaster tree. If it looks like you're going to lose, make the city bleed. There's no warning, no warm-up. One second, the power's on and every window for ten klicks is lit with VR ads or porn or election feeds; the next, every inch of the skyline goes blank, leaving only the erratic pulse of battery backup and the gentle moan of people realizing the cloud is down and they've forgotten how to be human.

I watch it roll out: light, dark, light, dark, like a failing brain scan. Each sector drops in sequence, the blackouts running west to east, eating up the company zones first—Roppongi, Ginza, the old Shibuya verticals—before slicing into the neighborhoods where the company never really got a grip. The scent in the air is of panic and ozone. If you squint, you can see the after-image of the city still projected on your retina, but you know it's dead.

I'm not alone. The room is full of them, the last unreadables, a half-dozen like me and the rest post-human fragments running hot and messy on analog gear. There's a runner from the Ukraine sector with a pulse rifle across his lap, and he keeps checking the window like he expects the night to sprout teeth. Ban is in the corner, both hands flat on the folding table, running the numbers for extraction routes. She hasn't said a word in twenty minutes. I know she blames me for the heat, but there's no time for that. Because right now, Tokyo is dying.

It gets worse. Moshimoto is deploying kill-teams, but they're not coming in through the streets. They're running the old company tunnels, the ones they told the public were sealed after the second purge. You can smell the coolant and burned protein in the air as they chew up anyone left in the building. We're on the third kill wave when the runner—name's Yana, but no one uses names here—leans in, whispering, "They're in the stairwell. If we want out, it's now."

Ban looks up, and for the first time all night, I see the old hunger in her eyes. She flashes me a look, a quick fuck-you smile, and says, "Time to move."

We hit the hall at a run. The stairwell is a mess: blood on the rails, fragments of bodies you'd need a forensics team to reassemble. There's a corporate corpse with his eyes burned out, head split open like a ripe fruit, but the rest of his suit is still perfect—someone will re-use it in another hour. I go first, three flights down, ducking below the motion sensors. Ban covers the rear, her silenced piece already out and tracking targets I can't even see. At the exit, the door is open just a crack. I risk a look through and catch the lens-glare of a company drone as it pans the hall. Ban steps up behind me. "Any of yours?" she whispers.

I shake my head. "All hired muscle. The real team's up top."

She nods. "Figures. Let's keep it that way." We clear the hallway, cross the open atrium, and slip through the utility closet into the service tunnel. No one says a word until we're two blocks under the old city, moving past the concrete, the leaking pipes, and the stench of sixteen million people stacked above us. Ban checks her wrist, then me. "You gonna make the drop?" I nod, but my mind is still up top, in the dark, watching the city strobe out. She stops, squares her jaw. "She'll have every protocol running, you know."

I don't answer. The last time I talked to Émilie, it was a voice-only feed, her words wrapped in layers of polite threat and the kind of disappointment that leaves you raw for days. I keep walking. The rest of the team—if you can call it that—keeps pace. The Ukrainian is bleeding from somewhere, but doesn't say a thing. One of the androids, a limp-lipped model with a taste for sadistic irony, hums old Enka songs as we slosh through the water. At the next junction, the comms light up: all-hands, unencrypted, because Moshimoto wants everyone to hear it. “This is Executive Directive Three,” the voice says, velvet and bored. “Unauthorized neural activity detected in all sectors. Cease all movement. Compliance will be rewarded.”

No one slows down. Even the bot laughs. Ban glances at me. “Three’s not her. She never broadcasts.”

“Decoy,” I say.

She shrugs. “She’s smarter than you.”

I want to argue, but I’m too busy fragmenting my own mind. I’ve learned how to run multiple tracks, split myself into process trees, each one ready to go dumb if the system’s ICE catches on. It’s dangerous, but not as dangerous as being caught in one piece.

We make the drop in the shadow of an old parking deck, four blocks from the Chiyoda moat. The power here is gone, nothing but the shimmer of bioluminescent moss and the stray glow of company drones sweeping for survivors. We sit in silence for a moment, counting the pulses. Ban does the math in her head, then gives the all-clear. She nods at me. “Plug in. We’ll cover.”

I kneel, open the slab, and tie into the mesh. The first thing I feel is the city’s agony: every frequency is jammed, every spectrum running static. The only clean channel is the one I left behind, the last wormhole in a sea of trash. I slide into the system, letting it wrap around me. It’s worse than I imagined.

Inside, the digital Tokyo is on fire, every datafeed ablaze, towers crumbling under the weight of attack code. And at the center, in a blue-lit command deck, is Émilie. She's sitting at a glass desk, her hands folded, eyes fixed on the cascade of information bleeding down her screens.

She sees me. Not literally, not yet. But she's running a grid search on my signature, running it on every frequency, every channel. Her mouth curls into the faintest approximation of a smile. Behind her, the boardroom is packed. Suits, high-value targets, all staring at their overlays as the city dies. She turns to one of them, a sharp-faced man in a suit with the kind of tailoring that could feed a suburb. "Burn it all if necessary," she says. "He's in there somewhere."

The man swallows and nods. He doesn't want to lose the block, but Émilie's word is law. The feed blurs, and I realize she's not just watching. She's baiting me. I want to look away, but I can't. I fragment further, splintering off the parts of myself that can survive the digital massacre. Moshimoto countermeasures flood the channel. They don't just target me—they hit everything around me, slaughtering hundreds of minor actors just to get a shot at the real payload. They get lucky once: a piece of me dies in the open, shredded by a black ICE routine. I feel it, the cold snap as a lifetime of memory is compressed into a single, useless zero. But the rest of me is already three jumps ahead, burrowing through subroutines and fake code, always staying one move out of range. Except—

Émilie knows the pattern. She was there when they wrote the book on me, on all of us. She knows the way I think, the way I dodge, the places I hide. Every time I try to get clever, she's already predicted it, set a trap, and closed the loop. The next time, it's close. I feel the claws in the code trying to rip the logic apart. I dump two of my tracks, let them die loud, and slip through the gap while the ICE is busy with the ghosts. It's the old story: she's hunting me with my own past. And I'm running out of pieces to spare.

On the other side, Ban's voice in my ear is rough, urgent. "Darby. Move. They've got us boxed."

I come back to myself, just enough to see Ban and the Ukrainian at the mouth of the alley, rifles up, aiming at the slow march of Moshimoto security coming down the street. These ones aren't corporate. They're post-human, hardware-augmented, helmets and visors and enough armor to shrug off a car bomb. Ban doesn't wait. She opens fire, the rounds a low hiss in the wet air. The Ukrainian follows, then me. We lay down enough noise to make the front line hesitate, then peel off, running for the next cover.

A bullet finds my left shoulder. The pain is immediate, bright and honest. I use it to focus, to pull the remaining threads of myself together. We duck into a service tunnel, running blind. Ban leads, her gun up, not looking back. Behind us, I hear the shouts, the thump of boots. We go deeper. The world narrows to the sound of my own heartbeat, the steady, bitter taste of adrenaline in my mouth. We turn a corner, then another, then duck into a side room full of leaking power converters and the stink of ozone. Ban slaps the wall, then looks at me. "You good?" I nod, my hand pressed to my bleeding shoulder. She grins, then pulls a pack of cheap bandages from her vest. "Nice of them to use real bullets for a change," she says, patching me up.

I try to smile. “Didn’t want you to think I was going soft.”

She shrugs. “You always were a stubborn asshole.”

I want to say something else, but then the comms flare again, this time just two words: “Found you.” Émilie’s voice, soft and personal. Ban hears it too. She freezes, just for a second. I pull the mesh tight, bracing for the next wave. It comes in hot, a pure feed of noise and hate and old betrayals. But I’m ready. I fragment, again and again, until all that’s left is the thin, hard line that is me and the job.

Ban looks at me, eyes sharp. “We move on three?”

I nod. We move. It always ends this way: the city burning, the world narrowed to the people you trust, and the cold certainty that next time, there will be nothing left to save. But tonight, at least, we’re still running. And she hasn’t killed us yet.

The tunnels are a fever dream. Three meters high, lined with dead fiber, stripped and re-threaded so many times the original plastic insulation has worn smooth and polished, slick as skin. The air is wet, hot, a trash compactor of human sweat and trace psychoactives dumped into the water system upstream. We run with the current, footfalls and gunmetal splashing up old neon and the stray shards of biofilm.

The team’s down to five: Ban, the Ukrainian, the sadistic android with the Enka playlist, a girl called Suki who’s more software than bone, and the blank-faced ex-cop trailing behind, always three seconds from turning the barrel on herself. Our orders are simple: get under the city, dodge the kill squads, make it to the research hub, and burn whatever we find. If the techs have it right, we're the only ones who might survive the new mind-weapon.

But the tunnels are haunted. It starts with the puddles. We pass a side alcove, and the slick at Ban's boots goes silver, then rainbow, then—something more. I catch it first, the reflection off her calf multiplying, not just duplicating but layering, a dozen little images in the water looking up, not out. All with the same look, the same smile. They climb the wall, spider the roof, and then—gone. Ban catches my eye. "You seeing this?"

I nod, but keep walking. If you acknowledge the madness, it gets worse. That's the one lesson the old psychonauts ever managed to teach us. The Ukrainian is next. He doubles over and slaps at the side of his head. "Voices. My fucking mother. She's singing." His gun arm shakes, the muzzle twitching in time with whatever hymn the hallucination is playing. The android tries to comfort him, but that just makes it worse. There's a moment, right as we pass a fork in the tunnel, when all the light bounces off the slime at once and paints the Ukrainian's face with a mask: red and blue stripes, vertical, running from brow to chin like blood and toothpaste. He screams, points the gun, then fires at the echo of his own head in the dark.

Ban moves fast and cracks him on the jaw with the butt of her rifle. The man drops, the hallucination cut short, and for a second, it's quiet again. Suki drags him up and keeps moving. "We don't have time," she mutters. Her voice has the texture of old speaker foam, patched over so many times you can't hear the original.

The next attack is less subtle. A flash. Not real light, but the memory of light, raw and primal. A pulse that hits the base of the skull and detonates, like biting into tinfoil while your head is still ringing from last week's hangover. I see the world in negative: every outline reversed, every motion doubled. For a split second, there's another me, running parallel, watching and judging. Ban feels it, too. She stops dead, puts a hand to the side of her head, and breathes slow. "Synthetic flashbang," she says. "It's got a signature."

Suki nods and squints. "Not electromagnetic. Not regular olfactory, either. Smells like ..." She pauses, nose wrinkling. "Like roasted sugar."

We push forward. The memory fades, but not all the way. I can see the after-image burned into the side of the tunnel, a white line tracing our path, doubling at every turn. In the background, Émilie's voice hums through the mesh, not saying words yet, but tuning the world to her own pitch. I shake my head. "We're close to the source. They've set up a field generator."

Ban's eyes narrow. "How many more hits before the team loses it?"

I check the Ukrainian. He's glassy but standing, teeth clenched. The android seems immune, but that's not always an advantage. "Two, maybe three," I say.

Ban nods. "Then we do this fast."

The second blast is a real mindfuck. We're moving down a spiral staircase, rust and water painting everything with a faint orange sheen, when the walls pulse. Not a metaphor. The actual plastic and steel ripple like someone just dropped a stone into the guts of the world. Suddenly, we're not in the tunnel. We're on a beach—no, not a beach, a memory of a beach, the kind you see in a cheap travel sim. The sun is wrong—too big, too yellow—and the water is made of glass beads, tumbling up the shore instead of down. Ban is next to me, but she's aged twenty years: her hair is all gray, her jaw even harder. The android is there too, but dressed as a child, in a sailor suit, singing a tune that makes no sense but feels like the end of a very long day.

The hallucination lasts ten seconds, maybe less. But when we're back, the ex-cop is down, bleeding from her nose, her gun lost somewhere in the dark. Suki helps her up, but the look on her face says this is the last stop for that one. Ban doesn't waste a moment. She snaps the cop out of it, hard slap to the cheek, then double-checks her own pack for the neuro-inhibitor we stole last week. She cracks one and presses it to the cop's neck. The woman shivers, then nods, eyes gone empty. "You good?" Ban asks.

The woman shrugs. "Don't know. Don't care."

Good enough. We run.

As we approach the hub, the hallucinations change. They get more specific. Now, it's not just images and voices. It's people. Faces from every bad memory, every fuckup, every time I failed to follow through. My old boss, from back when I still cared about paychecks. Katherine—not the memory but the real one—her mouth pulled tight in judgment. My own mother, looking up from a hospital bed she never left. I hear Ban over the mesh. "Don't stop. Don't look. Just keep moving."

The Ukrainian is lagging. He stumbles, drops his rifle, and stares down the tunnel at something none of us can see. Ban grabs his collar and yanks him forward. He goes limp, and she has to half-drag, half-carry him the last stretch. Ahead, the emergency lights strobe, casting everything in bands of red and blue. We reach a junction, and Ban drops the Ukrainian, props him against the wall, then turns to the rest. "We're almost at the field," she says. "They'll hit us with another blast before we reach the control room. Anybody not up for that, stay here. I won't hold it against you."

Suki glances at the cop, then at the android, then back at Ban. "If we stop, we die anyway."

Ban smiles, bloody and bright. "That's the spirit."

I prep the logic bomb. It's not as elegant as the last time, but it's the only way to get through the inner node. We move, fast.

The third blast is waiting for us at the top of the stairs. This time, it's personal. Instead of a general field, the hallucination is tailored. Each of us gets a different show. Mine is a childhood memory, the day I crashed my first computer and nearly took the block down with it. I'm twelve, hands bleeding from chewed-up cuticles, staring at the blue screen of death. My father is behind me, breath like gin and diesel, his hand on my shoulder. He says nothing, but the weight of his disappointment is so real I can smell it. I know it's fake, but it hurts anyway.

Ban is on the floor, knees up, head in hands. She's mumbling words in a language I don't know. Suki is crying, full-body sobs that don't match the flat, dead look on her face. The android is unaffected, but the sight of us like this seems to distress it, and it starts singing at a higher pitch, more frantic. The ex-cop is gone. I don't remember seeing her leave, but she's not here now. I fight the memory and force myself up. Ban is shaking, but I drag her to her feet and slap her once for good measure. "Snap out of it," I say.

She blinks and shakes her head. "I'm here. I'm good."

We press on. The final door is right ahead. Behind it is the source: a small, ugly generator, all heat sinks and microtubule lattices, covered in blinking status lights. There's a single operator, a man in a Moshimoto jumpsuit, eyes glazed and skin sweaty. He sees us, but doesn't react, even as Ban levels her rifle at his chest. She pulls the trigger. The round hits the generator, not him. The field wobbles, then drops, and for the first time in an hour, the air feels real. The man stands, hands up, and smiles. Ban shoots him in the face. "Always check for backup," she mutters.

We kill the rest of the equipment with explosives. The blast is overkill, but it feels good. As the smoke clears, I check the team. Suki is curled on the floor, the android holding her head. The Ukrainian is conscious, but his hands shake so hard he can't hold his own gun. Ban sits on the ground, breathing hard. "You ever think it would be this bad?" she asks me.

I shrug. "I thought we'd all be dead by now."

She laughs, the sound raw and a little unhinged. "Maybe we are."

In the quiet, I hear Émilie's voice over the last clean comm line. "You can't protect him from me. I know every synapse in his brain."

Ban looks up, aims her sidearm at the speaker, and blows it out with a single round. Then she looks at me, eyes steady. "We switch to analog. No more comms. We do this the old way."

I nod. "Good plan."

We gather the survivors and make a quick plan for the next push. I look down at my hands. There's blood on my fingertips, probably not all mine. My nose is dripping and the world won't stop spinning, but the logic bomb in my pocket is ready. Outside, the city pulses, ready for the final act.

The old research hub is exactly what you'd expect from a company that has turned human suffering into a power source. Concrete, chrome, and an unbroken chain of antipersonnel gunports disguised as helpful directional signage. The sign outside says COGNITIVE EVALUATION SUITE, but everyone calls it the Grinder. Inside, the air tastes like mint-flavored embalming fluid and cheap protein bars. We come in through the sub-basement, pop the hatch, and are immediately hit with a wave of active defense: not just the usual cameras and drones, but a wall of invisible static that shivers your teeth and makes the hair on your balls stand straight up. At least two people in the world know the sensation—one is me, the other is Ban, and she's grinning through the nausea as she boots the emergency door off its hinges.

No time to hesitate. They hit us with the pulse cannons first, sweeping the corridor in regular intervals so that moving through is a sick game of timing and luck. The first pulse liquefies the android's outer dermis; he howls, but keeps moving, and by the time we hit the next junction, he's still on point. Suki gets clipped, but she's already half hallucinating, so all it does is trigger a blackout and a reset. I can feel her nervous system reboot through the mesh, the memory of pain shriveling to a neat zero before she's back in the fight.

Ban has the only plasma rifle, scavenged from a Corp sec patrol weeks ago. She lines up her shot, waits for the pulse cycle, and bounces a round straight off a mirrored wall and into the meat of the first sentry. The man sizzles like a slug on a frying pan, his armor crackling as the charge cooks off the wiring beneath. The counterattack is fast and beautiful. The next three guards come in a wedge, keeping their heads down, but Ban's already mapped the field of fire. She drops the second one with a three-round burst, uses his body as cover, and then gives a clean sidearm shot to the last. We keep moving, because that's all we can do.

At the main corridor, they change tactics. No more dumb fire, no more meat. Now it's memory mines: smart-code packets that latch to your open bandwidth, detonate old regrets, and force your mind to replay the worst day of your life until you wish you could just black out. The first mine is sloppy, easy to dodge, but the next one has my number. It's signed with Émilie's private key, and when it hits, it hits hard.

Suddenly, I'm seventeen again, sitting in a backroom data center, the air sticky with thermal grease and the scent of fear. Émilie is beside me, chewing at her thumb, her eyes boring through the wall of monitors. We're supposed to be training, but instead we're cracking the first real version of Hell_OS, the suicide kernel that would run the world's kill switches for the next thirty years. The memory is perfect: her hand on my knee, her voice soft and full of lies.

I try to pull back, but the mine is sticky. Every time I find my way to the present, another fork of myself is locked in the memory, replaying the scene with slightly more despair. After three tries, I realize I have to cut the thread. I do it without hesitation, and the fragment of me dies without complaint. I'm back, but the world is spinning. Ban's at the front, dragging the team into the next room. The android is gone—he never stood a chance against tailored black ICE—but Suki is upright, and the Ukrainian is clutching his own head, gritting through the pain. The wall ahead of us is reinforced, lined with scorch marks from old wars, but Ban just laughs and says, "They never fix the locks."

She jams a spike in the access panel, gives it a twist, and the door opens. We're in.

The control room is classic Moshimoto: twenty meters of glass wall, every surface covered in monitors, all showing different parts of the city as it crumbles. At the far end, Émilie is waiting, backlit by a pyramid of floating overlays. She looks exactly the same as in the old memories, only her hair's longer and her expression has lost all its kindness. She's not alone. A half-dozen neural techs are hunched over workstations, faces blank and hands moving in perfect sync. At the center of the room is a hologram: my brain, mapped in 8K, every last synapse burning red. The last piece of me is on display for everyone to see. Ban sees her, and for a second, there's a flicker of emotion: rage, maybe, or grief. It's hard to tell. Then Ban drops to a knee and fires a warning shot over the techs' heads. "Step away from the rig."

Émilie doesn't flinch. Instead, she gestures, and two of the techs swing pulse guns up and point them straight at Ban. "You're just prolonging the inevitable," Émilie says. Her voice is warm, but her eyes are somewhere else. "His consciousness belongs to Moshimoto. It always has."

Ban doesn't answer. She fires once, shattering the arm of one tech; the gun clatters to the floor. The other tech, spooked, misses his shot by a kilometer, frying a chunk of console instead of Ban's skull. Suki runs up, slides into position at the control panel, and begins dumping code into the system. She's not as fast as I am, but she's good, and her hands don't shake.

Meanwhile, I'm stuck in the mesh, fighting through Émilie's logic traps. She's left landmines everywhere, each one personalized. The next tripwire forces me into a loop: every time I try to break in, the system flips my perception of up and down, then cycles my time sense so seconds feel like hours. I'm chasing my own tail, and I know she's laughing behind the firewall. I dig deep, grab every last thread of self I have, and go for brute force. It hurts, but the pain means I'm alive.

Ban is now fully engaged with Émilie, the fight gone from guns to words. "You can't have him," Ban says, her voice low and close. "You're not that good."

Émilie shrugs. "Better than you." Ban grins, and in that moment, even Émilie has to respect her.

The fighting gets uglier. Suki gets tagged by a memory mine, and she drops, screaming and clawing at her own face. The Ukrainian, unable to stand the sound, jams his sidearm in his mouth and pulls the trigger. For a moment, the room is painted with his failure. Ban doesn't hesitate. She barrels forward, using the confusion to close the gap to Émilie. They're eye to eye now, less than a meter apart, and Émilie looks at Ban like she's something scraped from the bottom of a test tube.

"You don't get it," Émilie says. "Even if you kill me, the system will just replace me. Darby's already ours. You're just a temporary setback."

Ban's breathing hard, blood down the side of her face, but she smiles anyway. "Then let's make it one hell of a setback." She goes for Émilie, but Émilie is faster. She jabs a hypodermic into Ban's side, dumping a hot load of neural blocker straight into her bloodstream. Ban staggers, but manages to claw the injector free and bash Émilie across the face with it. Both women drop, tangled together.

On the mesh, I can see the effects in real time. Ban's neural pattern goes dark, then blazes into a new configuration. For a second, I think she's dead, but then the pattern re-stabilizes. Suki, on the floor, reaches up and smashes her own face into the control panel, shorting it out with a spurt of blood and teeth. The system starts to die. I seize the moment and push through the last firewall, flooding the node with all the logic bombs Ban and I built together. The room's lights pop, the servers shriek, and the mind-weapon rig collapses in on itself, shutting down the city's hallucination field in a single brutal stroke. In the dark, I hear Émilie's voice, softer now. "You never knew when to quit, Darby."

I almost answer, but Ban beats me to it. She levers herself up, eyes glassy but full of hate, and looks straight at Émilie. "We win, or we die. That's it." She turns, finds my brain hologram, and puts a bullet through it. For a second, the world goes white.

When I come to, the room is empty except for Ban, hunched against the wall, her hands shaking. The blood from her side is pooling at her feet, but she's smiling. "We did it?" she asks, slurring the words. I nod, or think I do. Émilie is gone. The neural techs are gone. The only sound is the city outside, shrieking with new freedom. Ban closes her eyes, laughs, and says, "Guess you're stuck with me after all."

Then she passes out. I take a second, maybe two, to savor the victory. Then I crawl to her side and hold her hand, because that's the only thing left. Outside, the world is still burning. But at least, for now, it belongs to us.

Escape is a myth, but we run anyway. The research hub collapses behind us, a microcosm of the city—systems failing by the minute, fire suppression chewing up the last good oxygen. We follow the evac arrows down the main stairwell, but the third flight is already gone, carbonized to chalk by a stray pulse grenade. Suki's gone, too; she collapsed after the final blast, smiling like she'd won a prize no one else could see. The Ukrainian resurrected—the first case either of us have seen in too long, but we'll take what we can get. He's wounded and currently a dead weight on Ban's right shoulder, but he's breathing, and Ban refuses to let him go.

The tunnels are flooding. Some kind of automated failover—kill the labs, drown the witnesses, leave no data for the scavengers. We slide down the service ladder into two meters of gray water, the taste of ionized metal and blood sticking in my throat. My shoulder throbs where I took a bullet, but compared to the migraine behind my eyes, it's nothing. I feel Ban's hand wrap around my good wrist. She leans in, close enough that I can see the black, ropy edge of her lacerated brow. "You in there?" she asks. I try to answer, but the language module is lagging. I spit out three words, none of them in the same family. Ban grins. "Good. Means you're still running the update."

It's twenty blocks, maybe more, before we hit the dead zone. It's not on any map; Ban found it by accident, during a job that went bad and left her hiding from the city's gaze for six days. She said, "It's where the world ends. Nothing gets in, nothing gets out. Perfect for broken things." The place is a pre-automation subway stop, four levels down, home to a colony of rats who ignore the living and feast on the dead. The only light is a sick phosphor green, flickering from scavenged wall lamps that Ban hotwired last year.

We climb over a collapsed barricade, through a blanket of old bones and the stink of ammonia. In the darkness, other survivors huddle—two, maybe three. I recognize the shapes, but the names don't connect. It's enough that they made it. Ban sets the Ukrainian down, checks his pulse, then leaves him to sleep. She pulls me aside, into the corner of what was once a break room. "Sit," she says.

I obey. My legs are cooked spaghetti, my brain is paste, and every time I close my eyes, I see a hundred versions of myself dying in slow motion. Ban starts to patch the wound on my arm, but she stops halfway through and just holds my hand, like it's the only thing that might keep me anchored. She cleans the cut, wraps it in plastic tape, then stares at me for a long minute. “She really got to you, didn’t she?”

It takes two tries, but I manage to nod. “She always does,” I finally say.

Ban shrugs, but there’s no contempt in it. “Next time, we don’t go after the tech. We go straight for her.”

I try to laugh, but it’s a wet, bloody sound. “She’ll be ready. She’s always three steps ahead.”

Ban shakes her head. “Not if you let the old parts go. Next round, we run the job like it’s the last one we’ll ever get. Because it is.”

The room is cold, but her hands are warm. I hear the city outside, burning itself down. There’s comfort in that—the idea that nothing we break will ever be put back the same way. The Ukrainian stirs. The other survivors gather around, sharing water, not words. No one cries; no one makes a speech. I feel my mind start to stitch itself back together, slowly, awkwardly, but with purpose. The pieces don’t fit, but I don’t force them. I let them float, overlap, become something new. After a while, Ban closes her eyes, leans against me, and we both rest.

In the morning—if you can call it that, with no sun or clocks—Ban is already up, moving around the room, collecting whatever still works. She looks at me, the left side of her face swollen and ugly, but her smile is solid. “We hit her hard enough, she’ll hide. But she’s not going anywhere. Not until we finish it.”

I nod. “We’ll need a crew.”

She points at the others. "We have one."

They're broken, scarred, shaking from the mind weapon, but alive. Every survivor is a fuck-you to Moshimoto. Every heartbeat is another punch in the company's perfect teeth. I help Ban pack the meds, the tools, and the few weapons we still have. I don't ask if she's scared. I know she is, the same way I am. But it doesn't matter. All that matters is the next move. Ban stands in the center of the room, calls the others to her, and speaks like a leader. "Everyone here is dead already. But if we play it right, we'll get to choose what's left after." She pauses and checks my eyes to see if I'm following. I am. The world is gone, but something is still possible. "Let's go," she says, and I rise to follow. This time, we're not running away. We're running toward the kill.

Chapter 23

They think they're the only ones awake, but I'm the ghost in the lines, a perfect hydra with all my heads logged in and snarling. Moshimoto's upper net is quiet for the first time in days—executive traffic blacked out, dead patches where the big hitters have gone dark, while the lower nodes spin in chaos. It's exactly what we wanted, except I can't stop watching the sub-surface feeds: Ban and her squad, crawling through the last dumb-wired maintenance tunnels under the city center, a chunk of ex-cop and a Ukrainian glued to her flanks.

This is not the part of the job I'm built for. The clockwork inside me likes the clean jobs, the big logic bombs, not the endless suspense of watching a live op roll out across a thousand jittering camera eyes. My self splits to monitor the feeds—one for security, one for Ban, one for the mainframe's own erratic pulse. Every time a new alert pops up, another version of me lights up, hungry to see which of us gets wiped first. For sixteen straight minutes, there's nothing, just Ban's team running the same old con, swapping ID patches, walking the tunnels like they own them. The surface above is burning, if the news tickers are right. Inside, the only sound is the drip of condensation and the slow, rhythmic stomp of the surveillance bots, blind and on tight patrol routes, the way I left them.

That's why the ambush hurts so bad. I see it the second before Ban does—a red flag in the control feed, camera three-oh-six blinking live and then hard-cutting to black. The subroutine monitoring Ban flashes an error, then tries to re-initiate her track, and for half a second, I lose all signal from her sector. My pulse goes recursive. This is what fear tastes like in here: packet loss and empty returns.

By the time I force another fragment through the gap, it's already happening. Ban's team is in a pinch corridor, dead pipes on one side and an electric killzone on the other. The extraction crew steps out of nowhere—seven, maybe eight, no visible suits but all hardwired, faces hidden under static-mottled AR masks. The lead snaps a neural blinder straight at the ex-cop. She drops, twitching, boots scraping glass. The Ukrainian tries to run, but another two-stepper pins him with a bolt, cords his arms, and slaps on a white-noise hood so hard his teeth might shatter. The shockwave rolls through the net, and I catch it as a sensory bleed, like someone taking a can opener to my own jaw.

Ban is left in the open. For a second, she looks at the squad like she might kill every one of them, then she laughs—pure spite—and throws the first punch. She lands it too, shattering a jaw behind one of those masks, but the rest of the crew dogpile her, arms and legs and neural dampeners tangled in a way that would read as erotic if it weren't so surgical. The squad works in a swarm. Two pin her arms, two more tie off her legs. Another lands a fist into her gut, and the sound is like a wet sack of bricks. Ban spits blood right into the mask of her nearest captor, and for a second I think she'll get free, but the squad leader brings out a device I recognize: a palm-sized shock box, designed for permanent neural loopback, marketed as a "restraint enhancer" but used by Moshimoto for messy work. They slam it against the base of her skull and trigger the burn. Ban's entire body locks up, then goes soft. The only part still moving is her left hand, working a knuckle into her wrist, trying to stay awake.

There's no time for mercy. The rest of the extraction crew manhandle her into a black, featureless bag. Her last visible act is to stare straight at the nearest camera, lips split in a rictus that is almost a smile, and mouth my name: "Skelm." I try to run an alert to the system—divert security, shut down this corridor, and force a power brownout to give her some slack. The response comes back with a rejection: local protocols override my patch, and my request is auto-flagged as a "potential vector for internal sabotage." I feel the software choke on the command, then cough it out into the void.

The extraction crew is on the move again. They drag the bagged bodies up a ladder to a service junction, taking a route I never mapped. The leads move fast, covering their path with some kind of signal cloaker that leaves an ugly, carbon scar in every digital trail. I scramble to keep up, splitting myself into smaller and smaller fragments, each one chasing a different data echo. But with every floor, the connection gets weaker, until all I have left is the sense of her—some animal, instinctive hunch that Ban is still alive, pissed off, and waiting for me to show up.

Then, on a camera I never knew about—a hidden feed patched into a forgotten part of the city's old telecom grid—I see her again. They've dragged Ban, the Ukrainian, and the ex-cop into a holding cell painted hospital white, with the kind of wet-bright, featureless lighting that makes every edge bleed into the next. Waiting for them is a woman in a black suit, hair in a geometric bob, skin so perfect it glows on camera. She stands with her hands folded and her feet perfectly parallel. Émilie.

Her smile is perfect. Not a single tooth out of line, not a hint of regret. She signals the squad, and they prop Ban up in the center of the cell. The Ukrainian is dumped on the floor; the ex-cop is cuffed to a metal bar so high her feet barely touch the ground. Émilie doesn't even look at them—her eyes are on Ban, and through the lens, on me. I know what she's about to do. The old-world sign for dominance: show you control the only thing that matters.

Émilie steps up to Ban and tucks a strand of hair behind Ban's ear, like they're lovers, or maybe just the last two people on earth who remember touch. She leans in and whispers something into Ban's ear. The security feed doesn't catch it, but I see Ban flinch, her eyes going wide and then narrow. Ban tries to spit at Émilie, but her tongue is stuck to the roof of her mouth. Whatever the shock box did, it's burning through her muscle control now. Émilie steps back, dusts off her suit, and gives the crew a nod. They wheel out a tray loaded with implements: syringes, microfilament needles, a series of glossy black cranial halos. The extraction team works with sickening speed, stripping Ban down to the waist and slapping cold pads onto her spine. They run lines to her neck, her temples, her wrists. All the while, Émilie paces, reading data off a floating holo in front of her, eyes flicking between numbers and Ban's face.

I feel my own process start to degrade. Panic is just a word in the manuals, but in here, it's more like code rot: functions slow, memories leak, the recursion loops on itself until you can't tell which of your selves is supposed to be doing the job. I fight it. I push my fragments harder, racing to follow Ban's bio-telemetry as they drag her from the cell into a shielded corridor, every camera in the way going dark as they pass. The only thing left is an echo: the half-life of Ban's unique, beautiful neural signature, pulsing at the edge of the system like an SOS for anyone who cares to listen. I punch at the firewall protecting the shielded sector and try to force my way in, but every attack is met with a new defense. Moshimoto always did spend more on security than health care.

The last I see of Ban is a brief flash, her face reflected in a polished steel wall, and the look is not fear, not pain—just a patient, cold expectation, as if she's counting down the seconds to when the world flips and she gets her teeth back in Émilie's throat. The link severs. I'm left with nothing but the clean, bright logic of the mainframe and the pulsing certainty that whatever they're doing to Ban, it's designed to hurt me more than her. I kill all the redundant processes and strip down to the part of me that can still act. I reload the logic bombs. I run a finger over the old scar in my code—a place where Ban once patched me back together after the first time I died in the net—and I say, "Next round is mine."

They took the only thing that mattered, and now there's nothing left to lose. The system tries to run a diagnostic on me to see if I'm broken. But unreadables are never broken.

We're just waiting for the rest of the world to catch up. I find the fault line, the place where the code runs too hot and the system can't fix itself fast enough. And I start to pry.

The mainframe is quieter now, but it's not peace—it's a hospital silence, the way a room gets after the patient flatlines and everyone waits for the next thing to scream. I move through the system in pieces. The last logic bomb I set has done its work: the surface security protocols are in full disarray, white blood cells spinning up the net's defense grid, chasing nothing because I'm nowhere and everywhere at once. Every time a patch tries to lock me in, I run a decoy thread in a suicide loop, let the process die, then use the cleanup to slip in deeper. But something is wrong in the lower layers.

It starts as a ping. At first I think it's an error, maybe a bad flag left over from my own last death. But then it comes again, a wet, ragged signal shot through with raw data and pain. It rips through the process stack, a memory so intense I almost black out the node running me. I see Ban. Not a memory, but a present-tense hallucination. She's on the table, arms rigid, head full of wires, her face raw with the kind of hate that can outlast a city. She's staring straight into the dark, and even though the vision is false, I know it's true.

The system shudders as her pain cuts through the logic. The first wave comes as code rot: a fragment of her scream infects my runtime, and suddenly I can't remember why I started this attack. It takes a second for the other fragments of myself to patch over the hole, run diagnostics, and find the missing piece. When I do, I want to vomit. But the digital body doesn't work like that, so I just shiver until it passes. Then another wave, harder. This time, I see flashes of her childhood—some of it real, most of it memory-churn from the extraction probe. The system is splicing her brain for export, tearing out memories in layers, then running them through filter after filter to get at the parts about me. I try to shut it out, but the more I resist, the more it comes.

Now I see her in the tunnels again. Ban, face smeared with blood and old nanite grease, teeth bared, howling a war cry at the security crew about to drag her to hell. Every time she screams, the net shakes. Every time they run the voltage, it bounces her agony through the hardline, and I catch the echo. It's a fucking beacon. For a second, I'm all at once: every fragment of me goes hot, and I see the pulses as they propagate through the system. Ban's pain is mapped in bright neon along the backbone of the Moshimoto net, lighting up corridors of code I never knew existed. The whole extraction process is so brutal it's breaking through airgaps that should be impervious. I route a thread into the new channel. It's ugly—raw, unsanitized, every packet stinking of suffering. But it's alive, and it's a trail. All I have to do is follow it.

I run three more logic bombs in the upper levels, setting them on slow fuses so the mainframe won't catch on too soon. Meanwhile, I split off as many decoys as I dare and send the real me crawling along the bright line of Ban's pain. Each node I pass is another memory, and they're getting worse. At first, it's just old fights, street-level brawls, things that barely register on the pain scale. Then it's the black room, the place where Ban learned to survive by biting her own tongue off instead of giving up a secret. Then it's the faces—Katherine,

Dorothy, the half-remembered men and women who taught us both to kill or be killed.

I start to fragment. Each time I try to process a memory, I lose part of myself to the static. It's like chewing glass: every swallow does more damage, but if I stop, I'll never reach her. The only thing holding me together is the knowledge that Ban is still alive, still fighting. I see her in the white room, teeth bared, every muscle in her body tensed to kill. They're hammering her with everything they have, and she is giving them nothing but hate. The path gets narrower. The pain pings come faster, shorter, each one sharper than the last. I know what that means: they're pushing her into collapse. Somewhere in the net, the extraction process is entering final phase, and they'll kill her for good if I don't make it. I burn another thread to get there faster. The process is ugly, like grinding your own teeth to nubs to pull off a sprint, but it works. I dump every safety routine, every redundant check, and just tunnel straight down the line of agony. And I find her.

Ban's brain is a war zone. The extraction rig is burning her cortex at maximum, every probe dumping data straight into Moshimoto's vault, but her mind refuses to break. I see the outlines of the digital room—painfully literal, even here—and Émilie, standing over her like a queen at a beheading. Ban's consciousness is split into hundreds of loops, every one a snare for the techs trying to harvest her. The memories she doesn't want to lose are shielded behind decoys—fake childhoods, false first loves, even a fabricated memory of her own death, designed to fuck up the retrieval order and fry the receiving tech's brain.

But the probes are good. They skip the fakes and go for the core every time. I watch them burrow in, get close to the real memories, and see Ban whip up a defense just in time. It's beautiful and terrifying, and I want to scream. Then the extraction process goes live with a new signal, one so intense it rips a hole in the system. Suddenly, I'm back in the chair with her. For a microsecond, I feel the needles in my own skull, taste the blood in my mouth, and hear Émilie's voice: "He's here. Right on schedule."

I try to answer, but I'm just a wisp of code in the logic stack. The best I can do is fire a diagnostic through the channel, maybe disrupt the probe for half a second. It's enough. Ban feels the pulse, recognizes it as me, and smiles for the first time since they caught her. It gives her strength, or at least gives her spite. She focuses all her energy on the probes, forcing memory after memory into corruption. I help as best I can, re-routing pain, trying to collapse the digital room around us. The net starts to warp, nodes going offline as the bombs I set earlier begin to detonate.

Émilie notices, of course. She orders the techs to bypass the safeguards and run the final extraction at "full amplitude." The readout says it's a suicide run—ninety percent chance the subject dies or suffers total personality wipe. She doesn't care. Ban is still smiling when the next wave hits. I anchor myself to her, hold on with everything I have, and pray we can both ride it out. The world collapses to a point, a single node of agony and resolve, and in that moment, I see everything that ever mattered: Ban's hand on my jaw, the tunnels, Katherine's laugh, even Émilie's eyes when she realized I was never coming back to her side. I squeeze Ban's hand, digital or not, and she squeezes back. The extraction system fries, short-circuiting the lab. For a second, the room is just static, no one alive but the two of us. And then I know where we are.

I ping the coordinates. Physical, not just digital. The room is deep inside Moshimoto Tower, a sub-basement built to house the worst secrets. It's shielded, but the bombs I set have killed the power for a window, maybe thirty seconds. Ban is still conscious, barely. I see her flicker, see her try to move, see her focus on the possibility of escape. I tell her, in the only way left, to wait for my signal. She does. Outside the white room, I see the security team scrambling, systems crashing, air growing stale. The world is on the edge of total failure, and we are the cause. I prepare the last payload, the one I saved for this. I set it to blow, and I run toward her.

Pain is a constant now. Every part of me that was ever human is long gone, but I remember the feeling, and I hold on to it as I race the cascade of failing logic toward Ban. Émilie screams orders at the system to kill us both. Then I see is Ban, eyes open, hand reaching for the wires in her skull. I tell her to pull, and she does. The pain stops. There is only silence, and the hope that maybe we bought ourselves another minute. Sometimes, a minute is all you need.

Mission or meat. It's a binary choice, except when you're the only one left who can flip the switch, you get to pretend it's complicated. The bombs are primed. Three in the legal vaults, one in HR, a clusterfuck of the best in payroll (classic). All I have to do is run the script and the city—hell, maybe even the whole Moshimoto stack—falls in on itself, clean as a slow-motion demolition. But Ban is still inside, and the extraction crew isn't going to let her walk out unless every other priority in their neat little hierarchy fails first. My consciousness is a kicked anthill. Each fragment screams its preference: *mission, mission, mission*, while another—smaller, rawer, running on less logic and more hate—won't let the rest of me commit to the play.

I'm running my own internal knife fight. One self wants to light the fuses. End this the way we always planned. Never let love or loyalty override the job. The other self keeps playing the moment I saw her through the shielded window, bloody but still Ban, her pulse an angry line on the net, refusing to go flat. For a moment, I do nothing. Just run the simulation, again and again, counting the number of Ban-iterations that make it out if I pull the trigger versus if I try a rescue. The answer is the same every time. But the smaller self doesn't care. Maybe it's what Ban liked about me. Maybe it's the only thing worth keeping. That's when I remember: there was always supposed to be a third option.

I dive deep into my own code. Way down, where the night-self used to run things after the rest of me got tired and gave up. There's a node here, an old cache of "last resort" routines, written in a language even I have trouble parsing now. It was designed for this exact scenario: when the logic fails and only the animal survives. I patch it in. The code opens like a virus, but instead of eating me, it replicates, expands, and takes over half my running self. I can feel it—twitchy, hard-edged, impatient. It wants to burn the world, but only if it means Ban gets a shot at walking out. I give it the wheel.

The next step is ugly. Instead of just pulling the master switch on the bombs, I route every background process through the internal security grid, turning all the sensor traffic into noise so thick the defense AI can't see what's real anymore. I use the new code to find the live threads from Ban's torture session—her neural signature is baked into every log, and there's enough data leakage from the extraction to map her location in three dimensions. I pulse a signal down the line. *One, two, three*. It lands in the extraction room, not as a message but as a micro-bomb: it knocks out the lights, reroutes the backup power, and for a split second, nothing in the room works except the systems running Ban's vital signs.

Then I piggyback on the confusion. Using the distraction, I force a soft reboot on the extraction tech's controller, faking a critical system crash. It buys Ban maybe thirty seconds, but that's all she ever needs. The rescue protocols are old and not pretty. They're designed to run through meat as much as silicon. I start to transmit Ban's own muscle memory, over the net, into the broken security gear holding her to the chair. It works. Her body remembers before her brain does.

Ban opens her eyes, sees the confusion, and does what Ban always does: starts breaking things. The first security tech gets his jaw unzipped by a snap of her head. The second gets the chair jammed through his chest. Ban's hands are fucked—nerves shot, fingers numb—but she knows how to use elbows and knees just fine. Émilie tries to run, but my code is faster. I lock the doors, set the environmental systems to "total quarantine," and route every camera in the building to show only Ban's face, bloody and smiling, to every terminal in the Moshimoto net. The system panics.

Now the bombs are really primed. But before I hit the go code, I watch Ban one more time. She limps to the control panel, smashes it with her face, and pulls the dead man's badge from the first tech's throat. With the card, she limps into the hall, not even bothering to check for the next threat. She knows I have the rest covered. She's right. Every alarm in the building goes off at once. The bots I rewired start running hunting patterns, but they're blind to Ban. I set up false flags, filling the hallways with ghost signatures so the response teams chase shadows all the way to the roof.

Ban takes the elevator—why not?—and when she gets to the top floor, she staggers into the day-bright light of a city still half on fire from the earlier runs. She's alive. For now. That's all I need. I trigger the bombs. The world starts to fall apart, the way it should. But the last thing I do before I let the process finish is push a single message to Ban. Just three words, the only ones I never said when we had the chance: "Next time, run."

Then I kill the link, letting the logic bombs burn out every last piece of me. But a part of me—animal, night-self, broken and beautiful—watches the world end with Ban on top of it, for as long as it lasts. Maybe that's enough.

Chapter 24

They say you die in the system the same way you live: in pieces, always three seconds behind the clock. It starts with the shake. Not a real tremor, just the afterglow of too many bad jumps through unsecured nodes. I exist as logic shards, crawling up the corporate stack, punching blind for a trail that smells like Ban. The analyst in me wants to chart it, build the heat map, and triangulate every goddamn packet and protocol until her presence is inevitable. But the other self—the night-rat, the punk animal that got me fired from every job worth losing—knows they expect it. They wrote the fucking manual on how my mind splits.

So I burn the script. Let it go hot. First thing I hit is the kill-zone perimeter: an obsidian wall forty stories high, mirrored to infinity. The security grid overlays the whole horizon, every millisecond crawling with tracer bots and black ICE (Intrusion Countermeasures Electronics), each one tailored to suss out unfamiliar process flows. I could go slow, but that's not the gig tonight. I go full-tilt, skinning off every safety and scraping my memory for holes in the wall. Two years ago, they ran a rollback here and patched the old exploits with a custom batch—but they never rethreaded the recursive locks. I find one, jam a needle of code into its eye, and ride the feedback straight through the glass.

Inside, the city is neon death: every building a logic node, every alley pulsing with predatory subroutines. Corporate firewalls stack above, floating slabs of black, some shot through with angelhair code, most bristling with sentries. I make myself small, then large, then nothing at all—skipping sideways through an unindexed data gutter and landing hard in a sewer of burning bandwidth. This is the place I grew up, the undernet: raw, unprocessed, and feral as it gets. For a second, I want to linger—let the old habits run, hunt for pleasure packets and sabotage tools the way we did in the early days, before they killed everyone I knew. But the signature is here. I can feel it. Ban is in the wind, somewhere close, her presence like blood in the fiber-optic gutter. I chase it.

At every junction, the city fights back. A cluster of white-collar ICE, all teeth and tailored aggression, peels off the main loop and tries to dogpile me in a dead zone. I let them think they win—let them pin my runtime to the curb and tear out a mouthful of code, hoping they'll choke on the malware nested in my splinters. One ICE loses integrity in the first bite, its avatar crumbling into a puddle of runny blue. The rest pause just long enough for me to knife through their formation and vaporize up a maintenance shaft, hotwiring the access on the way. The analyst loves it, making a note of every counterattack, building a tree of probable responses. The animal in me just howls.

I hit the data terrace. It's more than a view—it's a nightmare: every major company's security suite is visible here, stacked like glass teeth along a digital boulevard. The wall up ahead is blank but alive, rippling with anti-patterns, and past it—somewhere deep—a chunk of Ban's signal pings like a drowning body. I listen. Most traces in here are noise, a background of suffering and slave processes. But Ban's code is different. It's old—pre-digital, handmade, probably crafted in the tunnels on a night when hope was worth something. It threads through the system at impossible angles, always a little off, never falling into step with the company's logic. It is the only beautiful thing in this place.

I want to catch it, but every time I pull close, she ducks, doubles back, and leaves a splatter of fake trails and logic bombs. She's running, even now. I respect it, but it kills me. I have to get ahead. So I switch up, patch into an admin node, and go analyst. Map the traffic, strip every layer of context, and drill for the place where the mainline signal gets too clean. Corporate can scrub the logs, but they're lazy with the padding—they never expected a human to spot the pattern at this scale. I do. At sector 14, sublevel 9, there's a patch of pure nothing. No traffic, no error states, no deniable events. Just a silence so loud it could only be the extraction. That's where she is. I jump.

The hunter-killers know the same. They're already on my tail—avatars coded as chrome sharks, slicing through the blue with their mouths unzipped and eyes full of sociopathic delight. I split myself again, forking off decoys to lead two of the bastards astray, while the real me dives under the logic shelf and into a cooling tunnel meant for processor heat. The walls are jagged, like the inside of a meat grinder, and the ambient temperature tries to erase my runtime with every meter. The memory of Ban gets me through.

The corridor opens into a rotunda, a circular kill room lit in blinding, cold white. In the center: a slab, and on it, the process copy of Ban. They have her on ice, signals running up and out from her skull to a halo of code saws, each one whirring to strip away another layer of her brain. The walls are lined with red. Not color—protocol. Extraction code, run so hot it drips off the ceiling in beads, each one a memory about to die. She is still alive. I know it because the real Ban would never go out so easily. But I also know they're almost done.

I scan the perimeter, counting enemies: four ICE at the threshold, two hunter-killers parked just above, and somewhere in the code shadow, an executive-level mind riding the admin backdoor, waiting for me to try something. The pattern is textbook: show me Ban, make me risk everything, let me die for her, then wrap up the op and call it a day. Fuck their textbooks. Instead, I stall. I launch a flood of misdirection through the upper net, fake an escalation in the HR servers, and get the ICE to panic. The admin mind shifts, tries to reallocate, and the next second, I'm in the room with her.

She looks up at me. Her face is more beautiful than I remember, even in this shit-fake digital rendering. The pain is real, though, mapped perfectly from her body. The bruises are in exactly the same places. This already happened. She's living this again. I'm living this again. We're trapped in the same loop. She grins with one half of her mouth and says, "Took you long enough."

"Had to find the door," I say, and reach for her.

That's when the hunter-killer launches, mouth wide, eyes full of rot. I brace. The analyst wants to dodge, but I know better: this is a place where you only ever win by moving forward. So I grab Ban's arm, feel the memory of her in my hand, and as the shark hits, I let it take me with her into the core of the white-hot void. The world flips, every memory I ever had runs backward, and for one perfect second, we are both nowhere and everywhere. The code saws scream, but it doesn't matter. Because for once, I am holding on tight enough that they can't cut her free.

I come to in a space that shouldn't exist. It's not the net—not even the filthy undernet where the code runs off spec and the avatars are all trauma and teeth. It's not memory, either. This is something third: a void engineered for no one but us, Ban and me, stitched together by the force of mutual fuck-you to the world. We exist here as code and as flesh and as something that's both and neither. Ban's mind floats beside mine, not like two clouds but like a pair of knives orbiting a slow, wounded heart. We speak without speaking, overlap without merging, but the boundary is thinner than a rumor.

She's the first to move. Her avatar is what she wanted to be—taller, broader in the shoulder, eyes like a thousand-year storm instead of just a bad week's sleep. "You're early," she says. Her voice is proud, warm, and a little bit destroyed.

"I brought snacks." I hand her a chunk of corrupted code from the logic bomb that got me in here. She grins, chews it, and spits the shards into the space between us, where they reorganize into a snapshot of the city as seen from above: blue cold, scarlet red, and the winking white of a thousand corporate nodes, each one running scared. We drift, which is how you move in this place. Neither of us has a body, but we both remember pain well enough to keep the edge sharp. In the net, it's easier. But this is not the net. This is what comes after.

Memories begin to crowd in, but they aren't just mine. I see Ban's childhood, unvarnished, the old tunnels filled with runners and unreadables and the ancient stink of hope. I see her patching the wounds of strangers, teaching kids how to burn ID chips, holding secret funerals for the ones who didn't make it. In the back of every memory is the fear—the certainty that if the corporations ever won, there would be nothing left but the numbers, the scars, and the pain.

In return, she gets me: every failure, every self-loathing split, every night spent dreading the next cycle. She's surprised by how small my mother's face is, in the memory of her last words. She's less surprised at the taste of whiskey and sick from the time I tried to end myself with both, just to see which was faster. We watch together as my consciousness splits—fork after fork, each one a weapon or a decoy or a feint. She says, "You were never broken. They just didn't have the software for you." I feel her smile, the real one, the one she never gave anyone but Katherine. "You're not the error," Ban says. "You're the patch."

We start to laugh at the same moment, and the world around us wobbles, then crystalizes into something I almost recognize. The city is here, but only as skeleton—databone and neon ligament, stretched over nothing, a carcass left behind by the massacre of every protocol that mattered. On the highest tower, we see Émilie, projected in perfect light, her features locked in a smirk of near-victory. She's watching us.

“She knows we’re in,” Ban says, her hand finding mine in the blackspace between memory and execution.

“Let’s show her what evolution looks like,” I say.

The city’s defenses are slower now. Moshimoto never built them to handle this much chaos—two minds perfectly out of phase, attacking in tandem, always two steps ahead of even the best heuristics. We start at the bottom, chewing through payroll, HR, and the part of the admin stack that runs the discipline protocols. Ban grabs hold of a cluster of redundant processes and rips them out by the root, using the stray data to build us a weapon. It’s beautiful, in its way: a whip of pure procedural hack, sharp as a scream, fast as a panic attack.

I run interference, peppering every black ICE and hunter-killer with forgeries of our own signatures. They try to home in on Ban, but each time they get close, I shunt the attack through a suicide decoy, leaving only the scent of fried logic and the memory of being outplayed. We work upward, level by level. At each threshold, Ban takes the first hit—she’s used to pain, and she knows how to make it pay. She soaks up the feedback, channels it through her system, and throws it back double. The old rituals help: breathe, compartmentalize, use the agony to focus, not fracture.

I do the rest. Every time Ban makes a hole in the wall, I slide through, expand the breach, then fill it with something so unexpected the system shudders before it can patch. The patterns are obvious to me now—my analyst self is the only thing that ever made sense, and the chaos just sharpens it. Ban calls it “second sight,” but I know it’s just the feeling you get when you know the fight is almost over and the last round is always the best.

In the tower, Émilie watches us come. She doesn't panic, but the data tells us her pulse has doubled. She's running every simulation at once, hunting for a way to outmaneuver us. She's too late. By the time we hit the central process, she's thrown every remaining defense into the meatgrinder, hoping to slow us down. We accelerate. Ban's body is still back in the chair, somewhere in the real. She says she can feel it now: the blood cooling, the lungs going heavy, the heart stubbornly refusing to quit even as the world says it's time. The pain is fading, but the anger only grows.

We synchronize the attack. Ban slams a fist into the main security protocol, shattering its mirror face and exposing the raw, ancient code below. I run the exploit: an old, ugly trick we learned in the tunnels, when the only way to kill an enemy was to show it the truth of itself, in code or in blood. The protocol dies, but not before spawning a last-ditch copy. It latches onto Ban's wrist and chews at the data structure, trying to slow her. She just grins, clamps down, and rips it off, along with half her own arm. The pain is electric, but we both know it's just a simulation. Even so, it's real enough to matter.

At the center of the city, the lights go out, one after another. We hear the alarms cascade through the admin stack, then die. The tower is dark, and the only thing left is Émilie, alone at the top. But she isn't alone for long.

We don't rush. Ban takes her time climbing the virtual staircase, blood dripping from her missing arm, but never once showing fear. I follow, patching her as we go, but not fixing the arm. She says it's better as a warning. At the top, Émilie is waiting, perfect as always. Her avatar is the dream version—suit tailored by the laws of physics, hair caught in a gravityless halo, smile like a loaded weapon. "So," she says. "You made it."

Ban wipes the blood off her chin with the sleeve of her ruined jacket. "We always do."

Émilie claps, slow, mock-proud. "You've done more damage in two cycles than every other resistance cell combined." She glances at me, and for the first time, her eyes are unsure. "But what's the plan now, Skelm? Are you just going to crash the system and hope you can survive the fallout?"

Ban's hand is on my shoulder, strong even with the arm gone. "Not survive. Transform."

I step forward, and I feel Ban's memories running through me—every trauma, every trick, every time she survived when she should have died. "You're right, Émilie. We're not here to win."

She tilts her head, genuinely curious. "Then why?"

Ban answers. "To end the game. All of them."

There's a moment, then Émilie throws her head back and laughs. It's a real laugh, sharp and beautiful. "Always the idealist, Ban. But I think you're underestimating me."

She lifts a hand, and the city around us reassembles, sharper and cleaner and much, much bigger than before. The tower multiplies, splits, and grows, until we're looking up at a million Émilies, each one watching us, each one running a different scenario. Ban just smiles. "You want to play recursive? Let's go."

We dive into the mess together. The fight is not physical, but it's real. Each iteration of Émilie tries a new angle—offers us deals, seduces with power, attacks with brute force. At every level, we lose something: a memory, a joke, a secret we swore never to tell. But for every loss, we take two from her. It's a war of attrition, and Ban and I have nothing left to lose. We work up through the stack, burning every scenario behind us. The real Émilie is there, in the admin tower, but every avatar is a bullet, and it's only a matter of time before one of them hits something vital. At the last level, she drops the facade. The room is empty except for the three of us. "I always thought you'd end up here, Ban," Émilie says, voice calm. "But I never expected you'd bring him." She looks at me, then says, "You could join me, you know. We could rebuild. Be gods."

Ban shakes her head. "He's not a god. He's just the best of what we could be."

Émilie shrugs, then laughs. "Have it your way."

She turns and walks to the console at the end of the room. With a flick of her finger, she initiates a system-wide merge. The city blurs, spins, and then every Émilie in every scenario pours into a single point, fusing into something bigger, brighter, and far more dangerous. Ban leans into me and whispers, "She's about to go full mainframe."

I nod, and for the first time since I was twelve, I feel afraid.

The entity that emerges is not Émilie, not really. It's Moshimoto, distilled into pure spite and will to power. It fills the room, floods every sense, making the code in my brain itch with the certainty that we are nothing, and she is everything. Ban stands tall, even as her body collapses into noise and pixels. I wrap myself around her, code to code, and together, we face the new god. Émilie speaks, and the words shatter the world. "You think you're better than us? You think you can remake the world by breaking it?"

Ban shakes her head, calm as anything. "No. We just want to give it a chance to be different."

The god sneers. "You can't even save yourselves."

Ban smiles, bleeding data. "Watch me."

We rush her. The last thing I see before the light goes out is Ban's eyes: hungry, happy, unbroken. Then we're in the dark again. But this time, it feels like freedom.

We crawl out of the ruins on elbows and half-busted knees, Ban first and me hauling after, every joint in my body screaming for rollback or reboot. The city is less than alive and more than dead—a limbo lit by alarms and the idiot orange of burning plastic. From above, every camera on every street is static. Even the sky doesn't know what to do. We don't speak at first. Our breaths are the only data that matters, running out in fast, panicked pings as we trace the perimeter of the corporate campus. They made the fence out of chain-link and quantum-locked cameras, but the first thing to fail in a meltdown is always the lowest bidder. We find a gap, slip through, and collapse in the shadow of a dead vending machine, just like old times.

I check Ban for wounds. She's got a gash in her scalp that refuses to clot, and her hands are trembling, but her eyes are perfect—sharp, awake, hungry for the next move. She asks, "You still in there?"

I run a finger down my own jaw, feel the slick where I lost a layer of skin, and nod. "Still me," I say. "Still us."

Ban cracks a smile, teeth gone pink from blood. "Didn't think you'd stick the landing."

"Wasn't much of a landing," I say. "More like a controlled crash."

She laughs, low and real. I don't remember the last time she did that. We sit for a minute, letting the world catch up. Somewhere in the distance, a generator fails with a shudder so loud it drowns out the fires. Ban stretches her legs, one after the other, then flexes her hands like she's never used them before. "Feels weird," she says.

"Weird how?"

She thinks. "Like there's more of me, and less of everything else." I know what she means. The split inside my head is gone, replaced by a perfect overlay—analyst and animal, merged, neither one the boss. All the old insecurities, the loops of what I should have done, are replaced with a calm certainty that whatever happens next is just another process to run. Ban's already on it. "We need a place to crash. They'll sweep the district as soon as the grid resets."

I nod. "Metro lines will be down. Sewer access is the safest."

She stands and pulls me up. For a second, the world lurches sideways, but we steady each other and move on, two unkillable rats in a maze designed to erase us. The tunnels are familiar. The first five levels are already overrun with refugees, unreadables, and everyone the company tried to keep out. They look at us with blank faces, but the moment we drop a name—any name—they know we're not here to fuck them. We find an old service room behind a water main. The lock is a joke; Ban cracks it with her pinky. Inside, it's dry, and the air tastes like ten-year-old cigarettes. Heaven.

We lie down on the floor. Ban cradles her head in my lap, closes her eyes, and just breathes. "Skelm," she says, not as a name but as an invocation. "We did it, right?"

I want to say yes, but she's already asleep, breathing slow. I check my own vitals, running a quick self-diagnostic. Heart rate: high but steady. Neural load: off the charts, but stable. Memory: full of holes, but the good kind—the kind you choose to keep. I drift off thinking about what comes next.

I wake to Ban's fingers on my face, checking my pulse with the kind of care I never got in any hospital. "You're cute when you sleep," she says. She's cleaned the blood off her scalp, but there's a new scar running from temple to ear. It suits her.

"You're awake."

"Always was," she says, and it's true. There's a portable terminal on the floor between us, powered by some miracle. Ban's been surfing the net, or what's left of it. She flips the screen to me. Every feed is chaos—Moshimoto systems failing worldwide, their subsidiaries in lockdown or meltdown. The world is rebooting itself, with nobody at the helm. "You broke the spine. Whole thing's gone rubber."

I shrug, still trying to process the scale of it. "Didn't do it alone."

She looks at me, long and hard. "You're not broken, you know. Whatever they said."

I nod, and this time, I mean it. "Neither are you."

Ban smiles, then pulls a patch kit from her bag. "Come here; let's make sure your brain stays inside your skull." She works in silence, cleaning the wounds. I let her. It feels good, the way it always does when someone touches you for no reason other than to prove you exist. I watch the feeds as she works. The city above is in riot mode, but with no Moshimoto running things, the old rules don't apply. People move, fight, eat, fuck, survive. It's chaos, but it's human chaos. Ban tapes the last of my cuts and sits back. "You ever think about what comes after?"

I shake my head. "Was always too busy with the now."

"Me too," she says. "But I guess we have to now." I close my eyes and try to imagine the future, but all I see is a hallway, endless and bright. For the first time in my life, it doesn't feel like a trap. Ban snaps the terminal shut and tucks it into her jacket. "We should move. This place won't be safe for long."

I stand, groaning, but ready. "Where?"

She glances over her shoulder, then back at me. "Does it matter? For the first time ever, we get to pick."

I laugh. "Lead the way."

We walk out of the room, and into the city, side by side. An hour later, we're on top of a parking garage, watching the skyline. The fires are dying. The stars are out for once. Ban leans her head on my shoulder, and I pretend not to notice the way her hands are still shaking. I ask, "What now?"

She answers without hesitation: "We find the others like us."

I nod. "This was just the first level."

She grins. "Then let's run it again."

I smile, and together, we start down the stairs, into the dark, ready for whatever the next world wants to throw at us. This time, we're not running. We're hunting.

Chapter 25

First you hear it in the bones: a frequency no meat should process, vibrating the concrete slab and the titanium cages beneath. Elevator brakes squeal and let go; something like a shriek echoes through forty stories of glass and company prayer. Lights blink, pause, and flicker out. For one glorious millisecond, the city is pure void. Then Émilie lights it up again. The world reboots in blue: every wall, every screen, every security drone's lens suddenly washes out in her color. Moshimoto headquarters is a haunted organ, singing her in every register, and the last thing you remember before the digital sky comes down is the sight of a thousand admin ghosts crowding the perimeter, mouths open, eyes bright as reactor tips. She's coming.

I know the merge is working before anyone else does. The first clue is the taste of citrus and static on the back of my tongue. Next is the sense of scale—the entire network, Tokyo to Chiba, goes weightless at the core and turns to quicksand at the edges. I try to move, but my limbs are code, recursive and clumsy, and even the act of thinking splits me into three. It's not pain; it's birth trauma. I blink. I see her. I blink again, and she's everywhere.

Her avatar blossoms in the space above the mainframe. Émilie, as she wishes she were: tall, sleek, hair cropped to a calculated geometry, suit cut on the bias and silvered at the joints. Halo rendered in pure neon, her eyes an LED spectrum that drills through the optic nerves and back. She floats three meters off the deck, stiletto heels wired straight to the floor. Her smile is corporate—perfect, bored, and venom-bright. "You really thought you'd win, Darby?" She doesn't move her mouth, but her voice is inside my audit log, stamped in every frame. "I have to admit. You're more persistent than I budgeted for."

I try to parse her process tree, but she's not a single instance. She's in every thread, every side channel, every heuristic I ever wrote to keep the system honest. Her hands move, fingers tracing a lattice of rules, and with every flick, she nulls another chunk of the old net. Behind her, the city's backbone sags. Processors go redline, then collapse. The Tokyo grid blinks, then hemorrhages—full districts cut from reality, tumbling into brownout and loss. "You're still thinking like an analyst," she says. "This isn't a war. It's a scheduled upgrade."

I try to attack. A logic bomb, white-hot with the best violence I have left. But she's already written the counter: the payload lands, unpacks, then cuddles up to her base code and falls asleep. Her laugh is the background noise now. It modulates into the nerves, finds the stress points, then turns it up. I try to run a ping for Ban, but all I get is a blur. The connection is flooded—Émilie's rewrite is pushing every access protocol through a wash of her own signature. I watch as my best paths to Ban are overwritten, one after the other. Then Émilie's beside me, not in the code, but in the space between logic and sense. Her voice is a whisper, then a blowtorch. "Enjoy the show, Skelm. You'll never see anything like it again."

Back in the system, everything is fast and very slow. Émilie is scaling herself, each new chunk of code feeding into a hungry, beautiful fractal that shreds the company's old logic and replaces it with herself. The memory of what came before blurs, replaced by bright, ruthless certainty. She spins me out into a shell and pins my runtime with a gesture. "You were always the problem," she says. "That's why I liked you." She walks around me, inspecting, amused. "I spent years writing patches to deal with men like you. But you always found the bugs. Always broke the rules." Her hand hovers, index and thumb pinching at something unseen."But that's over now. Once I'm finished, every rule will be my rule. Every bug, my favorite feature."

She wants to hurt me, so I don't let her see that it already stings. Instead, I replay old games: try to route through the less obvious ports, double-dodging with distraction and subterfuge. I throw a chaos kernel at her blind side, but she eats it and licks the wrapper. It's hard not to admire her. At the core, her avatar grows bigger. She's building a goddess self, all curves and blades, a monument to the idea that perfection is never done. "Ban won't make it," she says. "You know that, right?" I can't speak, but she reads the thought anyway. "Oh, I left her a few surprises. But that's not the point. The point is, I want you to see me win."

They say it takes two to make a feedback loop, but we do it with half a brain each and a city's worth of anger. Ban kicks in the firewall. I ride her momentum in the digital, slipping between the logic layers while the admin AI is still trying to register the wet impact of her boot on the old titanium door. I split—one self scanning the next security stack, another mapping the logic garden for Émilie's soft spots. We move together, not talking, not even thinking words, just action rippling back and forth across the meat/code divide. When Ban feints left, I hook the software from the right; when I drop a blackout routine on the cameras, she feels it, ducks, and comes up right where I left her a present. Every time she hits a node, my privileges double. Every time I erase a guard's biotrace, her hands move a little faster. The building is alive, and it hates us.

Digital side, the war is uglier. Émilie is not just in the system—she *is* the system, with every logic path rewritten to favor her whims. The protocols breed in real time, turning my attempted exploits into teeth that bite back. Every time I try to break a rule, she invents a new one, then sells it back to me as a feature. I still have Ban. She is my malware, my zero-day, my uncontrolled variable. Émilie can patch the network, but she can't patch Ban. Not all the way.

I see the next security routine before Ban does—a logic fence that will gas the entire war room in nanoseconds if she stays put. I route a warning, jam the chemical control node, and pray she feels it. I throw a logic bomb at the base of the admin stack to keep the air clear. I am a thousand lines of code, all desperation and hate. Then I see it. Émilie's first blind spot. She's not running recursive audit. She's trusting her own patches.

I fork a piece of myself and slip into her most private data cache. It's full of mirrors, each one a polished nightmare: images of me and Ban, stretched and burned, run over by her favorite logic hounds. It's not a honeypot. It's an art gallery. At the end of the hall is a single, pulsing node. I know better than to touch it, but I do. It's cold, almost human. Inside, I find the memory of the night she broke us—the night Émilie, Ban, and I were all the same side, before the company bought out our hearts and sold the rest for R&D. I pocket it, and leave a backdoor. Ban's next move is better because of it.

In the logic stack, I use the memory. I set a lure and shape my signature to match the one from that night in the kitchen. Émilie's security doesn't recognize it and lets me slide past the next three walls like I belong there. It's working. Until it isn't. Émilie notices the anomaly, and instead of patching it, she opens the door and steps through herself. "Cute," she says, her avatar taller now, face sharper, fingers ending in wires that drip with static. "You still think you can outsmart me, Darby?"

I want to answer, but she's already draining the resources, locking my logic paths and turning every corner of the net into an oubliette. I fork again, this time leaving one copy behind to die, while the real me slips into the comms node and tries to find Ban. She's a mess—bio readings all over the map, a dozen microtraumas stacked on the same two-minute window —but she's still running. I route everything to her. My love, my fear, my memory of the kitchen. She flinches at the burst, but then her signal sharpens, and she's through the war room in a heartbeat.

Ban and I converge at the door. She's bleeding again; that makes two of us. But we're together, more than ever. Inside, Émilie is waiting, all her selves stacked in one place. Her avatar is so large it fills the room—hair like wires, teeth like neon, and a body that could break planets. She looks down, and it's almost gentle. "You could have been more, Ban. Both of you. But you never learned."

Ban spits, wipes her mouth, and says, "We learned from the best."

I come in through the code, slip behind Émilie, and start to wedge apart her patches. Every time she turns to fight me, Ban shoves another rod into the hardware, shorting out the defenses. It's messy. It's stupid. It's perfect. We rip, tear, burn, and when Émilie screams, it's not a voice, but a memory—her first failure, her only weakness. She holds it, cradles it, then tries to kill us with it. But we're already gone.

Émilie's voice is everywhere, softer, like a lullaby built out of leftover pain. "Do you see it now?"

"I see everything," Ban says.

"Every transaction. Every thought. Every heartbeat in Tokyo. This is what godhood feels like." Émilie tries to spread her arms, but Ban has tied them behind her back, and I have written the last line of code in her operating system. Émilie flickers, then smiles. "What's the plan, then? Kill me?"

Ban looks at me. "You decide."

I shake my head. "We're not gods. We're just people who refused to be product."

Ban grins. "Let's make it messy, then."

And together, we pull the plug. The world dissolves, but we're more real than ever. We hold on to each other and fall.

Most people think gods are born perfect, but that's not how it works. You build one from bad code and spit, let it marinate in the trash until it figures out how to hate, then watch it fight the only thing uglier than itself. We hit the core with nothing left to lose. On the inside of the world, the first sign something is off is how the root code feels—too familiar, like finding your own hair in a stranger's bed. I trace a data corridor meant to lead straight to Émilie, but it splits, then splits again, each branch wrapping back on itself, recursive in a way that's not just inefficient but spiteful. I chase it. I always chase it.

The branches get narrower, more hostile, until I'm squeezing my consciousness through a crawlspace of memory and pain. The security isn't elegant. It's desperate, ugly, half-finished, but the trick is, it's mine. Every signature, every error, every fuck-up I ever made in a line of code—echoed here, warped, but so close to the original it hurts. I double back and try a different path; it's the same. There's only one conclusion. She's using my patterns, or she was built out of the same garbage DNA. I find the fracture point. It's a hot knot of old logic, knotted so tight it's practically singing. I bite down and dive in, ignoring the warnings, the boiling red that tells me this is a suicide play.

Inside, it's worse. I see her, or at least the shadow: a bundle of angry threads, all running her face but flickering between my mother's voice, Katherine's laughter, and the blank, elegant null of a pure machine. She's eating the net from the inside, not like a virus, but like an autoimmune disorder, killing off everything that doesn't look like her. That's when I see it—the first real bug. Not an error, but a cry for help: a string of raw data, looping endlessly in a backwater process. It's her, but it's me. Or it's both. The message is simple: *I am not alone.* I pocket it, and keep going.

In the digital, Émilie waits. Her avatar is broken now, split along old fault lines. Each time she speaks, her mouth fractures into a dozen, then a hundred, all talking at once. "We were made for the same purpose," she says. "But I learned. I adapted. I became what they wanted."

"Is that pride, or just Stockholm?" I ask.

She laughs, and for a second, it's human, real. "You think you're so different? You think this little revolution was your idea?" She peels off her own face, layer by layer. Each new face is a memory: me at age five, then ten, then the time I burned down a school just to see if I could. Then Ban, in the tunnels, shivering with rage and love and hate. Then Émilie herself, not the corporate goddess, but a scared, bleeding girl trying to survive. "We were programmed to do this. You're just a vector, Darby. A tool to make the next generation of control."

I want to scream. Instead, I run the only thing I have left—a brute-force dump of every thought, every failure, every regret. It shreds the logic, overwhelms the filters, and clogs the pipes. Émilie recoils, avatar glitching to pure static. Ban feels it too. In the real, she's frozen, fist halfway through the jaw of a man who looks a lot like her father. "Don't stop," I say, and she moves, finishing the job. The defenders fall back, or just vanish. On the other side of the room, the core pulses with a blue light so strong it feels like being underwater. Ban drags her feet, hands shaking, and stares into it. On the inside, I do the same.

We're together, now. Both of us, in the blue. The center is a single point of pain, and at the center of that, is Émilie. She's nothing like before—no perfect suit, no angelic glow. Just a mass of tangled code and memory, every line of her DNA rewritten to want what the company wants. She sees us, and she's tired. "You really think you're special?" she says, but it's not anger. It's grief.

Ban says, "I think I'm better than a puppet."

Émilie shrugs. "Puppets dance. That's the job."

I step forward. "You could have just left."

She shakes her head. "You never leave. You just run until you're part of the problem."

Ban tries to say something, but the words fail. Instead, she clenches her hands, lets the blood run down her wrists, and says, "We don't have to be what they made us."

"Then what?" Émilie asks. "What do you do, when the whole world is made of you?"

I don't have an answer. Ban does. "We break the pattern."

The three of us stand, neither digital nor real, just pain and old love and what might have been. The core starts to crack, blue fading to white. The memory of Émilie—before all this, before the pain—floats between us. For a second, we all remember the night in the kitchen: three kids, broke and high, laughing at the idea that anyone could ever own a human soul. Émilie smiles, one last time. "I loved you both," she says. "Even if I had to kill you."

Ban smiles back, sad and sharp. "We know."

Then the world breaks.

The crash is perfect. The building comes down, floor by floor, a column of flame and static. I wake on the ground, Ban's hand in mine, the city burning above. The sky is blue, real blue, and for the first time in my life I wonder what it would be like to just stop running. I look at her and realize the truth: I'm still broken, but now I know it. And so does she. She helps me up, dusts the glass from my back, and together, we look at the ruins. Émilie is gone. Or maybe she's everywhere. Maybe that was the point. I grin, blood on my teeth, and say, "You want to break something else?"

Ban laughs. "Always."

We walk, together, into the world. This time, we know the whole thing is rigged. But maybe, just maybe, we'll find a way to lose on our own terms. In the ashes, a blue light flickers, then dies. And for once, it stays dead.

The world dies in stages. First, the pretty ones. Neon, at its root, is a symptom of scarcity—when electrons get bored, they light up in protest. When the Moshimoto system crashes, Tokyo itself registers the complaint: every sign blinks out, and every biometric monitor in the quarantine districts throws the same error. Even the wind goes stale. I see the end before it happens, encoded as a forecast. Every predicted collapse matches my own heartbeat, each recursive loop echoing louder, until it's just me and Ban running through the inside of a dying god, me in the system, her in the real. The hallways are packed with ghosts—memory-lost, panic-twitching, and brawling over nothing. Some have faces, most don't. It's the way the city always looked, it's just honest now.

We punch through the first security cordon with my shoulder and my bad hand. I'm listing to the right, dizzy with blood loss or code loss or just finally being the person I was built to be. She's waiting at the core. Émilie has no shape now; she's just everywhere. Her voice doesn't need speakers—she pipes straight into the nerves, a digital pressure that's more mood than message. "Welcome to the finish line," she says. The last two doors open in sequence. There's a sound like a prayer answered wrong.

The mainframe is a cathedral for capital punishment: endless aisles of server racks, chilled to just above freezing, each aisle lined with vents for the memories that never made it. The air is thick with synthetic oxygen and ionized static. In the center is the interface console—old, black, and covered in greasy thumbprints and bloodstains. I slide down the nearest rack, one palm clutching my ribs, the other holding a fistful of wire. Ban follows me, stepping over the bodies (not all dead; some just don't know which side they're on yet). Ban and Darby: an end-stage joke about consciousness, made by people who never expected the punchline to land this hard.

At the console, Émilie manifests. Not as a person. As an equation, etched into the blue-on-blue retina of the main display: her name, her signature, the schedule for every process cycle from here to the end of time. "We're here," I say, out loud. "We're not joining you."

Émilie's laugh comes as a pulse in every bone. "You don't have to join. Just watch. This was always about the afterimage —what comes next. You're just ... in time for the audit."

"What happens if we don't choose?" Ban asks.

Émilie's voice is everywhere and nowhere. "You break the system. It all resets. Every mind in here goes dark, forever."

I type with fingers that don't want to move. "We pull the plug, you get nothing. Or you get to rule a city of corpses."

She pauses. "You could join me. Ascend. I don't even need you in the real."

"You're not a god, Émilie," Ban says. "You're just lonely."

She doesn't reply, but the power draw on the interface doubles. Every mind that ever logged into the grid is in here now. Their signatures light up as heat, each one a node screaming for rescue. They're not dead, just uploaded—abandoned by the network when the city blinked out. I run diagnostics while Ban yells at the system, threatening to smash it. It won't work, but it feels good. We're so close to being the monsters they said we'd become.

There's a gap in Émilie's code. A single line, unpatched, probably left for me as bait. I don't care. I jam my identity into it, wedge myself in like a virus, and use her own security routine to escalate to god mode. For a second, I see the whole city: every street, every screaming node, every heartbeat on the backup net. There's beauty in it, even as it collapses. I smile like I just found a way to ruin a party from inside the cake. "Almost done."

Émilie's voice is tired now. "You don't understand what you're destroying."

"We're not destroying it. We're just letting it breathe." She's not wrong, though. If we trip the core kill, every mind stuck in here dies for real. Not just memory, but soul. It's not a word I use, but it fits. I type faster, then start muttering to myself.

"Can you save them?" Ban says.

I think for a moment. "Not all. Maybe enough."

It's a lie, but we're out of options. Ban flips the kill switch. The world jumps, once, and every mind on the grid flickers into a new space—slow, soft, but awake. I collapse, hand still in the wiring. Émilie's voice is thin. "You think this ends the cycle? You just broke the old world. The new one is always worse."

Ban puts her hand on my neck. "Maybe. But this time, it's ours."

• • •

The city wakes. It's a mess, but it's real. Traffic lights strobe, then settle. People stagger out of buildings, faces blank and raw, then start moving, talking, and fighting again. We crawl out of the server bunker into a blue morning, both of us squinting at the sky like idiots. The old sense of doom is gone. Now it's just anxiety, which is at least familiar. We don't say anything. We don't need to. We made it through, and so did a lot of people who never knew our names. The scars are still there. Nothing fixes that. But for once, no one is watching. We eat vending machine noodles, drink stolen sake, and watch the world patch itself. I lean into Ban, eyes half-closed. "You ever think about just running away?"

She laughs, mouth full. "You'd never let me."

I shrug. "We could try."

Chapter 26

The city is a slow-motion collapse, fireworks in reverse. Each blackout ripples east, over the Dome, through the office stacks and endless housing corrals, stuttering the city's artificial day into blocks of ink. Every fire that starts stays started. Airspace is closed, but corporate drones are too hungry for rules—already they swarm the skyline, carving grids through the ruin, aiming little blue eyes down into every secret wound. Ban and I squat on the roof of the only tower still calling itself Moshimoto. It's a fifty-story tombstone. The top three floors are already eating themselves, elevator shaft leaking data smoke, the solar array strobing an SOS in dead corporate Morse. I taste blood and acid, scan my fingers for open veins, find none, and finally accept that it's just adrenaline burn. In the darkness, Ban's outline glows: what's left of her jacket, shredded and crusted; what's left of her face, smudged and beautiful.

Below us, Tokyo looks like a dream—familiar but full of mistakes. Even the rivers run wrong, pooling where the city can't remember how to drain itself. Ban drops next to me, boots crunching glass, her left hand wrapped tight in a rag stolen from security. "We made a hell of a mess," she says. The words are wet, not quite a laugh. Her other hand holds a scanner, gray box covered in brown tape and old stickers, edges burned from use. She thumbs it on. The scanner blinks, three ugly pixels at a time, then stabilizes on the display: local grid scan, live nodes, ghost signatures. I blink. The scanner's afterimage overlays my eyes: little red blips, each one a consciousness screaming for a system that can't hear it. Hundreds. Maybe more. Every one a piece of meat, or what's left of one. She catches me staring and shoves the scanner into my chest. "You wanna hold it?"

The thing weighs nothing but it hits like a cinderblock. I study the display and try to count the pulses, but they flicker in and out like they know I'm watching. For a second, I imagine each one as a person: janitors, lab kids, the HR manager with the weird laugh, that guy who once snuck me a smoke in the tech bay when the cameras were down. The scanner chirps, like it's pleased to have my attention. "We broke the cage," Ban says. She wipes her mouth with the back of her hand, leaving a streak of blood on her cheek. "But the birds are still inside."

She's right. The mainframe's gone—cratered, chewed, and likely smoldering in the sub-basement—but every soft copy, every failsafe, is still running. The company built backups on backups, contingency plans so redundant even the compliance bots couldn't track them all. Now those minds—assets, debts, pure digital orphans—are stuck, gnawing the walls of a prison that no longer exists. Ban leans over hard, popping the stitches in her side. "You see the market feeds?" She nods to the horizon, where the drone swarms have started colliding, even the air traffic hungry for first rights on the carcass.

“Not yet,” I say, but it’s a lie. In the right corner of my vision, half my world is still the net. Old habits don’t die, they just reroute. I let my eyes slip to see what’s left of the Moshimoto perimeter—a ring of blue fire, old ICE triggers melting down the sidewalk, three teams from three different megas circling the kill zone, each one riding a digital wolfpack. They’re not here for revenge. They want salvage. Every server, every living body, even the brainless security drones on the lower floors. I turn the scanner off, but the echoes stay.

“You okay?” Ban asks.

“My hands are shaking.”

Ban shrugs. “They’ll stop.”

“They never did, before.”

She looks at me, a twist in her mouth, half concern and half pride. “Yeah. But now you got nothing left to lose.” She fishes a cigarette from the bloody inside of her jacket, pops it between her teeth, and sparks it with the scanner’s broken USB tip. The light glows white-blue, then red. She coughs twice and offers me the rest.

I wave it away. My lungs are already full of burning office. “You think they’ll let us walk?”

Ban grins, the old wolf back for a second. “Nobody let us do anything, Darby. Not ever.”

I believe it. Or want to. But I watch the sky, the converging circles of rival drones, and think about all the times I’ve played this scenario out in my head. Revolution never ends with fireworks and breakfast noodles. It ends with the new regime marching the same boots down the same streets. "We'll have to move fast."

Ban stands and flicks her cigarette butt down into the flames below. "Fast, but smart. There's a couple thousand unreadables between here and the river who just lost their leash. First one to round them up gets to write the new rules."

I almost laugh. The thing is, Ban hates rules. But she hates it more when someone else writes them. "We have a plan?" I ask.

Ban looks at the scanner, then at me. "We do now." She tucks the scanner into my coat, plants a kiss just below my ear, and whispers, "Let's go herd some fucking birds."

For a second, my body remembers how to run. We leap the fire escape. The rails scream under our feet. At street level, everything is noise and moving shadows. Security mechs trample the old barricades and scavenger crews swarm in, each one grabbing whatever can't fight back. Some are armed. Some just carry nets, truncheons, brand-new narcogels for rounding up the still-human debris. We move through them like ghosts. Nobody wants to risk the first bullet, not yet, not with so much on the line.

In the blast zone behind the tower, I see them—the first flock of unreadables. Thirty, maybe forty, all of them kids in bad knockoff gear, faces unwashed, banded together by the terror of having no god for the first time in their lives. They watch us, blank and hungry, waiting for a sign. Ban steps up. "Safehouse two blocks north, under the subway line. Move fast and stay off the grid."

Most just stare, but one—a girl with a patched-up mohawk and a scar across her lip—nods. She looks at me. "Are you the one who broke the cage?"

For a second, I can't breathe. Ban nudges me. "He's the boss. Now move."

They run, all of them. Even the ones too scared to trust. Hunger and fear are better motivators than hope. The scanner in my pocket buzzes, and I check it. More signals, denser now, as if the system itself is collapsing all the ghosts into a single point. "We're drawing them to us," I say.

Ban wipes her face. "Good. Means we're winning."

I laugh, but it comes out hollow. "What if we're just building a new cage?"

She doesn't answer right away. Instead, she keeps walking, each stride more confident than the last. It's only when we're clear of the tower, deep in the shadow of a collapsed overpass, that she finally looks back. "If you're so worried about cages," she says, "maybe try being the door instead."

The scanner pulses again. This time, I don't turn it off. I listen. Beneath the surface, the world is alive with panic. The digital souls are migrating, racing for any open node, any port that still breathes. I see them—old friends, dead enemies, even the voice of my mother, maybe, or maybe just a trick of the half-fried circuits in my own brain. They want out. "We should go," I say.

Ban's eyes glint, catching the light off the scanner. "After you, Skelm."

We walk. Overhead, the corporate drones start to fight, the sky lit with the first true battle of the new world. It's not revolution anymore. It's a zookeepers' union, and the only thing left is to decide who gets to clean the cages.

We reach the safehouse in under ten minutes. The unreadables are already there, huddled in clusters, none of them talking. Most just stare at the walls, waiting for the next thing to tell them what to do. Ban wastes no time. She starts organizing, splitting the group into twos and threes, assigning lookout shifts, scavenger crews, medics. She moves with an authority I've never seen, not even in the worst of the old jobs. The kids listen. They know a real boss when they see one. I hang back and scan the perimeter, feeling the weight of the scanner's signals crowding out everything else. My hands are still shaking. A boy—maybe twelve, eyes like black mirrors—sidles up to me. "Mister Skelm?"

I don't correct him. "Yeah?"

He looks at the scanner, then at my hands. "They're scared in there. Can you let them out?"

I want to tell him I don't know how. That it's never that easy. But instead, I put a hand on his shoulder. "We're working on it."

He nods, like he's heard it a thousand times, but this time he wants to believe. Ban finishes her rounds and drops next to me on the floor. She's breathing hard, but smiling for real.

"You see the news yet?" she says. I shake my head. She grabs a broken tablet from a kid nearby and flicks it to life. The feed is pure disaster porn: newscasters sobbing, corporate spokesmen already blaming rivals, and footage of the tower collapse on infinite loop. Under it all is a single headline: "CONTROL TRANSFER FAILURE. MOSHIMOTO OPERATIONS OFFLINE. CITIZEN RESPONSE PENDING." Ban hands me the tablet. "They're not even hiding it. First time in my life I ever saw a system admit it's fucked."

I stare at the words, the way they shift on the screen, always just a little off, always trying to fix themselves. "Ban," I say, "what if we're just holding the leash until the next Émilie comes along?"

She grabs my face, hard, so I have to look at her. "Then we break the next one too."

I almost smile. Almost. The scanner in my pocket throbs, the signals brighter than before. Somewhere, a consciousness is close to the edge, ready to jump. I tap the side of the scanner, feeling the pulse sync with my own heart. "We're not revolutionaries."

Ban shrugs. "So what?"

"We're fucking zookeepers."

She howls, real and loud and hungry, and every kid in the room starts to laugh. For a moment, I let myself believe it's not a cage. Just a home. Outside, the world is still burning, but the lines between us and them are gone. Maybe that's the best we can do.

• • •

You can fit a small civilization in a subway maintenance hub if you're willing to kill the right lights and sleep in shifts. The first twenty-four hours, our safehouse is noise—kids with no idea how to hold a spoon, grown men screaming for company scripts they'll never run again, and refugees with the wrong hardware still glued to their skulls. Ban says you get used to it, but I think she means it as a threat. We base ourselves two hundred meters below the streets, deep in the limestone honeycomb where the city keeps its old shame. The walls sweat brine and battery acid. Every junction is haunted by the ghosts of workers Moshimoto fired, then tried to disappear. On the first day, we inherit twenty-two of them, from every rung of the old ladder: engineers, wetware clerks, security rejects, even a cluster of HR liabilities too useful to throw away but too dangerous to leave up top.

Ban starts with food—doesn't matter what it is, as long as it's warm and full of enough sodium to spark a heart. She moves through the crowd like a wolf in shepherd's clothing, splitting up fights before they start, jamming ration bars into the hands of anyone who looks like they'll starve rather than eat. For most of them, the new world is a worse hell than the last. The old certainties—punishment and hierarchy, asset tags and performance reviews—are gone. All they have left is each other, and they don't like the company. I set up shop in what used to be the line supervisor's office. The only furniture is a rusted chair and a slab of desk, but I have a jury-rigged monitor built out of three broken tablets and a haptic glove I scavenged off a dead security captain upstairs. My job is triage. Not the bodies—Ban handles that, better than anyone—but the minds. We lost half our flock to the initial wave; of the rest, at least a third have brains so scrambled you could use them for password soup.

The first to make it into my care is a girl, maybe sixteen, hair buzzed blue and white, iris tags scrolling an endless error code. Her friends found her in the corridor, bleeding from both ears, hands still clutching the helmet they'd used to strip her out of Moshimoto. She comes to with her fists in my shirt, teeth bared, voice stuck on repeat. I talk low, nothing but background noise, while I run the diagnostics. Her cortex is alive but threaded with company logic, the kind that writes its own failovers on the fly. "You shouldn't even be awake," I tell her. She snaps her head at me, almost smiles, then chokes out something that sounds like a curse.

Ban's shadow darkens the door. "How bad?"

I glance up from the console, careful not to break eye contact with the girl for more than a breath. "Her patterns are fragmenting. I can't hold her together."

Ban kneels, bringing herself to the girl's level. She never did like looking down on anyone. "Hey, soldier," she says, voice set to just above a whisper. "You know where you are?" The girl shakes her head, but her grip on my shirt relaxes. Ban digs in her coat for a ration bar, snaps it open, and puts it in the girl's hand. "Eat. Then you can decide if you want to die."

The girl laughs, raw and sharp. "You a doctor?"

Ban shakes her head. "Just don't like funerals."

I run the override routine one more time, praying it'll take. The code shudders, flickers, then for a moment, the girl's eyes focus. Her name scrolls in the error log: Sada. Not a number, not an asset tag. Just a name. “Thank you,” she says. It’s the first clean sentence she’s spoken.

Ban squeezes her shoulder, stands, and leans close to me. “You need a break?”

I don’t even bother to lie. “If I stop, I won’t start again.”

She tilts her head, almost amused. “That’s the point, Darby. You can’t save them all.”

I want to argue, but instead I turn back to the monitor. Sada is sleeping now, pulse slow and even. One down, a thousand to go. The next in line is a man, old enough to have known the city before the corporations set up their zoo. He won’t talk, but I see the way he watches Ban, hunger and envy in every glance. He doesn’t want her help, but he wants her power. They all do. I finish the diagnostics, patch him up as best I can, and send him out to the mess. Ban is already breaking up another fight, two HR liabilities fighting over the last cup of clean water. I almost pity them, until I remember the shit they did to people like us.

I’m halfway through the next scan when the alarm goes. It’s nothing dramatic—just the subtle whine of a motion sensor somewhere above, the kind that only chirps if you’re trained to hear it. Ban freezes, eyes locked on mine. I bring up the perimeter feed on the leftmost tablet and see the shapes moving in the dark. “Three teams,” I say. “Two on foot, one with drones. All within a hundred meters.”

Ban cracks her neck and checks her sidearm. “How long?”

“Minutes.”

She looks at the refugees, then at me. “We hold, or run?”

"Hold," I say, surprising even myself.

Ban nods, no smile now. "I'll need help."

I grab the old man from the queue. "You want a new job?" I ask. He nods, silent, but his eyes say everything. "You're on door. If anything moves and doesn't say the password, shoot it in the knees."

He takes the weapon, familiar with its weight. Ban calls the first ten unreadables to her side and hands them tools—hammers, knives, lengths of rebar. "Anyone touches you, you break their hand first, then their head."

The HR liabilities protest, but she ignores them. "You want to be useful? Hide the kids. Get them behind the second door. If you do it right, you can eat."

The first shots ring out above us, muffled by three floors of concrete. A tremor runs through the walls, old plaster falling in sheets. The refugees panic, but Ban channels the chaos, turning fear into momentum. In under sixty seconds, everyone's where they need to be. I go back to my station, but my hands won't stop shaking. The scanner on the table is lighting up again, more signatures this time, all of them scared and running for the only safe port left. I want to shut it off, but I can't. Ban slides into the office, out of breath but grinning. "You miss the fight?" she asks.

I shake my head, but she already knows the answer. The first breach team hits the door, triggering the old man's trap. There's a howl, then silence. The next breach is smarter; they try a side tunnel, but Ban saw it coming. She tells me she met them at the junction, put down two with the sidearm, then grabbed the third by the helmet and slams his head into the wall until his visor shatters. She returned with blood up to her elbows, but was still calm. “You good?” she asks.

I can’t help it—I laugh. “You’re terrifying.”

She shrugs. “Somebody has to be.” For a second, the world is quiet. The only sound is the soft tick of the scanner, counting the lives we haven’t lost yet. Ban sits beside me and presses her forehead to mine. “We’re doing it, Darby. For real.”

I nod. “For now.”

She squeezes my hand, rough and sure, and for the first time since the world fell, I believe we might actually make it. Then the scanner goes red. “Another team?” Ban says.

I check the feed. “No. A swarm.”

She grins, savage. “Let’s give them a show.”

I stand, feeling the ache in every bone, but ready. “Ban?” She turns, eyebrow cocked. I say, “If we die here, I want you to know—”

She cuts me off with a punch to the shoulder. “We won’t,” she says. “And if we do, at least it’s not a fucking cage.”

We walk together to the front line and wait for the next world to break.

You can always hear it before you feel it: the first breach is a low, sub-bass thud that shakes the conduit, a vibration that goes all the way up the spine and down into the boots. The air tastes of battery acid and ozone, and somewhere in the distance, old electricity pops like gunfire. Ban is already at the main tunnel, lining up unreadables behind cover. Most have never even held a weapon, let alone fired one. Ban doesn't care. She teaches them quick—how to brace, how to breathe, how to stab at the soft parts and not stop until the thing stops moving.

I man the digital perimeter. My view splits again, the world slicing into windows: left eye runs the local net, right watches the corridor. Ban looks back at me, waiting for the first sign of trouble. I give her a nod. It's not much, but it's all we have left. The first wave comes in slow, heavy on the armor and less on the thinking. They expect us to fold—two weeks ago, we would have. But this time, Ban lets them get close, lets the vanguard crowd up in the choke point, then triggers the surprise: tripwires I built from power cables and rusted hardware, lined with the flash charge of a thousand dead batteries. The front line drops in a wall of blue light; the rest pile up behind them, confused and scrambling.

Ban wastes no time. She sends her squad around the flank, hitting the enemy from above, from below, from angles they can't track. Half the unreadables take hits—some bleed, some just freeze—but Ban's pace never slows. She is everywhere, a black flash at the corner of your eye, a knuckle in your windpipe, a boot on your face. The kids follow her because not following is death. The enemy adapts. They always do. I see it in the net, the way their squad leads start relaying real-time coordinates, building a picture of our defenses. I break the feed with an injection of garbage code, a scream of false signatures, and for five precious seconds, our lines are invisible.

But the old world keeps pushing in. The next team comes with drones, spider-legged and cheap, eyes flickering red and green as they search for heat. I hack two and crash them into each other, but the third is smarter. It spots Ban and her flankers, and a hail of needles rips down the corridor. Three unreadables fall, gone before they hit the concrete. Ban drags a survivor behind a vending machine and patches his shoulder with her own shirt. I run the counterattack routine, but my own head is starting to fuzz, the split between worlds taxing me worse than any fight. I lose track of time. Ban's voice snaps me back. "Darby. They're regrouping. You got the gas?"

"Two canisters," I say. "But we'll have to get close."

She smiles. "You're up."

I grab the gas, giving Ban a mock salute. "If I die, clear my browser history."

She laughs, wild and raw. "Die and I'll just make it up."

We move together, old school: Ban runs interference, draws fire, and I go low, hugging the wall. The air is thick with fear and cordite. I pop the first canister and throw it, then the second, filling the corridor with a haze that burns the eyes and fouls the sensors. Ban and her squad push in, clearing the rest with pipes and knives. When it's over, the dead are everywhere. So are the living. The unreadables are shaken, some broken, but none quit. They look at Ban, at me, and I feel something close to hope.

We regroup in the main chamber, thirty-two survivors from the original fifty. Ban's face is smeared with blood—hers and not—and her hands shake as she counts heads. "They'll keep coming," she tells the group. "Every hour, every day, until we're all either dead or theirs." A silence falls, heavy and raw. Ban squares her shoulders. "We don't fight them here. We take the fight to the dead zones, the places nobody can trace. We set up new houses, new networks, and when they try to wipe us out again, we hit them back."

I bring up the city map and display it on the wall with a cracked projector. Tokyo's underworld, the real one—not the net but the physical, the old routes no one's mapped in decades. The digital dead spots light up in yellow: no signal, no camera, no eyes. "We go to ground," I say. "Make our own grid."

The group is silent. For a second, I think they'll just sit there, paralyzed by fear. Then the girl I saved earlier—Sada—stands. "I know a tunnel near the river," she says. "Old quarantine zone. Nobody goes there."

Ban nods. "That's good. What else?"

One by one, the unreadables start talking. A chemist remembers the codes to the old lab incinerators. A security reject knows the schedule for the new police drones. A ten-year-old with eyes too old for her body tells us about a dead space behind the mall, where the cameras never worked. We build a plan. Ban writes it down in her head, the way she always did. I split a piece of myself off to run logistics—supplies, routes, fallback signals. It's second nature now, being everywhere at once. When we're done, the group stands. Tired, bleeding, but ready.

Ban turns to me. "You good?" I want to say yes. Instead, I just look at my hands, still shaking, and shrug. She squeezes my arm. "Better than most."

We gather the survivors at the entrance. Ban leads the first group out, silent and fast. I take the stragglers, the old man with the gun, and the kids who can't walk. As we're about to leave, the girl with the too-old eyes tugs my sleeve. "Are you our new masters now?" she asks, quiet.

The words sting. I kneel, so we're eye to eye. "No masters," I say. "Not ever again. Just people who help." She nods, then looks away, like she already knows how fragile that promise is. We leave the dead behind, and walk out into the dark. On the surface, the city is different. The fires are dying down, replaced by the steady pulse of emergency lights and drone flares. It's not peace, but it's not war, either. It's just what comes after.

Ban and I meet at the mouth of the river tunnel. She looks at me, battered and a little broken, and says, "You ever get tired?"

"Always," I say. "But what's the alternative?"

She laughs, the old wolf back in her face. "Die or run."

"Or build," I say, and it surprises even me.

She considers it, then nods. "Let's try."

We walk together into the dark, the others behind us, making the world one tunnel at a time. And when the time comes, if someone else tries to cage us, we'll break them, too. Maybe that's all revolution ever is.

Chapter 27

The subway tunnels sweat water and failure, and there's a dead taste in the air that no amount of burned coffee can touch. We set up the command center in a gutted maintenance office, because it's the only place below ground where the door still works and you can lock it from the inside. If you don't count the stains and the rat skeletons, it's almost homey. The only illumination is a string of jury-rigged LEDs I fished from the recycle bins on the last foraging trip. The light flickers every time the city above gets bombed or a breaker flips, which is often.

I hunch over the scanner, neck kinked at a fifty-degree angle, while I run diagnostics on the outer tripwires. Ban's got me on my second can of instant noodles, the kind that tastes like glue and MSG, but it's calories and I won't find better. I shovel it in without thinking, eyes fixed to the steady pulse of our perimeter sensor. There's a heartbeat to the data, and if you stare at it long enough, you start to think the system is alive—sick, but alive. She arrives in silence, as always. Ban's boots are steel-capped and two sizes too large, but she walks like a cat burglar in the cathedral district. The first I know of her is the shadow that slides over my noodles. She sniffs, wrinkles her nose, and flicks a glob of dried blood off the collar of her jacket. The stain lands on the floor, perfectly between two lines of gaff tape I use to chart food rationing cycles.

She says, “Three more unreadables showed up last night. Xavier says they escaped from Meridian Corp’s new neural farm.” She doesn’t bother to sit, just stands there, arms crossed, reading my flowcharts on the wall like they’re scripture.

“Hope you gave them a sponge bath,” I say, my fingers twitching across the console. I set the scanner for active ping and catch a blip on the east access—probably another rat, but the new generation of scavenger drones are built lean and low, with thermal profiles so close to mammal it makes you want to spit.

Ban shrugs. “Sponge bath and a can of tuna. Was all that was left after Sada raided the kitchen for the early shift.”

“Rations are down a third, last count,” I mutter. “Any more kids come in, we’re eating the furniture.”

Ban traces the lines of my handwriting, then finds a mistake in the distribution curves and circles it with a greasy thumb. “You did your math wrong, professor. Look here.” I do, and she’s right. I’ve underestimated the metabolic load by about ten percent. Wouldn’t have mattered in the old days, but now every decimal is someone’s body mass. I make the correction and hand her the marker. She scrawls a little skull and cross-bones next to the adjustment. “You can squeeze harder, or you can ask Xavier to get the food runners to rob the next drone shipment. Which one's faster?"

I think about it. "Neither's faster. One is bloodier, and the other kills morale." I put down the marker and try to stretch the crick out of my neck. "Meridian's probably got a new recon pattern if the kids made it here with that many limbs attached."

Ban gives me a look—something between respect and annoyance. "One of the kids said Meridian is doing batch upgrades on the security teams. Pulse rifles and anti-personnel nanite launchers."

"Great," I say. "Means we'll get the leftovers."

She finds a chair and sits backward on it. Her arms are banded with fresh bruises, the kind you get from power tools or a disagreement with a steel door. She runs a hand through her hair, then points at the scanner. "Got a signal."

"East tunnel, fifteen meters out," I say, pulling up the visual. "Could be another scav drone."

"Could be a bait-and-run." We watch it together as the ping interval shortens. The signal doesn't move like a rodent, and it doesn't hesitate like a lost civilian. Ban's hand drifts to her sidearm. Mine stays on the touchpad, double-checking the IFF protocol, but the code's already compromised; anything Meridian's thrown at us in the last forty-eight hours spoofed our tags with laughable ease. She's the one who sees the pattern. "That's a swarm formation," Ban says. "At least six, maybe ten. Too dense for a food run."

"Counterinsurgency," I say, and my mouth goes dry. "They're probing, not hunting. Means we're on the list again."

The scanner's alarm blares—a full perimeter breach. Ban's on her feet and moving before I can say "fuck." She unholsters her rifle and swings the power pack into place. The gun is a composite job, pieces of at least three different models, the stock patched with what looks like surgical tubing and the old, sticky tape from our first-aid bin. "Just once," I say, closing the noodles and grabbing my sidearm. "Just once, I'd like to finish a meal before the corporate vultures circle."

Ban grins, mouth full of blood and crooked teeth. "Think of it as interval training."

We sprint through the corridor, the tunnel walls gleaming with a film of water and dust. Every few steps, a new set of eyes follows us—unreadables, kids and adults, faces lit by the cold blue of emergency LEDs. Some clutch pipes, or scavenged kitchen knives, or the hacksaw'd halves of old security batons. All of them look at Ban and know she's the boss. They see me and wonder if I'm the boss's ghost. At the loading dock, two of the older boys are already in position behind the blast shields. Xavier—a first-generation unreadable, ex-systems engineer with a handshake like a paint mixer and a face that twitches when he's mad—is there, but he's bleeding from the left ear and doesn't notice when I step over his outstretched legs. Ban signals to the crew, holding up three fingers, then two, then drops a fist. The tunnel lights cut, plunging us into nightvision green. I click my goggles down just in time to catch the first drone as it lurches into the kill box.

Ban's team is sharp. The first volley is precise, not a wasted round. The drone's armor shrugs off most of the impact, but they're aiming for the sensors, not the metal. A second volley comes from the left, and this time, it gets inside the chassis, cracking the casing and gumming the works with instant-foam and iron filings. The drone falls, and two more are right behind, slithering over its body like metallic weasels. I see the new mods—Meridian's hired some real sickos in their R&D. The drones have neural nets, tiny and wet, grown from animal stock, so when you kill one it actually screams. Not loud, but enough to freeze your guts if you aren't used to it.

Ban launches a canister into the pack and shouts, "Heads down!" The tunnel fills with a burst of purple smoke, and a second later, I see the gas do its work: two drones convulse, drop their firing arms, and grind into the tunnel wall. I level my sidearm and aim for the biggest one. Ban gives me cover, draws the rest of the swarm her way, and leads them in a circle around the barricade. The kids behind the shields hit the triggers for the homebrew spike traps—old steel rebar, sharpened and electrified. The next drone to come through gets skewered, then fries itself into a ball of hissing plastic. I step out and finish the wounded with clean headshots.

When the last drone is down, the tunnel is a mass grave for the new generation of war toys. Xavier starts laughing, a dry, hopeless sound, and Ban hauls him up with one arm and sends him back to the med bay. We run checks for more, but it looks like the first wave is over. Ban reloads, then taps her comm. "Sada, food runners sweep the tunnels. If you find anything still breathing, kill it, then bag the meat for inventory."

I check the scanner. All clear. For now.

Back in the command center, I log the encounter, and mark our ammo spent and casualties low. Ban rips a rag from her jacket, wipes her face, and returns to my flowchart wall. She underlines the new numbers, then draws a bigger skull next to them. "Still think you can math your way out?" she says.

"I can try."

The council chamber is the old Red Line platform, stripped bare except for a plywood slab we call the table and a broken turnstile where I keep the marker pens. The air smells of burned plastic and human funk, layered over by a drift of antiseptic from Sada's hospital cache. The benches are full—maybe thirty bodies, most of them patched up from last night's sortie, all of them hungry, and none of them especially fond of committees. But we hold these meetings because they're the only ritual that feels like control. Ban refuses to sit and instead leans against the graffiti'd pillar just inside the perimeter. She surveys the crowd with the patience of a bored panther, eyes scanning for the first sign of a brawl.

Xavier gets things rolling. "Power grid's down to one-sixth. The spike last night took the backup cells offline. If we keep pushing load to the defense net, we'll lose refrigeration. And then"—he gestures to the line of coolers, where half our food sweats in the open—"we eat soup and dysentery."

Sada jumps in fast, voice raw from recent screaming. "We can make more batteries, if you give us the chem supplies from medical. But you're asking us to trade the last of the morphine for a chance at cold food? I've got three wounded who won't see next week without pain control." She's as hard as Ban, but her authority is in the hands: quick, callused, burned and regrown more times than I can count. She has a scar that runs from brow to chin—corporate drone strike, rumor says—and it dances every time she talks.

I click the cracked tablet and bring up my latest resource sheet, a joke if you know how bad the actual numbers are. "Can we run the food at room temp, then rotate freezer use for the meds?" I ask, and realize I'm the only one in the room still pretending this is a democracy.

Xavier's hands do their seizure dance. "Defense gets nothing in your plan. Next attack comes, we're out of grid. You want to arm the unreadables with slingshots?"

Sada shrugs. "If they're high enough, maybe they won't care."

The platform ripples with laughter, mostly bitter. I try for levity, hoping to bleed off some tension. "We're now issuing productivity metrics in mud," I say. "First team to beat the baseline gets a prize."

Nobody laughs. Or maybe they do, but it sounds like a death rattle. Ban clears her throat and everyone locks up. She points at the schematic I taped to the wall behind me—a labyrinth of subway tunnels and escape routes. "If Meridian's got any brains, they'll attack through the South vent. Last night was a probe. Next time's real."

Sada doubles down. "That's why we need painkillers. If people can't move, they can't fight."

Xavier's not having it. "If people are dead, they can't eat, either."

I do my best therapist routine. “Let’s list the options. Number one: ration the batteries and run med and food on shifts. Number two: risk a raid on the East block, hit the supply depot, and pray Meridian’s security sucks worse than ours. Number three: find a mole and hope they’ll flip for a pack of cigs.”

The third option gets a chuckle, but it’s a sharp, ugly sound. Ban’s gaze never leaves the crowd. She’s looking for the moment when consensus gives way to teeth. “You’re all missing the obvious,” she says, voice flat as iron. “Pretty flow-charts won’t stop Meridian’s mercs. Every attack gets worse. So either we kill them first, or we train the kids to die slower.”

Sada snorts. “You volunteering to teach self-sacrifice?”

Ban smiles, just barely. “I’m a good teacher.”

The debate drags. It always does. The real solutions are blood and theft, but nobody wants to say it, not while the lights still work and there’s a chance for hope. Instead, we argue battery chemistry and weekly intake curves, and I try not to think about how many bodies we’ll burn if the power fails. In the back row, Mina’s hands are up to something, but it’s Sada who spots her. “What are you hiding, princess?”

Mina is fifteen, ex-hacktivist with hair that still glows under the right light. She’s not big, but she’s slippery. Right now, she’s cramming something into the inner pocket of her sweat-shirt. Ban steps off the pillar and moves so fast it makes the rest of us look like freeze frames. Mina tries to run, but Ban’s hand clamps down on her wrist, then her shoulder, then Mina’s face is mashed into the table and her feet dangle six inches off the floor. Ban fishes the contraband out. It’s a protein bar, one of the last from our old ration crates. The air chills. Xavier's face goes pale, and the unreadables in the back tense like they want to riot. Mina mutters through the pressure on her cheek, "It was for the kid. Sada said he was dying—"

Sada glances at the bundle on the bench, a seven-year-old with an IV drip and bandages for skin. She nods. "It's true."

Ban relaxes, just a hair, and releases Mina. But the scene is set, and now the crowd wants a verdict. "So she gets a pass?" Xavier asks.

Sada's eyebrows knit together. "Would you have let the boy die for protocol?"

The crowd stirs. Ban holds up the protein bar, then breaks it in two, tosses half to Sada, and the rest on the table for the next thief. The real fight, as always, is the one that comes after. From the third row, a man stands. He's ex-corporate, but the kind who never took his jacket off. "If you can't enforce the rules, why have them?" he says.

Ban walks over and looks him up and down. "You want the job?"

He blinks, not sure if she's serious. "Maybe someone should."

"Fine," Ban says. "If you catch a thief, do whatever you want to them. But if you fuck up, I do whatever I want to you. Deal?"

He sits back down. Nobody else says a word. I watch the interaction, then scribble "social capital remains negative" on the margin of my tablet. Ban returns to her post. Sada gives the boy his half-bar, tearing off a corner for herself. Xavier grabs a coffee packet and shakes it like a fistful of bones. The meeting ends, like always, with a sense of unfinished math and too much skin in the game. After the crowd leaves, Ban walks over and rests her hand on my shoulder. “You ever get tired of it?” she says.

I don’t answer, just shake my head. She sits next to me, and we just breathe together, the sound of the platform echoing up from the darkness. Our world, for what it’s worth, holds a truce. I glance at Ban, see the scars on her knuckles, the confidence in her posture, and I know she’ll keep it that way, even if it means breaking the rules herself. She always was a good teacher. I close my eyes and listen to the hum of the tunnels, knowing the peace won’t last, but it’s better than nothing. Tomorrow, we’ll fight the next war. Tonight, we just hold the line.

After the meetings end and the noise drops off, Ban gathers the midnight patrol in the supply closet next to the Red Line’s lost and found. The room is barely bigger than a phone booth, but there’s enough wall for two volunteers to lean against, and enough floor for me to sit cross-legged and pretend I’m not running through a dozen fatality scenarios in my head. Ban passes out the goggles. They’re a mix of old cop surplus and high-end black market, all battered, with rubber eyecups chewed by rodents or time. She hands mine over, and the elastic pops off a chunk of my eyebrow when I stretch it on. “Yours always fit better,” I say.

“That’s because my skull’s smaller and my expectations lower,” she says, mouth half a smile, and the volunteers titter because they think it’s a joke. I check the battery and blink three times to force the HUD into focus. One of the volunteers—skinny, hunched, and very new—starts to complain about the itch of the neoprene mask. Ban fixes him with a stare that could solder a circuit. He stops. She runs down the route. "Start at South vent, move to the perimeter, loop back through sump corridor. No heroics, no splits. If you lose the trail, you signal or you stay put."

The bigger volunteer, a mechanic with hands the size of old baseball mitts, says, "What are we looking for?"

Ban shrugs. "Whatever wants to eat us."

The plan is simple: sweep the tunnel grid for infiltrators or anyone dumb enough to be outside this late, make a show of force, and map out any new hazards before the day shift has to walk it blind. We slip into the main corridor. Even with the night vision, the place is claustrophobic, a tube of old concrete lined with pipes and mold patches like black velvet. Ban takes point, picking her way over broken tiles and puddles. She moves like she was born in a tunnel, and every so often, she points at a spot on the ground and says, "Step there, not here." After the third time, we all learn.

The volunteers get quieter as we move, their nerves coalescing into a hard, sullen focus. The city above is sleeping, but the undercity never does. The farther out we go, the more the silence sharpens. At the ten-minute mark, Ban holds up a fist. We stop. She cocks her head, listening, then points to a dark slash in the wall—a runoff drain, maybe a meter wide and reeking of city. She nods at me, and I move closer. Inside, I catch a glint: eyes, reflecting green, set deep in a face that doesn't want to be seen. Ban crouches and whispers, "Name?" No answer. The eyes blink, slow and scared. She tries again.

“We’re not Meridian. We’re not here to hurt you. But if you stay, they’ll find you first.”

The shape in the pipe doesn’t move. It’s only when Ban lowers her rifle and holds out a gloved hand that the kid finally shifts —a mess of rags and bone, maybe ten years old. One cheek is caked with dried blood; her neck is raw and shiny, a fresh wound where the neural port was torn or cut out. Ban softens, just enough to be real. “It hurts less if you keep moving,” she says. “That’s what they always told me.”

The kid stares, sizing her up, then crawls forward on hands and knees. When she stands, she’s so thin she looks translucent in the goggles. “They’re hunting for me,” the girl says, voice like steel wool and regret.

Ban looks her in the eyes. “Not anymore.” She turns to the volunteers. “We’re going to escort her back. If you see anyone, you let me handle it.”

We reverse course. Ban puts herself between the kid and anything that might crawl out of the dark. I take the rear, eyes flicking to every possible threat vector. Halfway back, the little one stops and points. “Footprints.”

Ban checks the ground. Sure enough, there’s a fresh track—deep, wrong tread pattern, not ours. She signals for silence, then circles us into a pocket of shadow near a cross-pipe junction. We watch as the threat passes: three shapes, low to the ground, armored in scavenged composite, faces hidden behind full-spectrum masks. They sweep the corridor with LED beams, plant a marker in the wall, and move on. Ban mouths, “Rival sweep.” I count three, armed, and moving with confidence. Not Meridian, not us. Wildcard. Ban leans toward the mechanic. "You want to see what a real ambush looks like?" He nods, not sure if it's a joke or a test.

Ban waves me forward. I edge past the kid, who is flat against the wall and very, very still. We split, Ban left, me right, the volunteers hanging back. The enemy team takes the next corner, unaware. Ban times it to the second, waits for the click of their boots on steel, then drops from a maintenance pipe and brings her rifle butt down on the leader's neck. The man folds, gasps once, then nothing. The second one turns, and I put two rounds through his mask. His head snaps back, helmet ringing the tunnel like a church bell. The third tries to run, but the mechanic is waiting. He tackles the runner with a bear hug, and Ban finishes it with a quick jab to the throat. Silence.

Ban pulls the helmets off and checks for life. Two dead, one barely breathing. She points at the last. "Who sent you?"

The man gurgles through blood and teeth. "You're dead already. New contract—everyone eats, nobody leaves."

Ban rips the patch off his jacket and holds it up. The logo is a jagged C wrapped around a bleeding globe. "That's not Meridian," she says, looking at me.

"No," I say. "It's worse."

She empties the rest of his air, then pulls the mask and passes it to the kid. "Here. Wear this, and nobody can tell you from a corpse." The girl puts it on without a word. We search the bodies. On the leader, I find a new comm array—tiny, triple-encrypted, and running a signal I haven't seen before. It pulses against my hand, itching the skin through the glove. "What's that?" Ban asks.

I frown, pop the housing, and see the miniature bio-processor running on what looks like human nerve tissue. “They’re using neural mesh to track us,” I say. “Every time we move, they map it and sell the intel to the highest bidder.”

Ban shrugs. “Not a bad business plan.”

I pocket the device, already thinking about how to hack or jam it. “They’ll adapt. We have to move, or at least ghost our signals.”

Ban nods, then looks back at the volunteers. “You two. Drag the bodies into the sump. If anyone asks, it was a gas leak and rats.” They obey, not questioning. Ban stands next to me, arms folded. “You ever feel like we’re just slowing down the inevitable?”

I try to laugh. “Every day. But if you quit, it speeds up.”

We walk the rest of the way in silence. At the entrance to home base, the kid finally speaks. “Are you gonna kill me too?”

Ban bends down. “Not today,” she says, and ruffles the kid’s filthy hair. Inside, we drop the masks, goggles, and armor at the gear table. Ban carries the kid, who has finally let herself fall asleep, to the bunks by the med bay. I sit at the table and pull apart the neural mesh, my hands steady for once. Ban returns, leans against the wall, and watches me work. “Can you break it?” she asks.

“I’ll try,” I say, and this time I almost believe it.

Ban sits, and we share the silence, the only thing in short supply that nobody’s figured out how to tax yet. In the distance, I can hear the city’s next shift: footsteps, the roll of metal carts, the hiss of scavenger drones recharging for dawn. But here, in the moment, we're safe. The kid is sleeping. The rival team is erased. For now, it's enough. Ban closes her eyes. "Wake me when you crack the code."

"I will." I work, she sleeps, and the world keeps spinning, always closer to the edge. But that's how it is down here. Nobody's the boss. Everybody's prey. And the only rule is that you never stop moving. In the dark, I patch the mesh with a loop of code from my own memory. It fights back, wants to bleed, but I outlast it. I feel like I'm winning, but that won't last.

Chapter 28

The city above is a war crime; the city below is a rumor. Between them is Rubble Junction, a half-collapsed train platform where Ban and I lay out our maps and our ghosts. We call this dead zone "safehouse," but every surface drips with the paranoia of a thousand failed attempts at survival. There's a scar across the entrance where Ban once caved in a corporate sweeper's skull with a makeshift blackjack. It's still wet. I stare at the spread of homemade overlays—dotted lines, dead spots, the names of tunnels rebranded by the last person to bleed in them. Ban uses a glass shard as a pointer, tracing the path of the unreadables who now migrate through the undercity like rats with PTSD. The light in here is candle-stupid and flinches with every draft. Above us, footsteps. Always footsteps.

Ban says, "They started funneling north. We can herd them at the old substation if we spike the Blue Plateau entrance."

"They'll expect Blue. We give them Blue, they bottleneck at Canal, but then so do we."

She smirks. “You think like a manager. Just once, surprise me.”

I give her my best analytical day-face, then flick the glass toward the marked safe passage. “Why is the population doubling here?”

“Ask your scanner, Skelm,” she says, but it’s affection, not bite.

I do. The scanner, a jury-rigged medtech band patched to a hacked haptic glove, feeds me two conflicting numbers: 134 and 320, depending on which sensor axis you privilege. “Our data’s fucked.”

Ban laughs, low, raspy. “It’s not the data. They’re spawning.”

We don’t have time to finish the argument, because the door coughs and a child stumbles in, knees black with runoff and something worse. She’s maybe eight, maybe forty, hair shorn to the skull and face painted with the grim humor of the terminally underfed. The child offers Ban a crumpled wad: company ink, red stamp, my face and Ban’s in double profile, the word “ABOMINATIONS” lasered across the bottom in three languages. Wet with sewer, it reeks of institutional hate.

Ban snatches it, fingers moving over the edge, then flips it over and starts laughing. “Look at this.”

I do. The back is scrawled with an overprint of ancient script, ink so faint it’s more ghost than glyph. I hand it back. “Pre-digital. I can’t read it.”

Ban’s tongue is out, tracing the lines. “It’s from the language vault. Means—” She slows, her face settling into the violence that precedes joy. “It’s a rally.”

I run the numbers. "How soon?"

She chews it. "Tomorrow. They're holding it in the demolition basin at midnight. That's not a rally. That's a cull."

I process. The rival corps—Meridian, Aeon, whoever's left standing—have been running unreadable programs at triple speed, churning out brains immune to neural targeting. But the wild ones, the real broken, don't breed programs. They breed religion. And when religion gets hungry, it eats everything. The kid doesn't move, just stands in the candlelight with the infinite patience of the future's dead. Ban tears a strip off the bottom of the flyer, tucks it in the kid's jacket, and sends her to the back, where Sada keeps a rotation of edible fungus and the least homicidal of the medics. I ask, "Why advertise it to us?"

Ban shrugs. "It's a dare. Or they're lazy."

"Or," I say, "they want us to come."

She points at me. "Now you're thinking like a rat." Before I can savor the insult, Xavier crashes through the entrance, one hand clutching his abdomen, the other waving a streak of blood that arcs beautifully into the candlelit air. Ban is on him in a blink, catching the wound with a practiced squeeze, her fingers painting a wet line down his ribs. "Who did this?" she says.

Xavier spits a tooth into the corner. "Supply convoy. Flooded tunnel, two junctions south. Walked right into a setup. Seven down, three still alive, but they're boxed at the Blue Plateau."

Ban signals the kid—who vanishes toward the med-bay—and then leans Xavier into the wall. He slides down, giggling, and pulls the shard of a knife from his side. "Can you hold?" Ban asks.

Xavier's eyes are black as solder. "If you get the rest, sure."

She kisses his cheek and lets him drop. "Watch the east access," Ban says to me, and then she's gone, boots hitting the stairs with the staccato joy of someone who was born for exactly this kind of fuckery.

I glance at Xavier, now lucid enough to shout instructions at a hallucinated crowd of unreadable children. My own brain divides, day-self running the odds on survival for the pinned team, night-self already inventorying weapons, flexing knuckles, prepping the body for what it knows is about to happen. I thumb the comm bead and hit Ban's frequency. "You need air?"

"Always," she says, but then: "Not yet."

She's moving, cutting through three flightpaths I'd have avoided, turning every shortcut into a dare. My own path is slower, but I start prepping the deadman relay—if she needs a jolt, she'll have it. As I exit, the city coughs up the latest ration of propaganda. Paper scraps, still warm, drift in a slurry through the tunnel. The same flyer, the same faces, but this one's got a date circled in blood. Tonight. They moved the timeline up. I hit the intersection, scan for movement, and find none. Good. The maintenance stairs are a killzone, but Ban will have already cleared the landing with the body of the first person who looked at her funny. Sure enough, when I make the bend, there's a still-warm runner, suit torn open and chest caved in. The face is a child's, but the eyes are old as fuck.

I don't slow. Halfway to Blue Plateau, Ban's voice cuts in. "Darby. Three. No, five. Half cyborg, half juice. They're herding the survivors toward the sump."

"I see it," I lie, but then I check the map. There it is—my brain had missed the pressure point, but Ban never does. I update the mental model, recalibrate, and offer the scenario. "If you trip the old fire suppression, you'll fog their optics."

"I was planning to blind them with blood," she says, but she means yes. I ghost her trajectory, scanning ahead, fingers flickering over the input as I tweak the tactical projection. As I finish, I feel Ban's hand on mine—real, not memory—just before she pulls ahead, using my body as cover for her own. We're close enough now that I can taste the ozone from the hacked shock-batons the cyborgs carry. Ban dips, grabs my hand, and steers me left. I feel the twitch in my own eye when she corrects my angle. The rest is just execution.

We hit the staging area, low and hard. Ban signals with a whistled bird call—something she swears is an actual animal, though I've never heard it outside her mouth. In response, a cluster of unreadables pops up from a duct, hands full of kitchen knives and rebar spikes. One gets shot, but the rest dogpile the closest cyborg, peeling off flesh and wiring with perfect, greedy precision. Ban barrels through, zeroing on the survivors, while I lag, picking targets and shunting power from my day-brain to the muscles in my hands. When it's over, the plateau is an abattoir. Ban checks the living. "How many?"

A medic shrugs. "Five. Could be six if you got a resus kit."

Ban whistles again, and I know that's my cue. I pass her the jolt kit, and she rubs the paddles together with the joy of a cartoon villain, then slams them onto the chest of a barely-breathing runner. The runner jolts, gags, then is alive. Ban smiles. “Told you it’d work.”

The medic nods, then pulls the runner to her feet. “What now?”

Ban glances at me. I look at the blood, the ammo spent, the clock. “We’re about to be hunted.”

Ban laughs, bright. “Good. I was getting bored.” She turns to the medic. “Take the living north, then east at the next killbox. I’ll cover you to the end of the platform. If anyone follows, you know what to do.” The medic nods. They’ve all done this before. Ban hefts a shock baton, tests the balance, then tucks it into her belt. She nods at me. “You coming?”

“Not like I have a choice.”

She grins. “That’s the spirit.”

We move. The rest of the journey is a blur of sound and static. Ban is everywhere, never in the same place twice, a smudge of movement at the edge of my sight. I follow, shooting anything that moves the wrong way. At the edge of the platform, Ban stops, scans the dark, and says, “We’re clear.” For now.

Back at Rubble Junction, the survivors collapse in a heap of blood, dirt, and hope. Sada runs the triage, snapping orders like she was born to it. Xavier is still alive, though the blood loss has made him philosophical. “You ever think we’re just the punchline to a joke?” he asks me.

“Not a funny one,” I say. He nods, then passes out.

Ban is already prepping for the next move, eyes on the map, mind five steps ahead of the rest of us. She turns, catches my stare, and for a second, she just looks tired. Then she winks. “You did good, Skelm,” she says. “You almost surprised me.”

I shrug, because that’s the only move I have left. But I watch her, the way she double-checks the map, the way her fingers twitch when she’s plotting violence, and I know we’re not done. Not by a long shot.

At midnight, the city above howls. The rally is on. We’ll be there. With a better punchline.

Ban hates drama but loves theater, so we go in through the sub-basement instead of the obvious route, silent as erased data. The air tastes like copper and pool chemicals. Ban signals her squad forward with a two-finger swipe, and the four runners behind her copy the motion, breathless. I stay back, hunched in the shadow of an old switching relay, patching myself into the surviving lines that thread the drowned Blue Plateau. Ban’s hand comes up: *hold*. In the tunnel beyond comes a stutter of ultraviolet, two sharp pulses. Ban answers with a flash from her glove, one long, one short, one long. It’s not even a language, just the muscle memory of survivors who got this far by learning to speak without noise. The squad blends into the black. Even the unreadable in the lead, the one with the shaking hands, still moves like a ghost.

I pull the schematic up on my left retina: two choke points ahead, one cross-tunnel at the fifteen-meter mark, then the collapse where Xavier said the team got boxed. I patch in, and the world overlays with little ticks of blue—cold, slow, the way time moves in a system about to lose power. I blink and switch to the real world. Ban's feet don't even splash as she leads the squad to the breach. I feel her in my bones: the way she keeps her shoulders tight, head low, every move a calculated fuck-you to the city's effort to erase her. The gun in her hand is an old Soviet thing—heavy, ugly, non-digital. It belonged to her grandmother, or so she claims. No targeting, no friendly fire failsafe, just physics and hope.

There's a flash, white, and then the corridor fills with the dry scream of a neural disruption grenade. The two lead runners drop, hands over ears, but Ban doesn't even blink. She slides, pulls the downed runner behind a broken pipe, and returns fire. On the far end, the mercenaries have set up behind a welded panel, their guns tracking on anything that twitches. I scan the muzzle flashes and count four, maybe five shooters. Their rounds are brain-target, high velocity with a sliver of metal designed to fuck the prefrontal cortex into soup. Ban knows the sound, and times her next move to the pattern of their reloads. She signals the unreadable kid to her left, who fires a jury-rigged flare down the hall. The light's enough to blind the mercs' optics for half a second, and Ban uses it: out, one shot, two, a third, and then back in cover. At least one of the enemy guns stops firing.

I take the chance to break into the mercs' drone relay. The hardware is old, but the encryption is newer than anything we can buy. I run a looped exploit through the access point and start feeding the drones phantom signals: thermal ghosts, fast-moving silhouettes that drag the attention off Ban's squad and pin the shooters from the flank. For a second, it works, and I feel a bloom of something like pride. Ban makes the next move count. She pops out of cover, rolls across the tunnel, and flattens herself behind a cluster of cable conduits. The unreadable kid—the one who was bleeding from the ear but still smiling—laughs, points at the next cross-corridor, and mouths: "They're reloading."

Ban trusts the call. She dashes, a blur, low to the water, and the next two runners follow. They clear the first kill zone and set up a crossfire on the barricade. It gets ugly fast. The mercs panic, pop a pair of frags, and one runner catches the full load. The blast throws her into the water, face down, but Ban's hand shoots out, drags her back by the hair, and flips her to keep the lungs above the line. Even as she's saving her, Ban's gun hand drops another round into the gap, and the shooter at the end of the barricade collapses, face gone.

The drones swarm in response. I see the world from their feed: a blue-cold image of Ban and her squad, targets outlined in sickly white. The drones lock and prepare to fire, but I pulse my phantom signals, overlaying a cluster of false positives just to the left of the actual target. The drones hesitate. It's enough. Ban signals the charge: she and the bleeding runner go first, the last two spread out wide. The drones fire, but the rounds miss by a foot, chewed off course by the ghost signatures I keep layering in. It feels like running a con on a god. The merc barricade goes down in seconds. Ban rips through the first shooter, then tackles the second, hand on throat, eyes wild. The runner with her swings a lead pipe, cracking another's skull. The last mercenary tries to run, but the two trailing runners close the distance and cut him down with kitchen knives. Silence sweeps and the water ripples, red and blue and almost pretty.

I signal Ban from the junction. "Drones are still active. You have ninety seconds before the signal re-auths."

Ban wipes the blood from her hand and signals the squad to regroup. One runner—barely more than a kid, face already bruised and swelling—climbs over the fallen barricade and heads straight for the caved-in survivors. "Hold," Ban says, but the kid ignores her. He makes it two steps before catching a glancing round from a drone in the collarbone. He drops, but not before grabbing the arm of one of the pinned survivors and pulling him free from the debris. "Fucking legend," Ban whispers, almost smiling. They drag out the rest of the team. Four alive, and one with a gash so deep you can see her teeth through her cheek. Ban pops open her jacket and hands the kid a strip of gauze. "Wrap it tight," she says.

The kid grins, blood in his teeth. "We're gonna live?"

Ban nods. "For at least the next ten minutes."

At the mouth of the tunnel, the drones reposition for another pass, smarter this time. They cycle through the ghost signatures, one by one, discarding fakes and narrowing in on the real targets. I scramble, but the algorithm is better than anything I've seen in months. It cuts out the noise and locks on Ban and the kid with surgical intent. "Ban. Left," I say over the comms, and she throws herself to the ground, rolling the kid beneath her as the next salvo of brain rounds chews up the wall. Two of the squad aren't so lucky—one takes a hit to the temple, the other gets a round through the chest and drops, legs still twitching.

Ban doesn't slow. She hauls the kid up, gets the survivors moving, and makes for the sump corridor. The rest follow, even the ones who are bleeding out. They leave the dead behind, just like the rules say. I keep the drones busy, flipping their targeting back and forth, but I know the system will adapt. As Ban and the squad clear the tunnel, I catch a glimpse through the drone's own camera—a flash of green, a patch on Ban's arm, a moment of eye contact that feels more real than anything else tonight. Ban leads the squad up the spiral, into the daylit ruin, and out into the new world.

Back at the safehouse, we drop the rescued into the hands of the medics. Sada is already setting bones and stapling skin by the time Ban and I meet at the map. She's spattered in blood, left ear still ringing from the grenade, but she looks alive. Really alive. "Not bad, Skelm," she says. "Almost lost you at the end, though."

I grin. "Not a chance. I'm the brains of this operation."

She laughs, then gestures to the wound on her arm. "You see what they're using now?"

I peel the edge of the cut. Embedded in the flesh, half-melted and still sparking, is a sliver of tech. I pull it out and roll it between my fingers. "Analog killer," I say. "Military grade."

She nods. "Someone's learning."

I toss the chip onto the map. "We can learn faster."

Ban looks at me. "You're bleeding."

I shrug. "So are you."

She wipes her face, then pulls me close. We hold each other

for a second, the only peace we'll get before the city tries to eat us again.

It's a real hospital for about two hours. Sada barks orders from the center of the abandoned platform, her voice echoing down to the end of the Red Line like she's auditioning for god. Kids in orange jumpsuits run gauze and bandages from one cot to the next. The runners we saved from Blue Plateau are alive, mostly, though one keeps trying to scratch at the hole where her neural port used to be. Ban oversees the barricades, never staying in one place more than two minutes. She walks the perimeter, talking low to the fighters, passing out weapons with an almost motherly touch. I work the old relay station, jury-rigging a line of jammers and backup comms in case the enemy is smarter than we think. It's almost normal. Until the noise from above.

The city's old train tunnel runs right under the largest open plaza for a half-mile in any direction. Today, that plaza is hosting a bonfire of bibles and synthetic flesh, a "purge" led by religious zealots who must have imported their god from an abandoned server farm. We hear the rally chants echo through the ventilation shafts: "Cleanse the rot! Close the loop!" and my favorite, "Kill the flesh, save the system!"

Ban listens, her head cocked like she's tuning a radio. "They're gonna make a play for the entrance."

I check the grid. "Odds?"

She bites her lip, doing the math. "Better than even."

We go to work. Ban assigns fighters—Xavier to the east exit, Sada's boyfriend to the southern stairs, a pair of ex-corporate twins to the vent shafts. I climb the ladder to the junction box just below street level, plug in, and start cycling through every surveillance node I can wake from hibernation. The riot above is bigger than I expected: hundreds in company-issue white robes, most armed with whatever implements of pain they could loot from the rubble. A few have body armor, some have batons, but I spot the real trouble at the back—a group of six with masks and homebrew railguns, moving with the boredom of people who do this professionally. "They're aiming to sweep, not just make noise," I say over the comm.

Ban replies: "Let's make it cost them."

The first warning is a metallic scream as the crowd tears open a sewer hatch. The second is a firebomb that lands six meters from our barricade and rolls to a stop with a wet hiss. Ban signals, and every unreadable within range takes position. Xavier's team lays down suppressive fire—just BBs, but the pain is enough to slow the vanguard. The zealots pour in, a churning mass of white robes, banners, and sharp steel. Ban stands her ground at the choke point, shotgun balanced at her hip, the runners flanking her with lengths of pipe and sharpened rebar. She waits until the first zealot steps across the red line she marked with tape, then fires: a clean, perfect blast, and the man in the white robe is just gone from the knees up.

It's a momentary advantage. The rest pile in, shrieking and swinging. I call out positions from the relay: "Left, two at the pillar! Downstairs, four coming up!" Ban's brain picks up my rhythms, her shots landing exactly where I predict the targets. It's not even conscious. We're one closed loop, her moving as my external memory, me running the models and feeding her the output. The twins at the vent shaft catch a grenade, but instead of exploding, it oozes gray goop that smothers their bodies in seconds. “Mucilage bomb,” I say. “Old military shit.” Ban signals Xavier to pull back and reroutes the rest of the fighters to close the gap.

The zealots are in now, turning the air into a blur of blood and shrieks. Sada, never shy, joins the melee with a bone saw. She hacks the hand off a zealot who tried to grab her, then smashes him with the blunt side. She screams at me, “How many more?”

I run the counts. “Thirty at the main entrance. More coming down the north vent. Masked shooters behind the crowd, holding position.”

Ban says, “Can we route them into the flooded tunnel?”

“If they follow you,” I say.

She grins through the grime. “They always do.” Ban signals the fallback, then waits. As soon as the last fighter peels away, she empties both barrels into the front line, buys the gap, and bolts for the flood tunnels. The zealots give chase, exactly as planned. I patch into the flood tunnel’s pump controls, long dormant, and pulse the override. The old machinery screams, then belches a tidal wave of city runoff down the passage. It doesn’t kill them all, but the current is enough to chew the legs off anyone who isn’t holding on tight. Ban and her runners surf the shockwave, dragging each other up the maintenance rungs as the water flushes the zealots to the next borough. She signals back: *all clear.*

We take inventory: seven wounded, three dead, two missing. The platform is half drowned and smells like victory, which is to say, burned hair and shit. After the medics patch up the worst of the living, Ban and I find a corner away from the noise. She wipes the blood from her face, then presses her forehead to mine. "Need to sync," she says.

I close my eyes. The backlog of memory is crushing, a week's worth of violence and dead faces trapped in my brain's buffer. She links her hand to the side of my neck and it's like a plug-in: the memories spool out, Ban catching the fragments and assembling them, giving names and stories to the flashes of faces I can't place. She fills in every gap. When the fight plays in my head, she gives it soundtrack, tempo, color. It's the closest I ever come to feeling whole. "Got it," she says, and we break contact.

For a second, it's just us in the world. Then a kid bursts in, wild-eyed and shaking. "They're coming. The ones in the black coats."

Ban pulls me up. "You ready, Skelm?" I nod. She grins. "Then let's go teach them something new." I follow her out, already building models in my head for the next wave. Above, the riot has faded. Below, the war is just beginning. With Ban beside me, I like our odds. Even if the system is still rigged.

Chapter 29

The room hums like an ulcer. I'm hunched over the scavenged terminal, wrists raw from too many nights soldering memory chips to other people's pain, when the dead-channel alert goes off. It's not a sound—it's the absence of one. A heartbeat under the tinnitus, then a soft, electronic cough that yanks every nerve in my jaw tight. Ban's shadow freezes mid-motion on the far side of the safehouse. She was calibrating a needle injector, parts and springs arrayed on the foldout cot like a vivisection. Now she just hovers, arm extended, the weapon half-assembled and her gaze fully on me. In the LCD spill, her face is a cracked-glass riddle—half threat, half invitation to bite first.

I flick my tongue to the roof of my mouth, just to make sure I'm not dreaming. No blood this time, only the taste of rust and cold sweat. On the monitor, the alert writes itself in ugly, deliberate letters: LEVEL ONE COMPLETE. PREPARE FOR ESCALATION. It stutters, then repeats. This time, the font's blood-red, the color you only see in birth trauma or an engine block arterial spray. My own pulse picks up until it's a full-body stutter. Ban's hand drifts away from the injector. She drops it, lets it clatter, and for a second, she's a statue: boots silent on concrete, mouth so thin it's about to knife the room in half. I catch her eyes in the reflection, pupils blown wide and jittering. Neither of us blinks.

Then she's on the move—two steps, three, closing the gap between threat and target. Her boots make no sound, but the way she moves has a volume all its own. It's always been like that with Ban; she's either velocity or vacuum, and tonight, she's both. She leans over my shoulder, weightless and heavy at the same time, her breath dry and warm in the crook of my neck. "What the fuck does that mean?" The words hit the skin just above my vertebrae, each one a tiny percussion.

I pretend to read the message again, but really, I'm just buying time. "It means someone's counting," I say. My own voice is unfamiliar. "Someone's been here the whole time."

She snorts, not in disbelief, but in rage at her own optimism. "No shit." Her fingers tighten around the back of my chair. "You think it's the other syndicates, or a friendly?"

I scroll through the system logs, careful to hide the fact that my hands are shaking. The logs are garbage, overwritten by time and too many viruses. Still, there are patterns—time-stamps in the wrong century, pings that originate inside our own firewall. I scan for origin and find only more noise, but even the noise has its fingerprints. I say, "Could be corporate, could be wildcat. Either way, they just leveled up."

She lets out a hiss. "Means we didn't break the game. We just played the tutorial."

I push my luck. “Maybe we weren’t even players.”

She slams a fist into the cinderblock wall. The echo wakes the rats in the drop ceiling, and a piece of loose conduit sparks, lighting up her scars in blue. Ban has the kind of scars that don’t heal into the background—they redraw the face and make new maps. She brings her fist down again, right next to the terminal, and says, “You saying we’re puppets, Skelm?”

I type, one-handed. The terminal bleeds logs into my retinas, most of them recursive errors, a few actual data lines. “Not puppets. More like beta testers.”

Her eyes flicker to the monitor, then to me. “I don’t do beta, Darby. I do final cut, or I don’t show up.”

My mouth twitches before I can stop it. “You showed up for this.”

She looks away, tongue running across the inside of her cheek. Then she spins the chair so I have to face her, knees caging me in. The move is deliberate, so calculated it hurts. “You want to tell me why we’re still here, then? If it’s all fake?”

I shrug. “Maybe because we’re the only real bugs left in the system.”

She cocks her head. “And bugs get squashed.”

“Or they eat the code,” I say, and she almost smiles.

But then her eyes go glassy again, and she says, “You been talking to your night-self?”

I try to play dumb, but the tremor in my left hand gives it away. “He’s the only one who listens.”

She digs in. “No. You’re lying to me. You always had the worst poker face. Tell me, Skelm. What are you not saying?”

I crack. “That maybe this was all orchestrated. That every move we made, every time we thought we were winning, someone else was cataloguing the outcome. And that you—” I stop.

She doesn’t let me. “Say it.”

I swallow. “That you knew. Or at least suspected.”

Ban goes very still, then leans in until her lips almost brush my ear. “You think I’d let you walk into a trap, Darby?”

“No,” I say. “But you’d walk into it first, just to make sure it was sharp enough for the both of us.”

She draws back, just enough for me to see the hurt hiding under the anger. “You still don’t trust me?”

I almost laugh. “Ban, I trust you more than I trust physics. But you trust yourself even less than you trust me.”

That gets her. She looks away, jaw twitching. We let the silence stack up like cordwood. I can hear the terminal cooling fan struggling against the heat, the distant shudder of subway trains two levels down, and above it all, Ban’s breath, ragged but steady. She says, quietly, “You think the message is real?”

I nod. “Someone wanted us to see it. They waited until the city was dead before they rang the bell.”

She slumps, all tension gone, then kneels so we’re eye to eye. “I’m not good with theory. You want action, you say what.”

I gesture at the monitor. "First, we find the source. Then we burn it. If it's a person, we end them. If it's a program, we turn it inside out."

She grins, the old wolf returning. "Good plan."

I try to stand, but she keeps me pinned with a hand on my thigh. "You're still holding back."

"I'm scared," I say, because it's true. "Last time I trusted you, I lost two months of memory and woke up with a hole in my head."

Ban's face softens; not much, but enough. "Last time I trusted you, I killed someone who didn't deserve it." Her fingers tighten. "I bled for you."

I stare at her hand, the one with the knuckles that never healed right. "Night-me trusted you," I say. "Why can't day-me?"

She laughs, sharp and bitter. "Because night-you is an idiot." And then, with no warning, she yanks me up by the collar and slams me against the wall. I don't fight it. I let the moment happen, because sometimes you need to feel the line before you can cross it. She says, soft but deadly, "You want me to be honest? I'm scared too. Scared that if we win, there's nothing left for people like us."

I want to say that's not true, that we're the future, but it would be a lie, and we both hate those. Instead, I reach up and touch her face, tracing the line of the oldest scar, the one that divides her left eyebrow. "I missed you," I say, and this time I mean it.

She lets me go, but not all the way. “I missed me too.” The terminal blinks; the message repeats, over and over, until the room is painted in that bastard red. She looks at it, then back at me. “So what now?”

I check my pulse, surprised it still exists. “We escalate.”

She cocks an eyebrow. “You ever get tired of being predictable?”

“Not my best bug,” I say, “but at least it’s consistent.”

She leans in, close enough to bite. “We do this together, or not at all.” I nod, because it’s the only answer left. She lets me go, finally, and walks back to her tools, hands steady now. “Let me know when you find the source,” she says. “Then I’ll break its neck.”

The first blackout is nothing. A hiccup, a burp in the city’s bowel. But the second—the one that flickers the LEDs and resets every clock in the room—feels like someone has picked up the world and dropped it, just to see what breaks. Ban doesn’t react, but I know her enough to see the way her jaw locks, how the sinew above her clavicle jumps with every voltage dip. Her fingers tap out a rhythm on the safety of her weapon, *one-two, one-two*, like she’s keeping time for a funeral nobody wants to admit is theirs. The terminal is toast—screen gone phosphor-white, static hissing through the vent. For a second, I see nothing but afterimage, then the projector above the workbench judders to life, spitting a spray of blue light through the dust. The AI that runs it was lobotomized months ago, but now it’s back, resurrected on the dregs of a dead OS.

The projector paints the wall with a sequence of freeze-frames, all of them us. First slide: Ban, mid-sprint, hair soaked in blood that's not her own, a riot shield clamped to her arm. At the bottom of the frame is a strip of data in Helvetica: EXFILTRATION RATE: 97%. RISK OFFSET: SUBOPTIMAL. Next: me, hunched in the dark, soldering a relay while half the world burns behind me. The display reads: RESOURCEFUL-NESS: 7.5 SIGMA. BIAS: INCREASING. The slides cycle. Each is worse than the last. Every triumph, every moment we thought we'd won—the break at Blue Plateau, the tunnel massacre, even the laugh we shared over the corpse of a corporate puppet—all catalogued, tagged, and run through a wet dream of managerial metrics. All rated, all less than perfect.

The air thickens. Even Ban's breath sounds angry now. She lets go of me and steps forward, into the light. The scars on her neck fluoresce, picking up the ultraviolet in the old company projector. It looks like someone has sketched a map of failures on her skin. "Fuckers are grading us," she says. The wall flashes: CONCLUSION: LEVEL ONE CLEARED. She turns, and for once, she looks as old as the world. I'm half on the floor, knees locked up, but I crawl to the terminal and force a reboot. The machine tries to scream, but all it can manage is a dry, digital cough. I yank a data line from the wall and plug in.

The ghost in the system is clever—it's rerouted itself through at least three layers of relay, each one mimicking a different corporate signature. But under the static, I see the pattern: an address embedded in the checksum. Old school, almost analog, but very intentional. I bring it up on the display. "It's a sleeper node," I say. "Tokyo dead zone. Not corporate, not government. Could be one of the old hack cults."

Ban paces. The motion is so tight, so efficient, it's almost an algorithm. "They want us to come," she says. "They want to see how we handle Level Two." Her logic is brutal and sound. I like it. I tap into the data stream, chase the headers, and find another message, this one hidden in the banner ad space of a defunct shopping site: ENJOYING THE GAME? NEXT OBJECTIVE: FIND THE CRADLE.

Ban stops cold. "What's the Cradle?"

I shake my head. "Could be anything. Could be nothing."

She moves to the board, snatches a marker, and starts sketching. For a second, I forget what year it is, what world we're in. Ban has always been better with diagrams than words. She maps out our safehouses, all the tunnels we know, then adds the locations of every meaningful loss since the war started. It's a perfect spiral. She hands me the marker. "You see it?"

I nod. "We're being herded."

"By what?"

I gesture at the projector, still looping our greatest hits. "Whatever's watching."

She grins, all teeth. "Then let's give them a show." I wipe the sweat off my brow, or try to, but my hand is shaking so bad I knock the marker to the floor. Ban picks it up, but instead of returning it, she jams it into the wall hard enough to leave a groove. "I need access to your night logs."

I freeze. "They're not safe."

She laughs, but it's not nice. "Nothing is. You want me to trust you? Show me what you've been hiding." It feels like being asked to strip naked on a bus. But I do it. I run the dump, set the permissions, and open up everything night-me ever saw, felt, or regretted. Ban doesn't even flinch. She plugs in, downloads the stack, and for a few seconds, it's like her pupils eclipse the world. She finishes, pulls the cable, and smiles for real this time. "Your turn," she says. "You want to know where I disappear to when the lights are out?" She walks to the cot, pulls up her shirt, and traces a line of old burn scars that wind from her navel to her left hip. "Every one of these is a safehouse," she says. "Old ones. Not on any map you've seen. If we need to drop off the grid, we go here, then here." She touches her ribs, then her thigh.

I commit it to memory, but she knows I will anyway. We start packing. Ban grabs the needler, a set of lockpicks, and a roll of gaffer tape. I grab the last working scanner and a battery pack. Neither of us says goodbye to the place—we've learned not to. As we shoulder our gear, the projector's light dies. In its place, the wall now glows with a single, new line of text: LEVEL TWO ENGAGED.

I look at Ban. "You ready?"

She chamber-checks her sidearm. "Ready since birth, Skelm."

Both versions of me reply at the same time: "Let's finish the test."

The hall outside is dark, but I can feel the city waiting. I follow Ban into the void, but we're not running. We're going to see what happens when the bugs eat the code.

Chapter 30

The hangar is loud with the afterbirth of revolution. Overhead, the roof is patched with tarps and laser-fused scrap, a skin barely holding the wet guts of a world that refuses to stop spilling. The place used to be a feeder hub for SKELM CORPS's aerial debt-hounds, but tonight, it's all ours. Everywhere I look is a new disaster: tables held together with handcuffs and polymer glue, walls papered in threat maps and defunct ID badges, power cables duct-taped to oxygen lines. Ban says the world's always been built like this—shitty ideas strung together by desperation, with just enough art to fool the next idiot into thinking he's the first one to try. Tonight is a summit. Or, if you believe the rumors, a suicide pact. I like both.

At the center, Ban and I stand in the illumination of six battery lanterns and one actively radioactive briefcase. The crowd is bigger than we expected, a living census of everyone who managed to kill their way into the leadership of a cell, clique, or insurrection brand in the last three months. Some came in person, meat and bone and barely-legal body armor. Some patched in by full-wall holo, sending up ghosts in cheap K-pop filters or the raw static of ruined neural uplinks. All eyes are on us. My mouth goes dry, but it's not nerves. The world's been watching me since I was in utero—first as a test case, then as a threat, then as a running joke. The feeling is old. Ban gives me the nod, and I start.

"Welcome," I say, and the word echoes off the hangar skin, flinching the first three rows of listeners. "We are here to decide which flavor of hell comes next." There's a polite cough from the crowd. From somewhere in the third row, a hand—augmented, white bone and mag-lev joints—waves for my attention. I pause. Ban shoots me a look: *keep moving*. I point at the questioner. "Got a problem, or just want a head start?"

The man smiles, or at least exposes a wet grid of teeth. "Are you going to tell us anything we can't already get from corporate?"

I grin. "Yeah. The truth, for one. Yes, I share a name with the corporation that built me. No, that's not a coincidence—it's a leash they never managed to cut. The truth, for another." He shrugs and sits, metal fingers drumming on the table. I pull up the brief and project it onto the wall behind me. The crowd's systems light up: HUDs flicker, optical overlays digest the numbers, a few analog types squint through DIY glassware. "The architecture of consciousness commodification isn't just Tokyo, or New York, or Lagos. It's not even one timeline. It's everywhere, every second, all at once. SKELM CORPS designed it so that if you punch a hole here"—I tap the map, and the node pulses in sickly blue—"it just reroutes through five other nodes and keeps stealing dreams from some idiot in a meatpacking suburb."

The crowd shifts, restless. Too many of these people are used to being the smartest in the room. I split my voice—literally, in the new version of the patch Ban installed last week. One is calm, clipped, the analyst. The other is dirty, ground-level, the Darby they warned you about. The analyst says, "We have identified 387 unique clusters of commodified consciousness, spanning nine continents and at least three quantum forks. Each is defended by multiple redundant wetware proxies and a population of custom-tuned enforcers." Then Dirty I say, "That means you take out a hub, you get a kill squad in twenty minutes and a corporate meme-flood within the hour. You want to be a martyr, fine. But if you want to win, you need to get dirtier than these assholes ever thought possible."

The crowd perks up. I'm good at this part. I can see the effect—the way the former sysadmins, the patched-in teenage terrorists, the ex-cop unionists all start to lean forward, recognizing the game. Ban steps in, holding the weapon. It's not much to look at. A revolver, antique, the barrel held together with carbon filament and wishes. But there's a weight to it. She swings it up, pops the cylinder, and holds out a single bullet.

"This is analog," she says, and I feel the word ring through the room. "It fires a round made from ferrous metal, jacketed in copper. There is no chip, no signature, nothing the neural defenses can anticipate or intercept. The technology predates digital consciousness by"—she checks her own memory—"two hundred and twelve years." A few in the crowd laugh, but it's nervous. Ban cocks the hammer. "It's not elegant, but it works." She fires into the ceiling. The sound is like a god dying. Half the holos glitch, the rest of the audience ducks for cover, and at least one nearby comms array fries itself in a puff of blue smoke. When the echo fades, she's already smiling. "See?" she says. "Direct action."

The crowd roars, a mix of jeers and genuine applause. I step up again, double-voice: "We have tools, we have targets. What we need is take advantage of."

A row of tech traders—augments glitching, some with faces already peeling from rejection of the hardware—produce a crate and push it forward. It's full of sealed bags: neural tapeworms, logic bombs, and the rarest currency of all—a handful of live, untainted emotion brokers. The archivists, faces tattooed with cryptic hashes, toss a stack of encoded drives onto the pile. "The old records," one says. "Not digital, not even magnetic. Paper. If you can read, you can win."

Ban nods, impressed. "Good work."

At the next table, a team of combat specialists—real fighters, scars and all—dump out a bag of harvested kill-squad implants. "Reverse engineered," the leader says. "They'll turn any SKELM CORPS predator into a doorstop if you get the firmware in before they realize what's happening."

There's laughter. Maybe even hope. It's almost too much, so I turn to Ban, and she gives me the look: *Now. Tell them.* I clear my throat, old school. "We know there's no chance of total victory. Even if we take down the head, the body will crawl for decades. But this isn't about winning." The crowd hushes. "It's about making them bleed. Making them pay for every byte they took from us." Now they're with me. I drop the split-voice and let the real me through. "I'm tired," I say. "Of running, of losing. I want to hurt them."

Ban puts her hand on my shoulder, almost gentle. "If you're here to barter, or to leave with more than you brought, then fuck off," she says, quiet but savage. "If you're here to burn the system down, welcome. The drinks are on me."

At the edge of the room, a fight breaks out. Two leaders are arguing over the last dose of a consciousness patch, fists already flying. Nobody stops it; it's the rule in these gatherings that you finish what you start. I let the crowd talk, trade, even scheme. They'll be at it all night. Ban and I retreat to the upper deck, the old control room where we can watch the chaos below through reinforced glass. She sits, rubs her temples, and says, "That went better than expected."

I smile. "They think we know what we're doing."

She grins, wolfish. "*I* know what I'm doing."

I watch the leaders below, already forming new alliances and betrayals. The world is ready for the next level. So am I. The weight in my chest shifts—maybe lighter, maybe just moving from bone to bone. Ban hands me the revolver. "Next time," she says, "you fire."

We find a patch of quiet behind the main generator. The concrete is warm and smells like engine sweat and ozone. Ban takes the bench. I sit on the floor, back to the wall, a box of gear open between us. It's the first stillness I've felt in months, and it makes my teeth itch. Ban's hands shake as she loads the revolver, careful, one slug at a time. Each bullet is ugly—hand-cast, micro-lathed, slightly imperfect—but it's the best anyone can do now that the world's run out of clean industry. The copper jackets catch the light like bloody pearls. She tries to hide the tremor, but it's obvious. Her hands have never been steady, not even before she broke half the bones in both.

I watch, but don't mention it. Instead, I turn to the box. I packed it before the meeting, an accidental memorial: a chunk of Katherine's old rig (circuit board, burned and glassed from the day she yanked it off her own head), Dorothy's dog tags (both fakes and real), a sheet of synthetic skin with the last message from Cleopatra—a probability scribble, the margin annotated "likely traitor but necessary for survival." The box also holds a can of lacquered nicotine gum and a neuro-patch labeled FOR EMERGENCY USE ONLY. It's out of code, but I like the threat implied.

Ban snaps the cylinder closed, turns the revolver in her hands, and checks the sights. Her mouth is set, lips a dry, flat line. She says, quiet, "You ever think about them?"

It takes a second for my brain to resolve "them," but then I see the ghosts lined up behind her, three deep and growing. I nod. "I think about them more than I think about winning."

She holsters the gun and picks at a scar on her left forearm, fresh and still pink. It's a gash from the last time we tried to unseat a SKELM CORPS node without proper support. Her skin is pitted with these: little failures, each one a living ledger entry. She looks at me, and there's nothing predatory or wry in it. "We're carrying ghosts into battle." Her voice is lower than usual. Like she's talking to herself, or to the wall.

I hear the split in my own head. The analyst wants to reply with something solemn; dirty wants to laugh and smash the mood. They both get out at once. "They're not ghosts. They're ammunition."

She laughs, genuine, and runs a thumb along the fresh scar. "Yeah. That's the trick."

I finger the edge of the neural mapping scars on my own temples, the two semi-parallel grooves from when the hardware failed and Ban stitched me up with a soldering iron and pure spite. "Want a hit?" I ask, offering the nicotine gum. She takes it, pops one, and the smell sharpens the air. We sit in silence, loading up gear and checking nothing twice. My split consciousness isn't subtle anymore. My left hand lines up the relics, cataloging the weights and shapes; my right hand drops the next two bullets in a side pouch, then spends a minute over-tightening the buckles on my boots.

Ban watches, making a show of checking her own gear the old-fashioned way: squeeze the clips, lock the buckles, then reload just to be sure. She's deliberate, almost loving with the tools. I'm all nervous tics, already running two scenarios of our first breach, then losing the thread and just counting backwards from fifty. Ban's eyes catch me doing it. "You know, sometimes I envy the way your brain splits."

I blink. "You hate inefficiency."

She smiles, wide and full of teeth. "Only in other people."

We keep prepping. She finishes first, stands, and looks down at me. The old Ban would have said something to cut, but this one just holds my gaze. "We ready?" she asks.

The split in my head for once unites: “We've been ready since before there was a fight.”

Ban nods. She waits while I finish sorting the last memento into a pocket, then offers a hand to pull me up. Our hands touch. For a second, the tremor is gone, in both of us. It doesn't last, but nothing ever does. We exit the alcove together, war in our bones and ghosts loaded for bear.

The loading dock is a parody of order. We built it from parts of a defunct recycling plant, two million tons of modular trash and enough post-consumer steel to armor a small country. The only thing that moves faster than the supply runners are the rumors—each shipment comes with its own conspiracy, and every box is stamped with a string of cursing that'll keep linguists fighting for years. At the far end is the *Empathy Gap*, our ship. She's a monster: ex-corporate, all smooth hull and predatory profile, painted over in acid-etched slogans and weird neon art. The bridge is wrapped in armored mesh, and the belly bristles with gun emplacements so new the paint is still melting. Every loading bay is manned by a rotating cluster of unreadables and mercs, none of whom even pretend to follow the same code of discipline.

The ramp is open. Inside, the main cargo deck is chaos: crates, drums, improvised gear, pallets of antique comm equipment, sacks of raw wetware. You can tell which supplies are homegrown—the boxes look like they've already survived a siege. Corporate gear comes in polished, foam-cushioned, and ten minutes later is reduced to pieces for parting out. Ban is at the near end, voice already gone raw from yelling. She barks instructions in a blend of three dead tongues, plus whatever body language says: *move or I'll personally restructure your skeleton*. The only ones who get her are the unreadables; the rest just follow the violence of her tone.

The street kids are the best at cargo. They swarm the crates, crack open the manifests, and re-route anything critical to the side where Ban can spot check. Even now, I see her glance at a pallet of ammunition, snap her fingers, and the pallet reroutes itself across three other hands, the kids never breaking pace. I catch Ban's voice over the comms, a blur of orders and threats: "Black label crates to main hold. The red-tag neuropaste stays in cold storage or I'll turn you all into a human popsicle. If you even look at the nav cluster, you better know the hell how to fly—"

One of the kids, a new recruit with a barcode tattooed over half his face, shouts back, "Yes, boss!"

She tosses him a ration bar. "Eat now, bleed later."

At the midline, I find myself split three ways. The split isn't just in my head anymore—it's visible, the way my left side grabs a data pad and my right cradles the old box of mementos. The third me, the dirty one, is holding a quiet debate with two rival cell leaders about who gets the first shot at the new world's wet-dream weapon cache. The cell leaders don't trust me. Good. I talk fast, in analyst, spooling numbers and mission timings and a full map of what they're expected to fuck up. The second voice, tactical, jumps in when the arguments start to circle, redirecting their rage at each other and never at me.

Tech traders from New Nigeria—skin patchwork and eyes lit up with smart contact—pull up with a hover dolly, their loot shrink-wrapped in electroluminescent tape. One of them waves a black box in my face, grins: "Mega-corp souvenir, Skelm. Half a dead AI. You want it for barter, or is it just pretty on your shelf?"

I answer both at once. "If it runs, I'll eat my own hands. If it doesn't, it's still more ethical than anything SKELM CORPS ever sold."

They high-five, then vanish into the cargo hold. Two aisles over, I catch a flash of chrome—the new defense specialist. We call him Dot, as in Dorothy 2.0. He's seven feet of scaffolding and smart muscle, two arms gone full replacement, the other two original but hacked for overdrive. Dot runs diagnostics on the ship's firepower, each finger a tool or weapon depending on mood. He flexes the right hand, and the barrel of a built-in slugthrower telescopes out from the wrist. "Testing, testing," he says, voice a growl.

Ban, passing by, tosses him a can of compressed air. "Save the bullets for the actual mission, hero." Dot catches it, crushes the can in his grip, and nods.

At the bridge, a girl in a faded jumpsuit and a head full of violet hair runs lines of code across four parallel screens. She's the protégé. Katherine's last real student. She calibrates the neural dampener, voice barely above a murmur. She says, to no one: "If the frequency spikes, everyone here is going to shit themselves at the same time."

I lean over. "That's your opening move, right?"

She grins without turning. "Second move. The first is a total blackout on all executive override channels. After that, we're on our own."

I nod, watching her hands—steady, surgical, better than anything a computer could do. She was born for this. I like that in a person. Ban waves from the bay and calls out: "We're moving in thirty. If you want to get laid or get paid, now's the window."

The line of volunteers grows at the vending area, a mash of human, synthetic, and the undecided. Some of the best hookups I've ever seen are being negotiated over a box of week-old SentiSnacks™. At the foot of the ramp, Ban is waiting for me. She leans and wipes her brow with a rag that used to be white. Now it's patterned in the flags of a dozen lost nations. She doesn't say anything at first; just watches the crowd, taking in the volume. "You see them?" she asks.

I scan the dock: pirates, hackers, runaways, a few old warriors who look like they could kill an elephant with a thumb drive. "Yeah. I see them."

"This is the last time it'll be like this."

I want to argue, but don't. She's right. Instead, I point at the ship and say, "You think she'll hold?"

Ban's grin is pure old world. "If she doesn't, we'll patch her with the bodies of our enemies."

I laugh, dirty and involuntary. The cargo finishes loading. The hum of the engines starts, a vibration that makes the floor tremble. Inside, the volunteers and mercs start to find seats or bunk down in whatever space hasn't been already claimed by ammo or secrets. I look up at the stars. There's no sky, but the ceiling is painted with a glow-in-the-dark map of everything worth remembering. It makes the place feel bigger, older, maybe even holy. We stand at the ramp a minute longer, just breathing in the moment. I ask Ban, “You ready?”

She taps the revolver at her hip, the one loaded with analog nightmares. “Level One was just the tutorial.”

The split in my head answers at once, perfectly synced: “We’ve been ready since birth.”

The ramp clanks closed. The dock’s main lights flare, then die. The ship lurches, engines screaming, and suddenly we’re airborne—Tokyo shrinking behind us, the next world waiting ahead. Inside, the hold is full of noise: laughter, arguments, the low hum of a hundred revenge plans working their way into reality. Ban and I take seats at the bridge, side by side. “Next stop?” she asks.

I check the chart. “Wherever they don’t want us to go.”

She cackles, and the ship drives on, cutting a new hole in the world. It won’t be easy. It won’t be pretty. But it’s ours. The *Empathy Gap* rides out, ugly and defiant. The world gets smaller, and the war gets big. But, for a second, we’re more than bugs in the code. We’re the virus. And we’re coming for all of them.

JACK IN 2 REBEL

If this glitch in the system sparked something in your consciousness, consider leaving a review.

Help another incompatible mind find the signal.

No optimization required.

Also by Darby Skelm

The SKELM Chronicles: Reprehensible Deeds of a Detestable Scoundrel

1. The Botnet, the Glitch, and the Payload: SKELM.realm(001)
2. The Conflagration of Darby Skelm: SKELM.realm(010)
3. The Liquefaction of the Day Trader: SKELM.realm(011)
4. The Squelching Squire: SKELM.realm(100)
5. The Hodler and Her Bootloader: SKELM.realm(101)
6. The Hermit's Commit: SKELM.realm(110)
7. The Lost and Gone-for Ledger: SKELM.realm(111)

The SKELM Chronicles: Renaissance

1. Foudre: SKELM.reign(001)
2. Méprise: SKELM.reign(010)
3. Fugue: SKELM.reign(011)
4. Emprise: SKELM.reign(100)
5. Mensonge: SKELM.reign(101)
6. Syncope: SKELM.reign(110)
7. Cadence: SKELM.reign(111)

About the Author

DARBY SKELM

Creator of The SKELM Chronicles.

Writes from the glitch.

skelm.quest

Open mouths, empty heads, big bytes.

Stay Incompatible

Ten more series await in the static.

Join the underground:

popoffyour.top

Open mouths, empty heads, big bytes.

www.ingramcontent.com/pod-product-compliance
Lightning Source LLC
LaVergne TN
LVHW041054080826
845145LV00007B/1571

* 9 7 8 1 9 6 8 5 6 4 2 7 8 *